THE COLD
EQUATIONS
& OTHER STORIES

THE COLD
EQUATIONS

& OTHER STORIES

TOM GODWIN

EDITED AND COMPILED BY
ERIC FLINT

THE COLD EQUATIONS

This is a work of fiction. All the characters and events portrayed in this book are fictional, and any resemblance to real people or incidents is purely coincidental.

Copyright © 2003 by Tom Godwin.
The Survivors was first published by Gnome Press in 1958, and reissued in 1960 by Pyramid Books under the title *Space Prison*. "The Harvest" was first published in *Venture* in July, 1957. "Brain Teaser" was first published in *If* in October, 1956. "Mother of Invention" was first published in *Astounding* in December, 1953. "—And Devious the Line of Duty" was first published in *Analog* in December, 1962. "Empathy" was first published in *Fantastic* in October, 1959. "No Species Alone" was first published in *Universe* in November, 1954. "The Gulf Between" was first published in *Astounding* in October, 1953. "The Cold Equations" was first published in *Astounding* in August, 1954.

A Baen Books Original

Baen Publishing Enterprises
P.O. Box 1403
Riverdale, NY 10471
www.baen.com

ISBN: 0-7434-3601-6

Cover art by Clyde Caldwell

First printing, April 2003

Library of Congress Cataloging-in-Publication Data

Godwin, Tom.
    The cold equations & other stories / by Tom Godwin ; edited and
    compiled by Eric Flint.
        p. cm.
    ISBN 0-7434-3601-6 (pbk.)
    1. Science fiction, American. 2. Space flight—Fiction. I. Title: Cold
    equations and other stories. II. Flint, Eric. III. Title.

PS3557.O3175C65 2003
813'.54—dc21   2002043995

Distributed by Simon & Schuster
1230 Avenue of the Americas
New York, NY 10020

Production by Windhaven Press, Auburn, NH
Printed in the United States of America

10   9   8   7   6   5   4   3   2   1

CONTENTS

THE COLD
EQUATIONS
& OTHER STORIES

PREFACE
by Barry Malzberg

The title story of this volume, "The Cold Equations," is perhaps the most famous and controversial of all science fiction short stories. When it first appeared in the August 1954 issue of *Astounding*, it generated more mail from readers than any story previously published in the magazine. Since then, it has been reprinted thousands of times (almost all college courses on science fiction routinely include it on reading lists). It has been the basis of a television movie and a *Twilight Zone* episode, and prior to that had been adapted for radio and television many, many times.

Its impact remains. In the late 1990's it was the subject of a furious debate in the intellectually ambitious (or simply pretentious; you decide) *New York Review of Science Fiction* in which the story was anatomized as anti-feminist, proto-feminist, hard-edged realism, squishy fantasy for the self-deluded, misogynistic past routine pathology, crypto-fascist, etc., etc. One correspondent suggested barely-concealed pederasty.

The debaters' affect over a story more than four decades old was extraordinary, and the debate did not end so much as it kind of expired from exhaustion. Godwin's adoptive daughter, Diane Sullivan, said in conclusion that Godwin himself had always felt women were "To be loved and protected" and A.J. Budrys in a

1

similarly funerary tone noted that " 'The Cold Equations' was the best short story that Godwin ever wrote and he didn't write it."

But, of course, he did. I'll have more to say about the history of the short story in my afterword (see below), but for now that's enough. Here, in one volume, are the best writings of Tom Godwin. It begins with his most popular novel, *The Survivors*, and closes with his legendary story, "The Cold Equations."

Editor's note: This is my personal favorite of all of Godwin's writings. Some of my fondness for this short novel, I'll admit, is perhaps simply nostalgia. The first two science fiction novels I ever read were Robert Heinlein's Citizen of the Galaxy *and . . . this one. Between them, the two stories instilled a love of science fiction in a thirteen-year-old boy which has now lasted for more than four decades. But leaving that aside, I think this story more than any other captures those themes which recur constantly in Godwin's fiction: the value of courage and loyalty.*

Godwin had a grim side to him, which is reflected in The Survivors *as it is in most of his stories, but—also as in most—it is ultimately a story of triumph. More so, in some ways, than in any other science fiction novel I've ever read.*

Eric Flint

THE SURVIVORS

Part 1

For seven weeks the *Constellation* had been plunging through hyperspace with her eight thousand colonists; fleeing like a hunted thing with her communicators silenced and her drives moaning and thundering. Up in the control room, Irene had been told, the needles of the dials danced against the red danger lines day and night.

She lay in bed and listened to the muffled, ceaseless roar of the drives and felt the singing vibration of the hull. *We should be almost safe by now*, she thought. *Athena is only forty days away.*

Thinking of the new life awaiting them all made her too restless to lie still any longer. She got up, to sit on the edge of the bed and switch on the light. Dale was gone—he had been summoned to adjust one of the machines in the ship's X-ray room—and Billy was asleep, nothing showing of him above the covers but a crop of brown hair and the furry nose of his ragged teddy bear.

She reached out to straighten the covers, gently, so as not to awaken him. It happened then, the thing they had all feared.

From the stern of the ship came a jarring, deafening explosion. The ship lurched violently, girders screamed, and the light flicked out.

In the darkness she heard a rapid-fire *thunk-thunk-thunk* as the automatic guard system slid inter-compartment doors shut against sections of the ship suddenly airless. The doors were still thudding shut when another explosion came, from toward the bow. Then there was silence; a feeling of utter quiet and motionlessness.

The fingers of fear enclosed her and her mind said to her, like the cold, unpassionate voice of a stranger: *The Gerns have found us.*

The light came on again, a feeble glow, and there was the soft, muffled sound of questioning voices in the other compartments. She dressed, her fingers shaking and clumsy, wishing that Dale would come to reassure her; to tell her that nothing really serious had happened, that it had not been the Gerns.

It was very still in the little compartment—strangely so. She had finished dressing when she realized the reason: the air circulation system had stopped working.

That meant the power failure was so great that the air regenerators, themselves, were dead. And there were eight thousand people on the *Constellation* who would have to have air to live . . .

The *Attention* buzzer sounded shrilly from the public address system speakers that were scattered down the ship's corridors. A voice she recognized as that of Lieutenant Commander Lake spoke:

"War was declared upon Earth by the Gern Empire ten days ago. Two Gern cruisers have attacked us and their blasters have destroyed the stern and bow of the ship. We are without a drive and without power but for a few emergency batteries. I am the *Constellation*'s only surviving officer and the Gern commander is boarding us to give me the surrender terms.

"None of you will leave your compartments until ordered to do so. Wherever you may be, remain there. This is necessary to avoid confusion and to have as many as possible in known locations for future instructions. I repeat: you will not leave your compartments."

The speaker cut off. She stood without moving and heard again the words: *I am the* Constellation's *only surviving officer . . .*

The Gerns had killed her father.

He had been second-in-command of the Dunbar expedition that had discovered the world of Athena and his knowledge of Athena was valuable to the colonization plans. He had been quartered among the ship's officers—and the Gern blast had destroyed that section of the ship.

She sat down on the edge of the bed again and tried to

reorient herself; to accept the fact that her life and the lives of all the others had abruptly, irrevocably, been changed.

The Athena Colonization Plan was ended. They had known such a thing might happen—that was why the *Constellation* had been made ready for the voyage in secret and had waited for months for the chance to slip through the ring of Gern spy ships; that was why she had raced at full speed, with her communicators silenced so there would be no radiations for the Gerns to find her by. Only forty days more would have brought them to the green and virgin world of Athena, four hundred light-years beyond the outermost boundary of the Gern Empire. There they should have been safe from Gern detection for many years to come; for long enough to build planetary defenses against attack. And there they would have used Athena's rich resources to make ships and weapons to defend mineral-depleted Earth against the inexorably increasing inclosure of the mighty, coldly calculating colossus that was the Gern Empire.

Success or failure of the Athena Plan had meant ultimate life or death for Earth. They had taken every precaution possible but the Gern spy system had somehow learned of Athena and the *Constellation*. Now, the cold war was no longer cold and the Plan was dust . . .

Billy sighed and stirred in the little-boy sleep that had not been broken by the blasts that had altered the lives of eight thousand people and the fate of a world.

She shook his shoulder and said, "Billy."

He raised up, so small and young to her eyes that the question in her mind was like an anguished prayer: *Dear God—what do Gerns do to five-year-old boys?*

He saw her face, and the dim light, and the sleepiness was suddenly gone from him. "What's wrong, Mama? And why are you scared?"

There was no reason to lie to him.

"The Gerns found us and stopped us."

"Oh," he said. In his manner was the grave thoughtfulness of a boy twice his age, as there always was. "Will they—will they kill us?"

"Get dressed, honey," she said. "Hurry, so we'll be ready when they let Daddy come back to tell us what to do."

✧   ✧   ✧

They were both ready when the *Attention* buzzer sounded in the corridors. Lake spoke, his tone grim and bitter:

"There is no power for the air regenerators and within twenty hours we will start smothering to death. Under these circumstances I could not do other than accept the survival terms the Gern commander offered us.

"He will speak to you now and you will obey his orders without protest. Death is the only alternative."

Then the voice of the Gern commander came, quick and harsh and brittle:

"This section of space, together with planet Athena, is an extension of the Gern Empire. This ship has deliberately invaded Gern territory in time of war with intent to seize and exploit a Gern world. We are willing, however, to offer a leniency not required by the circumstances. Terran technicians and skilled workers in certain fields can be used in the factories we shall build on Athena. The others will not be needed and there is not room on the cruisers to take them.

"Your occupation records will be used to divide you into two groups: the Acceptables and the Rejects. The Rejects will be taken by the cruisers to an Earth-type planet near here and left, together with the personal possessions in their compartments and additional, and ample, supplies. The Acceptables will then be taken on to Athena and at a later date the cruisers will return the Rejects to Earth.

"This division will split families but there will be no resistance to it. Gern guards will be sent immediately to make this division and you will wait in your compartments for them. You will obey their orders promptly and without annoying them with questions. At the first instance of resistance or rebellion this offer will be withdrawn and the cruisers will go their way again."

In the silence following the ultimatum she could hear the soft, wordless murmur from the other compartments, the undertone of anxiety like a dark thread through it. In every compartment parents and children, brothers and sisters, were seeing one another for the last time . . .

The corridor outside rang to the tramp of feet; the sound of a dozen Gerns walking with swift military precision. She held her breath, her heart racing, but they went past her door and on to the corridor's end.

There she could faintly hear them entering compartments, demanding names, and saying, "*Out—out!*" Once she heard a Gern say, "Acceptables will remain inside until further notice. Do not open your doors after the Rejects have been taken out."

Billy touched her on the hand. "Isn't Daddy going to come?"

"He—he can't right now. We'll see him pretty soon."

She remembered what the Gern commander had said about the Rejects being permitted to take their personal possessions. She had very little time in which to get together what she could carry . . .

There were two small bags in the compartment and she hurried to pack them with things she and Dale and Billy might need, not able to know which of them, if any, would be Rejects. Nor could she know whether she should put in clothes for a cold world or a hot one. The Gern commander had said the Rejects would be left on an Earth-type planet but where could it be? The Dunbar Expedition had explored across five hundred light-years of space and had found only one Earth-type world: Athena.

The Gerns were almost to her door when she had finished and she heard them enter the compartments across from her own. There came the hard, curt questions and the command: "Outside—hurry!" A woman said something in pleading question and there was the soft thud of a blow and the words: "Outside—do not ask questions!" A moment later she heard the woman going down the corridor, trying to hold back her crying.

Then the Gerns were at her own door.

She held Billy's hand and waited for them with her heart hammering. She held her head high and composed herself with all the determination she could muster so that the arrogant Gerns would not see that she was afraid. Billy stood beside her as tall as his five years would permit, his teddy bear under his arm, and only the way his hand held to hers showed that he, too, was scared.

The door was flung open and two Gerns strode in.

They were big, dark men, with powerful, bulging muscles. They surveyed her and the room with a quick sweep of eyes that were like glittering obsidian, their mouths thin, cruel slashes in the flat, brutal planes of their faces.

"Your name?" snapped the one who carried a sheaf of occupation records.

"It's"—she tried to swallow the quaver in her voice and make it cool and unfrightened—"Irene Lois Humbolt—Mrs. Dale Humbolt."

The Gern glanced at the papers. "Where is your husband?"

"He was in the X-ray room at—"

"You are a Reject. Out—down the corridor with the others."

"My husband—will he be a—"

"*Outside!*"

It was the tone of voice that had preceded the blow in the other compartment and the Gern took a quick step toward her. She seized the two bags in one hand, not wanting to release Billy, and swung back to hurry out into the corridor. The other Gern jerked one of the bags from her hand and flung it to the floor. "Only one bag per person," he said, and gave her an impatient shove that sent her and Billy stumbling through the doorway.

She became part of the Rejects who were being herded like sheep down the corridors and into the port airlock. There were many children among them, the young ones frightened and crying, and often with only one parent or an older brother or sister to take care of them. And there were many young ones who had no one at all and were dependent upon strangers to take their hands and tell them what they must do.

When she was passing the corridor that led to the X-ray room she saw a group of Rejects being herded up it. Dale was not among them and she knew, then, that she and Billy would never see him again.

"*Out from the ship—faster—faster—*"

The commands of the Gern guards snapped like whips around them as she and the other Rejects crowded and stumbled down the boarding ramp and out onto the rocky ground. There was the pull of a terrible gravity such as she had never experienced and they were in a bleak, barren valley, a cold wind moaning down it and whipping the alkali dust in bitter clouds. Around the valley stood ragged hills, their white tops laying out streamers of wind-driven snow, and the sky was dark with sunset.

"*Out from the ship—faster—*"

It was hard to walk fast in the high gravity, carrying the bag in one hand and holding up all of Billy's weight she could with the other.

"They lied to us!" a man beside her said to someone. "Let's turn and fight. Let's take—"

A Gern blaster cracked with a vivid blue flash and the man plunged lifelessly to the ground. She flinched instinctively and fell over an unseen rock, the bag of precious clothes flying from her hand. She scrambled up again, her left knee half numb, and turned to retrieve it.

The Gern guard was already upon her, his blaster still in his hand. "Out from the ship—faster."

The barrel of his blaster lashed across the side of her head. "Move on—move on!"

She staggered in a blinding blaze of pain and then hurried on, holding tight to Billy's hand, the wind cutting like knives of ice through her thin clothes and blood running in a trickle down her cheek.

"He hit you," Billy said. "He hurt you." Then he called the Gern a name that five-year-old boys were not supposed to know, with a savagery that five-year-old boys were not supposed to possess.

When she stopped at the outer fringe of Rejects she saw that all of them were out of the cruiser and the guards were going back into it. A half mile down the valley the other cruiser stood, the Rejects out from it and its boarding ramps already withdrawn.

When she had buttoned Billy's blouse tighter and wiped the blood from her face the first blast of the drives came from the farther cruiser. The nearer one blasted a moment later and they lifted together, their roaring filling the valley. They climbed faster and faster, dwindling as they went. Then they disappeared in the black sky, their roaring faded away, and there was left only the moaning of the wind around her and somewhere a child crying.

And somewhere a voice asking, "Where are we? In the name of God—what have they done to us?"

She looked at the snow streaming from the ragged hills, felt the hard pull of the gravity, and knew where they were. They were on Ragnarok, the hell-world of 1.5 gravity and fierce beasts and raging fevers where men could not survive. The name came from an old Teutonic myth and meant: *The last day for gods and men*. The Dunbar Expedition had discovered Ragnarok and her father had told her of it, of how it had killed six of the eight men who had left the ship and would have killed all of them if they had remained any longer.

She knew where they were and she knew the Gerns had lied to them and would never send a ship to take them to Earth. Their abandonment there had been intended as a death sentence for all of them.

And Dale was gone and she and Billy would die helpless and alone . . .

"It will be dark—so soon." Billy's voice shook with the cold. "If Daddy can't find us in the dark, what will we do?"

"I don't know," she said. "There's no one to help us and how can I know—what we should do—"

She was from the city. How could she know what to do on an alien, hostile world where armed explorers had died? She had tried to be brave before the Gerns but now—now night was at hand and out of it would come terror and death for herself and Billy. They would never see Dale again, never see Athena or Earth or even the dawn on the world that had killed them . . .

She tried not to cry, and failed. Billy's cold little hand touched her own, trying to reassure her.

"Don't cry, Mama. I guess—I guess everybody else is scared, too."

Everyone else . . .

She was not alone. How could she have thought she was alone? All around her were others, as helpless and uncertain as she. Her story was only one out of four thousand.

"I guess they are, Billy," she said. "I never thought of that, before."

She knelt to put her arms around him, thinking: *Tears and fear are futile weapons; they can never bring us any tomorrows. We'll have to fight whatever comes to kill us no matter how scared we are. For ourselves and for our children. Above all else, for our children* . . .

"I'm going back to find our clothes," she said. "You wait here for me, in the shelter of that rock, and I won't be gone long."

Then she told him what he would be too young to really understand.

"I'm not going to cry any more and I know, now, what I must

do. I'm going to make sure that there is a tomorrow for you, always, to the last breath of my life."

The bright blue star dimmed and the others faded away. Dawn touched the sky, bringing with it a coldness that frosted the steel of the rifle in John Prentiss's hands and formed beads of ice on his gray mustache. There was a stirring in the area behind him as the weary Rejects prepared to face the new day and the sound of a child whimpering from the cold. There had been no time the evening before to gather wood for fires—

"Prowlers!"

The warning cry came from an outer guard and black shadows were suddenly sweeping out of the dark dawn.

They were things that might have been half wolf, half tiger; each of them three hundred pounds of incredible ferocity with eyes blazing like yellow fire in their white-fanged tiger-wolf faces. They came like the wind, in a flowing black wave, and ripped through the outer guard line as though it had not existed. The inner guards fired in a chattering roll of gunshots, trying to turn them, and Prentiss's rifle licked out pale tongues of flame as he added his own fire. The prowlers came on, breaking through, but part of them went down and the others were swerved by the fire so that they struck only the outer edge of the area where the Rejects were grouped.

At that distance they blended into the dark ground so that he could not find them in the sights of his rifle. He could only watch helplessly and see a dark-haired woman caught in their path, trying to run with a child in her arms and already knowing it was too late. A man was running toward her, slow in the high gravity, an axe in his hands and his cursing a raging, savage snarl. For a moment her white face was turned in helpless appeal to him and the others; then the prowlers were upon her and she fell, deliberately, going to the ground with her child hugged in her arms beneath her so that her body would protect it.

The prowlers passed over her, pausing for an instant to slash the life from her, and raced on again. They vanished back into the outer darkness, the farther guards firing futilely, and there was a silence but for the distant, hysterical sobbing of a woman.

It had happened within seconds; the fifth prowler attack that night and the mildest.

❖   ❖   ❖

Full dawn had come by the time he replaced the guards killed by the last attack and made the rounds of the other guard lines. He came back by the place where the prowlers had killed the woman, walking wearily against the pull of gravity. She lay with her dark hair tumbled and stained with blood, her white face turned up to the reddening sky, and he saw her clearly for the first time.

It was Irene.

He stopped, gripping the cold steel of the rifle and not feeling the rear sight as it cut into his hand.

Irene . . . He had not known she was on Ragnarok. He had not seen her in the darkness of the night and he had hoped she and Billy were safe among the Acceptables with Dale.

There was the sound of footsteps and a bold-faced girl in a red skirt stopped beside him, her glance going over him curiously.

"The little boy," he asked, "do you know if he's all right?"

"The prowlers cut up his face but he'll be all right," she said. "I came back after his clothes."

"Are you going to look after him?"

"Someone has to and"—she shrugged her shoulders—"I guess I was soft enough to elect myself for the job. Why—was his mother a friend of yours?"

"She was my daughter," he said.

"Oh." For a moment the bold, brassy look was gone from her face, like a mask that had slipped. "I'm sorry. And I'll take care of Billy."

The first objection to his assumption of leadership occurred an hour later. The prowlers had withdrawn with the coming of full daylight and wood had been carried from the trees to build fires. Mary, one of the volunteer cooks, was asking two men to carry her some water when he approached. The smaller man picked up one of the clumsy containers, hastily improvised from canvas, and started toward the creek. The other, a big, thick-chested man, did not move.

"We'll have to have water," Mary said. "People are hungry and cold and sick."

The man continued to squat by the fire, his hands extended to its warmth. "Name someone else," he said.

"But—"

She looked at Prentiss in uncertainty. He went to the thick-chested man, knowing there would be violence and welcoming it as something to help drive away the vision of Irene's pale, cold face under the red sky.

"She asked you to get her some water," he said. "Get it."

The man looked up at him, studying him with deliberate insolence, then he got to his feet, his heavy shoulders hunched challengingly.

"I'll have to set you straight, old timer," he said. "No one has appointed you the head cheese around here. Now, there's the container you want filled and over there"—he made a small motion with one hand—"is the creek. Do you know what to do?"

"Yes," he said. "I know what to do."

He brought the butt of the rifle smashing up. It struck the man under the chin and there was a sharp cracking sound as his jawbone snapped. For a fraction of a second there was an expression of stupefied amazement on his face then his eyes glazed and he slumped to the ground with his broken jaw setting askew.

"All right," he said to Mary. "Now you go ahead and name somebody else."

He found that the prowlers had killed seventy during the night. One hundred more had died from the Hell Fever that often followed exposure and killed within an hour.

He went the half mile to the group that had arrived on the second cruiser as soon as he had eaten a delayed breakfast. He saw, before he had quite reached the other group, that the *Constellation*'s Lieutenant Commander, Vincent Lake, was in charge of it.

Lake, a tall, hard-jawed man with pale blue eyes under pale brows, walked forth to meet him as soon as he recognized him.

"Glad to see you're still alive," Lake greeted him. "I thought that second Gern blast got you along with the others."

"I was visiting midship and wasn't home when it happened," he said.

He looked at Lake's group of Rejects, in their misery and uncertainty so much like his own, and asked, "How was it last night?"

"Bad—damned bad," Lake said. "Prowlers and Hell Fever, and no wood for fires. Two hundred died last night."

"I came down to see if anyone was in charge here and to tell them that we'll have to move into the woods at once—today. We'll have plenty of wood for the fires there, some protection from the wind, and by combining our defenses we can stand off the prowlers better."

Lake agreed. When the brief discussion of plans was finished he asked, "How much do you know about Ragnarok?"

"Not much," Prentiss answered. "We didn't stay to study it very long. There are no heavy metals here, or resources of any value. We gave Ragnarok a quick survey and when the sixth man died we marked it on the chart as uninhabitable and went on our way.

"As you probably know, that bright blue star is Ragnarok's other sun. Its position in the advance of the yellow sun shows the season to be early spring. When summer comes Ragnarok will swing between the two suns and the heat will be something no human has ever endured. Nor the cold, when winter comes.

"I know of no edible plants, although there might be some. There are a few species of rodent-like animals—they're scavengers—and a herbivore we called the woods goat. The prowlers are the dominant form of life on Ragnarok and I suspect their intelligence is a good deal higher than we would like it to be. There will be a constant battle for survival with them.

"There's another animal, not as intelligent as the prowlers but just as dangerous—the unicorn. The unicorns are big and fast and they travel in herds. I haven't seen any here so far—I hope we don't. At the lower elevations are the swamp crawlers. They're unadulterated nightmares. I hope they don't go to these higher elevations in the summer. The prowlers and the Hell Fever, the gravity and heat and cold and starvation, will be enough for us to have to fight."

"I see," Lake said. He smiled, a smile that was as bleak as moonlight on an arctic glacier. "Earth-type—remember the promise the Gerns made the Rejects?" He looked out across the camp, at the snow whipping from the frosty hills, at the dead and the dying and a little girl trying vainly to awaken her brother.

"They were condemned, without reason, without a chance to live," he said. "So many of them are so young . . . and when you're young it's too soon to have to die."

Prentiss returned to his own group. The dead were buried in shallow graves and inventory was taken of the promised "ample supplies." These were only the few personal possessions the Rejects had been permitted to take plus a small amount of food the Gerns had taken from the *Constellation*'s stores. The Gerns had been forced to provide the Rejects with at least a little food— had they openly left them to starve, the Acceptables, whose families were among the Rejects, might have rebelled.

Inventory of the firearms and ammunition showed the total to be discouragingly small. They would have to learn how to make and use bows and arrows as soon as possible.

With the first party of guards and workmen following him, Prentiss went to the tributary valley that emptied into the central valley a mile to the north. It was as good a camp site as could be hoped for; wide and thickly spotted with groves of trees, a creek running down its center.

The workmen began the construction of shelters and he climbed up the side of the nearer hill. He reached its top, his breath coming fast in the gravity that was the equivalent of a burden half his own weight, and saw what the surrounding terrain was like.

To the south, beyond the barren valley, the land could be seen dropping in its long sweep to the southern lowlands where the unicorns and swamp crawlers lived. To the north the hills climbed gently for miles, then ended under the steeply sloping face of an immense plateau. The plateau reached from western to eastern horizon, still white with the snows of winter and looming so high above the world below that the clouds brushed it and half obscured it.

He went back down the hill as Lake's men appeared. They started work on what would be a continuation of his own camp and he told Lake what he had seen from the hill.

"We're between the lowlands and the highlands," he said. "This will be as near to a temperate altitude as Ragnarok has. We survive here—or else. There's no other place for us to go."

An overcast darkened the sky at noon and the wind died down to almost nothing. There was a feeling of waiting tension in the air and he went back to the Rejects, to speed their move into the woods. They were already going in scattered groups, accompanied by prowler guards, but there was no organization and it would be too long before the last of them were safely in the new camp.

He could not be two places at once—he needed a subleader to oversee the move of the Rejects and their possessions into the woods and their placement after they got there.

He found the man he wanted already helping the Rejects get started: a thin, quiet man named Henry Anders who had fought well against the prowlers the night before, even though his determination had been greater than his marksmanship. He was the type people instinctively liked and trusted; a good choice for the subleader whose job it would be to handle the multitude of details in camp while he, Prentiss, and a second subleader he would select, handled the defense of the camp and the hunting.

"I don't like this overcast," he told Anders. "Something's brewing. Get everyone moved and at work helping build shelters as soon as you can."

"I can have most of them there within an hour or two," Anders said. "Some of the older people, though, will have to take it slow. This gravity—it's already getting the hearts of some of them."

"How are the children taking the gravity?" he asked.

"The babies and the very young—it's hard to tell about them yet. But the children from about four on up get tired quickly, go to sleep, and when they wake up they've sort of bounced back out of it."

"Maybe they can adapt to some extent to this gravity." He thought of what Lake had said that morning: *So many of them are so young . . . and when you're young it's too soon to have to die.* "Maybe the Gerns made a mistake—maybe Terran children aren't as easy to kill as they thought. It's your job and mine and others to give the children the chance to prove the Gerns wrong."

He went his way again to pass by the place where Julia, the girl who had become Billy's foster-mother, was preparing to go to the new camp.

It was the second time for him to see Billy that morning. The first time Billy had still been stunned with grief, and at the sight of his grandfather he had been unable to keep from breaking.

"The Gern hit her," he had sobbed, his torn face bleeding anew as it twisted in crying. "He hurt her, and Daddy was gone and then—and then the other things killed her—"

But now he had had a little time to accept what had happened and he was changed. He was someone much older, almost a man, trapped for a while in the body of a five-year-old boy.

"I guess this is all, Billy," Julia was saying as she gathered up her scanty possessions and Irene's bag. "Get your teddy bear and we'll go."

Billy went to his teddy bear and knelt down to pick it up. Then he stopped and said something that sounded like "*No.*" He laid the teddy bear back down, wiping a little dust from its face as in a last gesture of farewell, and stood up to face Julia empty-handed.

"I don't think I'll want to play with my teddy bear any more," he said. "I don't think I'll ever want to play at all anymore."

Then he went to walk beside her, leaving his teddy bear lying on the ground behind him and with it leaving forever the tears and laughter of childhood.

The overcast deepened, and at midafternoon dark storm clouds came driving in from the west. Efforts were intensified to complete the move before the storm broke, both in his section of the camp and in Lake's. The shelters would be of critical importance and they were being built of the materials most quickly available; dead limbs, brush, and the limited amount of canvas and blankets the Rejects had. They would be inadequate protection but there was no time to build anything better.

It seemed only a few minutes until the black clouds were overhead, rolling and racing at an incredible velocity. With them came the deep roar of the high wind that drove them and the wind on the ground began to stir restlessly in response, like some monster awakening to the call of its kind.

Prentiss knew already who he wanted as his other subleader. He found him hard at work helping build shelters; Howard Craig, a powerfully muscled man with a face as hard and grim as a cliff of granite. It had been Craig who had tried to save Irene from the prowlers that morning with only an axe as a weapon.

Prentiss knew him slightly—and Craig still did not know Irene had been his daughter. Craig had been one of the field engineers for what would have been the Athena Geological Survey. He had had a wife, a frail, blonde girl who had been the first of all to die of Hell Fever the night before, and he still had their three small children.

"We'll stop with the shelters we already have built," he told Craig. "It will take all the time left to us to reinforce them against the wind. I need someone to help me, in addition to Anders. You're the one I want.

"Send some young and fast-moving men back to last night's camp to cut all the strips of prowler skins they can get. Everything about the shelters will have to be lashed down to something solid. See if you can find some experienced outdoorsmen to help you check the jobs.

"And tell Anders that women and children only will be placed in the shelters. There will be no room for anyone else and if any man, no matter what the excuse, crowds out a woman or child I'll personally kill him."

"You needn't bother," Craig said. He smiled with savage mirthlessness. "I'll be glad to take care of any such incidents."

Prentiss saw to it that the piles of wood for the guard fires were ready to be lighted when the time came. He ordered all guards to their stations, there to get what rest they could. They would have no rest at all after darkness came.

He met Lake at the north end of his own group's camp, where it merged with Lake's group and no guard line was needed. Lake told him that his camp would be as well prepared as possible under the circumstances within another hour. By then the wind in the trees was growing swiftly stronger, slapping harder and harder at the shelters, and it seemed doubtful that the storm would hold off for an hour.

But Lake was given his hour, plus half of another. Then deep dusk came, although it was not quite sundown. Prentiss ordered all the guard fires lighted and all the women and children into the shelters. Fifteen minutes later the storm finally broke.

It came as a roaring downpour of cold rain. Complete darkness came with it and the wind rose to a velocity that made the trees lean. An hour went by and the wind increased, smashing at the shelters with a violence they had not been built to withstand. The prowler skin lashings held but the canvas and blankets were ripped into streamers that cracked like rifle shots in the wind before they were torn completely loose and flung into the night.

One by one the guard fires went out and the rain continued, growing colder and driven in almost horizontal sheets by the wind. The women and children huddled in chilled misery in what meager protection the torn shelters still gave and there was nothing that could be done to help them.

The rain turned to snow at midnight, a howling blizzard through which Prentiss's light could penetrate but a few feet as he made his rounds. He walked with slogging weariness, forcing himself on. He was no longer young—he was fifty—and he had had little rest.

He had known, of course, that successful leadership would involve more sacrifice on his part than on the part of those he led. He could have shunned responsibility and his personal welfare would have benefited. He had lived on alien worlds almost half his life; with a rifle and a knife he could have lived, until Ragnarok finally killed him, with much less effort than that required of him as leader. But such an action had been repugnant to him, unthinkable. What he knew of survival on hostile worlds might help the others to survive.

So he had assumed command, tolerating no objections and disregarding the fact that he would be shortening his already short time to live on Ragnarok. It was, he supposed, some old instinct that forbade the individual to stand aside and let the group die.

The snow stopped an hour later and the wind died to a frigid moaning. The clouds thinned, broke apart, and the giant star looked down upon the land with its cold, blue light.

The prowlers came then.

They feinted against the east and west guard lines, then hit the south line in massed, ferocious attack. Twenty got through, past the slaughtered south guards, and charged into the interior of the camp. As they did so the call, prearranged by him in case of such an event, went up the guard lines:

"Emergency guards, east and west—*close in!*"

In the camp, above the triumphant, demoniac yammering of the prowlers, came the screams of women, the thinner cries of children, and the shouting and cursing of men as they tried to fight the prowlers with knives and clubs. Then the emergency guards—every third man from the east and west lines—came plunging through the snow, firing as they came.

The prowlers launched themselves away from their victims and toward the guards, leaving a woman to stagger aimlessly with blood spurting from a severed artery and splashing dark in the starlight on the blue-white snow. The air was filled with the cracking of gunfire and the deep, savage snarling of the prowlers. Half of the prowlers broke through, leaving seven dead guards before them. The others lay in the snow where they had fallen and the surviving emergency guards turned to hurry back to their stations, reloading as they went.

The wounded woman had crumpled down in the snow and a first aid man knelt over her. He straightened, shaking his head, and joined the others as they searched for injured among the prowlers' victims.

They found no injured; only the dead. The prowlers killed with grim efficiency.

"John—"

John Chiara, the young doctor, hurried toward him. His dark eyes were worried behind his frosted glasses and his eyebrows were coated with ice.

"The wood is soaked," he said. "It's going to be some time before we can get fires going. There are babies that will freeze to death before then."

Prentiss looked at the prowlers lying in the snow and motioned toward them. "They're warm. Have their guts and lungs taken out."

"What—"

Then Chiara's eyes lighted with comprehension and he hurried away without further questions.

Prentiss went on, to make the rounds of the guards. When he returned he saw that his order had been obeyed.

The prowlers lay in the snow as before, their savage faces still twisted in their dying snarls, but snug and warm inside them babies slept.

The prowlers attacked again and again and when the wan sun lifted to shine down on the white, frozen land there were five hundred dead in Prentiss's camp: three hundred by Hell Fever and two hundred by prowler attacks.

Five hundred—and that had been only one night on Ragnarok.

Lake reported over six hundred dead. "I hope," he said with bitter hatred, "that the Gerns slept comfortably last night."

"We'll have to build a wall around the camp to hold out the prowlers," Prentiss said. "We don't dare keep using up what little ammunition we have at the rate we've used it the last two nights."

"That will be a big job in this gravity," Lake said. "We'll have to crowd both groups in together to let its circumference be as small as possible."

It was the way Prentiss had planned to do it. One thing would have to be settled with Lake: there could not be two independent leaders over the merged groups . . .

Lake, watching him, said, "I think we can get along. Alien worlds are your specialty rather than mine. And according to the Ragnarok law of averages, there will be only one of us pretty soon, anyway."

All were moved to the center of the camp area that day and when the prowlers came that night they found a ring of guards and fires through which they could penetrate only with heavy sacrifices.

There was warmth to the sun the next morning and the snow began to melt. Work was commenced on the stockade wall. It would have to be twelve feet high so the prowlers could not jump over it and, since the prowlers had the sharp claws and climbing ability of cats, its top would have to be surmounted with a row of sharp outward-and-downward projecting stakes. These would be set in sockets in the top rail and tied down with strips of prowler skin.

The trees east of camp were festooned for a great distance with the remnants of canvas and cloth the wind had left there. A party of boys, protected by the usual prowler guards, was sent out to climb the trees and recover it. All of it, down to the smallest fragment, was turned over to the women who were physically incapable of helping work on the stockade wall. They began patiently sewing the rags and tatters back into usable form again.

The first hunting party went out and returned with six of the tawny-yellow sharp-horned woods goats, each as large as an Earth deer. The hunters reported the woods goats to be hard to stalk and dangerous when cornered. One hunter was killed and another injured because of not knowing that.

They also brought in a few of the rabbit-sized scavenger

animals. They were all legs and teeth and bristly fur, the meat almost inedible. It would be a waste of the limited ammunition to shoot any more of them.

There was a black barked tree which the Dunbar Expedition had called the lance tree because of its slender, straightly outthrust limbs. Its wood was as hard as hickory and as springy as cedar. Prentiss found two amateur archers who were sure they could make efficient bows and arrows out of the lance tree limbs. He gave them the job, together with helpers.

The days turned suddenly hot, with nights that still went below freezing. The Hell Fever took a constant, relentless toll. They needed adequate shelters—but the dwindling supply of ammunition and the nightly prowler attacks made the need for a stockade wall even more imperative. The shelters would have to wait.

He went looking for Dr. Chiara one evening and found him just leaving one of the makeshift shelters.

A boy lay inside it, his face flushed with Hell Fever and his eyes too bright and too dark as he looked up into the face of his mother who sat beside him. She was dry-eyed and silent as she looked down at him but she was holding his hand in hers, tightly, desperately, as though she might that way somehow keep him from leaving her.

Prentiss walked beside Chiara and when the shelter was behind them he asked, "There's no hope?"

"None," Chiara said. "There never is with Hell Fever."

Chiara had changed. He was no longer the stocky, cheerful man he had been on the *Constellation*, whose brown eyes had smiled at the world through thick glasses and who had laughed and joked as he assured his patients that all would soon be well with them. He was thin and his face was haggard with worry. He had, in his quiet way, been fully as valiant as any of those who had fought the prowlers. He had worked day and night to fight a form of death he could not see and against which he had no weapon.

"The boy is dying," Chiara said. "He knows it and his mother knows it. I told them the medicine I gave him might help. It was a lie, to try to make it a little easier for both of them before the end comes. The medicine I gave him was a salt tablet—that's all I have."

And then, with the first bitterness Prentiss had ever seen him display, Chiara said, "You call me 'Doctor.' Everyone does. I'm not—I'm only a first-year intern. I do the best I know how to do but it isn't enough—it will never be enough."

"What you have to learn here is something no Earth doctor knows or could teach you," he said. "You have to have time to learn—and you need equipment and drugs."

"If I could have antibiotics and other drugs . . . I wanted to get a supply from the dispensary but the Gerns wouldn't let me go."

"Some of the Ragnarok plants might be of value if a person could find the right ones. I just came from a talk with Anders about that. He'll provide you with anything possible in the way of equipment and supplies for research—anything in the camp you need to try to save lives. He'll be at your shelter tonight to see what you want. Do you want to try it?"

"Yes—of course." Chiara's eyes lighted with new hope. "It might take a long time to find a cure—maybe we never would—but I'd like to have help so I could try. I'd like to be able, some day once again, to say to a scared kid, 'Take this medicine and in the morning you'll be better,' and know I told the truth."

The nightly prowler attacks continued and the supply of ammunition diminished. It would be some time before men were skilled in the use of the bows and arrows that were being made; and work on the wall was pushed ahead with all speed possible. No one was exempt from labor on it who could as much as carry the pointed stakes. Children down to the youngest worked alongside the men and women.

The work was made many times more exhausting by the 1.5 gravity. People moved heavily at their jobs and even at night there was no surcease from the gravity. They could only go into a coma-like sleep in which there was no real rest and from which they awoke tired and aching. Each morning there would be some who did not awaken at all, though their hearts had been sound enough for working on Earth or Athena.

The killing labor was recognized as necessary, however, and there were no complaints until the morning he was accosted by Peter Bemmon.

He had seen Bemmon several times on the *Constellation*; a big, soft-faced man who had attached much importance to his role as a minor member of the Athena Planning Board. But even on the *Constellation* Bemmon had felt he merited a still higher position, and his ingratiating attitude when before his superiors had become one of fault-finding insinuations concerning their ability as compared with his when their backs were turned.

This resentment had taken new form on Ragnarok, where his former position was of utterly no importance to anyone and his lack of any skills or outdoor experience made him only one worker among others.

The sun was shining mercilessly hot the day Bemmon chose to challenge Prentiss's wisdom as leader. Bemmon was cutting and sharpening stakes, a job the sometimes-too-lenient Anders had given him when Bemmon had insisted his heart was on the verge of failure from doing heavier work. Prentiss was in a hurry and would have gone on past him but Bemmon halted him with a sharp command:

"You—wait a minute!"

Bemmon had a hatchet in his hand, but only one stake lay on the ground; and his face was red with anger, not exertion. Prentiss stopped, wondering if Bemmon was going to ask for a broken jaw, and Bemmon came to him.

"How long," Bemmon asked, anger making his voice a little thick, "do you think I'll tolerate this absurd situation?"

"What situation?" Prentiss asked.

"This stupid insistence upon confining me to manual labor. I'm the single member on Ragnarok of the Athena Planning Board and surely you can see that the bumbling confusion of these people"—Bemmon indicated the hurrying, laboring men, women and children around them—"can be transformed into efficient, organized effort only through proper supervision. Yet my abilities along such lines are ignored and I've been forced to work as a common laborer—a wood chopper!"

He flung the hatchet down viciously, into the rocks at his feet, breathing heavily with resentment and challenge. "I demand the respect to which I'm entitled."

"Look," Prentiss said.

He pointed to the group just then going past them. A sixteen-year-old girl was bent almost double under the weight of the pole she was carrying, her once pretty face flushed and sweating. Behind her two twelve-year-old boys were dragging a still larger pole. Behind them came several small children, each of them carrying as many of the pointed stakes as he or she could walk under, no matter if it was only one. All of them were trying to hurry, to accomplish as much as possible, and no one was complaining even though they were already staggering with weariness.

"So you think you're entitled to more respect?" Prentiss asked. "Those kids would work harder if you were giving them orders from under the shade of a tree—is that what you want?"

Bemmon's lips thinned and hatred was like a sheen on his face. Prentiss looked from the single stake Bemmon had cut that morning to Bemmon's white, unblistered hands. He looked at the hatchet that Bemmon had thrown down in the rocks and at the V notch broken in its keen-edged blade. It had been the best of the very few hatchets they had . . .

"The next time you even nick that hatchet I'm going to split your skull with it," he said. "Pick it up and get back to work. I mean *work*. You'll have broken blisters on every finger tonight or you'll go on the log-carrying force tomorrow. Now, move!"

What Bemmon had thought to be his wrath deserted him before Prentiss's fury. He stooped to obey the order but the hatred remained on his face and when the hatchet was in his hands he made a last attempt to bluster:

"The day may come when we'll refuse to tolerate any longer your sadistic displays of authority."

"Good," Prentiss said. "Anyone who doesn't like my style is welcome to try to change it—or to try to replace me. With knives or clubs, rifles or broken hatchets, Bemmon—any way you want it and any time you want it."

"I—" Bemmon's eyes went from the hatchet in his half raised hand to the long knife in Prentiss's belt. He swallowed with a convulsive jerk of his Adam's apple and his hatchet-bearing arm suddenly wilted. "I don't want to fight—to replace you—"

He swallowed again and his face forced itself into a sickly attempt at an ingratiating smile. "I didn't mean to imply any disrespect for you or the good job you're doing. I'm very sorry."

Then he hurried away, like a man glad to escape, and began to chop stakes with amazing speed.

But the sullen hatred had not been concealed by the ingratiating smile; and Prentiss knew Bemmon was a man who would always be his enemy.

✧   ✧   ✧

The days dragged by in the weary routine, but overworked muscles slowly strengthened and people moved with a little less laborious effort. On the twentieth day the wall was finally completed and the camp was prowler proof.

But the spring weather was a mad succession of heat and cold and storm that caused the Hell Fever to take its toll each day and there was no relaxation from the grueling labor. Weatherproof shelters had to be built as rapidly as possible.

So the work of constructing them began; wearily, sometimes almost hopelessly, but without complaint other than to hate and curse the Gerns more than ever.

There was no more trouble from Bemmon; Prentiss had almost forgotten him when he was publicly challenged one night by a burly, threatening man named Haggar.

"You've bragged that you'll fight any man who dares disagree with you," Haggar said loudly. "Well, here I am. We'll use knives and before they even have time to bury you tonight I'm goin' to have your stooges kicked out and replaced with men who'll give us competent leadership instead of blunderin' authoritarianism."

Prentiss noticed that Haggar seemed to have a little difficulty pronouncing the last word, as though he had learned it only recently.

"I'll be glad to accommodate you," Prentiss said mildly. "Go get yourself a knife."

Haggar already had one, a long-bladed butcher knife, and the duel began. Haggar was surprisingly adept with his knife but he had never had the training and experience in combat that interstellar explorers such as Prentiss had. Haggar was good, but considerably far from good enough.

Prentiss did not kill him. He had no compunctions about doing such a thing, but it would have been an unnecessary waste of needed manpower. He gave Haggar a carefully painful and bloody lesson that thoroughly banished all his lust for conflict without seriously injuring him. The duel was over within a minute after it began.

Bemmon, who had witnessed the challenge with keen interest and then watched Haggar's defeat with agitation, became excessively friendly and flattering toward Prentiss afterward. Prentiss felt sure, although he had no proof, that it had been

Bemmon who had spurred the simple-minded Haggar into challenging him to a duel.

If so, the sight of what had happened to Haggar must have effectively dampened Bemmon's desire for revenge because he became almost a model worker.

As Lake had predicted, he and Prentiss worked together well. Lake calmly took a secondary role, not at all interested in possession of authority but only in the survival of the Rejects. He spoke of the surrender of the *Constellation* only once, to say:

"I knew there could be only Ragnarok in this section of space. I had to order four thousand people to go like sheep to what was to be their place of execution so that four thousand more could live as slaves. That was my last act as an officer."

Prentiss suspected that Lake found it impossible not to blame himself subconsciously for what circumstances had forced him to do. It was irrational—but conscientious men were quite often a little irrational in their sense of responsibility.

Lake had two subleaders: a genial, red-haired man named Ben Barber, who would have been a farmer on Athena but who made a good subleader on Ragnarok; and a lithe, cat-like man named Karl Schroeder.

Schroeder claimed to be twenty-four but not even the scars on his face could make him look more than twenty-one. He smiled often, a little too often. Prentiss had seen smiles like that before. Schroeder was the type who could smile while he killed a man—and he probably had.

But, if Schroeder was a born fighter and perhaps killer, they were characteristics that he expended entirely upon the prowlers. He was Lake's right-hand man; a deadly marksman and utterly without fear.

One evening, when Lake had given Schroeder some instructions concerning the next day's activities, Schroeder answered him with the half-mocking smile and the words, "I'll see that it's done, Commander."

"Not 'Commander,'" Lake said. "I—all of us—left our ranks, titles and honors on the *Constellation*. The past is dead for us."

"I see," Schroeder said. The smile faded away and he looked into Lake's eyes as he asked, "And what about our past dishonors, disgraces and such?"

"They were left on the *Constellation,* too," Lake said. "If anyone wants dishonor he'll have to earn it all over again."

"That sounds fair," Schroeder said. "That sounds as fair as anyone could ever ask for."

He turned away and Prentiss saw what he had noticed before: Schroeder's black hair was coming out light brown at the roots. It was a color that would better match his light complexion and it was the color of hair that a man named Schrader, wanted by the police on Venus, had had.

Hair could be dyed, identification cards could be forged—but it was all something Prentiss did not care to pry into until and if Schroeder gave him reason to. Schroeder was a hard and dangerous man, despite his youth, and sometimes men of that type, when the chips were down, exhibited a higher sense of duty than the soft men who spoke piously of respect for Society— and then were afraid to face danger to protect the society and the people they claimed to respect.

A lone prowler came on the eleventh night following the wall's completion. It came silently, in the dead of night, and it learned how to reach in and tear apart the leather lashings that held the pointed stakes in place and then jerk the stakes out of their sockets. It was seen as it was removing the third stake—which would have made a large enough opening for it to come through—and shot. It fell back and managed to escape into the woods, although staggering and bleeding.

The next night the stockade was attacked by dozens of prowlers who simultaneously began removing the pointed stakes in the same manner employed by the prowler of the night before. Their attack was turned back with heavy losses on both sides and with a dismayingly large expenditure of precious ammunition.

There could be no doubt about how the band of prowlers had learned to remove the stakes: the prowler of the night before had told them before it died. It was doubtful that the prowlers had a spoken language, but they had some means of communication. They worked together and they were highly intelligent, probably about halfway between dog and man.

The prowlers were going to be an enemy even more formidable than Prentiss had thought.

The missing stakes were replaced the next day and the others were tied down more securely. Once again the camp was prowler proof—but only for so long as armed guards patrolled inside the walls to kill attacking prowlers during the short time it would take them to remove the stakes.

The hunting parties suffered unusually heavy losses from prowler attacks that day and that evening, as the guards patrolled inside the walls, Lake said to Prentiss:

"The prowlers are so damnably persistent. It isn't that they're hungry—they don't kill us to eat us. They don't have any reason to kill us—they just hate us."

"They have a reason," Prentiss said. "They're doing the same thing we're doing: fighting for survival."

Lake's pale brows lifted in question.

"The prowlers are the rulers of Ragnarok," Prentiss said. "They fought their way up here, as men did on Earth, until they're master of every creature on their world. Even of the unicorns and swamp crawlers. But now we've come and they're intelligent enough to know that we're accustomed to being the dominant species, ourselves.

"There can't be two dominant species on the same world—and they know it. Men or prowlers—in the end one is going to have to go down before the other."

"I suppose you're right," Lake said. He looked at the guards, a fourth of them already reduced to bows and arrows that they had not yet had time to learn how to use. "If we win the battle for supremacy it will be a long fight, maybe over a period of centuries. And if the prowlers win—it may all be over within a year or two."

The giant blue star that was the other component of Ragnarok's binary grew swiftly in size as it preceded the yellow sun farther each morning. When summer came the blue star would be a sun as hot as the yellow sun and Ragnarok would be between them. The yellow sun would burn the land by day and the blue sun would sear it by the night that would not be night. Then would come the brief fall, followed by the long, frozen winter when the yellow sun would shine pale and cold, far to the south, and the blue sun would be a star again, two hundred and fifty million miles away and invisible behind the cold yellow sun.

The Hell Fever lessened with the completion of the shelters

but it still killed each day. Chiara and his helpers worked with unfaltering determination to find a cure for it but the cure, if there was one, eluded them. The graves in the cemetery were forty long by forty wide and more were added each day. To all the fact became grimly obvious: they were swiftly dying out and they had yet to face Ragnarok at its worst.

The old survival instincts asserted themselves and there were marriages among the younger ones. One of the first to marry was Julia.

She stopped to talk to Prentiss one evening. She still wore the red skirt, now faded and patched, but her face was tired and thoughtful and no longer bold.

"Is it true, John," she asked, "that only a few of us might be able to have children here and that most of us who tried to have children in this gravity would die for it?"

"It's true," he said. "But you already knew that when you married."

"Yes . . . I knew it." There was a little silence. "All my life I've had fun and done as I pleased. The human race didn't need me and we both knew it. But now—none of us can be apart from the others or be afraid of anything. If we're selfish and afraid there will come a time when the last of us will die and there will be nothing on Ragnarok to show we were ever here.

"I don't want it to end like that. I want there to be children, to live after we're gone. So I'm going to try to have a child. I'm not afraid and I won't be."

When he did not reply at once she said, almost self-consciously, "Coming from me that all sounds a little silly, I suppose."

"It sounds wise and splendid, Julia," he said, "and it's what I thought you were going to say."

Full spring came and the vegetation burst into leaf and bud and bloom, quickly, for its growth instincts knew in their mindless way how short was the time to grow and reproduce before the brown death of summer came. The prowlers were suddenly gone one day, to follow the spring north, and for a week men could walk and work outside the stockade without the protection of armed guards.

Then the new peril appeared, the one they had not expected: the unicorns.

The stockade wall was a blue-black rectangle behind them and the blue star burned with the brilliance of a dozen moons, lighting the woods in blue shadow and azure light. Prentiss and the hunter walked a little in front of the two riflemen, winding to keep in the starlit glades.

"It was on the other side of the next grove of trees," the hunter said in a low voice. "Fred was getting ready to bring in the rest of the woods goats. He shouldn't have been more than ten minutes behind me—and it's been over an hour."

They rounded the grove of trees. At first it seemed there was nothing before them but the empty, grassy glade. Then they saw it lying on the ground no more than twenty feet in front of them.

It was—it had been—a man. He was broken and stamped into hideous shapelessness and something had torn off his arms.

For a moment there was dead silence, then the hunter whispered, "*What did that?*"

The answer came in a savage, squealing scream and the pound of cloven hooves. A formless shadow beside the trees materialized into a monstrous charging bulk; a thing like a gigantic gray bull, eight feet tall at the shoulders, with the tusked, snarling head of a boar and the starlight glinting along the curving, vicious length of its single horn.

"*Unicorn!*" Prentiss said, and jerked up his rifle.

The rifles cracked in a ragged volley. The unicorn squealed in fury and struck the hunter, catching him on its horn and hurling him thirty feet. One of the riflemen went down under the unicorn's hooves, his cry ending almost as soon as it began.

The unicorn ripped the sod in deep furrows as it whirled back to Prentiss and the remaining rifleman; not turning in the manner of four-footed beasts of Earth but rearing and spinning on its hind feet. It towered above them as it whirled, the tip of its horn fifteen feet above the ground and its hooves swinging around like great clubs.

Prentiss shot again, his sights on what he hoped would be a vital area, and the rifleman shot an instant later.

The shots went true. The unicorn's swing brought it on around but it collapsed, falling to the ground with jarring heaviness.

"We got it!" the rifleman said. "We—"

It half scrambled to its feet and made a noise; a call that went

out through the night like the blast of a mighty trumpet. Then
it dropped back to the ground, to die while its call was still echoing from the nearer hills.

From the east came an answering trumpet blast; a trumpet-
ing that was sounded again from the south and from the north.
Then there came a low and muffled drumming, like the pounding
of thousands of hooves.

The rifleman's face was blue-white in the starlight. "The others
are coming—we'll have to run for it!"

He turned, and began to run toward the distant bulk of the
stockade.

"No!" Prentiss commanded, quick and harsh. "Not the
stockade!"

The rifleman kept running, seeming not to hear him in his
panic. Prentiss called to him once more:

"Not the stockade—*you'll lead the unicorns into it!*"

Again the rifleman seemed not to hear him.

The unicorns were coming in sight, converging in from the
north and east and south, the rumble of their hooves swelling
to a thunder that filled the night. The rifleman would reach the
stockade only a little ahead of them and they would go through
the wall as though it had been made of paper.

For a while the area inside the stockade would be filled with
dust, with the squealing of the swirling, charging unicorns and
the screams of the dying. Those inside the stockade would have
no chance whatever of escaping. Within two minutes it would
be over, the last child would have been found among the shattered shelters and trampled into lifeless shapelessness in the
bloody ground.

Within two minutes all human life on Ragnarok would be
gone.

There was only one thing for him to do.

He dropped to one knee so his aim would be steady and the
sights of his rifle caught the running man's back. He pressed the
trigger and the rifle cracked viciously as it bucked against his
shoulder.

The man spun and fell hard to the ground. He twisted, to raise
himself up a little and look back, his face white and accusing
and unbelieving.

"*You shot me!*"

Then he fell forward and lay without moving.

Prentiss turned back to face the unicorns and to look at the trees in the nearby grove. He saw what he already knew: they were young trees and too small to offer any escape for him. There was no place to run, no place to hide.

There was nothing he could do but wait; nothing he could do but stand in the blue starlight and watch the devil's herd pound toward him and think, in the last moments of his life, how swiftly and unexpectedly death could come to man on Ragnarok.

The unicorns held the Rejects prisoners in their stockade the rest of the night and all the next day. Lake had seen the shooting of the rifleman and had watched the unicorn herd kill John Prentiss and then trample the dead rifleman.

He had already given the order to build a quick series of fires around the inside of the stockade walls when the unicorns paused to tear their victims to pieces, grunting and squealing in triumph as bones crushed between their teeth and they flung the pieces to one side.

The fires were started and green wood was thrown on them, to make them smolder and smoke for as long as possible. Then the unicorns were coming on to the stockade and every person inside it went into the concealment of the shelters.

Lake had already given his last order: There would be absolute quiet until and if the unicorns left; a quiet that would be enforced with fist or club wherever necessary.

The unicorns were still outside when morning came. The fires could not be refueled; the sight of a man moving inside the stockade would bring the entire herd charging through. The hours dragged by, the smoke from the dying fires dwindled to thin streamers. The unicorns grew increasingly bolder and suspicious, crowding closer to the walls and peering through the openings between rails.

The sun was setting when one of the unicorns trumpeted; a sound different from that of the call to battle. The others threw up their heads to listen, then they turned and drifted away. Within minutes the entire herd was gone out of sight through the woods, toward the north.

Lake waited and watched until he was sure the unicorns were

gone for good. Then he ordered the All Clear given and hurried to the south wall, to look down across the barren valley and hope he would not see what he expected to see.

Barber came up behind him, to sigh with relief. "That was close. It's hard to make so many people stay absolutely quiet for hour after hour. Especially the children—they don't understand."

"We'll have to leave," Lake said.

"Leave?" Barber asked. "We can make this stockade strong enough to hold out unicorns."

"Look to the south," Lake told him.

Barber did so and saw what Lake had already seen; a broad, low cloud of dust moving slowly toward them.

"Another herd of unicorns," Lake said. "John didn't know they migrated—the Dunbar Expedition wasn't here long enough to learn that. There'll be herd after herd coming through and no time for us to strengthen the walls. We'll have to leave tonight."

Preparations were made for the departure; preparations that consisted mainly of providing each person with as much in the way of food or supplies as he or she could carry. In the 1.5 gravity, that was not much.

They left when the blue star rose. They filed out through the northern gate and the rear guard closed it behind them. There was almost no conversation among them. Some of them turned to take a last look at what had been the only home they had ever known on Ragnarok, then they all faced forward again, to the northwest, where the foothills of the plateau might offer them sanctuary.

They found their sanctuary on the second day; a limestone ridge honey-combed with caves. Men were sent back at once to carry the food and supplies left in the stockade to the new home.

They returned, to report that the second herd of unicorns had broken down the walls and ripped the interior of the stockade into wreckage. Much of the food and supplies had been totally destroyed.

Lake sent them back twice more to bring everything, down to the last piece of bent metal or torn cloth. They would find uses for all of it in the future.

✧　　　✧　　　✧

The cave system was extensive, containing room for several times their number. The deeper portions of the caves could not be lived in until ventilation ducts were made, but the outer caves were more than sufficient in number. Work was begun to clear them of fallen rubble, to pry down all loose material overhead and to level the floors. A spring came out of the ridge not far from the caves and the approach to the caves was so narrow and steep that unicorns could scramble up it only with difficulty and one at a time. And should they ever reach the natural terrace in front of the caves they would be too large to enter and could do no more than stand outside and make targets of themselves for the bowmen within.

Anders was in charge of making the caves livable, his working force restricted almost entirely to women and children. Lake sent Barber out, with a small detachment of men, to observe the woods goats and learn what plants they ate. And then learn, by experimenting, if such plants could be safely eaten by humans.

The need for salt would be tremendously increased when summer came. Having once experienced a saltless two weeks in the desert Lake doubted that any of them could survive without it. All hunting parties, as well as Barber's party, were ordered to investigate all deposits that might contain salt as well as any stream or pond that was white along the banks.

The hunting parties were of paramount importance and they were kept out to the limits of their endurance. Every man physically able to do so accompanied them. Those who could not kill game could carry it back to the caves. There was no time to spare; already the unicorns were decreasing in numbers and the woods goats were ranging farther and farther north.

At the end of twenty days Lake went in search of Barber and his party, worried about them. Their mission was one that could be as dangerous as any hunting trip. There was no proof that humans and Ragnarok creatures were so similar as to guarantee that food for one might not be poison for the other. It was a very necessary mission, however; dried meat, alone, would bring grave deficiency diseases during the summer which dried herbs and fruits would help prevent.

When he located Barber's party he found Barber lying under a tree, pale and weak from his latest experiment but recovering.

"I was the guinea pig yesterday," Barber said. "Some little purple berries that the woods goats nibble at sometimes, maybe to get a touch of some certain vitamin or something. I ate too many, I guess, because they hit my heart like the kick of a mule."

"Did you find anything at all encouraging?" Lake asked.

"We found four different herbs that are the most violent cathartics you ever dreamed of. And a little silvery fern that tastes like vanilla flavored candy and paralyzes you stiff as a board on the third swallow. It's an hour before you come back out of it.

"But on the good side we found three different kinds of herbs that seem to be all right. We've been digging them up and hanging them in the trees to dry."

Lake tried the edible herbs and found them to be something like spinach in taste. There was a chance they might contain the vitamins and minerals needed. Since the hunting parties were living exclusively on meat he would have to point out the edible herbs to all of them so they would know what to eat should any of them feel the effects of diet deficiency.

He traveled alone as he visited the various hunting parties, finding such travel to be safer each day as the dwindling of the unicorns neared the vanishing point. It was a safety he did not welcome; it meant the last of the game would be gone north long before sufficient meat was taken.

None of the hunting parties could report good luck. The woods goats, swift and elusive at best, were vanishing with the unicorns. The last cartridge had been fired and the bowmen, while improving all the time, were far from expert. The unicorns, which should have been their major source of meat, were invulnerable to arrows unless shot at short range in the side of the neck just behind the head. And at short range the unicorns invariably charged and presented no such target.

He made the long, hard climb up the plateau's southern face, to stand at last on top. It was treeless, a flat, green table that stretched to the north for as far as he could see. A mountain range, still capped with snow, lay perhaps a hundred miles to the northwest; in the distance it looked like a white, low-lying cloud on the horizon. No other mountains or hills marred the endless sweep of the high plain.

The grass was thick and here and there were little streams of water produced by the recently melted snow. It was a paradise land for the herbivores of Ragnarok but for men it was a harsh, forbidding place. At that elevation the air was so thin that only a moderate amount of exertion made the heart and lungs labor painfully. Hard and prolonged exertion would be impossible.

It seemed unlikely that men could hunt and dare unicorn attacks at such an elevation but two hunting parties were ahead of him; one under the grim Craig and one under the reckless Schroeder, both parties stripped down to the youngest, strongest men among all the Rejects.

He found Schroeder early one morning, leading his hunters toward a small band of woods goats. Two unicorns were grazing in between and the hunters were swinging downwind from them. Schroeder saw him coming and walked back a little way to meet him.

"Welcome to our breathtaking land," Schroeder greeted him. "How are things going with the rest of the hunting parties?"

Schroeder was gaunt and there was weariness beneath his still lithe movements. His whiskers were an untamed sorrel bristling and across his cheekbone was the ugly scar of a half healed wound. Another gash was ripped in his arm and something had battered one ear. He reminded Lake of a battle-scarred, indomitable tomcat who would never, for as long as he lived, want to relinquish the joy of conflict and danger.

"So far," he answered, "you and Craig are the only parties to manage to tackle the plateau."

He asked about Schroeder's luck and learned it had been much better than that of the others due to killing three unicorns by a method Schroeder had thought of.

"Since the bowmen have to be to one side of the unicorns to kill them," Schroeder said, "it only calls for a man to be the decoy and let the unicorns chase him between the hidden bowmen. If there's no more than one or two unicorns and if the decoy doesn't have to run very far and if the bowmen don't miss it works well."

"Judging from your beat-up condition," Lake said, "you must have been the decoy every time."

"Well—" Schroeder shrugged his shoulders. "It was my idea."

"I've been wondering about another way to get in shots at close range," Lake said. "Take the skin of a woods goat, give it the original shape as near as possible, and a bowman inside it might be able to fake a grazing woods goat until he got the shot he wanted.

"The unicorns might never suspect where the arrows came from," he concluded. "And then, of course, they might."

"I'll try it before the day is over, on those two unicorns over there," Schroeder said. "At this elevation and in this gravity my own method is just a little bit rough on a man."

Lake found Craig and his men several miles to the west, all of them gaunt and bearded as Schroeder had been.

"We've had hell," Craig said. "It seems that every time we spot a few woods goats there will be a dozen unicorns in between. If only we had rifles for the unicorns . . ."

Lake told him of the plan to hide under woods goats' skins and of the decoy system used by Schroeder.

"Maybe we won't have to use Schroeder's method," he said. "We'll see if the other works—I'll give it the first try."

This he was not to do. Less than an hour later one of the men who helped dry the meat and carry it to the caves returned to report the camp stricken by a strange, sudden malady that was killing a hundred a day. Dr. Chiara, who had collapsed while driving himself on to care for the sick, was sure it was a deficiency disease. Anders was down with it, helpless, and Bemmon had assumed command; setting up daily work quotas for those still on their feet and refusing to heed Chiara's requests concerning treatment of the disease.

Lake made the trip back to the caves in a fraction of the length of time it had taken him to reach the plateau, walking until he was ready to drop and then pausing only for an hour or two of rest. He spotted Barber's camp when coming down off the plateau and he swung to one side, to tell Barber to have a supply of the herbs sent to the caves at once.

He reached the caves, to find half the camp in bed and the other half dragging about listlessly at the tasks given them by Bemmon. Anders was in grave condition, too weak to rise, and Dr. Chiara was dying.

He squatted down beside Chiara's pallet and knew there could be no hope for him. On Chiara's pale face and in his eyes was the shadow of his own foreknowledge.

"I finally saw what it was"—Chiara's words were very low, hard to hear—"and I told Bemmon what to do. It's a deficiency disease, complicated by the gravity into some form not known on Earth."

He stopped to rest and Lake waited.

"Beri-beri—pellagra—we had deficiency diseases on Earth. But none so fatal—so quickly. I told Bemmon—ration out fruits and vegetables to everybody. Hurry—or it will be too late."

Again he stopped to rest, the last vestige of color gone from his face.

"And you?" Lake asked, already knowing the answer.

"For me—too late. I kept thinking of viruses—should have seen the obvious sooner. Just like—"

His lips turned up a little at the corners and the Chiara of the dead past smiled for the last time at Lake.

"Just like a damned fool intern . . ."

That was all, then, and the chamber was suddenly very quiet. Lake stood up to leave, and to speak the words that Chiara could never hear:

"We're going to need you and miss you—Doctor."

He found Bemmon in the food storage cavern, supervising the work of two teen-age boys with critical officiousness although he was making no move to help them. At sight of Lake he hurried forward, the ingratiating smile sliding across his face.

"I'm glad you're back," he said. "I had to take charge when Anders got sick and he had everything in such a mess. I've been working day and night to undo his mistakes and get the work properly under way again."

Lake looked at the two thin-faced boys who had taken advantage of the opportunity to rest. They leaned wearily against the heavy pole table Bemmon had had them moving, their eyes already dull with incipient sickness and watching him in mute appeal.

"Have you obeyed Chiara's order?" he asked.

"Ah—no," Bemmon said. "I felt it best to ignore it."

"Why?" Lake asked.

"It would be a senseless waste of our small supply of fruit and vegetable foods to give them to people already dying. I'm afraid"—the ingratiating smile came again—"we've been letting him exercise an authority he isn't entitled to. He's really hardly more than a medical student and his diagnoses are only guesses."

"He's dead," Lake said flatly. "His last order will be carried out."

He looked from the two tired boys to Bemmon, contrasting their thinness and weariness with the way Bemmon's paunch still bulged outward and his jowls still sagged with their load of fat.

"I'll send West down to take over in here," he said to Bemmon. "You come with me. You and I seem to be the only two in good health here and there's plenty of work for us to do."

The fawning expression vanished from Bemmon's face. "I see," he said. "Now that I've turned Anders's muddle into organization, you'll hand my authority over to another of your favorites and demote me back to common labor?"

"Setting up work quotas for sick and dying people isn't organization," Lake said. He spoke to the two boys, "Both of you go lie down. West will find someone else." Then to Bemmon, "Come with me. We're both going to work at common labor."

They passed by the cave where Bemmon slept. Two boys were just going into it, carrying armloads of dried grass to make a mattress under Bemmon's pallet. They moved slowly, heavily. Like the two boys in the food storage cave they were dull-eyed with the beginning of the sickness.

Lake stopped, to look more closely into the cave and verify something else he thought he had seen: Bemmon had discarded the prowler skins on his bed and in their place were soft wool blankets; perhaps the only unpatched blankets the Rejects possessed.

"Go back to your caves," he said to the boys. "Go to bed and rest."

He looked at Bemmon. Bemmon's eyes flinched away, refusing to meet his.

"What few blankets we have are for babies and the very youngest children," he said. His tone was coldly unemotional but he could not keep his fists from clenching at his sides. "You will return them at once and sleep on animal skins, as all the men and women do. And if you want grass for a mattress you will carry it yourself, as even the young children do."

Bemmon made no answer, his face a sullen red and hatred shining in the eyes that still refused to meet Lake's.

"Gather up the blankets and return them," Lake said. "Then come on up to the central cave. We have a lot of work to do."

He could feel Bemmon's gaze burning against his back as he turned away and he thought of what John Prentiss had once said:

"I know he's no good but he never has guts enough to go quite far enough to give me an excuse to whittle him down."

Barber's men arrived the next day, burdened with dried herbs. These were given to the seriously ill as a supplement to the ration of fruit and vegetable foods and were given, alone, to those not yet sick. Then came the period of waiting; of hoping that it was all not too late and too little.

A noticeable change for the better began on the second day. A week went by and the sick were slowly, steadily, improving. The not-quite-sick were already back to normal health. There was no longer any doubt: the Ragnarok herbs would prevent a recurrence of the disease.

It was, Lake thought, all so simple once you knew what to do. Hundreds had died, Chiara among them, because they did not have a common herb that grew at a slightly higher elevation. Not a single life would have been lost if he could have looked a week into the future and had the herbs found and taken to the caves that much sooner.

But the disease had given no warning of its coming. Nothing, on Ragnarok, ever seemed to give warning before it killed.

Another week went by and hunters began to trickle in, gaunt and exhausted, to report all the game going north up the plateau and not a single creature left below. They were the ones who had tried and failed to withstand the high elevation of the plateau. Only two out of three hunters returned among those who had challenged the plateau. They had tried, all of them, to the best of their ability and the limits of their endurance.

The blue star was by then a small sun and the yellow sun blazed hotter each day. Grass began to brown and wither on the hillsides as the days went by and Lake knew summer was very near. The last hunting party, but for Craig's and Schroeder's, returned. They had very little meat but they brought with them a large quantity of something almost as important: salt.

They had found a deposit of it in an almost inaccessible region of cliffs and canyons. "Not even the woods goats can get in there," Stevens, the leader of that party, said. "If the salt was in an accessible place there would have been a salt lick there and goats in plenty."

"If woods goats care for salt the way Earth animals do," Lake said. "When fall comes we'll make a salt lick and find out."

Two more weeks went by and Craig and Schroeder returned with their surviving hunters. They had followed the game to the eastern end of the snow-capped mountain range but there the migration had drawn away from them, traveling farther each day than they could travel. They had almost waited too long before turning back: the grass at the southern end of the plateau was turning brown and the streams were dry. They got enough water, barely, by digging seep holes in the dry stream beds.

Lake's method of stalking unicorns under the concealment of a woods goat skin had worked well only a few times. After that the unicorns learned to swing downwind from any lone woods goats. If they smelled a man inside the goat skin they charged him and killed him.

With the return of the last hunters everything was done that could be done in preparation for summer. Inventory was taken of the total food supply and it was even smaller than Lake had feared. It would be far from enough to last until fall brought the game back from the north and he instituted rationing much stricter than before.

The heat increased as the yellow sun blazed hotter and the blue sun grew larger. Each day the vegetation was browner and a morning came when Lake could see no green wherever he looked.

They numbered eleven hundred and ten that morning, out of what had so recently been four thousand. Eleven hundred and ten thin, hungry scarecrows who, already, could do nothing more than sit listlessly in the shade and wait for the hell that was coming. He thought of the food supply, so pitifully small, and of the months it would have to last. He saw the grim, inescapable future for his charges: famine. There was nothing he could do to prevent it. He could only try to forestall complete starvation for all by cutting rations to the bare existence level.

And that would be bare existence for the stronger of them. The weaker were already doomed.

He had them all gather in front of the caves that evening when the terrace was in the shadow of the ridge. He stood before them and spoke to them:

"All of you know we have only a fraction of the amount of food we need to see us through the summer. Tomorrow the present ration will be cut in half. That will be enough to live on, just barely. If that cut isn't made the food supply will be gone long before fall and all of us will die.

"If anyone has any food of any kind it must be turned in to be added to the total supply. Some of you may have thought of your children and kept a little hidden for them. I can understand why you should do that—but you must turn it in. There may possibly be some who hid food for themselves, personally. If so, I give them the first and last warning: turn it in tonight. If any hidden cache of food is found in the future the one who hid it will be regarded as a traitor and murderer.

"All of you, but for the children, will go into the chamber next to the one where the food is stored. Each of you—and there will be no exceptions regardless of how innocent you are—will carry a bulkily folded cloth or garment. Each of you will go into the chamber alone. There will be no one in there. You will leave the food you have folded in the cloth, if any, and go out the other exit and back to your caves. No one will ever know whether the cloth you carried contained food or not. No one will ever ask.

"Our survival on this world, if we are to survive at all, can be only by working and sacrificing together. There can be no selfishness. What any of you may have done in the past is of no consequence. Tonight we start anew. From now on we trust one another without reserve.

"There will be one punishment for any who betray that trust—death."

Anders set the example by being the first to carry a folded cloth into the cave. Of them all, Lake heard later, only Bemmon voiced any real indignation; warning all those in his section of the line that the order was the first step toward outright dictatorship and a police-and-spy system in which Lake and the other leaders would deprive them all of freedom and dignity. Bemmon insisted upon exhibiting the emptiness of the cloth he carried; an action that, had he succeeded in persuading the others to follow his example, would have mercilessly exposed those who did have food they were returning.

But no one followed Bemmon's example and no harm was done. As for Lake, he had worries on his mind of much greater importance than Bemmon's enmity.

The weeks dragged by, each longer and more terrible to endure than the one before it as the heat steadily increased. Summer solstice arrived and there was no escape from the heat, even in the deepest caves. There was no night; the blue sun rose in the east as the yellow sun set in the west. There was no life of any kind to be seen, not even an insect. Nothing moved across the burned land but the swirling dust devils and shimmering, distorted mirages.

The death rate increased with appalling swiftness. The small supply of canned and dehydrated milk, fruit and vegetables was reserved exclusively for the children but it was far insufficient in quantity. The Ragnarok herbs prevented any recurrence of the fatal deficiency disease but they provided virtually no nourishment to help fight the heat and gravity. The stronger of the children lay wasted and listless on their pallets while the ones not so strong died each day.

Each day thin and hollow-eyed mothers would come to plead with him to save their children. " . . . it would take so little to save his life . . . Please—before it's too late . . ."

But there was so little food left and the time was yet so long until fall would bring relief from the famine that he could only answer each of them with a grim and final "No."

And watch the last hope flicker and die in their eyes and watch them turn away, to go and sit for the last hours beside their children.

Bemmon became increasingly irritable and complaining as the rationing and heat made existence a misery; insisting that Lake and the others were to blame for the food shortage, that their hunting efforts had been bungling and faint-hearted. And he implied, without actually saying so, that Lake and the others had forbidden him to go near the food chamber because they did not want a competent, honest man to check up on what they were doing.

There were six hundred and three of them the blazing

afternoon when the girl, Julia, could stand his constant, vindictive, fault-finding no longer. Lake heard about it shortly afterward, the way she had turned on Bemmon in a flare of temper she could control no longer and said:

"Whenever your mouth is still you can hear the children who are dying today—but you don't care. All you can think of is yourself. You claim Lake and the others were cowards—but you didn't dare hunt with them. You keep insinuating that they're cheating us and eating more than we are—but *your* belly is the only one that has any fat left on it—"

She never completed the sentence. Bemmon's face turned livid in sudden, wild fury and he struck her, knocking her against the rock wall so hard that she slumped unconscious to the ground.

"She's a liar!" he panted, glaring at the others. "She's a rotten liar and anybody who repeats what she said will get what she got!"

When Lake learned of what had happened he did not send for Bemmon at once. He wondered why Bemmon's reaction had been so quick and violent and there seemed to be only one answer:

Bemmon's belly *was* still a little fat. There could be but one way he could have kept it so.

He summoned Craig, Schroeder, Barber and Anders. They went to the chamber where Bemmon slept and there, almost at once, they found his cache. He had it buried under his pallet and hidden in cavities along the walls; dried meat, dried fruits and milk, canned vegetables. It was an amount amazingly large and many of the items had presumably been exhausted during the deficiency disease attack.

"It looks," Schroeder said, "like he didn't waste any time feathering his nest when he made himself leader."

The others said nothing but stood with grim, frozen faces, waiting for Lake's next action.

"Bring Bemmon," Lake said to Craig.

Craig returned with him two minutes later. Bemmon stiffened at the sight of his unearthed cache and color drained away from his face.

"Well?" Lake asked.

"I didn't"—Bemmon swallowed—"I didn't know it was there."

And then quickly, "You can't prove I put it there. You can't prove you didn't just now bring it in yourselves to frame me."

Lake stared at Bemmon, waiting. The others watched Bemmon as Lake was doing and no one spoke. The silence deepened and Bemmon began to sweat as he tried to avoid their eyes. He looked again at the damning evidence and his defiance broke.

"It—if I hadn't take it it would have been wasted on people who were dying," he said. He wiped at his sweating face. "I won't ever do it again—I swear I won't."

Lake spoke to Craig. "You and Barber take him to the lookout point."

"What—" Bemmon's protest was cut off as Craig and Barber took him by the arms and walked him swiftly away.

Lake turned to Anders. "Get a rope," he ordered.

Anders paled a little. "A—rope?"

"What else does he deserve?"

"Nothing," Anders said. "Not—not after what he did."

On the way out they passed the place where Julia lay. Bemmon had knocked her against the wall with such force that a sharp projection of rock had cut a deep gash in her forehead. A woman was wiping the blood from her face and she lay limply, still unconscious; a frail shadow of the bold girl she had once been with the new life she would try to give them an almost unnoticeable little bulge in her starved thinness.

The lookout point was an outjutting spur of the ridge, six hundred feet from the caves and in full view of them. A lone tree stood there, its dead limbs thrust like white arms through the brown foliage of the limbs that still lived. Craig and Barber waited under the tree, Bemmon between them. The lowering sun shone hot and bright on Bemmon's face as he squinted back toward the caves at the approach of Lake and the other two.

He twisted to look at Barber. "What is it—why did you bring me here?" There was the tremor of fear in his voice. "What are you going to do to me?"

Barber did not answer and Bemmon turned back toward Lake. He saw the rope in Anders' hand and his face went white with comprehension.

"*No!*"

Ht threw himself back with a violence that almost tore him loose. "*No—no!*"

Schroeder stepped forward to help hold him and Lake took the rope from Anders. He fashioned a noose in it while Bemmon struggled and made panting, animal sounds, his eyes fixed in horrified fascination on the rope.

When the noose was finished he threw the free end of the rope over the white limb above Bemmon. He released the noose and Barber caught it, to draw it snug around Bemmon's neck.

Bemmon stopped struggling then and sagged weakly. For a moment it appeared that he would faint. Then he worked his mouth soundlessly until words came:

"You won't—you can't—really hang me?"

Lake spoke to him:

"We're going to hang you. What you stole would have saved the lives of ten children. You've watched the children cry because they were so hungry and you've watched them become too weak to cry or care any more. You've watched them die each day and each night you've secretly eaten the food that was supposed to be theirs.

"We're going to hang you, for the murder of children and the betrayal of our trust in you. If you have anything to say, say it now."

"You can't! I had a right to live—to eat what would have been wasted on dying people!" Bemmon twisted to appeal to the ones who held him, his words quick and ragged with hysteria. "You can't hang me—I don't want to die!"

Craig answered him, with a smile that was like the thin snarl of a wolf:

"Neither did two of my children."

Lake nodded to Craig and Schroeder, not waiting any longer. They stepped back to seize the free end of the rope and Bemmon screamed at what was coming, tearing loose from the grip of Barber.

Then his scream was abruptly cut off as he was jerked into the air. There was a cracking sound and he kicked spasmodically, his head setting grotesquely to one side.

Craig and Schroeder and Barber watched him with hard, expressionless faces but Anders turned quickly away, to be suddenly and violently sick.

"He was the first to betray us," Lake said. "Snub the rope and leave him to swing there. If there are any others like him, they'll know what to expect."

The blue sun rose as they went back to the caves. Behind them Bemmon swung and twirled aimlessly on the end of the rope. Two long, pale shadows swung and twirled with him; a yellow one to the west and a blue one to the east.

Bemmon was buried the next day. Someone cursed his name and someone spit on his grave and then he was part of the dead past as they faced the suffering ahead of them.

Julia recovered, although she would always wear a ragged scar on her forehead. Anders, who had worked closely with Chiara and was trying to take his place, quieted her fears by assuring her that the baby she carried was still too small for there to be much danger of the fall causing her to lose it.

Three times during the next month the wind came roaring down out of the northwest, bringing a gray dust that filled the sky and enveloped the land in a hot, smothering gloom through which the suns could not be seen.

Once black clouds gathered in the distance, to pour out a cloudburst. The 1.5 gravity gave the wall of water that swept down the canyon a far greater force and velocity than it would have had on Earth and boulders the size of small houses were tossed into the air and shattered into fragments. But all the rain fell upon the one small area and not a drop fell at the caves.

One single factor was in their favor and but for it they could not have survived such intense, continual heat: there was no humidity. Water evaporated quickly in the hot, dry air and sweat glands operated at the highest possible degree of efficiency. As a result they drank enormous quantities of water—the average adult needed five gallons a day. All canvas had been converted into water bags and the same principle of cooling-by-evaporation gave them water that was only warm instead of sickeningly hot as it would otherwise have been.

But despite the lack of humidity the heat was still far more intense than any on Earth. It never ceased, day or night, never let them have a moment's relief. There was a limit to how long human flesh could bear up under it, no matter how valiant the will. Each day the toll of those who had reached that limit was greater, like a swiftly rising tide.

There were three hundred and forty of them when the first rain came; the rain that meant the end of summer. The yellow sun moved southward and the blue sun shrank steadily. Grass grew again and the woods goats returned, with them the young that had been born in the north, already half the size of their mothers.

For a while there was meat, and green herbs. Then the prowlers came, to make hunting dangerous. Females with pups were seen but always at a great distance as though the prowlers, like humans, took no chances with the lives of their children.

The unicorns came close behind the first prowlers, their young amazingly large and already weaned. Hunting became doubly dangerous then but the bowmen, through necessity, were learning how to use their bows with increasing skill and deadliness.

A salt lick for the woods goats was hopefully tried, although Lake felt dubious about it. They learned that salt was something the woods goats could either take or leave alone. And when hunters were in the vicinity they left it alone.

The game was followed for many miles to the south. The hunters returned the day the first blizzard came roaring and screaming down over the edge of the plateau; the blizzard that marked the beginning of the long, frigid winter. By then they were prepared as best they could be. Wood had been carried in great quantities and the caves fitted with crude doors and a ventilation system. And they had meat—not as much as they would need but enough to prevent starvation.

Lake took inventory of the food supply when the last hunters returned and held check-up inventories at irregular and unannounced intervals. He found no shortages. He had expected none—Bemmon's grave had long since been obliterated by drifting snow but the rope still hung from the dead limb, the noose swinging and turning in the wind.

Anders had made a Ragnarok calendar that spring, from data given him by John Prentiss, and he had marked the corresponding Earth dates on it. By a coincidence, Christmas came near the middle of the winter. There would be the same rationing of food on Christmas day but little brown trees had been cut for the children and decorated with such ornaments as could be made from the materials at hand.

There was another blizzard roaring down off the plateau Christmas morning; a white death that thundered and howled outside the caves at a temperature of more than eighty degrees below zero. But inside the caves it was warm by the fires and under the little brown trees were toys that had been patiently whittled from wood or sewn from scraps of cloth and animal skins while the children slept. They were crude and humble toys but the pale, thin faces of the children were bright with delight when they beheld them.

There was the laughter of children at play, a sound that had not been heard for many months, and someone singing the old, old songs. For a few fleeting hours that day, for the first and last time on Ragnarok, there was the magic of an Earth Christmas.

That night a child was born to Julia, on a pallet of dried grass and prowler skins. She asked for her baby before she died and they let her have it.

"I wasn't afraid, was I?" she asked. "But I wish it wasn't so dark—I wish I could see my baby before I go."

They took the baby from her arms when she was gone and removed from it the blanket that had kept her from learning that her child was still-born.

There were two hundred and fifty of them when the first violent storms of spring came. By then eighteen children had been born. Sixteen were still-born, eight of them deformed by the gravity, but two were like any normal babies on Earth. There was only one difference: the 1.5 gravity did not seem to affect them as much as it had the Earth-born babies.

Lake, himself, married that spring; a tall, gray-eyed girl who had fought alongside the men the night of the storm when the prowlers broke into John Prentiss's camp. And Schroeder married, the last of them all to do so.

That spring Lake sent out two classes of bowmen: those who would use the ordinary short bow and those who would use the longbows he had had made that winter. According to history the English longbowmen of medieval times had been without equal in the range and accuracy of their arrows and such extra-powerful weapons should eliminate close-range stalking of woods goats and afford better protection from unicorns.

The longbows worked so well that by mid-spring he could

detach Craig and three others from the hunting and send them on a prospecting expedition. Prentiss had said Ragnarok was devoid of metals but there was the hope of finding small veins the Dunbar Expedition's instruments had not detected. They would have to find metal or else, in the end, they would go back into a flint axe stage.

Craig and his men returned when the blue star was a sun again and the heat was more than men could walk and work in. They had traveled hundreds of miles in their circuit and found no metals.

"I want to look to the south when fall comes," Craig said. "Maybe it will be different down there."

They did not face famine that summer as they had the first summer. The diet of meat and dried herbs was rough and plain but there was enough of it.

Full summer came and the land was again burned and lifeless. There was nothing to do but sit wearily in the shade and endure the heat, drawing what psychological comfort they could from the fact that summer solstice was past and the suns were creeping south again even though it would be many weeks before there was any lessening of the heat.

It was then, and by accident, that Lake discovered there was something wrong about the southward movement of the suns.

He was returning from the lookout that day and he realized it was exactly a year since he and the others had walked back to the caves while Bemmon swung on the limb behind them.

It was even the same time of day; the blue sun rising in the east behind him and the yellow sun bright in his face as it touched the western horizon before him. He remembered how the yellow sun had been like the front sight of a rifle, set in the deepest V notch of the western hills—

But now, exactly a year later, it was not in the V notch. It was on the north side of the notch.

He looked to the east, at the blue sun. It seemed to him that it, too, was farther north than it had been although with it he had no landmark to check by.

But there was no doubt about the yellow sun: it was going south, as it should at that time of year, but it was lagging behind schedule. The only explanation Lake could think of was one that would mean still another threat to their survival; perhaps greater than all the others combined.

The yellow sun dropped completely behind the north slope of the V notch and he went on to the caves. He found Craig and Anders, the only two who might know anything about Ragnarok's axial tilts, and told them what he had seen.

"I made the calendar from the data John gave me," Anders said. "The Dunbar men made observations and computed the length of Ragnarok's year—I don't think they would have made any mistake."

"If they didn't," Lake said, "we're in for something."

Craig was watching him, closely, thoughtfully. "Like the Ice Ages of Earth?" he asked.

Lake nodded and Anders said, "I don't understand."

"Each year the north pole tilts toward the sun to give us summer and away from it to give us winter," Lake said. "Which, of course, you know. But there can be still another kind of axial tilt. On Earth it occurs at intervals of thousands of years. The tilting that produces the summers and winters goes on as usual but as the centuries go by the summer tilt toward the sun grows less, the winter tilt away from it greater. The north pole leans farther and farther from the sun and ice sheets come down out of the north—an Ice Age. Then the north pole's progression away from the sun stops and the ice sheets recede as it tilts back toward the sun."

"I see," Anders said. "And if the same thing is happening here, we're going away from an ice age but at a rate thousands of times faster than on Earth."

"I don't know whether it's Ragnarok's tilt, alone, or if the orbits of the suns around each other add effects of their own over a period of years," Lake said. "The Dunbar Expedition wasn't here long enough to check up on anything like that."

"It seemed to me it was hotter this summer than last," Craig said. "Maybe only my imagination—but it won't be imagination in a few years if the tilt toward the sun continues."

"The time would come when we'd have to leave here," Lake said. "We'd have to go north up the plateau each spring. There's no timber there—nothing but grass and wind and thin air. We'd have to migrate south each fall."

"Yes . . . migrate." Anders's face was old and weary in the harsh reflected light of the blue sun and his hair had turned almost white in the past year. "Only the young ones could ever adapt enough to go up the plateau to its north portion. The rest of us . . . but we haven't many years, anyway. Ragnarok is for the young—and if they have to migrate back and forth like animals just to stay alive they will never have time to accomplish anything or be more than stone age nomads."

"I wish we could know how long the Big Summer will be that we're going into," Craig said. "And how long and cold the Big Winter, when Ragnarok tilts away from the sun. It wouldn't change anything—but I'd like to know."

"We'll start making and recording daily observations," Lake said. "Maybe the tilt will start back the other way before it's too late."

Fall seemed to come a little later that year. Craig went to the south as soon as the weather permitted but there were no minerals there; only the metal-barren hills dwindling in size until they became a prairie that sloped down and down toward the southern lowlands where all the creatures of Ragnarok spent the winter.

"I'll try again to the north when spring comes," Craig said. "Maybe that mountain on the plateau will have something."

Winter came, and Elaine died in giving him a son. The loss of Elaine was an unexpected blow; hurting more than he would ever have thought possible.

But he had a son . . . and it was his responsibility to do whatever he could to insure the survival of his son and of the sons and daughters of all the others.

His outlook altered and he began to think of the future, not in terms of years to come but in terms of generations to come. Someday one of the young ones would succeed him as leader but the young ones would have only childhood memories of Earth. He was the last leader who had known Earth and the civilization of Earth as a grown man. What he did while he was leader would incline the destiny of a new race.

He would have to do whatever was possible for him to do and he would have to begin at once. The years left to him could not be many.

He was not alone; others in the caves had the same thoughts

he had regarding the future even though none of them had any plan for accomplishing what they spoke of. West, who had held degrees in philosophy on Earth, said to Lake one night as they sat together by the fire:

"Have you noticed the way the children listen when the talk turns to what used to be on Earth, what might have been on Athena, and what would be if only we could find a way to escape Ragnarok?"

"I've noticed," he said.

"These stories already contain the goal for the future generations," West went on. "Someday, somehow, they will go to Athena, to kill the Gerns there and free the Terran slaves and reclaim Athena as their own."

He had listened to them talk of the interstellar flight to Athena as they sat by their fires and worked at making bows and arrows. It was only a dream they held, yet without that dream there would be nothing before them but the vision of generation after generation living and dying on a world that could never give them more than existence.

The dream was needed. But it, alone, was not enough. How long, on Earth, had it been from the Neolithic age to advanced civilization—how long from the time men were ready to leave their caves until they were ready to go to the stars?

Twelve thousand years.

There were men and women among the Rejects who had been specialists in various fields. There were a few books that had survived the trampling of the unicorns and others could be written with ink made from the black lance tree bark upon parchment made from the thin inner skin of unicorn hides.

The knowledge contained in the books and the learning of the Rejects still living should be preserved for the future generations. With the help of that learning perhaps they really could, someday, somehow, escape from their prison and make Athena their own.

He told West of what he had been thinking. "We'll have to start a school," he said. "This winter—tomorrow."

West nodded in agreement. "And the writings should be commenced as soon as possible. Some of the textbooks will require more time to write than Ragnarok will give the authors."

A school for the children was started the next day and the

writing of the books began. The parchment books would serve two purposes. One would be to teach the future generations things that would not only help them survive but would help them create a culture of their own as advanced as the harsh environment and scanty resources of Ragnarok permitted. The other would be to warn them of the danger of a return of the Gerns and to teach them all that was known about Gerns and their weapons.

Lake's main contribution would be a lengthy book: TERRAN SPACESHIPS; TYPES AND OPERATION. He postponed its writing, however, to first produce a much smaller book but one that might well be more important: INTERIOR FEATURES OF A GERN CRUISER. Terran Intelligence knew a little about Gern cruisers and as second-in-command of the *Constellation* he had seen and studied a copy of that report. He had an excellent memory for such things, almost photographic, and he wrote the text and drew a multitude of sketches.

He shook his head ruefully at the result. The text was good but, for clarity, the accompanying illustrations should be accurate and in perspective. And he was definitely not an artist.

He discovered that Craig could take a pen in his scarred, powerful hand and draw with the neat precision of a professional artist. He turned the sketches over to him, together with the mass of specifications. Since it might someday be of such vital importance, he would make four copies of it. The text was given to a teen-age girl, who would make three more copies of it . . .

Four days later Schroeder handed Lake a text with some rough sketches. The title was: OPERATION OF GERN BLASTERS.

Not even Intelligence had ever been able to examine a Gern hand blaster. But a man named Schrader, on Venus, had killed a Gern with his own blaster and then disappeared with both infuriated Gerns and Gern-intimidated Venusian police in pursuit. There had been a high reward for his capture . . .

He looked it over and said, "I was counting on your giving us this."

Only the barest trace of surprise showed on Schroeder's face but his eyes were intently watching Lake. "So you knew all the time who I was?"

"I knew."

"Did anyone else on the *Constellation* know?"

"You were recognized by one of the ship's officers. You would have been tried in two more days."

"I see," Schroeder said. "And since I was guilty and couldn't be returned to Earth or Venus I'd have been executed on the *Constellation*." He smiled sardonically. "And you, as second-in-command, would have been my execution's master of ceremonies."

Lake put the parchment sheets back together in their proper order. "Sometimes," he said, "a ship's officer has to do things that are contrary to all his own wishes."

Schroeder drew a deep breath, his face somber with the memories he had kept to himself.

"It was two years ago when the Gerns were still talking friendship to the Earth government while they shoved the colonists around on Venus. This Gern . . . there was a girl there and he thought he could do what he wanted to her because he was a mighty Gern and she was nothing. He did. That's why I killed him. I had to kill two Venusian police to get away—that's where I put the rope around my neck."

"It's not what we did but what we do that we'll live or die by on Ragnarok," Lake said. He handed Schroeder the sheets of parchment. "Tell Craig to make at least four copies of this. Someday our knowledge of Gern blasters may be something else we'll live or die by."

The school and writing were interrupted by the spring hunting. Craig made his journey to the Plateau's snowcapped mountain but he was unable to keep his promise to prospect it. The plateau was perhaps ten thousand feet in elevation and the mountain rose another ten thousand feet above the plateau. No human could climb such a mountain in a 1.5 gravity.

"I tried," he told Lake wearily when he came back. "Damn it, I never tried harder at anything in my life. It was just too much for me. Maybe some of the young ones will be better adapted and can do it when they grow up."

Craig brought back several sheets of unusually transparent mica, each sheet a foot in diameter, and a dozen large water-clear quartz crystals.

"Float, from higher up on the mountain," he said. "The mica and crystals are in place up there if we could only reach them.

Other minerals, too—I panned traces in the canyon bottoms. But no iron."

Lake examined the sheets of mica. "We could make windows for the outer caves of these," he said. "Have them double thickness with a wide air space between, for insulation. As for the quartz crystals . . ."

"Optical instruments," Craig said. "Binoculars, microscopes— it would take us a long time to learn how to make glass as clear and flawless as those crystals. But we have no way of cutting and grinding them."

Craig went to the east that fall and to the west the next spring. He returned from the trip to the west with a twisted knee that would never let him go prospecting again.

"It will take years to find the metals we need," he said. "The indications are that we never will but I wanted to keep on try- ing. Now, my damned knee has me chained to these caves . . ."

He reconciled himself to his lameness and confinement as best he could and finished his textbook: GEOLOGY AND MINERAL IDENTIFICATION.

He also taught a geology class during the winters. It was in the winter of the year four on Ragnarok that a nine-year-old boy entered his class; the silent, scar-faced Billy Humbolt.

He was by far the youngest of Craig's students, and the most attentive. Lake was present one day when Craig asked, curiously:

"It's not often a boy your age is so interested in mineral- ogy and geology, Billy. Is there something more than just interest?"

"I have to learn all about minerals," Billy said with matter- of-fact seriousness, "so that when I'm grown I can find the metals for us to make a ship."

"And then?" Craig asked.

"And then we'd go to Athena, to kill the Gerns who caused my mother to die, and my grandfather, and Julia, and all the others. And to free my father and the other slaves if they're still alive."

"I see," Craig said.

He did not smile. His face was shadowed and old as he looked at the boy and beyond him; seeing again, perhaps, the frail blonde girl and the two children that the first quick, violent months had taken from him.

"I hope you succeed," he said. "I wish I was young so I could dream of the same thing. But I'm not . . . so let's get back to the identification of the ores that will be needed to make a ship to go to Athena and to make blasters to kill Gerns after you get there."

Lake had a corral built early the following spring, with camouflaged wings, to trap some of the woods goats when they came. It would be an immense forward step toward conquering their new environment if they could domesticate the goats and have goat herds near the caves all through the year. Gathering enough grass to last a herd of goats through the winter would be a problem—but first, before they worried about that, they would have to see if the goats could survive the summer and winter extremes of heat and cold.

They trapped ten goats that spring. They built them brush sunshades—before summer was over the winds would have stripped the trees of most of their dry, brown leaves—and a stream of water was diverted through the corral.

It was all work in vain. The goats died from the heat in early summer, together with the young that had been born.

When fall came they trapped six more goats. They built them shelters that would be as warm as possible and carried them a large supply of the tall grass from along the creek banks; enough to last them through the winter. But the cold was too much for the goats and the second blizzard killed them all.

The next spring and fall, and with much more difficulty, they tried the experiment with pairs of unicorns. The results were the same.

Which meant they would remain a race of hunters. Ragnarok would not permit them to be herdsmen.

The years went by, each much like the one before it but for the rapid aging of the Old Ones, as Lake and the others called themselves, and the growing up of the Young Ones. No woman among the Old Ones could any longer have children, but six more normal, healthy children had been born. Like the first two, they were not affected by the gravity as Earth-born babies had been.

Among the Young Ones, Lake saw, was a distinguishable difference. Those who had been very young the day the Gerns had left them to die had adapted better than those who had been a few years older.

The environment of Ragnarok had struck at the very young with merciless savagery. It had subjected them to a test of survival that was without precedent on Earth. It had killed them by the hundreds but among them had been those whose young flesh and blood and organs had resisted death by adapting to the greatest extent possible.

The day of the Old Ones was almost done and the future would soon be in the hands of the Young Ones. They were the ninety unconquerables out of what had been four thousand Rejects; the first generation of what would be a new race.

It seemed to Lake that the years came and went ever faster as the Old Ones dwindled in numbers at an accelerating rate. Anders had died in the sixth year, his heart failing him one night as he worked patiently in his crude little laboratory at carrying on the work started by Chiara to find a cure for the Hell Fever. Barber, trying to develop a strain of herbs that would grow in the lower elevation of the caves, was killed by a unicorn as he worked in his test plot below the caves. Craig went limping out one spring day on the eighth year to look at a new mineral a hunter had found a mile from the caves. A sudden cold rain blew up, chilling him before he could return, and he died of Hell Fever the same day.

Schroeder was killed by prowlers the same year, dying with his back to a tree and a bloody knife in his hand. It was the way he would have wanted to go—once he had said to Lake:

"When my time comes I would rather it be against the prowlers. They fight hard and kill quick and then they're through with you. They don't tear you up after you're dead and slobber and gloat over the pieces, the way the unicorns do."

The springs came a little earlier each year, the falls a little later, and the observations showed the suns progressing steadily northward. But the winters, though shorter, were seemingly as cold as ever. The long summers reached such a degree of heat on the ninth year that Lake knew they could endure no more than two or three years more of the increasing heat.

Then, in the summer of the tenth year, the tilting of Ragnarok—the apparent northward progress of the suns—stopped. They were in the middle of what Craig had called Big

Summer and they could endure it—just barely. They would not have to leave the caves.

The suns started their drift southward. The observations were continued and carefully recorded. Big Fall was coming and behind it would be Big Winter.

Big Winter . . . the threat of it worried Lake. How far to the south would the suns go—how long would they stay? Would the time come when the plateau would be buried under hundreds of feet of snow and the caves enclosed in glacial ice?

There was no way he could ever know or even guess. Only those of the future would ever know.

On the twelfth year only Lake and West were left of the Old Ones. By then there were eighty-three left of the Young Ones, eight Ragnarok-born children of the Old Ones and four Ragnarok-born children of the Young Ones. Not counting himself and West, there were ninety-five of them.

It was not many to be the beginnings of a race that would face an ice age of unknown proportions and have over them, always, the threat of a chance return of the Gerns.

The winter of the fifteenth year came and he was truly alone, the last of the Old Ones. White-haired and aged far beyond his years, he was still leader. But that winter he could do little other than sit by his fire and feel the gravity dragging at his heart. He knew, long before spring, that it was time he chose his successor.

He had hoped to live to see his son take his place—but Jim was only thirteen. Among the others was one he had been watching since the day he told Craig he would find metals to build a ship and kill the Gerns: Bill Humbolt.

Bill Humbolt was not the oldest among those who would make leaders but he was the most versatile of them all, the most thoughtful and stubbornly determined. He reminded Lake of that fierce old man who had been his grandfather and had it not been for the scars that twisted his face into grim ugliness he would have looked much like him.

A violent storm was roaring outside the caves the night he told the others that he wanted Bill Humbolt to be his successor. There were no objections and, without ceremony and with few words, he terminated his fifteen years of leadership.

He left the others, his son among them, and went back to the cave where he slept. His fire was low, down to dying embers, but he was too tired to build it up again. He lay down on his pallet and saw, with neither surprise nor fear, that his time was much nearer than he had thought. It was already at hand.

He lay back and let the lassitude enclose him, not fighting it. He had done the best he could for the others and now the weary journey was over.

His thoughts dissolved into the memory of the day fifteen years before. The roaring of the storm became the thunder of the Gern cruisers as they disappeared into the gray sky. Four thousand Rejects stood in the cold wind and watched them go, the children not yet understanding that they had been condemned to die. Somehow, his own son was among them—

He tried feebly to rise. There was work to do—a lot of work to do . . .

Part 2

It was early morning as Bill Humbolt sat by the fire in his cave and studied the map Craig had made of the plateau's mountain. Craig had left the mountain nameless and he dipped his pen in ink to write: *Craig Mountains.*

"Bill—"

Delmont Anders entered very quietly, what he had to tell already evident on his face.

"He died last night, Bill."

It was something he had been expecting to come at any time but the lack of surprise did not diminish the sense of loss. Lake had been the last of the Old Ones, the last of those who had worked and fought and shortened the years of their lives that the Young Ones might have a chance to live. Now he was gone— now a brief era was ended, a valiant, bloody chapter written and finished.

And he was the new leader who would decree how the next chapter should be written, only four years older than the boy who was looking at him with an unconscious appeal for reassurance on his face . . .

"You'd better tell Jim," he said. "Then, a little later, I want to talk to everyone about the things we'll start doing as soon as spring comes."

"You mean, the hunting?" Delmont asked.

"No—more than just the hunting."

He sat for a while after Delmont left, looking back down the years that had preceded that day, back to that first morning on Ragnarok.

He had set a goal for himself that morning when he left his toy bear in the dust behind him and walked beside Julia into the new and perilous way of life. He had promised himself that some day he would watch the Gerns die and beg for mercy as they died and he would give them the same mercy they had given his mother.

As he grew older he realized that his hatred, alone, was a futile thing. There would have to be a way of leaving Ragnarok and there would have to be weapons with which to fight the Gerns. These would be things impossible and beyond his reach unless he had the help of all the others in united, coordinated effort.

To make certain of that united effort he would have to be their leader. So for eleven years he had studied and trained until there was no one who could use a bow or spear quite as well as he could, no one who could travel as far in a day or spot a unicorn ambush as quickly. And there was no one, with the exception of George Ord, who had studied as many textbooks as he had.

He had reached his first goal—he was leader. For all of them there existed the second goal: the hope of someday leaving Ragnarok and taking Athena from the Gerns. For many of them, perhaps, it was only wishful dreaming but for him it was the prime driving force of his life.

There was so much for them to do and their lives were so short in which to do it. For so long as he was leader they would not waste a day in idle wishing . . .

When the others were gathered to hear what he had to say he spoke to them:

"We're going to continue where the Old Ones had to leave off. We're better adapted than they were and we're going to find metals to make a ship if there are any to be found.

"Somewhere on Ragnarok, on the northwest side of a range

similar to the Craig Mountains on the plateau, is a deep valley that the Dunbar Expedition called the Chasm. They didn't investigate it closely since their instruments showed no metals there but they saw strata in one place that was red; an iron discoloration. Maybe we can find a vein there that was too small for them to have paid any attention to. So we'll go over the Craigs as soon as the snow melts from them."

"That will be in early summer," George Ord said, his black eyes thoughtful. "Whoever goes will have to time their return for either just before the prowlers and unicorns come back from the north or wait until they've all migrated down off the plateau."

It was something Humbolt had been thinking about and wishing they could remedy. Men could elude unicorn attacks wherever there were trees large enough to offer safety and even prowler attacks could be warded off wherever there were trees for refuge; spears holding back the prowlers who would climb the trees while arrows picked off the ones on the ground. But there were no trees on the plateau, and to be caught by a band of prowlers or unicorns there was certain death for any small party of two or three. For that reason no small parties had ever gone up on the plateau except when the unicorns and prowlers were gone or nearly so. It was an inconvenience and it would continue for as long as their weapons were the slow-to-reload bows.

"You're supposed to be our combination inventor-craftsman," he said to George. "No one else can compare with you in that respect. Besides, you're not exactly enthusiastic about such hard work as mountain climbing. So from now on you'll do the kind of work you're best fitted for. Your first job is to make us a better bow. Make it like a crossbow, with a sliding action to draw and cock the string and with a magazine of arrows mounted on top of it."

George studied the idea thoughtfully. "The general principle is simple," he said. "I'll see what I can do."

"How many of us will go over the Craig Mountains, Bill?" Dan Barber asked.

"You and I," Humbolt answered. "A three-man party under Bob Craig will go into the Western Hills and another party under Johnny Stevens will go into the Eastern Hills."

He looked toward the adjoining cave where the guns had been stored for so long, coated with unicorn tallow to protect them from rust.

"We could make gun powder if we could find a deposit of saltpeter. We already know where there's a little sulphur. The guns would have to be converted to flintlocks, though, since we don't have what we need for cartridge priming material. Worse, we'd have to use ceramic bullets. They would be inefficient—too light, and destructive to the bores. But we would need powder for mining if we ever found any iron. And, if we can't have metal bullets to shoot the Gerns, we can have bombs to blast them with."

"Suppose," Johnny Stevens said, "that we never do find the metals to make a ship. How will we ever leave Ragnarok if that happens?"

"There's another way—a possible way—of leaving here without a ship of our own. If there are no metals we'll have to try it."

"Why wait?" Bob Craig demanded. "Why not try it now?"

"Because the odds would be about ten thousand to one in favor of the Gerns. But we'll try it if everything else fails."

George made, altered, and rejected four different types of crossbows before he perfected a reloading bow that met his critical approval. He brought it to where Humbolt stood outside the caves early one spring day when the grass was sending up the first green shoots on the southern hillsides and the long winter was finally dying.

"Here it is," he said, handing Humbolt the bow. "Try it."

He took it, noting the fine balance of it. Projecting down from the center of the bow, at right angles to it, was a stock shaped to fit the grip of the left hand. Under the crossbar was a sliding stock for the right hand, shaped like the butt of a pistol and fitted with a trigger. Mounted slightly above and to one side of the crossbar was a magazine containing ten short arrows.

The pistol grip was in position near the forestock. He pulled it back the length of the crossbar and it brought the string with it, stretching it taut. There was a click as the trigger mechanism locked the bowstring in place and at the same time a concealed spring arrangement shoved an arrow into place against the string.

He took quick aim at a distant tree and pressed the trigger. There was a twang as the arrow was ejected. He jerked the sliding pistol grip forward and back to reload, pressing the trigger an instant later. Another arrow went its way.

By the time he had fired the tenth arrow in the magazine he was shooting at the rate of one arrow per second. On the trunk of the distant tree, like a bristle of stiff whiskers, the ten arrows were driven deep into the wood in an area no larger than the chest of a prowler or head of a unicorn.

"This is better than I hoped for," he said to George. "One man with one of these would equal six men with ordinary bows."

"I'm going to add another feature," George said. "Bundles of arrows, ten to the bundle in special holders, to carry in the quivers. To reload the magazine you'd just slap down a new bundle of arrows, in no more time than it would take to put one arrow in an ordinary bow. I figured that with practice a man should be able to get off forty arrows in not much more than twenty seconds."

George took the bow and went back in the cave to add his new feature. Humbolt stared after him, thinking, *If he can make something like that out of wood and unicorn gut, what would he be able to give us if he could have metal?*

Perhaps George would never have the opportunity to show what he could do with metal. But Humbolt already felt sure that George's genius would, if it ever became necessary, make possible the alternate plan for leaving Ragnarok.

The weeks dragged into months and at last enough snow was gone from the Craigs that Humbolt and Dan Barber could start. They met no opposition. The prowlers had long since disappeared into the north and the unicorns were very scarce. They had no occasion to test the effectiveness of the new automatic crossbows in combat; a lack of opportunity that irked Barber.

"Any other time, if we had ordinary bows," he complained, "the unicorns would be popping up to charge us from all directions."

"Don't fret," Humbolt consoled him. "This fall, when we come back, they will be."

They reached the mountain and stopped near its foot where a creek came down, its water high and muddy with melting snows. There they hunted until they had obtained all the meat they could carry. They would see no more game when they went up the mountain's canyons. A poisonous weed replaced most of the grass in all the canyons and the animals of Ragnarok had learned long before to shun the mountain.

They found the canyon that Craig and his men had tried to explore and started up it. It was there that Craig had discovered the quartz and mica and so far as he had been able to tell the head of that canyon would be the lowest of all the passes over the mountain.

The canyon went up the mountain diagonally so that the climb was not steep although it was constant. They began to see mica and quartz crystals in the creek bed and at noon on the second day they passed the last stunted tree. Nothing grew higher than that point but the thorny poison weeds and they were scarce.

The air was noticeably thinner there and their burdens heavier. A short distance beyond they came to a small rock monument; Craig's turn-back point.

The next day they found the quartz crystals in place. A mile farther was the vein the mica had come from. Of the other minerals Craig had hoped to find, however, there were only traces.

The fourth day was an eternity of struggling up the now-steeper canyon under loads that seemed to weigh hundreds of pounds; forcing their protesting legs to carry them fifty steps at a time, at the end of which they would stop to rest while their lungs labored to suck in the thin air in quick, panting breaths.

It would have been much easier to have gone around the mountain. But the Chasm was supposed to be like a huge cavity scooped out of the plateau beyond the mountain, rimmed with sheer cliffs a mile high. Only on the side next to the mountain was there a slope leading down into it.

They stopped for the night where the creek ended in a small spring. There the snow still clung to the canyon's walls and there the canyon curved, offering them the promise of the summit just around the bend as it had been doing all day.

The sun was hot and bright the next morning as they made their slow way on again. The canyon straightened, the steep walls of it flattening out to make a pair of ragged shoulders with a saddle between them.

They climbed to the summit of the saddle and there, suddenly before them, was the other side of the world—and the Chasm.

Far below them was a plateau, stretching endlessly like the one they had left behind them. But the chasm dominated all else. It was a gigantic, sheer-walled valley, a hundred miles long by forty miles wide, sunk deep in the plateau with the tops of its mile-high walls level with the floor of the plateau. The mountain under them dropped swiftly away, sloping down and down to the level of the plateau and then on, down and down again, to the bottom of the chasm that was so deep its floor was half hidden by the morning shadows.

"My God!" Barber said. "It must be over three miles under us to the bottom, on the vertical. Ten miles of thirty-three percent grade—if we go down we'll never get out again."

"You can turn back here if you want to," Humbolt said.

"Turn back?" Barber's red whiskers seemed to bristle. "Who in hell said anything about turning back?"

"Nobody," Humbolt said, smiling a little at Barber's quick flash of anger.

He studied the chasm, wishing that they could have some way of cutting the quartz crystals and making binoculars. It was a long way to look with the naked eye . . .

Here and there the chasm thrust out arms into the plateau. All the arms were short, however, and even at their heads the cliffs were vertical. The morning shadows prevented a clear view of much of the chasm and he could see no sign of the red-stained strata that they were searching for.

In the southwest corner of the chasm, far away and almost imperceptible, he saw a faint cloud rising up from the chasm's floor. It was impossible to tell what it was and it faded away as he watched.

Barber saw it, too, and said, "It looked like smoke. Do you suppose there could be people—or some kind of intelligent things—living down there?"

"It might have been the vapor from hot springs, condensed by the cool morning air," he said. "Whatever it was, we'll look into it when we get there."

The climb down the steep slope into the chasm was swifter than that up the canyon but no more pleasant. Carrying a heavy pack down such a grade exerted a torturous strain upon the backs of the legs.

The heat increased steadily as they descended. They reached the floor of the valley the next day and the noonday heat was so great that Humbolt wondered if they might not have trapped themselves into what the summer would soon transform into a monstrous oven where no life at all could exist. There could never be any choice, of course—the mountains were passable only when the weather was hot.

The floor of the valley was silt, sand and gravel—they would find nothing there. They set out on a circuit of the chasm's walls, following along close to the base.

In many places the mile-high walls were without a single ledge to break their vertical faces. When they came to the first such place they saw that the ground near the base was riddled with queer little pits, like tiny craters of the moon. As they looked there was a crack like a cannon shot and the ground beside them erupted into an explosion of sand and gravel. When the dust had cleared away there was a new crater where none had been before.

Humbolt wiped the blood from his face where a flying fragment had cut it and said, "The heat of the sun loosens rocks under the rim. When one falls a mile in a one point five gravity, it's traveling like a meteor."

They went on, through the danger zone. As with the peril of the chasm's heat, there was no choice. Only by observing the material that littered the base of the cliffs could they know what minerals, if any, might be above them.

On the fifteenth day they saw the red-stained stratum. Humbolt quickened his pace, hurrying forward in advance of Barber. The stratum was too high up on the wall to be reached but it was not necessary to examine it in place—the base of the cliff was piled thick with fragments from it.

He felt the first touch of discouragement as he looked at them. They were a sandstone, light in weight. The iron present was only what the Dunbar Expedition had thought it to be; a mere discoloration.

They made their way slowly along the foot of the cliff, examining piece after piece in the hope of finding something more than iron stains. There was no variation, however, and a mile farther on they came to the end of the red stratum. Beyond that point the rocks were gray, without a vestige of iron.

"So that," Barber said, looking back the way they had come, "is what we were going to build a ship out of—iron stains!"

Humbolt did not answer. For him it was more than a disappointment. It was the death of a dream he had held since the year he was nine and had heard that the Dunbar Expedition had seen iron-stained rock in a deep chasm—the only iron-stained rock on the face of Ragnarok. Surely, he had thought, there would be enough iron there to build a small ship. For eleven years he had worked toward the day when he would find it. Now, he had found it—and it was nothing. The ship was as far away as ever . . .

But discouragement was as useless as iron-stained sandstone. He shook it off and turned to Barber.

"Let's go," he said. "Maybe we'll find something by the time we circle the chasm."

For seven days they risked the danger of death from downward plunging rocks and found nothing. On the eighth day they found the treasure that was not treasure.

They stopped for the evening just within the mouth of one of the chasm's tributaries. Humbolt went out to get a drink where a trickle of water ran through the sand and as he knelt down he saw the flash of something red under him, almost buried in the sand.

He lifted it out. It was a stone half the size of his hand; darkly translucent and glowing in the light of the setting sun like blood.

It was a ruby.

He looked, and saw another gleam a little farther up the stream. It was another ruby, almost as large as the first one. Near it was a flawless blue sapphire. Scattered here and there were smaller rubies and sapphires, down to the size of grains of sand.

He went farther upstream and saw specimens of still another stone. They were colorless but burning with internal fires. He rubbed one of them hard across the ruby he still carried and there was a gritting sound as it cut a deep scratch in the ruby.

"I'll be damned," he said aloud.

There was only one stone hard enough to cut a ruby—the diamond.

✧   ✧   ✧

It was almost dark when he returned to where Barber was resting beside their packs.

"What did you find to keep you out so late?" Barber asked curiously.

He dropped a double handful of rubies, sapphires and diamonds at Barber's feet.

"Take a look," he said. "On a civilized world what you see there would buy us a ship without our having to lift a finger. Here they're just pretty rocks.

"Except the diamonds," he added. "At least we now have something to cut those quartz crystals with."

They took only a few of the rubies and sapphires the next morning but they gathered more of the diamonds, looking in particular for the gray-black and ugly but very hard and tough carbonado variety. Then they resumed their circling of the chasm's walls.

The heat continued its steady increase as the days went by. Only at night was there any relief from it and the nights were growing swiftly shorter as the blue sun rose earlier each morning. When the yellow sun rose the chasm became a blazing furnace around the edge of which they crept like ants in some gigantic oven.

There was no life in any form to be seen; no animal or bush or blade of grass. There was only the barren floor of the chasm, made a harsh green shade by the two suns and writhing and undulating with heat waves like a nightmare sea, while above them the towering cliffs shimmered, too, and sometimes seemed to be leaning far out over their heads and already falling down upon them.

They found no more minerals of any kind and they came at last to the place where they had seen the smoke or vapor.

There the walls of the chasm drew back to form a little valley a mile long by half a mile wide. The walls did not drop vertically to the floor there but sloped out at the base into a fantastic formation of natural roofs and arches that reached almost to the center of the valley from each side. Green things grew in the shade under the arches and sparkling waterfalls cascaded down over many of them. A small creek carried the water out of the valley, going out into the chasm a little way before the hot sands absorbed it.

They stood and watched for some time, but there was no movement in the valley other than the waving of the green plants as a breeze stirred them. Once the breeze shifted to bring them the fresh, sweet scent of growing things and urge them to come closer.

"A place like that doesn't belong here," Barber said in a low voice. "But it's there. I wonder what else is there?"

"Shade and cool water," Humbolt said. "And maybe things that don't like strangers. Let's go find out."

They watched warily as they walked, their crossbows in their hands. At the closer range they saw that the roofs and arches were the outer remains of a system of natural caves that went back into the valley's walls. The green vegetation grew wherever the roofs gave part-time shade, consisting mainly of a holly-leafed bush with purple flowers and a tall plant resembling corn.

Under some of the roofs the corn was mature, the orange-colored grains visible. Under others it was no more than half grown. He saw the reason and said to Barber:

"There are both warm and cold springs here. The plants watered by the warm springs would grow almost the year around; the ones watered by the cold springs only in the summer. And what we saw from the mountain top would have been vapor rising from the warm springs."

They passed under arch after arch without seeing any life. When they came to the valley's upper end and still had seen nothing it seemed evident that there was little danger of an encounter with any intelligent-and-hostile creatures. Apparently nothing at all lived in the little valley.

Humbolt stopped under a broad arch where the breeze was made cool and moist by the spray of water it had come through. Barber went on, to look under the adjoining arch.

Caves led into the wall from both arches and as he stood there Humbolt saw something lying in the mouth of the nearest cave. It was a little mound of orange corn; lying in a neat pile as though whatever had left it there had intended to come back after it.

He looked toward the other arch but Barber was somewhere

out of sight. He doubted that whatever had left the corn could be much of a menace—dangerous animals were more apt to eat flesh than corn—but he went to the cave with his crossbow ready.

He stopped at the mouth of the cave to let his eyes become accustomed to the darkness inside it. As he did so the things inside came out to meet him.

They emerged into full view; six little animals the size of squirrels, each of them a different color. They walked on short hind legs like miniature bears and the dark eyes in the bear-chipmunk faces were fixed on him with intense interest. They stopped five feet in front of him, there to stand in a neat row and continue the fascinated staring up at him.

The yellow one in the center scratched absently at its stomach with a furry paw and he lowered the bow, feeling a little foolish at having bothered to raise it against animals so small and harmless.

Then he half brought it up again as the yellow one opened its mouth and said in a tone that held distinct anticipation:

"I think we'll eat you for supper."

He darted glances to right and left but there was nothing near him except the six little animals. The yellow one, having spoken, was staring silently at him with some curiosity on its furry face. He wondered if some miasma or some scent from the vegetation in the valley had warped his mind into sudden insanity and asked:

"You think you'll do what?"

It opened its mouth again, to stutter, "I—I—" Then, with a note of alarm, "*Hey . . .*"

It said no more and the next sound was that of Barber hurrying toward him and calling, "Hey—Bill—where are you?"

"Here," he answered, and he was already sure that he knew why the little animal had spoken to him.

Barber came up and saw the six chipmunk-bears. "Six of them!" he exclaimed. "There's one in the next cave—the damned thing spoke to me!"

"I thought so," he replied. "You told it we'd have it for supper and then it said, 'You think you'll do what?' didn't it?"

Barber's face showed surprise. "How did you know that?"

"They're telepathic between one another," he said. "The yellow one there repeated what the one you spoke to heard you say and it repeated what the yellow one heard me say. It has to be telepathy between them."

"Telepathy—" Barber stared at the six little animals, who stared back with their fascinated curiosity undiminished. "But why should they want to repeat aloud what they receive telepathically?"

"I don't know. Maybe at some stage in their evolution only part of them were telepaths and the telepaths broadcasted danger warnings to the others that way. So far as that goes, why does a parrot repeat what it hears?"

There was a scurry of movement behind Barber and another of the little animals, a white one, hurried past them. It went to the yellow one and they stood close together as they stared up. Apparently they were mates . . .

"That's the other one—those are the two that mocked us," Barber said, and thereby gave them the name by which they would be known: mockers.

The mockers were fresh meat—but they accepted the humans with such friendliness and trust that Barber lost all his desire to have one for supper or for any other time. They had a limited supply of dried meat and there would be plenty of orange corn. They would not go hungry.

They discovered that the mockers had living quarters in both the cool caves and the ones warmed by the hot springs. There was evidence that they hibernated during the winters in the warm caves.

There were no minerals in the mockers' valley and they set out to continue their circuit of the chasm. They did not get far until the heat had become so great that the chasm's tributaries began going dry. They turned back then, to wait in the little valley until the fall rains came.

When the long summer was ended by the first rain they resumed their journey. They took a supply of the orange corn and two of the mockers; the yellow one and its mate. The other mockers watched them leave, standing silent and solemn in front of their caves as though they feared they might never see their two fellows or the humans again.

The two mockers were pleasant company, riding on their shoulders and chattering any nonsense that came to mind. And sometimes saying things that were not at all nonsense, making Humbolt wonder if mockers could partly read human minds and dimly understand the meaning of some of the things they said.

They found a place where saltpeter was very thinly and erratically distributed. They scraped off all the films of it that were visible and procured a small amount. They completed their circuit and reached the foot of the long, steep slope of the Craigs without finding anything more.

It was an awesome climb that lay before them; up a grade so steep and barred with so many low ledges that when their legs refused to carry them farther they crawled. The heat was still very serious and there would be no water until they came to the spring beyond the mountain's summit. A burning wind, born on the blazing floor of the chasm, following them up the mountain all day. Their leather canteens were almost dry when night came and they were no more than a third of the way to the top.

The mockers had become silent as the elevation increased and when they stopped for the night Humbolt saw that they would never live to cross the mountain. They were breathing fast, their hearts racing, as they tried to extract enough oxygen from the thin air. They drank a few drops of water but they would not touch the corn he offered them.

The white mocker died at midmorning the next day as they stopped for a rest. The yellow one crawled feebly to her side and died a few minutes later.

"So that's that," Humbolt said, looking down at them. "The only things on Ragnarok that ever trusted us and wanted to be our friends—and we killed them."

They drank the last of their water and went on. They made dry camp that night and dreams of cold streams of water tormented their exhausted sleep. The next day was a hellish eternity in which they walked and fell and crawled and walked and fell again.

Barber weakened steadily, his breathing growing to a rattling panting. He spoke once that afternoon, to try to smile with dry, swollen lips and say between his panting gasps, "It would be hell—to have to die—so thirsty like this."

After that he fell with increasing frequency, each time slower and weaker in getting up again. Half a mile short of the summit he fell for the last time. He tried to get up, failed, and tried to crawl. He failed at that, too, and collapsed face down in the rocky soil.

Humbolt went to him and said between his own labored intakes of breath, "Wait, Dan—I'll go on—bring you back water."

Barber raised himself with a great effort and looked up. "No use," he said. "My heart—too much—"

He fell forward again and that time he was very still, his desperate panting no more.

It seemed to Humbolt that it was half a lifetime later that he finally reached the spring and the cold, clear water. He drank, the most ecstatic pleasure he had ever experienced in his life. Then the pleasure drained away as he seemed to see Dan Barber trying to smile and seemed to hear him say, "It would be hell—to have to die—so thirsty like this."

He rested for two days before he was in condition to continue on his way. He reached the plateau and saw that the woods goats had been migrating south for some time. On the second morning he climbed up a gentle roll in the plain and met three unicorns face to face.

They charged at once, squealing with anticipation. Had he been equipped with an ordinary bow he would have been killed within seconds. But the automatic crossbow poured a rain of arrows into the faces of the unicorns that caused them to swing aside in pain and enraged astonishment. The moment they had swung enough to expose the area just behind their heads the arrows became fatal.

One unicorn escaped, three arrows bristling in its face. It watched him from a distance for a little while, squealing and shaking its head in baffled fury. Then it turned and disappeared over a swell in the plain, running like a deer.

He resumed his southward march, hurrying faster than before. The unicorn had headed north and that could be for but one purpose: to bring enough reinforcements to finish the job.

He reached the caves at night. No one was up but George Ord, working late in his combination workshop-laboratory.

George looked up at the sound of his entrance and saw that he was alone. "So Dan didn't make it?" he asked.

"The chasm got him," he answered. And then, wearily, "The chasm—we found the damned thing."

"The red stratum—"

"It was only iron stains."

"I made a little pilot smelter while you were gone," George said. "I was hoping the red stratum would be ore. The other prospecting parties—none of them found anything."

"We'll try again next spring," he said. "We'll find it somewhere, no matter how long it takes."

"Our time may not be so long. The observations show the sun to be farther south than ever."

"Then we'll make double use of the time we do have. We'll cut the hunting parties to the limit and send out more prospecting parties. We're going to have a ship to meet the Gerns again."

"Sometimes," George said, his black eyes studying him thoughtfully, "I think that's all you live for, Bill: for the day when you can kill Gerns."

George said it as a statement of a fact, without censure, but Humbolt could not keep an edge of harshness out of his voice as he answered:

"For as long as I'm leader that's all we're all going to live for."

He followed the game south that fall, taking with him Bob Craig and young Anders. Hundreds of miles south of the caves they came to the lowlands; a land of much water and vegetation and vast herds of unicorns and woods goats. It was an exceedingly dangerous country, due to the concentration of unicorns and prowlers, and only the automatic crossbows combined with never ceasing vigilance enabled them to survive.

There they saw the crawlers; hideous things that crawled on multiple legs like three-ton centipedes, their mouths set with six mandibles and dripping a stinking saliva. The bite of a crawler was poisonous, instantly paralyzing even to a unicorn, though not instantly killing them. The crawlers ate their victims at once, however, ripping the helpless and still living flesh from its bones.

Although the unicorns feared the crawlers, the prowlers hated them with a fanatical intensity and made use of their superior quickness to kill every crawler they found; ripping at the crawler until the crawler, in an insanity of rage, bit itself and died of its own poison.

They had taken one of the powerful longbows with them, in addition to their crossbows, and they killed a crawler with it one day. As they did so a band of twenty prowlers came suddenly upon them.

Twenty prowlers, with the advantage of surprise at short range, could have slaughtered them. Instead, the prowlers continued on their way without as much as a challenging snarl.

"Now why," Bob Craig wondered, "did they do that?"

"They saw we had just killed a crawler," Humbolt said. "The crawlers are their enemies and I guess letting us live was their way of showing appreciation."

Their further explorations of the lowlands revealed no minerals—nothing but alluvial material of unknown depth—and there was no reason to stay longer except that return to the caves was impossible until spring came. They built attack-proof shelters in the trees and settled down to wait out the winter.

They started north with the first wave of woods goats, nothing but lack of success to show for their months of time and effort.

When they were almost to the caves they came to the barren valley where the Gerns had herded the Rejects out of the cruisers and to the place where the stockade had been. It was a lonely place, the stockade walls fallen and scattered and the graves of Humbolt's mother and all the others long since obliterated by the hooves of the unicorn legions. Bitter memories were reawakened, tinged by the years with nostalgia, and the stockade was far behind them before the dark mood left him.

The orange corn was planted that spring and the number of prospecting parties was doubled.

The corn sprouted, grew feebly, and died before maturity. The prospecting parties returned one by one, each to report no success. He decided, that fall, that time was too precious to waste—they would have to use the alternate plan he had spoken of.

He went to George Ord and asked him if it would be possible to build a hyperspace transmitter with the materials they had.

"It's the one way we could have a chance to leave here

without a ship of our own," he said. "By luring a Gern cruiser here and then taking it away from them."

George shook his head. "A hyperspace transmitter *might* be built, given enough years of time. But it would be useless without power. It would take a generator of such size that we'd have to melt down every gun, knife, axe, every piece of steel and iron we have. And then we'd be five hundred pounds short. On top of that, we'd have to have at least three hundred pounds more of copper for additional wire."

"I didn't realize it would take such a large generator," he said after a silence. "I was sure we could have a transmitter."

"Get me the metal and we can," George said. He sighed restlessly and there was almost hatred in his eyes as he looked at the inclosing walls of the cave. "You're not the only one who would like to leave our prison. Get me eight hundred pounds of copper and iron and I'll make the transmitter, some way."

Eight hundred pounds of metal . . . On Ragnarok that was like asking for the sun.

The years went by and each year there was the same determined effort, the same lack of success. And each year the suns were farther south, marking the coming of the end of any efforts other than the one to survive.

In the year thirty when fall came earlier than ever before, he was forced to admit to himself the bleak and bitter fact: he and the others were not of the generation that would escape from Ragnarok. They were Earth-born—they were not adapted to Ragnarok and could not scour a world of 1.5 gravity for metals that might not exist.

And vengeance was a luxury he could not have.

A question grew in his mind where there had been only his hatred for the Gerns before. *What would become of the future generations on Ragnarok?*

With the question a scene from his childhood kept coming back to him; a late summer evening in the first year on Ragnarok and Julia sitting beside him in the warm starlight . . .

"You're my son, Billy," she had said. "The first I ever had. Now, before so very long, maybe I'll have another one."

Hesitantly, not wanting to believe, he had asked, "What some of them said about how you might die then—it won't really happen, will it, Julia?"

"It . . . might." Then her arm had gone around him and she had said, "If I do I'll leave in my place a life that's more important than mine ever was.

"Remember me, Billy, and this evening, and what I said to you, if you should ever be leader. Remember that it's only through the children that we can ever survive and whip this world. Protect them while they're small and helpless and teach them to fight and be afraid of nothing when they're a little older. Never, never let them forget how they came to be on Ragnarok. Someday, even if it's a hundred years from now, the Gerns will come again and they must be ready to fight, for their freedom and for their lives."

He had been too young then to understand how truly she had spoken and when he was old enough his hatred for the Gerns had blinded him to everything but his own desires. Now, he could see . . .

The children of each generation would be better adapted to Ragnarok and full adaptation would eventually come. But all the generations of the future would be potential slaves of the Gern Empire, free only so long as they remained unnoticed.

It was inconceivable that the Gerns should never pass by Ragnarok through all time to come. And when they finally came the slow, uneventful progression of decades and centuries might have brought a false sense of security to the people of Ragnarok, might have turned the stories of what the Gerns did to the Rejects into legends and then into myths that no one any longer believed.

The Gerns would have to be brought to Ragnarok before that could happen.

He went to George Ord again and said:

"There's one kind of transmitter we could make a generator for—a plain normal-space transmitter, dot-dash, without a receiver."

George laid down the diamond cutting wheel he had been working on.

"It would take two hundred years for the signal to get to Athena at the speed of light," he said. "Then, forty days after it got there, a Gern cruiser would come hell-bent to investigate."

"I want the ones of the future to know that the Gerns will

be here no later than two hundred years from now. And with always the chance that a Gern cruiser in space might pick up the signal at any time before then."

"I see," George said. "The sword of Damocles hanging over their heads, to make them remember."

"You know what would happen to them if they ever forgot. You're as old as I am—you know what the Gerns did to us."

"I'm older than you are," George said. "I was nine when the Gerns left us here. They kept my father and mother and my sister was only three. I tried to keep her warm by holding her but the Hell Fever got her that first night. She was too young to understand why I couldn't help her more . . ."

Hatred burned in his eyes at the memory, like some fire that had been banked but had never died. "Yes, I remember the Gerns and what they did. I wouldn't want it to have to happen to others—the transmitter will be made so that it won't."

The guns were melted down, together with other items of iron and steel, to make the castings for the generator. Ceramic pipes were made to carry water from the spring to a water-wheel. The long, slow job of converting the miscellany of electronic devices, many of them broken, into the components of a transmitter proceeded.

It was five years before the transmitter was ready for testing. It was early fall of the year thirty-five then, and the water that gushed from the pipe splashed in cold drops against Humbolt as the waterwheel was set in motion.

The generator began to hum and George observed the output of it and the transmitter as registered by the various meters he had made.

"Weak, but it will reach the Gern monitor station on Athena," he said. "It's ready to send—what do you want to say?"

"Make it something short," he said. "Make it *'Ragnarok calling.'* "

George poised his finger over the transmitting key. "This will set forces in motion that can never be recalled. What we do here this morning is going to cause a lot of Gerns—or Ragnarok people—to die."

"It will be the Gerns who die," he said. "Send the signal."

"Like you, I believe the same thing," George said. "I have to believe it because that's the way I want it to be. I hope we're right. It's something we'll never know."

He began depressing the key.

A boy was given the job of operating the key and the signal went out daily until the freezing of winter stopped the waterwheel that powered the generator.

The sending of the signals was resumed when spring came and the prospecting parties continued their vain search for metals.

The suns continued moving south and each year the springs came later, the falls earlier. In the spring of forty-five he saw that he would have to make his final decision.

By then they dwindled until they numbered only sixty-eight; the Young Ones gray and rapidly growing old. There was no longer any use to continue the prospecting—if any metals were to be found they were at the north end of the plateau where the snow no longer melted during the summer. They were too few to do more than prepare for what the Old Ones had feared they might have to face—Big Winter. That would require the work of all of them.

Sheets of mica were brought down from the Craigs, the summits of which were deeply buried under snow even in midsummer. Stoves were made of fireclay and mica, which would give both heat and light and would be more efficient than open fireplaces. The innermost caves were prepared for occupation, with multiple doors to hold out the cold and with laboriously excavated ventilation ducts and smoke outlets.

There were sixty of them in the fall of fifty, when all had been done that could be done to prepare for what might come.

"There aren't many of the Earth-born left now," Bob Craig said to him one night as they sat in the flickering light of a stove. "And there hasn't been time for there to be many of the Ragnarok-born. The Gerns wouldn't get many slaves if they should come now."

"They could use however many they found," he answered. "The younger ones, who are the best adapted to this gravity, would be exceptionally strong and quick on a one-gravity world. There are dangerous jobs where a strong, quick slave is a lot more efficient and expendable than complex, expensive machines."

"And they would want some specimens for scientific study," Jim Lake said. "They would want to cut into the young ones and see how they're built that they're adapted to this one and a half gravity world."

He smiled with the cold mirthlessness that always reminded Humbolt of his father—of the Lake who had been the *Constellation*'s lieutenant commander. "According to the books the Gerns never did try to make it a secret that when a Gern doctor or biologist cuts into the muscles or organs of a non-Gern to see what makes them tick, he wants them to be still alive and ticking as he does so."

Seventeen-year-old Don Chiara spoke, to say slowly, thoughtfully:

"Slavery and vivisection . . . If the Gerns should come now when there are so few of us, and if we should fight the best we could and lose, it would be better for whoever was the last of us to put a knife in the hearts of the women and children than to let the Gerns have them."

No one made any answer. There was no answer to make, no alternative to suggest.

"In the future there will be more of us and it will be different," he said at last. "On Earth the Gerns were always stronger and faster than humans but when the Gerns come to Ragnarok they're going to find a race that isn't really human any more. They're going to find a race before which they'll be like woods goats before prowlers."

"If only they don't come too soon," Craig said.

"That was the chance that had to be taken," he replied.

He wondered again as he spoke, as he had wondered so often in the past years, if he had given them all their death sentence when he ordered the transmitter built. Yet, the future generations could not be permitted to forget . . . and steel could not be tempered without first thrusting it into the fire.

He was the last of the Young Ones when he awoke one night in the fall of fifty-six and found himself burning with the Hell Fever. He did not summon any of the others. They could do nothing for him and he had already done all he could for them.

He had done all he could for them . . . and now he would leave forty-nine men, women and children to face the unknown forces of Big Winter while over them hung the sword he had forged: the increasing danger of detection by the Gerns.

The question came again, sharp with the knowledge that it was far too late for him to change any of it. *Did I arrange the execution of my people?*

Then, through the red haze of the fever, Julia spoke to him out of the past; sitting again beside him in the summer twilight and saying:

Remember me, Billy, and this evening, and what I said to you . . . teach them to fight and be afraid of nothing . . . never let them forget how they came to be on Ragnarok . . .

She seemed very near and real and the doubt faded and was gone. *Teach them to fight . . . never let them forget . . .* The men of Ragnarok were only fur-clad hunters who crouched in caves but they would grow in numbers as time went by. Each generation would be stronger than the generation before it and he had set forces in motion that would bring the last generation the trial of combat and the opportunity for freedom. How well they fought on that day would determine their destiny but he was certain, once again, what that destiny would be.

It would be to walk as conquerors before beaten and humbled Gerns.

Part 3

It was winter of the year eighty-five and the temperature was one hundred and six degrees below zero. Walter Humbolt stood in front of the ice tunnel that led back through the glacier to the caves and looked up into the sky.

It was noon but there was no sun in the starlit sky. Many weeks before the sun had slipped below the southern horizon. For a little while a dim halo had marked its passage each day; then that, too, had faded away. But now it was time for the halo to appear again, to herald the sun's returning.

Frost filled the sky, making the stars flicker as it swirled endlessly downward. He blinked against it, his eyelashes trying to freeze to his lower eyelids at the movement, and turned to look at the north.

There the northern lights were a gigantic curtain that filled a third of the sky, rippling and waving in folds that pulsated in red and green, rose and lavender and violet. Their reflection gleamed on the glacier that sloped down from the caves and glowed softly on the other glacier; the one that covered the transmitter station. The transmitter had long ago been taken into the caves but the generator and waterwheel were still there, frozen in a tomb of ice.

For three years the glacier had been growing before the caves and the plateau's southern face had been buried under snow for ten years. Only a few woods goats ever came as far north as the country south of the caves and they stayed only during the brief period between the last snow of spring and the first snow of fall. Their winter home was somewhere down near the equator. What had been called the Southern Lowlands was a frozen, lifeless waste.

Once they had thought about going to the valley in the chasm where the mockers would be hibernating in their warm caves. But even if they could have gone up the plateau and performed the incredible feat of crossing the glacier-covered, blizzard-ripped Craigs, they would have found no food in the mockers' valley— only a little corn the mockers had stored away, which would soon have been exhausted.

There was no place for them to live but in the caves or as nomads migrating with the animals. And if they migrated to the equator each year they would have to leave behind them all the books and tools and everything that might someday have given them a civilized way of life and might someday have shown them how to escape from their prison.

He looked again to the south where the halo should be, thinking: *They should have made their decision in there by now. I'm their leader—but I can't force them to stay here against their will. I could only ask them to consider what it would mean if we left here.*

Snow creaked underfoot as he moved restlessly. He saw something lying under the blanket of frost and went to it. It was an arrow that someone had dropped. He picked it up, carefully, because the intense cold had made the shaft as brittle as glass. It would regain its normal strength when taken into the caves—

There was the sound of steps and Fred Schroeder came out

of the tunnel, dressed as he was dressed in bulky furs. Schroeder looked to the south and said, "It seems to be starting to get a little lighter there."

He saw that it was; a small, faint paling of the black sky.

"They talked over what you and I told them," Schroeder said. "And about how we've struggled to stay here this long and how, even if the sun should stop drifting south this year, it will be years of ice and cold at the caves before Big Spring comes."

"If we leave here the glacier will cover the caves and fill them with ice," he said. "All we ever had will be buried back in there and all we'll have left will be our bows and arrows and animal skins. We'll be taking a one-way road back into the stone age, for ourselves and our children and their children."

"They know that," Schroeder said. "We both told them."

He paused. They watched the sky to the south turn lighter. The northern lights flamed unnoticed behind them as the pale halo of the invisible sun slowly brightened to its maximum. Their faces were white with near-freezing then and they turned to go back into the caves. "They had made their decision," Schroeder went on. "I guess you and I did them an injustice when we thought they had lost their determination, when we thought they might want to hand their children a flint axe and say, 'Here— take this and let it be the symbol of all you are or all you will ever be.'

"Their decision was unanimous—we'll stay for as long as it's possible for us to survive here."

Howard Lake listened to Teacher Morgan West read from the diary of Walter Humbolt, written during the terrible winter of thirty-five years before:

"Each morning the light to the south was brighter. On the seventh morning we saw the sun—and it was not due until the eighth morning!

"It will be years before we can stop fighting the enclosure of the glacier but we have reached and passed the dead of Big Winter. We have reached the bottom and the only direction we can go in the future is up."

"And so," West said, closing the book, "we are here in the caves tonight because of the stubbornness of Humbolt and Schroeder and all the others. Had they thought only of their own welfare,

had they conceded defeat and gone into the migratory way of
life, we would be sitting beside grass campfires somewhere to
the south tonight, our way of life containing no plans or aspira-
tions greater than to follow the game back and forth through
the years.

"Now, let's go outside to finish tonight's lesson."

Teacher West led the way into the starlit night just outside
the caves, Howard Lake and the other children following him.
West pointed to the sky where the star group they called the
Athena Constellation blazed like a huge arrowhead high in the
east.

"There," he said, "beyond the top of the arrowhead, is where
we were going when the Gerns stopped us a hundred and twenty
years ago and left us to die on Ragnarok. It's so far that Athena's
sun can't be seen from here, so far that it will be another hundred and fifteen years before our first signal gets there. Why is
it, then, that you and all the other groups of children have to
learn such things as history, physics, the Gern language, and the
way to fire a Gern blaster?"

The hand of every child went up. West selected eight-year-
old Clifton Humbolt. "Tell us, Clifton," he said.

"Because," Clifton answered, "a Gern cruiser might pass by a
few light-years out at any time and pick up our signals. So we
have to know all we can about them and how to fight them
because there aren't very many of us yet."

"The Gerns will come to kill us," little Marie Chiara said, her
dark eyes large and earnest. "They'll come to kill us and to make
slaves out of the ones they don't kill, like they did with the others
a long time ago. They're awful mean and awful smart and we
have to be smarter than they are."

Howard looked again at the Athena constellation, thinking,
*I hope they come just as soon as I'm old enough to fight them,
or even tonight . . .*

"Teacher," he asked, "how would a Gern cruiser look if it came
tonight? Would it come from the Athena arrowhead?"

"It probably would," West answered. "You would see its rocket
blast, like a bright trail of fire—"

A bright trail of fire burst suddenly into being, coming from
the constellation of Athena and lighting up the woods and hills
and their startled faces as it arced down toward them.

"*It's them!*" a treble voice exclaimed and there was a quick flurry of movement as Howard and the other older children shoved the younger children behind them.

Then the light vanished, leaving a dimming glow where it had been.

"Only a meteor," West said. He looked at the line of older children who were standing protectingly in front of the younger ones, rocks in their hands with which to ward off the Gerns, and he smiled in the way he had when he was pleased with them.

Howard watched the meteor trail fade swiftly into invisibility and felt his heartbeats slow from the first wild thrill to gray disappointment. Only a meteor . . .

But someday he might be leader and by then, surely, the Gerns would come. If not, he would find some way to make them come.

Ten years later Howard Lake was leader. There were three hundred and fifty of them then and Big Spring was on its way to becoming Big Summer. The snow was gone from the southern end of the plateau and once again game migrated up the valleys east of the caves.

There were many things to be done now that Big Winter was past and they could have the chance to do them. They needed a larger pottery kiln, a larger workshop with a wooden lathe, more diamonds to make cutting wheels, more quartz crystals to make binoculars and microscopes. They could again explore the field of inorganic chemistry, even though results in the past had produced nothing of value, and they could, within a few years, resume the metal prospecting up the plateau—the most important project of all.

Their weapons seemed to be as perfect as was possible but when the Gerns came they would need some quick and certain means of communication between the various units that would fight the Gerns. A leader who could not communicate with his forces and coordinate their actions would be helpless. And they had on Ragnarok a form of communication, if trained, that the Gerns could not detect or interfere with electronically: the mockers.

The Craigs were still white and impassable with snow that summer but the snow was receding higher each year. Five years later, in the summer of one hundred and thirty-five, the Craigs were passable for a few weeks.

Lake led a party of eight over them and down into the chasm. They took with them two small cages, constructed of wood and glass and made airtight with the strong medusabush glue. Each cage was equipped with a simple air pump and a pressure gauge.

They brought back two pairs of mockers as interested and trusting captives, together with a supply of the orange corn and a large amount of diamonds. The mockers, in their pressure-maintained cages, were not even aware of the increase in elevation as they were carried over the high summit of the Craigs.

To Lake and the men with him the climb back up the long, steep slope of the mountain was a stiff climb to make in one day but no more than that. It was hard to believe that it had taken Humbolt and Barber almost three days to climb it and that Barber had died in the attempt. It reminded him of the old crossbows that Humbolt and the others had used. They were thin, with a light pull, such as the present generation boys used. It must have required courage for the Old Ones to dare unicorn attacks with bows so thin that only the small area behind the unicorn's jaw was vulnerable to their arrows . . .

When the caves were reached, a very gradual reduction of pressure in the mocker cages was started; one that would cover a period of weeks. One pair of mockers survived and had two young ones that fall. The young mockers, like the first generation of Ragnarok-born children of many years before, were more adapted to their environment than their parents were.

The orange corn was planted, using an adaptation method somewhat similar to that used with the mockers. It might have worked had the orange corn not required such a long period of time in which to reach maturity. When winter came only a few grains had formed.

They were saved for next year's seeds, to continue the slow adaptation process.

By the fifth year the youngest generation of mockers was well adapted to the elevation of the caves but for a susceptibility to a quickly fatal form of pneumonia which made it necessary to keep them from exposing themselves to the cold or to any sudden changes of temperature.

Their intelligence was surprising and they seemed to be parti-
ally receptive to human thoughts, as Bill Humbolt had written.
By the end of the fifteenth year their training had reached such
a stage of perfection that a mocker would transmit or not transmit with only the unspoken thought of its master to tell it which
it should be. In addition, they would transmit the message to
whichever mocker their master's thought directed. Presumably
all mockers received the message but only the mocker to whom
it was addressed would repeat it aloud.

They had their method of communication. They had their
automatic crossbows for quick, close fighting, and their long-
range longbows. They were fully adapted to the 1.5 gravity and
their reflexes were almost like those of prowlers—Ragnarok had
long ago separated the quick from the dead.

There were eight hundred and nineteen of them that year, in
the early spring of one hundred and fifty, and they were ready
and impatient for the coming of the Gerns.

Then the transmitter, which had been in operation again for
many years, failed one day.

George Craig had finished checking it when Lake arrived. He
looked up from his instruments, remarkably similar in appearance to a sketch of the old George Ord—a resemblance that had
been passed down to him by his mother—and said:

"The entire circuit is either gone or ready to go. It's already
operated for a lot longer than it should have."

"It doesn't matter," Lake said. "It's served its purpose. We won't
rebuild it."

George watched him questioningly.

"It's served its purpose," he said again. "It didn't let us forget that the Gerns will come again. But that isn't enough, now.
The first signal won't reach Athena until the year two thirty-
five. It will be the dead of Big Winter again then. They'll have
to fight the Gerns with bows and arrows that the cold will make
as brittle as glass. They won't have a chance."

"No," George said. "They won't have a chance. But what can
we do to change it?"

"It's something I've been thinking about," he said. "We'll build
a hyperspace transmitter and bring the Gerns before Big Winter
comes."

"We will?" George asked, lifting his dark eyebrows. "And what do we use for the three hundred pounds of copper and five hundred pounds of iron we would have to have to make the generator?"

"Surely we can find five hundred pounds of iron somewhere on Ragnarok. The north end of the plateau might be the best bet. As for the copper—I doubt that we'll ever find it. But there are seams of a bauxite-like clay in the Western Hills—they're certain to contain aluminum to at least some extent. So we'll make the wires of aluminum."

"The ore would have to be refined to pure aluminum oxide before it could be smelted," George said. "And you can't smelt aluminum ore in an ordinary furnace—only in an electric furnace with a generator that can supply a high amperage. And we would have to have cryolite ore to serve as the solvent in the smelting process."

"There's a seam of cryolite in the Eastern Hills, according to the old maps," said Lake. "We could make a larger generator by melting down everything we have. It wouldn't be big enough to power the hyperspace transmitter but it should be big enough to smelt aluminum ore."

George considered the idea. "I think we can do it."

"How long until we can send the signal?" he asked.

"Given the extra metal we need, the building of the generator is a simple job. The transmitter is what will take years—maybe as long as fifty."

Fifty years . . .

"Can't anything be done to make it sooner?" he asked.

"I know," George said. "You would like for the Gerns to come while you're still here. So would every man on Ragnarok. But even on Earth the building of a hyperspace transmitter was a long, slow job, with all the materials they needed and all the special tools and equipment. Here we'll have to do everything by hand and for materials we have only broken and burned-out odds and ends. It will take about fifty years—it can't be helped."

Fifty years . . . but that would bring the Gerns before Big Winter came again. And there was the rapidly increasing chance that a Gern cruiser would at any day intercept the first signals. They were already more than halfway to Athena.

"Melt down the generator," he said. "Start making a bigger one.

Tomorrow men will go out after bauxite and cryolite and four of us will go up the plateau to look for iron."

Lake selected Gene Taylor, Tony Chiara and Steve Schroeder to go with him. They were well on their way by daylight the next morning, on the shoulder of each of them a mocker which observed the activity and new scenes with bright, interested eyes.

They traveled light, since they would have fresh meat all the way, and carried herbs and corn only for the mockers. Once, generations before, it had been necessary for men to eat herbs to prevent deficiency diseases but now the deficiency diseases, like Hell Fever, were unknown to them.

They carried no compasses since the radiations of the two suns constantly created magnetic storms that caused compass needles to swing as much as twenty degrees within an hour. Each of them carried a pair of powerful binoculars, however; binoculars that had been diamond-carved from the ivory-like black unicorn horn and set with lenses and prisms of diamond-cut quartz.

The foremost bands of woods goats followed the advance of spring up the plateau and they followed the woods goats. They could not go ahead of the goats—the goats were already pressing close behind the melting of the snow. No hills or ridges were seen as the weeks went by and it seemed to Lake that they would walk forever across the endless rolling floor of the plain.

Early summer came and they walked across a land that was green and pleasantly cool at a time when the vegetation around the caves would be burned brown and lifeless. The woods goats grew less in number then as some of them stopped for the rest of the summer in their chosen latitudes.

They continued on and at last they saw, far to the north, what seemed to be an almost infinitesimal bulge on the horizon. They reached it two days later; a land of rolling green hills, scared here and there with ragged outcroppings of rock, and a land that climbed slowly and steadily higher as it went into the north.

They camped that night in a little vale. The floor of it was white with the bones of woods goats that had tarried too long the fall before and got caught by an early blizzard. There was still flesh on the bones and scavenger rodents scuttled among the carcasses, feasting.

"We'll split up now," he told the others the next morning.

He assigned each of them his position; Steve Schroeder to parallel his course thirty miles to his right, Gene Taylor to go thirty miles to his left, and Tony Chiara to go thirty miles to the left of Taylor.

"We'll try to hold those distances," he said. "We can't look over the country in detail that way but it will give us a good general survey of it. We don't have too much time left by now and we'll make as many miles into the north as we can each day. The woods goats will tell us when it's time for us to turn back."

They parted company with casual farewells but for Steve Schroeder, who smiled sardonically at the bones of the woods goats in the vale and asked:

"Who's supposed to tell the woods goats?"

Tip, the black, white-nosed mocker on Lake's shoulder, kept twisting his neck to watch the departure of the others until he had crossed the next hill and the others were hidden from view.

"All right, Tip," he said then. "You can unwind your neck now."

"Unwind—all right—all right," Tip said. Then, with a sudden burst of energy which was characteristic of mockers, he began to jiggle up and down and chant in time with his movements, "All right all right all right all right—"

"Shut up!" he commanded. "If you want to talk nonsense I don't care—but don't say 'all right' any more."

"All right," Tip agreed amiably, settling down. "Shut up if you want to talk nonsense. I don't care."

"And don't slaughter the punctuation like that. You change the meaning entirely."

"But don't say all right any more," Tip went on, ignoring him. "You change the meaning entirely."

Then, with another surge of animation, Tip began to fish in his jacket pocket with little hand-like paws. "Tip hungry—Tip hungry."

Lake unbuttoned the pocket and gave Tip a herb leaf. "I notice there's no nonsensical chatter when you want to ask for something to eat."

Tip took the herb leaf but he spoke again before he began to eat; slowly, as though trying seriously to express a thought:

"Tip hungry—no nonsensical."

"Sometimes," he said, turning his head to look at Tip, "you

mockers give me the peculiar feeling that you're right on the edge of becoming a new and intelligent race and no fooling."

Tip wiggled his whiskers and bit into the herb leaf. "No fooling," he agreed.

He stopped for the night in a steep-walled hollow and built a small fire of dead moss and grass to ward off the chill that came with dark. He called the others, thinking first of Schroeder so that Tip would transmit to Schroeder's mocker:

"Steve?"

"Here," Tip answered, in a detectable imitation of Schroeder's voice. "No luck."

He thought of Gene Taylor and called, "Gene?"

There was no answer and he called Chiara. "Tony—could you see any of Gene's route today?"

"Part of it," Chiara answered. "I saw a herd of unicorns over that way. Why—doesn't he answer?"

"No."

"Then," Chiara said, "they must have got him."

"Did you find anything today, Tony?" he asked.

"Nothing but pure andesite. Not even an iron stain."

It was the same kind of barren formation that he, himself, had been walking over all day. But he had not expected success so soon . . .

He tried once again to call Gene Taylor:

"Gene . . . Gene . . . are you there, Gene?"

There was no answer. He knew there would never be.

The days became weeks with dismaying swiftness as they penetrated farther into the north. The hills became more rugged and there were intrusions of granite and other formations to promise a chance of finding metal; a promise that urged them on faster as their time grew shorter.

Twice he saw something white in the distance. Once it was the bones of another band of woods goats that had huddled together and frozen to death in some early blizzard of the past and once it was the bones of a dozen unicorns.

The nights grew chillier and the suns moved faster and faster to the south. The animals began to migrate, an almost imperceptible movement in the beginning but one that increased each day. The first frost came and the migration began in earnest. By the third day it was a hurrying tide.

Tip was strangely silent that day. He did not speak until the noon sun had cleared the cold, heavy mists of morning. When he spoke it was to give a message from Chiara:

"Howard . . . last report . . . Goldie is dying . . . pneumonia . . ."

Goldie was Chiara's mocker, his only means of communication—and there would be no way to tell him when they were turning back.

"Turn back today, Tony," he said. "Steve and I will go on for a few days more."

There was no answer and he said quickly, "Turn back—turn back! Acknowledge that, Tony."

"Turning back . . ." the acknowledgment came. " . . . tried to save her . . ."

The message stopped and there was a silence that Chiara's mocker would never break again. He walked on, with Tip sitting very small and quiet on his shoulder. He had crossed another hill before Tip moved, to press up close to him the way mockers did when they were lonely and to hold tightly to him.

"What is it, Tip?" he asked.

"Goldie is dying," Tip said. And then again, like a soft, sad whisper, "Goldie is dying . . ."

"She was your mate . . . I'm sorry."

Tip made a little whimpering sound, and the man reached up to stroke his silky side.

"I'm sorry," he said again. "I'm sorry as hell, little fellow."

For two days Tip sat lonely and silent on his shoulder, no longer interested in the new scenes nor any longer relieving the monotony with his chatter. He refused to eat until the morning of the third day.

By then the exodus of woods goats and unicorns had dwindled to almost nothing; the sky a leaden gray through which the sun could not be seen. That evening he saw what he was sure would be the last band of woods goats and shot one of them.

When he went to it he was almost afraid to believe what he saw.

The hair above its feet was red, discolored with the stain of iron-bearing clay.

He examined it more closely and saw that the goat had apparently watered at a spring where the mud was material washed down from an iron-bearing vein or formation. It had done so fairly recently—there were still tiny particles of clay adhering to the hair.

The wind stirred, cold and damp with its warning of an approaching storm. He looked to the north, where the evening had turned the gray clouds black, and called Schroeder:

"Steve—any luck?"

"None," Schroeder answered.

"I just killed a goat," he said. "It has iron stains on its legs it got at some spring farther north. I'm going on to try to find it. You can turn back in the morning."

"No," Schroeder objected. "I can angle over and catch up with you in a couple of days."

"You'll turn back in the morning," he said. "I'm going to try to find this iron. But if I get caught by a blizzard it will be up to you to tell them at the caves that I found iron and to tell them where it is—you know the mockers can't transmit that far."

There was a short silence; then Schroeder said, "All right—I see. I'll head south in the morning."

Lake took a route the next day that would most likely be the one the woods goats had come down, stopping on each ridge top to study the country ahead of him through his binoculars. It was cloudy all day but at sunset the sun appeared very briefly, to send its last rays across the hills and redden them in mockery of the iron he sought.

Far ahead of him, small even through the glasses and made visible only because of the position of the sun, was a spot at the base of a hill that was redder than the sunset had made the other hills.

He was confident it would be the red clay he was searching for and he hurried on, not stopping until darkness made further progress impossible.

Tip slept inside his jacket, curled up against his chest, while the wind blew raw and cold all through the night. He was on his way again at the first touch of daylight, the sky darker than ever and the wind spinning random flakes of snow before him.

He stopped to look back to the south once, thinking, *If I turn back now I might get out before the blizzard hits.*

Then the other thought came: *These hills all look the same. If I don't go to the iron while I'm this close and know where it is, it might be years before I or anyone else could find it again.*

He went on and did not look back again for the rest of the day.

By midafternoon the higher hills around him were hidden under the clouds and the snow was coming harder and faster as the wind drove the flakes against his face. It began to snow with a heaviness that brought a half darkness when he came finally to the hill he had seen through the glasses.

A spring was at the base of it, bubbling out of red clay. Above it the red dirt led a hundred feet to a dike of granite and stopped. He hurried up the hillside that was rapidly whitening with snow and saw the vein.

It set against the dike, short and narrow but red-black with the iron it contained. He picked up a piece and felt the weight of it. It was heavy—it was pure iron oxide.

He called Schroeder and asked, "Are you down out of the high hills, Steve?"

"I'm in the lower ones," Schroeder answered, the words coming a little muffled from where Tip lay inside his jacket. "It looks black as hell up your way."

"I found the iron, Steve. Listen—these are the nearest to landmarks I can give you . . ."

When he had finished he said, "That's the best I can do. You can't see the red clay except when the sun is low in the south-west but I'm going to build a monument on top of the hill to find it by."

"About you, Howard," Steve asked, "what are your chances?"

The wind was rising to a high moaning around the ledges of the granite dike and the vein was already invisible under the snow.

"It doesn't look like they're very good," he answered. "You'll probably be leader when you come back next spring—I told the council I wanted that if anything happened to me. Keep things going the way I would have. Now—I'll have to hurry to get the monument built in time."

"All right," Schroeder said. "So long, Howard . . . good luck."

He climbed to the top of the hill and saw boulders there he could use to build the monument. They were large—he might crush Tip against his chest in picking them up—and he took off his jacket, to wrap it around Tip and leave him lying on the ground.

He worked until he was panting for breath, the wind driving the snow harder and harder against him until the cold seemed to have penetrated to the bone. He worked until the monument was too high for his numb hands to lift any more boulders to its top. By then it was tall enough that it should serve its purpose.

He went back to look for Tip, the ground already four inches deep in snow and the darkness almost complete.

"Tip," he called. "Tip—Tip—" He walked back and forth across the hillside in the area where he thought he had left him, stumbling over rocks buried in the snow and invisible in the darkness, calling against the wind and thinking, *I can't leave him to die alone here.*

Then, from a bulge he had not seen in the snow under him, there came a frightened, lonely wail:

"Tip cold—Tip cold—"

He raked the snow off his jacket and unwrapped Tip, to put him inside his shirt next to his bare skin. Tip's paws were like ice and he was shivering violently, the first symptom of the pneumonia that killed mockers so quickly.

Tip coughed, a wrenching, rattling little sound, and whimpered, "Hurt—hurt—"

"I know," he said. "Your lungs hurt—damn it to hell, I wish I could have let you go home with Steve."

He put on the cold jacket and went down the hill. There was nothing with which he could make a fire—only the short half-green grass, already buried under the snow. He turned south at the bottom of the hill, determining the direction by the wind, and began the stubborn march southward that could have but one ending.

He walked until his cold-numbed legs would carry him no farther. The snow was warm when he fell for the last time; warm and soft as it drifted over him, and his mind was clouded with a pleasant drowsiness.

This isn't so bad, he thought, and there was something like surprise through the drowsiness. *I can't regret doing what I had to do—doing it the best I could . . .*

Tip was no longer coughing and the thought of Tip was the only one that was tinged with regret: *I hope he wasn't still hurting when he died.*

He felt Tip stir very feebly against his chest then, and he did not know if it was his imagination or if in that last dreamlike state it was Tip's thought that came to him; warm and close and reassuring him:

No hurt no cold now—all right now—we sleep now . . .

Part 4

When spring came Steve Schroeder was leader, as Lake had wanted. It was a duty and a responsibility that would be under circumstances different from those of any of the leaders before him. The grim fight was over for a while. They were adapted and increasing in number; going into Big Summer and into a renascence that would last for fifty years. They would have half a century in which to develop their environment to its fullest extent. Then Big Fall would come, to destroy all they had accomplished, and the Gerns would come, to destroy them.

It was his job to make certain that by then they would be stronger than either.

He went north with nine men as soon as the weather permitted. It was hard to retrace the route of the summer before, without compasses, among the hills which looked all the same as far as their binoculars could reach, and it was summer when they saw the hill with the monument. They found Lake's bones a few miles south of it, scattered by the scavengers as were the little bones of his mocker. They buried them together, man and mocker, and went silently on toward the hill.

They had brought a little hand-cranked diamond drill with them to bore holes in the hard granite and black powder for blasting. They mined the vein, sorting out the ore from the waste and saving every particle.

The vein was narrow at the surface and pinched very rapidly. At a depth of six feet it was a knife-blade seam; at ten feet it was only a red discoloration in the bottom of their shaft.

"That seems to be all of it," he said to the others. "We'll send men up here next year to go deeper and farther along its course but I have an idea we've just mined all of the only iron vein on Ragnarok. It will be enough for our purpose."

They sewed the ore in strong rawhide sacks and then prospected, without success, until it was time for the last unicorn band to pass by on its way south. They trapped ten unicorns and hobbled their legs, with other ropes reaching from horn to hind leg on each side to prevent them from swinging back their heads or even lifting them high.

They had expected the capture and hobbling of the unicorns to be a difficult and dangerous job and it was. But when they were finished the unicorns were helpless. They could move awkwardly about to graze but they could not charge. They could only stand with lowered heads and fume and rumble.

The ore sacks were tied on one frosty morning and the men mounted. The horn-leg ropes were loosened so the unicorns could travel, and the unicorns went into a frenzy of bucking and rearing, squealing with rage as they tried to impale their riders.

The short spears, stabbing at the sensitive spot behind the jaw-bones of the unicorns, thwarted the backward flung heads and the unicorns were slowly forced into submission. The last one conceded temporary defeat and the long journey to the south started, the unicorns going in the run that they could maintain hour after hour.

Each day they pushed the unicorns until they were too weary to fight at night. Each morning, rested, the unicorns resumed the battle. It became an expected routine for both unicorns and men.

The unicorns were released when the ore was unloaded at the foot of the hill before the caves and Schroeder went to the new waterwheel, where the new generator was already in place. There George Craig told him of the unexpected obstacle that had appeared.

"We're stuck," George said. "The aluminum ore isn't what we thought it would be. It's scarce and very low grade, of such a complex nature that we can't refine it to the oxide with what we have to work with on Ragnarok."

"Have you produced any aluminum oxide at all?"

"A little. We might have enough for the wire in a hundred years if we kept at it hard enough."

"What else do you need—was there enough cryolite?" he asked.

"Not much of it, but enough. We have the generator set up, the smelting box built and the carbon lining and rods ready. We have everything we need to smelt aluminum ore—except the aluminum ore."

"Go ahead and finish up the details, such as installing the lining," he said. "We didn't get this far to be stopped now."

But the prospecting parties, making full use of the time left them before winter closed down, returned late that fall to report no sign of the ore they needed.

Spring came and he was determined they would be smelting aluminum before the summer was over even though he had no idea where the ore would be found. They needed aluminum ore of a grade high enough that they could extract the pure aluminum oxide. Specifically, they needed aluminum oxide . . .

Then he saw the answer to their problem, so obvious that all of them had overlooked it.

He passed by four children playing a game in front of the caves that day; some kind of a checker-like game in which differently colored rocks represented the different children. One boy was using red stones; some of the rubies that had been brought back as curios from the chasm. Rubies were of no use or value on Ragnarok; only pretty rocks for children to play with . . .

Only pretty rock?—*rubies and sapphires were corundum, were pure aluminum oxide!*

He went to tell George and to arrange for a party of men to go into the chasm after all the rubies and sapphires they could find. The last obstacle had been surmounted.

The summer sun was hot the day the generator hummed into life. The carbon-lined smelting box was ready and the current flowed between the heavy carbon rods suspended in the cryolite and the lining, transforming the cryolite into a liquid. The crushed rubies and sapphires were fed into the box, glowing and glittering in blood-red and sky-blue scintillations of light, to be deprived by the current of their life and fire and be changed into something entirely different.

When the time came to draw off some of the metal they

opened the orifice in the lower corner of the box. Molten aluminum flowed out into the ingot mold in a little stream; more beautiful to them than any gems could ever be, bright and gleaming in its promise that more than six generations of imprisonment would soon be ended.

The aluminum smelting continued until the supply of rubies and sapphires in the chasm had been exhausted but for small and scattered fragments. It was enough, with some aluminum above the amount needed for the wire.

It was the year one hundred and fifty-two when they smelted the aluminum. In eight more years they would reach the middle of Big Summer; the suns would start their long drift southward, not to return for one hundred and fifty years. Time was passing swiftly by for them and there was none of it to waste...

The making of ceramics was developed to an art, as was the making of different types of glass. Looms were built to spin thread and cloth from woods goat wool, and vegetables dyes were discovered. Exploration parties crossed the continent to the eastern and western seas; salty and lifeless seas that were bordered by immense deserts. No trees of any kind grew along their shores and ships could not be built to cross them.

Efforts were continued to develop an inorganic field of chemistry, with discouraging results, but in one hundred and fifty-nine the orange corn was successfully adapted to the elevation and climate of the caves.

There was enough that year to feed the mockers all winter, supply next year's seeds, and leave enough that it could be ground and baked into bread for all to taste.

It tasted strange, but good. It was, Schroeder thought, symbolic of a great forward step. It was the first time in generations that any of them had known any food but meat. The corn would make them less dependent upon hunting and, of paramount importance, it was the type of food to which they would have to become accustomed in the future—they could not carry herds of woods goats and unicorns with them on Gern battle cruisers.

The lack of metals hindered them wherever they turned in their efforts to build even the simplest machines or weapons. Despite its dubious prospects, however, they made a rifle-like gun.

The barrel of it was thick, of the hardest, toughest ceramic material they could produce. It was a cumbersome, heavy thing, firing with a flintlock action, and it could not be loaded with much powder lest the charge burst the barrel.

The flintlock ignition was not instantaneous, the light-weight porcelain bullet had far less penetrating power than an arrow, and the thing boomed and belched out a cloud of smoke that would have shown the Gerns exactly where the shooter was located.

It was an interesting curio and the firing of it was something spectacular to behold but it was a weapon apt to be much more dangerous to the man behind it than to the Gern it was aimed at. Automatic crossbows were far better.

Woods goats had been trapped and housed during the summers in shelters where sprays of water maintained a temperature cool enough for them to survive. Only the young were kept when fall came, to be sheltered through the winter in one of the caves. Each new generation was subjected to more heat in the summer and more cold in the winter than the generation before it and by the year one hundred and sixty the woods goats were well on their way toward adaptation.

The next year they trapped two unicorns, to begin the job of adapting and taming future generations of them. If they succeeded they would have utilized the resources of Ragnarok to the limit—except for what should be their most valuable ally with which to fight the Gerns: the prowlers.

For twenty years prowlers had observed a truce wherein they would not go hunting for men if men would stay away from their routes of travel. But it was a truce only and there was no indication that it could ever evolve into friendship.

Three times in the past, half-grown prowlers had been captured and caged in the hope of taming them. Each time they had paced their cages, looking longingly into the distance, refusing to eat and defiant until they died.

To prowlers, as to some men, freedom was more precious than life. And each time a prowler had been captured the free ones had retaliated with a resurgence of savage attacks.

There seemed no way that men and prowlers could ever meet on common ground. They were alien to one another, separated by the gulf of an origin on worlds two hundred and fifty light-years apart. Their only common heritage was the will of each to battle.

But in the spring of one hundred and sixty-one, for a little while one day, the gulf was bridged.

Schroeder was returning from a trip he had taken alone to the east, coming down the long canyon that led from the high face of the plateau to the country near the caves. He hurried, glancing back at the black clouds that had gathered so quickly on the mountain behind him. Thunder rumbled from within them, an almost continuous roll of it as the clouds poured down their deluge of water.

A cloudburst was coming and the sheer-walled canyon down which he hurried had suddenly become a death trap, its sunlit quiet soon to be transformed into roaring destruction. There was only one place along its nine-mile length where he might climb out and the time was already short in which to reach it.

He had increased his pace to a trot when he came to it, a talus of broken rock that sloped up steeply for thirty feet to a shelf. A ledge eleven feet high stood over the shelf and other, lower, ledges set back from it like climbing steps.

At the foot of the talus he stopped to listen, wondering how close behind him the water might be. He heard it coming, a sound like the roaring of a high wind up the canyon, and he scrambled up the talus of loose rock to the shelf at its top. The shelf was not high enough above the canyon's floor—he would be killed there—and he followed it fifty feet around a sharp bend. There it narrowed abruptly, to merge into the sheer wall of the canyon. Blind alley . . .

He ran back to the top of the talus where the edge of the ledge, ragged with projections of rock, was unreachably far above him. As he did so the roaring was suddenly a crashing, booming thunder and he saw the water coming.

It swept around the bend at perhaps a hundred miles an hour, stretching from wall to wall of the canyon, the crest of it seething and slashing and towering forty sheer feet above the canyon's floor.

A prowler was running in front of it, running for its life and losing.

There was no time to watch. He leaped upward, as high as

possible, his crossbow in his hand. He caught the end of the bow over one of the sharp projections of rock on the ledge's rim and began to pull himself up, afraid to hurry lest the rock cut the bowstring in two and drop him back.

It held and he stood on the ledge, safe, as the prowler flashed up the talus below.

It darted around the blind-alley shelf and was back a moment later. It saw that its only chance would be to leap up on the ledge where he stood and it tried, handicapped by the steep, loose slope it had to jump from.

It failed and fell back. It tried again, hurling itself upward with all its strength, and its claws caught fleetingly on the rough rock a foot below the rim. It began to slide back, with no time left it for a third try.

It looked up at the rim of safety that it had not quite reached and then on up at him, its eyes bright and cold with the knowledge that it was going to die and its enemy would watch it.

Schroeder dropped flat on his stomach and reached down, past the massive black head, to seize the prowler by the back of the neck. He pulled up with all his strength and the claws of the prowler tore at the rocks as it climbed.

When it was coming up over the ledge, safe, he rolled back from it and came to his feet in one swift, wary motion, his eyes on it and his knife already in his hand. As he did so the water went past below them with a thunder that deafened. Logs and trees shot past, boulders crashed together, and things could be seen surging in the brown depths; shapeless things that had once been woods goats and the battered gray bulk of a unicorn. He saw it all with a sideward glance, his attention on the prowler.

It stepped back from the rim of the ledge and looked at him; warily, as he looked at it. With the wariness was something like question, and almost disbelief.

The ledge they stood on was narrow but it led out of the canyon and to the open land beyond. He motioned to the prowler to precede him and, hesitating a moment, it did so.

They climbed out of the canyon and out onto the grassy slope of the mountainside. The roar of the water was a distant rumble there and he stopped. The prowler did the same and they watched each other again, each of them trying to understand what the thoughts of the other might be. It was something they could not know—they were too alien to each other and had been enemies too long.

Then a gust of wind swept across them, bending and rippling the tall grass, and the prowler swung away to go with it and leave him standing alone.

His route was such that it diverged gradually from that taken by the prowler. He went through a grove of trees and emerged into an open glade on the other side. Up on the ridge to his right he saw something black for a moment, already far away.

He was thirty feet from the next grove of trees when he saw the gray shadow waiting silently for his coming within them.

Unicorn!

His crossbow rattled as he jerked back the pistol grip. The unicorn charged, the underbrush crackling as it tore through it and a vine whipping like a rope from its lowered horn.

His first arrow went into its chest. It lurched, fatally wounded but still coming, and he jerked back on the pistol grip for the quick shot that would stop it.

The rock-frayed bow string broke with a singing sound and the bow end snapped harmlessly forward.

He had counted on the bow and its failure came a fraction of a second too late for him to dodge far enough. His sideward leap was short, and the horn caught him in midair, ripping across his ribs and breaking them, shattering the bone of his left arm and tearing the flesh. He was hurled fifteen feet and he struck the ground with a stunning impact, pain washing over him in a blinding wave.

Through it, dimly, he saw the unicorn fall and heard its dying trumpet blast as it called to another. He heard an answering call somewhere in the distance and then the faraway drumming of hooves.

He fought back the blindness and used his good arm to lift himself up. His bow was useless, his spear lay broken under the unicorn, and his knife was gone. His left arm swung helplessly and he could not climb the limbless lower trunk of a lance tree with only one arm.

He went forward, limping, trying to hurry to find his knife while the drumming of hooves raced toward him. It would be a battle already lost that he would make with the short knife but he would have blood for his going . . .

The grass grew tall and thick, hiding the knife until he could hear the unicorn crashing through the trees. He saw it ten feet ahead of him as the unicorn tore out from the edge of the woods thirty feet away.

It squealed, shrill with triumph, and the horn swept up to impale him. There was no time left to reach the knife, no time left for anything but the last fleeting sight of sunshine and glade and arching blue sky—

Something from behind him shot past and up at the unicorn's throat, a thing that was snarling black savagery with yellow eyes blazing and white fangs slashing—the prowler!

It ripped at the unicorn's throat, swerving its charge, and the unicorn plunged past him. The unicorn swung back, all the triumph gone from its squeal, and the prowler struck again. They became a swirling blur, the horn of the unicorn swinging and stabbing and the attacks of the prowler like the swift, relentless thrusting of a rapier.

He went to his knife and when he turned back with it in his hand the battle was already over.

The unicorn fell and the prowler turned away from it. One foreleg was bathed in blood and its chest was heaving with a panting so fast that it could not have been caused by the fight with the unicorn.

It must have been watching me, he thought, with a strange feeling of wonder. *It was watching from the ridge and it ran all the way.*

Its yellow eyes flickered to the knife in his hand. He dropped the knife in the grass and walked forward, unarmed, wanting the prowler to know that he understood; that for them in that moment the gulf of two hundred and fifty light-years did not exist.

He stopped near it and squatted in the grass to begin binding up his broken arm so the bones would not grate together. It watched him, then it began to lick at its bloody shoulder; standing so close to him that he could have reached out and touched it.

Again he felt the sense of wonder. They were alone together in the glade, he and a prowler, each caring for his hurts. There was a bond between them that for a little while made them like brothers. There was a bridge for a little while across the gulf that had never been bridged before . . .

When he had finished with his arm and the prowler had lessened the bleeding of its shoulder it took a step back toward the ridge. He stood up, knowing it was going to leave.

"I suppose the score is even now," he said to it, "and we'll never see each other again. So good hunting—and thanks."

It made a sound in its throat; a queer sound that was neither bark nor growl, and he had the feeling it was trying to tell him something. Then it turned and was gone like a black shadow across the grass and he was alone again.

He picked up his knife and bow and began the long, painful journey back to the caves, looking again and again at the ridge behind him and thinking: *They have a code of ethics. They fight for their survival—but they pay their debts.*

Ragnarok was big enough for both men and prowlers. They could live together in friendship as men and dogs of Earth lived together. It might take a long time to win the trust of the prowlers but surely it could be done.

He came to the rocky trail that led to the caves and there he took a last look at the ridge behind him; feeling a poignant sense of loss and wondering if he would ever see the prowler again or ever again know the strange, wild companionship he had known that day.

Perhaps he never would . . . but the time would come on Ragnarok when children would play in the grass with prowler pups and the time would come when men and prowlers, side by side, would face the Gerns.

In the year that followed there were two incidents when a prowler had the opportunity to kill a hunter on prowler territory and did not do so. There was no way of knowing if the prowler in each case had been the one he had saved from the cloudburst or if the prowlers, as a whole, were respecting what a human had done for one of them.

Schroeder thought of again trying to capture prowler pups— very young ones—and decided it would be a stupid plan. Such an act would destroy all that had been done toward winning the trust of the prowlers. It would be better to wait, even though time was growing short, and find some other way.

The fall of one hundred and sixty-three came and the suns were noticeably moving south. That was the fall that his third child, a girl, was born. She was named Julia, after the Julia of long ago, and she was of the last generation that would be born in the caves.

Plans were already under way to build a town in the valley a mile from the caves. The unicorn-proof stockade wall that would enclose it was already under construction, being made of stone blocks. The houses would be of diamond-sawed stone, thick-walled, with dead-air spaces between the double walls to insulate against heat and cold. Tall, wide canopies of lance tree poles and the palm-like medusabush leaves would be built over all the houses to supply additional shade.

The woods goats were fully adapted that year and domesticated to such an extent that they had no desire to migrate with the wild goats. There was a small herd of them then, enough to supply a limited amount of milk, cheese and wool.

The adaptation of the unicorns proceeded in the following years, but not their domestication. It was their nature to be ill-tempered and treacherous and only the threat of the spears in the hands of their drivers forced them to work; work that they could have done easily had they not diverted so much effort each day to trying to turn on their masters and kill them. Each night they were put in a massive-walled corral, for they were almost as dangerous as wild unicorns.

The slow, painstaking work on the transmitter continued while the suns moved farther south each year. The move from the caves to the new town was made in one hundred and seventy-nine, the year that Schroeder's wife died.

His two sons were grown and married and Julia, at sixteen, was a woman by Ragnarok standards; blue-eyed and black-haired as her mother, a Craig, had been, and strikingly pretty in a wild, reckless way. She married Will Humbolt that spring, leaving her father alone in the new house in the new town.

Four months later she came to him to announce with pride and excitement:

"I'm going to have a baby in only six months! If it's a boy he'll be the right age to be leader when the Gerns come and we're going to name him John, after the John who was the first leader we ever had on Ragnarok."

Her words brought to his mind a question and he thought of what old Dale Craig, the leader who had preceded Lake, had written:

*We have survived, the generations that the Gerns thought
would never be born. But we must never forget the characteristics that insured that survival: an unswerving loyalty of every
individual to all the others and the courage to fight, and die
if necessary.*

*In any year, now, the Gerns will come. There will be no one
to help us. Those on Athena are slaves and it is probable that Earth
has been enslaved by now. We will stand or fall alone. But if we
of today could know that the ones who meet the Gerns will still
have the courage and loyalty that made our survival possible, then
we would know that the Gerns are already defeated . . .*

The era of danger and violence was over for a little while. The
younger generation had grown up during a time of peaceful
development of their environment. It was a peace that the coming
of the Gerns would shatter—but had it softened the courage and
loyalty of the younger generation?

A week later he was given his answer.

He was climbing up the hill that morning, high above the town
below, when he saw the blue of Julia's wool blouse in the
distance. She was sitting up on a hillside, an open book in her
lap and her short spear lying beside her.

He frowned at the sight. The main southward migration of
unicorns was over but there were often lone stragglers who might
appear at any time. He had warned her that someday a unicorn
would kill her—but she was reckless by nature and given to
restless moods in which she could not stand the confinement
of the town.

She jerked up her head as he watched, as though at a faint
sound, and he saw the first movement within the trees behind
her—a unicorn.

It lunged forward, its stealth abandoned as she heard it, and
she came to her feet in a swift, smooth movement; the spear
in her hand and the book spilling to the ground.

The unicorn's squeal rang out and she whirled to face it, with
two seconds to live. He reached for his bow, knowing his help
would come too late.

She did the only thing possible that might enable her to survive: she shifted her balance to take advantage of the fact that
a human could jump to one side a little more quickly than a
four-footed beast in headlong charge. As she did so she brought

up the spear for the thrust into the vulnerable area just behind the jawbone.

It seemed the needle point of the black horn was no more than an arm's length from her stomach when she jumped aside with the lithe quickness of a prowler, swinging as she jumped and thrusting the spear with all her strength into the unicorn's neck.

The thrust was true and the spear went deep. She released it and flung herself backward to dodge the flying hooves. The force of the unicorn's charge took it past her but its legs collapsed under it and it crashed to the ground, sliding a little way before it stopped. It kicked once and lay still.

She went to it, to retrieve her spear, and even from the distance there was an air of pride about her as she walked past her bulky victim.

Then she saw the book, knocked to one side by the unicorn's hooves. Tatters of its pages were blowing in the wind and she stiffened, her face growing pale. She ran to it to pick it up, the unicorn forgotten.

She was trying to smooth the torn leaves when he reached her. It had been one of the old textbooks, printed on real paper, and it was fragile with age. She had been trusted by the librarian to take good care of it. Now, page after page was torn and unreadable . . .

She looked up at him, shame and misery on her face.

"Father," she said. "The book—I—"

He saw that the unicorn was a bull considerably larger than the average. Men had in the past killed unicorns with spears but never, before, had a sixteen-year-old girl done so . . .

He looked back at her, keeping his face emotionless, and asked sternly, "You what?"

"I guess—I guess I didn't have any right to take the book out of town. I wish I hadn't . . ."

"You promised to take good care of it," he told her coldly. "Your promise was believed and you were trusted to keep it."

"But—but I didn't mean to damage it—I didn't mean to!" She was suddenly very near to tears. "I'm not a—a *bemmon!*"

"Go back to town," he ordered. "Tonight bring the book to the town hall and tell the council what happened to it."

She swallowed and said in a faint voice, "Yes, father."

She turned and started slowly back down the hill, not seeing the unicorn as she passed it, the bloody spear trailing disconsolately behind her and her head hanging in shame.

He watched her go and it was safe for him to smile. When night came and she stood before the council, ashamed to lift her eyes to look at them, he would have to be grim and stern as he told her how she had been trusted and how she had betrayed that trust. But now, as he watched her go down the hill, he could smile with his pride in her and know that his question was answered; that the younger generation had lost neither courage nor loyalty.

Julia saved a child's life that spring and almost lost her own. The child was playing under a half-completed canopy when a sudden, violent wind struck it and transformed it into a death-trap of cracking, falling timbers. She reached him in time to fling him to safety but the collapsing roof caught her before she could make her own escape.

Her chest and throat were torn by the jagged ends of the broken poles and for a day and a night her life was a feebly flickering spark. She began to rally on the second night and on the third morning she was able to speak for the first time, her eyes dark and tortured with her fear:

"My baby—what did it do to him?"

She convalesced slowly, haunted by the fear. Her son was born five weeks later and her fears proved to have been groundless. He was perfectly normal and healthy.

And hungry—and her slowly healing breasts would be dry for weeks to come.

By a coincidence that had never happened before and could never happen again there was not a single feeding-time foster-mother available for the baby. There were many expectant mothers but only three women had young babies—and each of them had twins to feed.

But there was a small supply of frozen goat milk in the ice house, enough to see young Johnny through until it was time for the goat herd to give milk. He would have to live on short rations until then but it could not be helped.

Johnny was a month old when the opportunity came for the men of Ragnarok to have their ultimate ally.

The last of the unicorns were going north and the prowlers had long since gone. The blue star was lighting the night like a small sun when the breeze coming through Schroeder's window brought the distant squealing of unicorns.

He listened, wondering. It was a sound that did not belong. Everyone was safely in the town, most of them in bed, and there should be nothing outside the stockade for the unicorns to fight.

He armed himself with spear and crossbow and went outside. He let himself out through the east gate and went toward the sounds of battle. They grew louder as he approached, more furious, as though the battle was reaching its climax.

He crossed the creek and went through the trees beyond. There, in a small clearing no more than half a mile from the town, he came upon the scene.

A lone prowler was making a stand against two unicorns. Two other unicorns lay on the ground, dead, and behind the prowler was the dark shape of its mate lying lifelessly in the grass. There was blood on the prowler, purple in the blue starlight, and gloating rang in the squeals of the unicorns as they lunged at it. The leaps of the prowler were faltering as it fought them, the last desperate defiance of an animal already dying.

He brought up the bow and sent a volley of arrows into the unicorns. Their gloating squeals died and they fell. The prowler staggered and fell beside them.

It was breathing its last when he reached it but in the way it looked up at him he had the feeling that it wanted to tell him something, that it was trying hard to live long enough to do so. It died with the strange appeal in its eyes and not until then did he see the scar on its shoulder; a scar such as might have been made long ago by the rip of a unicorn's horn.

It was the prowler he had known nineteen years before.

The ground was trampled all around by the unicorns, showing that the prowlers had been besieged all day. He went to the other prowler and saw it was a female. Her breasts showed that she had had pups recently but she had been dead at least two days. Her hind legs had been broken sometime that spring and they were still only half healed, twisted and almost useless.

Then, that was why the two of them were so far behind the other prowlers. Prowlers, like the wolves, coyotes and foxes of Earth, mated for life and the male helped take care of the young.

She had been injured somewhere to the south, perhaps in a fight with unicorns, and her mate had stayed with her as she hobbled her slow way along and killed game for her. The pups had been born and they had had to stop. Then the unicorns had found them and the female had been too crippled to fight . . .

He looked for the pups, expecting to find them trampled and dead. But they were alive, hidden under the roots of a small tree near their mother.

Prowler pups—*alive!*

They were very young, small and blind and helpless. He picked them up and his elation drained away as he looked at them. They made little sounds of hunger, almost inaudible, and they moved feebly, trying to find their mother's breasts and already so weak that they could not lift their heads.

Small chunks of fresh meat had been left beside the pups and he thought of what the prowler's emotions must have been as his mate lay dead on the ground and he carried meat to their young, knowing they were too small to eat it but helpless to do anything else for them.

And he knew why there had been the appeal in the eyes of the prowler as it died and what it had tried to tell him: *Save them . . . as you once saved me.*

He carried the pups back past the prowler and looked down at it in passing. "I'll do my best," he said.

When he reached his house he laid the pups on his bed and built a fire. There was no milk to give them—the goats would not have young for at least another two weeks—but perhaps they could eat a soup of some kind. He put water on to boil and began shredding meat to make them a rich broth.

One of them was a male, the other a female, and if he could save them they would fight beside the men of Ragnarok when the Gerns came. He thought of what he would name them as he worked. He would name the female Sigyn, after Loki's faithful wife who went with him when the gods condemned him to Hel, the Teutonic underworld. And he would name the male Fenrir, after the monster wolf who would fight beside Loki when Loki led the forces of Hel in the final battle on the day of Ragnarok.

But when the broth was prepared, and cooled enough, the pups could not eat it. He tried making it weaker, tried it mixed with corn and herb soup, tried corn and herb soups alone. They could eat nothing he prepared for them.

When gray daylight entered the room he had tried everything possible and had failed. He sat wearily in his chair and watched them, defeated. They were no longer crying in their hunger and when he touched them they did not move as they had done before.

They would be dead before the day was over and the only chance men had ever had to have prowlers as their friends and allies would be gone.

The first rays of sunrise were coming into the room, revealing fully the frail thinness of the pups, when there was a step outside and Julia's voice:

"Father?"

"Come in, Julia," he said, not moving.

She entered, still a pale shadow of the reckless girl who had fought a unicorn, even though she was slowly regaining her normal health. She carried young Johnny in one arm, in her other hand his little bottle of milk. Johnny was hungry—there was never quite enough milk for him—but he was not crying. Ragnarok children did not cry . . .

She saw the pups and her eyes went wide.

"Prowlers—baby prowlers! Where did you get them?"

He told her and she went to them, to look down at them and say, "If you and their father hadn't helped each other that day they wouldn't be here, nor you, nor I, nor Johnny—none of us in this room."

"They won't live out the day," he said. "They have to have milk—and there isn't any."

She reached down to touch them and they seemed to sense that she was something different. They stirred, making tiny whimpering sounds and trying to move their heads to nuzzle at her fingers.

Compassion came to her face, like a soft light.

"They're so young," she said. "So terribly young to have to die . . ."

She looked at Johnny and at the little bottle that held his too-small morning ration of milk.

"Johnny—Johnny—" Her words were almost a whisper. "You're hungry—but we can't let them die. And someday, for this, they will fight for your life."

She sat on the bed and placed the pups in her lap beside Johnny. She lifted a little black head with gentle fingers and a little pink mouth ceased whimpering as it found the nipple of Johnny's bottle.

Johnny's gray eyes darkened with the storm of approaching protest. Then the other pup touched his hand, crying in its hunger, and the protest faded as surprise and something like sudden understanding came into his eyes.

Julia withdrew the bottle from the first pup and transferred it to the second one. Its crying ceased and Johnny leaned forward to touch it again, and the one beside it.

He made his decision with an approving sound and leaned back against his mother's shoulder, patiently awaiting his own turn and their presence accepted as though they had been born his brother and sister.

The golden light of the new day shone on them, on his daughter and grandson and the prowler pups, and in it he saw the bright omen for the future.

His own role was nearing its end but he had seen the people of Ragnarok conquer their environment in so far as Big Winter would ever let it be conquered. The last generation was being born, the generation that would meet the Gerns, and now they would have their final ally. Perhaps it would be Johnny who led them on that day, as the omen seemed to prophesy.

He was the son of a line of leaders, born to a mother who had fought and killed a unicorn. He had gone hungry to share what little he had with the young of Ragnarok's most proud and savage species and Fenrir and Sigyn would fight beside him on the day he led the forces of the hell-world in the battle with the Gerns who thought they were gods.

Could the Gerns hope to have a leader to match?

Part 5

John Humbolt, leader, stood on the wide stockade wall and watched the lowering sun touch the western horizon—far south of where it had set when he was a child. Big Summer was over

and now, in the year two hundred, they were already three years
into Big Fall. The Craigs had been impassable with snow for five
years and the country at the north end of the plateau, where the
iron had been found, had been buried under never-melting snow
and growing glaciers for twenty years.

There came the soft tinkling of ceramic bells as the herd of
milk goats came down off the hills. Two children were following
and six prowlers walked with them, to protect them from wild
unicorns.

There were not many of the goats. Each year the winters were
longer, requiring the stocking of a larger supply of hay. The time
would come when the summers would be so short and the winters so long that they could not keep goats at all. And by then,
when Big Winter had closed in on them, the summer seasons
would be too short for the growing of the orange corn. They
would have nothing left but the hunting.

They had, he knew, reached and passed the zenith of the
development of their environment. From a low of forty-nine
men, women and children in dark caves they had risen to a town
of six thousand. For a few years they had had a way of life that
was almost a civilization but the inevitable decline was already
under way. The years of frozen sterility of Big Winter were
coming and no amount of determination or ingenuity could alter
them. Six thousand would have to live by hunting—and one
hundred, in the first Big Winter, had found barely enough game.

They would have to migrate in one of two different ways: they
could go to the south as nomad hunters—or they could go to
other, fairer worlds in ships they took from the Gerns.

The choice was very easy to make and they were almost ready.

In the workshop at the farther edge of town the hyperspace
transmitter was nearing completion. The little smelter was waiting
to receive the lathe and other iron and steel and turn them into
the castings for the generator. Their weapons were ready, the
mockers were trained, the prowlers were waiting. And in the
massive corral beyond town forty half-tame unicorns trampled
the ground and hated the world, wanting to kill something. They
had learned to be afraid of Ragnarok men but they would not
be afraid to kill Gerns . . .

The children with the goats reached the stockade and two
of the prowlers, Fenrir and Sigyn, turned to see him standing

on the wall. He made a little motion with his hand and they came running, to leap up beside him on the ten-foot-high wall.

"So you've been checking up on how well the young ones guard the children?" he asked.

Sigyn lolled out her tongue and her white teeth grinned at him in answer. Fenrir, always the grimmer of the two, made a sound in his throat in reply.

Prowlers developed something like a telepathic rapport with their masters and could sense their thoughts and understand relatively complex instructions. Their intelligence was greater, and of a far more mature order, than that of the little mockers but their vocal cords were not capable of making the sounds necessary for speech.

He rested his hands on their shoulders, where their ebony fur was frosted with gray. Age had not yet affected their quick, flowing movement but they were getting old—they were only a few weeks short of his own age. He could not remember when they had not been with him . . .

Sometimes it seemed to him he could remember those hungry days when he and Fenrir and Sigyn shared together in his mother's lap—but it was probably only his imagination from having heard the story told so often. But he could remember for certain when he was learning to walk and Fenrir and Sigyn, full grown then, walked tall and black beside him. He could remember playing with Sigyn's pups and he could remember Sigyn watching over them all, sometimes giving her pups a bath and his face a washing with equal disregard for their and his protests. Above all he could remember the times when he was almost grown; the wild, free days when he and Fenrir and Sigyn had roamed the mountains together. With a bow and a knife and two prowlers beside him he had felt that there was nothing on Ragnarok that they could not conquer; that there was nothing in the universe they could not defy together . . .

There was a flicker of black movement and a young messenger prowler came running from the direction of the council hall, a speckle-faced mocker clinging to its back. It leaped up on the wall beside him and the mocker, one that had been trained to remember and repeat messages verbatim, took a breath so deep that its cheeks bulged out. It spoke, in a quick rush like a child that is afraid it might forget some of the words:

"You will please come to the council hall to lead the discussion regarding the last preparations for the meeting with the Gerns. The transmitter is complete."

The lathe was torn down the next day and the smelter began to roar with its forced draft. Excitement and anticipation ran through the town like a fever. It would take perhaps twenty days to build the generator, working day and night so that not an hour of time would be lost, forty days for the signal to reach Athena, and forty days for the Gern cruiser to reach Ragnarok—

In one hundred days the Gerns would be there!

The men who would engage in the fight for the cruiser quit trimming their beards. Later, when it was time for the Gerns to appear, they would discard their woolen garments for ones of goat skin. The Gerns would regard them as primitive inferiors at best and it might be of advantage to heighten the impression. It would make the awakening of the Gerns a little more shocking.

An underground passage, leading from the town to the concealment of the woods in the distance, had long ago been dug. Through it the women and children would go when the Gerns arrived.

There was a level area of ground, just beyond the south wall of town, where the cruiser would be almost certain to land. The town had been built with that thought in mind. Woods were not far from both sides of the landing site and unicorn corrals were hidden in them. From the corrals would come the rear flanking attack against the Gerns.

The prowlers, of course, would be scattered among all the forces.

The generator was completed and installed on the nineteenth night. Charley Craig, a giant of a man whose red beard gave him a genially murderous appearance, opened the valve of the water pipe. The new wooden turbine stirred and belts and pulleys began to spin. The generator hummed, the needles of the dials climbed, flickered, and steadied.

Norman Lake looked from them to Humbolt, his pale gray

eyes coldly satisfied. "Full output," he said. "We have the power we need this time."

Jim Chiara was at the transmitter and they waited while he threw switches and studied dials. Every component of the transmitter had been tested but they had not had the power to test the complete assembly.

"That's it," he said at last, looking up at them. "She's ready, after almost two hundred years of wanting her."

Humbolt wondered what the signal should be and saw no reason why it should not be the same one that had been sent out with such hope a hundred and sixty-five years ago.

"All right, Jim," he said. "Let the Gerns know we're waiting for them—make it 'Ragnarok calling' again."

The transmitter key rattled and the all-wave signal that the Gerns could not fail to receive went out at a velocity of five light-years a day:

Ragnarok calling—Ragnarok calling—Ragnarok calling—

It was the longest summer Humbolt had ever experienced. He was not alone in his impatience—among all of them the restlessness flamed higher as the slow days dragged by, making it almost impossible to go about their routine duties. The gentle mockers sensed the anticipation of their masters for the coming battle and they became nervous and apprehensive. The prowlers sensed it and they paced about the town in the dark of night; watching, listening, on ceaseless guard against the mysterious enemy their masters waited for. Even the unicorns seemed to sense what was coming and they rumbled and squealed in their corrals at night, red-eyed with the lust for blood and sometimes attacking the log walls with blows that shook the ground.

The interminable days went their slow succession and summer gave way to fall. The hundredth day dawned, cold and gray with the approach of winter; the day of the Gerns.

But no cruiser came that day, nor the next.

He stood again on the stockade wall in the evening of the third day, Fenrir and Sigyn beside him. He listened for the first dim, distant sound of the Gern cruiser and heard only the moaning of the wind around him.

Winter was coming. Always, on Ragnarok, winter was coming or the brown death of summer. Ragnarok was a harsh and barren prison, and no amount of desire could ever make it otherwise. Only the coming of a Gern cruiser could ever offer them the bloody, violent opportunity to regain their freedom.

But what if the cruiser never came?

It was a thought too dark and hopeless to be held. They were not asking a large favor of fate, after two hundred years of striving for it; only the chance to challenge the Gern Empire with bows and knives . . .

Fenrir stiffened, the fur lifting on his shoulders and a muted growl coming from him. Then Humbolt heard the first whisper of sound; a faint, faraway roaring that was not the wind.

He watched and listened and the sound came swiftly nearer, rising in pitch and swelling in volume. Then it broke through the clouds, tall and black and beautifully deadly. It rode down on its rockets of flame, filling the valley with its thunder, and his heart hammered with exultation.

It had come—the cruiser had come!

He turned and dropped the ten feet to the ground inside the stockade. The warning signal was being sounded from the center of town; a unicorn horn that gave out the call they had used in the practice alarms. Already the women and children would be hurrying along the tunnels that led to the temporary safety of the woods beyond town. The Gerns might use their turret blasters to destroy the town and all in it before the night was over. There was no way of knowing what might happen before it ended. But whatever it was, it would be the action they had all been wanting.

He ran to where the others would be gathering, Fenrir and Sigyn loping beside him and the horn ringing wild and savage and triumphant as it announced the end of two centuries of waiting.

The cruiser settled to earth in the area where it had been expected to land, towering high above the town with its turret blasters looking down upon the houses.

Charley Craig and Norman Lake were waiting for him on the high steps of his own house in the center of town where the elevation gave them a good view of the ship yet where the fringes of the canopy would conceal them from the ship's scanners. They were heavily armed, their prowlers beside them and their mockers on their shoulders.

Elsewhere, under the connected rows of concealing canopies, armed men were hurrying to their prearranged stations. Most of them were accompanied by prowlers, bristling and snarling as they looked at the alien ship. A few men were deliberately making themselves visible not far away, going about unimportant tasks with only occasional and carefully disinterested glances toward the ship. They were the bait, to lure the first detachment into the center of town . . .

"Well?" Normal Lake asked, his pale eyes restless with his hunger for violence. "There's our ship—when do we take her?"

"Just as soon as we get them outside it," he said. "We'll use the plan we first had—wait until they send a full force to rescue the first detachment and then hit them with everything we have."

His black, white-nosed mocker was standing in the open doorway and watching the hurrying men and prowlers with worried interest: Tip, the great-great-great-great grandson of the mocker that had died with Howard Lake north of the plateau. He reached down to pick him up and set him on his shoulder, and said:

"Jim?"

"The longbows are ready," Tip's treble imitation of Jim Chiara's voice answered. "We'll black out their searchlights when the time comes."

"Andy?" he asked.

"The last of us for this section are coming in now," Andy Taylor answered.

He made his check of all the subleaders, then looked up to the roof to ask, "All set, Jimmy?"

Jimmy Stevens' grinning face appeared over the edge. "Ten crossbows are cocked and waiting up here. Bring us our targets."

They waited, while the evening deepened into near-dusk. Then the airlock of the cruiser slid open and thirteen Gerns emerged, the one leading them wearing the resplendent uniform of a subcommander.

"There they come," he said to Lake and Craig. "It looks like we'll be able to trap them in here and force the commander to send out a full-sized force. We'll all attack at the sound of the horn and if you can hit their rear flanks hard enough with the unicorns to give us a chance to split them from this end some of us should make it to the ship before they realize up in the control room that they should close the airlocks.

"Now"—he looked at the Gerns who were coming straight toward the stockade wall, ignoring the gate to their right—"you'd better be on your way. We'll meet again before long in the ship."

Fenrir and Sigyn looked from the advancing Gerns to him with question in their eyes after Lake and Craig were gone, Fenrir growling restlessly.

"Pretty soon," he said to them. "Right now it would be better if they didn't see you. Wait inside, both of you."

They went reluctantly inside, to merge with the darkness of the interior. Only an occasional yellow gleam of their eyes showed that they were crouched to spring just inside the doorway.

He called to the nearest unarmed man, not loud enough to be heard by the Gerns:

"Cliff—you and Sam Anders come here. Tell the rest to fade out of sight and get armed."

Cliff Schroeder passed the command along and he and Sam Anders approached. He looked back at the Gerns and saw they were within a hundred feet of the—for them—unscalable wall of the stockade. They were coming without hesitation—

A pale blue beam lashed down from one of the cruiser's turrets and a fifty-foot section of the wall erupted into dust with a sound like thunder. The wind swept the dust aside in a gigantic cloud and the Gerns came through the gap, looking neither to right nor left.

"That, I suppose," Sam Anders said from beside him, "was Lesson Number One for degenerate savages like us: Gerns, like gods, are not to be hindered by man-made barriers."

The Gerns walked with a peculiar gait that puzzled him until he saw what it was. They were trying to come with the arrogant military stride affected by the Gerns and in the 1.5 gravity they were succeeding in achieving only a heavy clumping.

They advanced steadily and as they drew closer he saw that in the right hand of each Gern soldier was a blaster while in the left hand of each could be seen the metallic glitter of chains.

Schroeder smiled thinly. "It looks like they want to subject about a dozen of us to some painful questioning."

No one else was any longer in sight and the Gerns came

straight toward the three on the steps. They stopped forty feet away at a word of command from the officer and Gerns and Ragnarok men exchanged silent stares; the faces of the Ragnarok men bearded and expressionless, the faces of the Gerns hairless and reflecting a contemptuous curiosity.

"Narth!" The communicator on the Gern officer's belt spoke with metallic authority. "What do they look like? Did we come two hundred light-years to view some animated vegetables?"

"No, Commander," Narth answered. "I think the discard of the Rejects two hundred years ago has produced for us an unexpected reward. There are three natives under the canopy before me and their physical perfection and complete adaptation to this hellish gravity is astonishing."

"They could be used to replace expensive machines on some of the outer world mines," the commander said, "providing their intelligence isn't too abysmally low. What about that?"

"They can surely be taught to perform simple manual labor," Narth answered.

"Get on with your job," the commander said. "Try to pick some of the most intelligent looking ones for questioning—I can't believe these cattle sent that message and they're going to tell us who did. And pick some young, strong ones for the medical staff to examine—ones that won't curl up and die after the first few cuts of the knife."

"We'll chain these three first," Narth said. He lifted his hand in an imperious gesture to Humbolt and the other two and ordered in accented Terran: "Come here!"

No one moved and he said again, sharply, "*Come here!*"

Again no one moved and the minor officer beside Narth said, "Apparently they can't even understand Terran now."

"Then we'll give them some action they can understand," Narth snapped, his face flushing with irritation. "We'll drag them out by their heels!"

The Gerns advanced purposefully, three of them holstering their blasters to make their chains ready. When they had passed under the canopy and could not be seen from the ship Humbolt spoke:

"All right, Jimmy."

The Gerns froze in midstride, suspicion flashing across their faces.

"Look up on the roof," he said in Gern.

They looked, and the suspicion became gaping dismay.

"You can be our prisoners or you can be corpses," he said. "We don't care which."

The urgent hiss of Narth's command broke their indecision: "*Kill them!*"

Six of them tried to obey, bringing up their blasters in movements that seemed curiously heavy and slow, as though the gravity of Ragnarok had turned their arms to wood. Three of them almost lifted their blasters high enough to fire at the steps in front of them before arrows went through their throats. The other three did not get that far.

Narth and the remaining six went rigidly motionless and he said to them:

"Drop your blasters—quick!"

Their blasters thumped to the ground and Jimmy Stevens and his bowmen slid off the roof. Within a minute the Gerns were bound with their own chains, but for the officer, and the blasters were in the hands of the Ragnarok men.

Jimmy looked down the row of Gerns and shook his head. "So these are Gerns?" he said. "It was like trapping a band of woods goats."

"Young ones," Schroeder amended. "And almost as dangerous."

Narth's face flushed at the words and his eyes went to the ship. The sight of it seemed to restore his courage and his lips drew back in a snarl.

"You fools—you stupid, megalomaniac dung-heaps—do you think you can kill Gerns and live to boast about it?"

"Keep quiet," Humbolt ordered, studying him with curiosity. Narth, like all the Gerns, was different from what they had expected. It was true the Gerns had strode into their town with an attempt at arrogance but they were harmless in appearance, soft of face and belly, and the snarling of the red-faced Narth was like the bluster of a cornered scavenger-rodent.

"I promise you this," Narth was saying viciously, "if you don't release us and return our weapons this instant I'll personally oversee the extermination of you and every savage in this village with the most painful death science can contrive and I'll—"

Humbolt reached out his hand and flicked Narth under the

chin. Narth's teeth cracked loudly together and his face twisted with the pain of a bitten tongue.

"Tie him up, Jess," he said to the man near him. "If he opens his mouth again, shove your foot in it."

He spoke to Schroeder. "We'll keep three of the blasters and send two to each of the other front groups. Have that done."

Dusk was deepening into darkness and he called Chiara again. "They'll turn on their searchlights any minute and make the town as light as day," he said. "If you can keep them blacked out until some of us have reached the ship, I think we'll have won."

"They'll be kept blacked out," Chiara said. "With some flint-headed arrows left over for the Gerns."

He called Lake and Craig, to be told they were ready and waiting.

"But we're having hell keeping the unicorns quiet," Craig said. "They want to get to killing something."

He pressed the switch of the communicator but it was dead. They had, of course, transferred to some other wave length so he could not hear the commands. It was something he had already anticipated.

Fenrir and Sigyn were still obediently inside the doorway, almost frantic with desire to rejoin him. He spoke to them and they bounded out, snarling at three Gerns in passing and causing them to blanch to a dead-white color.

He set Tip on Sigyn's shoulders and said, "Sigyn, there's a job for you and Tip to do. A dangerous job. Listen—both of you . . ."

The yellow eyes of Sigyn and the dark eyes of the little mocker looked into his as he spoke to them and accompanied his words with the strongest, clearest mental images he could project:

"Sigyn, take Tip to the not-men thing. Leave him hidden in the grass to one side of the big hole in it. Tip, you wait there. When the not-men come out you listen, and tell what they say.

"Now, do you both understand?"

Sigyn made a sound that meant she did but Tip clutched at his wrist with little paws suddenly gone cold and wailed, "*No! Scared—scared—*"

"You have to go, Tip," he said, gently disengaging his wrist. "And Sigyn will hide near to you and watch over you." He spoke to Sigyn. "When the horn calls you run back with him."

Again she made the sound signifying understanding and

he touched them both in what he hoped would not be the last farewell.

"All right, Sigyn—go now."

She vanished into the gloom of coming night, Tip hanging tightly to her. Fenrir stood with the fur lifted on his shoulders and a half snarl on his face as he watched her go and watched the place where the not-men would appear.

"Where's Freckles?" he asked Jimmy.

"Here," someone said, and came forward with Tip's mate.

He set Freckles on his shoulder and the first searchlight came on, shining down from high up on the cruiser. It lighted up the area around them in harsh white brilliance, its reflection revealing the black shadow that was Sigyn just vanishing behind the ship.

Two more searchlights came on, to illuminate the town. Then the Gerns came.

They poured out through the airlock and down the ramp, there to form in columns that marched forward as still more Gerns hurried down the ramp behind them. The searchlights gleamed on their battle helmets and on the blades of the bayonets affixed to their rifle-like long-range blasters. Hand blasters and grenades hung from their belts, together with stubby flame guns.

They were a solid mass reaching halfway to the stockade before the last of them, the commanding officers, appeared. One of them stopped at the foot of the ramp to watch the advance of the punitive force and give the frightened but faithful Tip the first words to transmit to Freckles:

"The full force is on its way, Commander."

A reply came, in Freckles' simulation of the metallic tones of the communicator:

"The key numbers of the confiscated blasters have been checked and the disturbance rays of the master integrator set. You'll probably have few natives left alive to take as prisoners after those thirteen charges explode but continue with a mopping up job that the survivors will never forget."

So the Gerns could, by remote control, set the total charges of stolen blasters to explode upon touching the firing stud? It was something new since the days of the Old Ones . . .

He called Chiara and the other groups, quickly, to tell them what he had learned. "We'll get more blasters—ones they can't know the numbers of—when we attack," he finished.

He took the blaster from his belt and laid it on the ground. The front ranks of the Gerns were almost to the wall by then, a column wider than the gap that had been blasted through it, coming with silent purposefulness.

Two blaster beams lanced down from the turrets, to smash at the wall. Dust billowed and thunder rumbled as they swept along. A full three hundred feet of the wall had been destroyed when they stopped and the dust hid the ship and made dim glows of the searchlights.

It had no doubt been intended to impress them with the might of the Gerns but in doing so it hid the Ragnarok forces from the advancing Gerns for a few second.

"Jim—black out their lights before the dust clears," he called. "Joe—the horn! We attack now!"

The first longbow arrow struck a searchlight and its glow grew dimmer as the arrow's burden—a thin tube of thick lance tree ink—splattered against it. Another followed—

Then the horn rang out, harsh and commanding, and in the distance a unicorn screamed in answer. The savage cry of a prowler came, like a sound to match, and the attack was on.

He ran with Fenrir beside him and to his left and right ran the others with their prowlers. The lead groups converged as they went through the wide gap in the wall. They ran on, into the dust cloud, and the shadowy forms of the Gerns were suddenly before them.

A blaster beam cut into them and a Gern shouted, "*The natives!*" Other beams sprang into life, winking like pale blue eyes through the dust and killing all they touched. The beams dropped as the first volley of arrows tore through the massed front ranks, to be replaced by others.

They charged on, into the blue winking of the blasters and the red lances of the flame guns with the crossbows rattling and strumming in answer. The prowlers lunged and fought beside them and ahead of them; black hell-creatures that struck the Gerns too swiftly for blaster to find before throats were torn out; the sound of battle turned into a confusion of raging snarls, frantic shouts and dying screams.

A prowler shot past him to join Fenrir—Sigyn—and he felt Tip dart up to his shoulder. She made a sound of greeting in passing, a sound that was gone as her jaws closed on a Gern.

The dust cloud cleared a little and the searchlights looked down on the scene; no longer brilliantly white but shining through the red-black lance tree ink as a blood-red glow. A searchlight turret slid shut and opened a moment later, the light wiped clean. The longbows immediately transformed it into a red glow.

The beam of one of the turret blasters stabbed down, to blaze a trail of death through the battle. It ceased as its own light revealed to the Gern commander that the Ragnarok forces were so intermixed with the Gern forces that he was killing more Gerns than Ragnarok men.

By then the fighting was so hand to hand that knives were better than crossbows. The Gerns fell like harvested corn; too slow and awkward to use their bayonets against the faster Ragnarok men and killing as many of one another as men when they tried to use their blasters and flame guns. From the rear there came the command of a Gern officer, shouted high and thin above the sound of battle:

"Back to the ship—leave the natives for the ship's blasters to kill!"

The unicorns arrived then, to cut off their retreat.

They came twenty from the east and twenty from the west in a thunder of hooves, squealing and screaming in their blood lust, with prowlers a black wave going before them. They struck the Gerns; the prowlers slashing lanes through them while the unicorns charged behind, trampling them, ripping into them with their horns and smashing them down with their hooves as they vented the pent-up rage of their years of confinement. On the back of each was a rider whose long spear flicked and stabbed into the throats and bellies of Gerns.

The retreat was halted and transformed into milling confusion. He led his own group in the final charge, the prearranged wedge attack, and they split the Gern force in two.

The ship was suddenly just beyond them.

He gave the last command to Lake and Craig: "*Now*—into the ship!"

He scooped up a blaster from beside a fallen Gern and ran toward it. A Gern officer was already in the airlock, his face pale and strained as he looked back and his hand on the closing switch. He shot him and ran up the ramp as the officer's body rolled down it.

Unicorn hooves pounded behind him and twenty of them swept past, their riders leaping from their backs to the ramp. Twenty men and fifteen prowlers charged up the ramp as a warning siren shrieked somewhere inside the ship. At the same time the airlocks, operated from the control room, began to slide swiftly shut.

He was through first, with Fenrir and Sigyn. Lake and Craig, together with six men and four prowlers, squeezed through barely in time. Then the airlocks were closed and they were sealed in the ship.

Alarm bells added their sound to the shrieking of the siren and from the multiple-compartment shafts came the whir of elevators dropping with Gern forces to kill the humans trapped inside the ship.

They ran past the elevator shafts without pausing, light and swift in the artificial gravity that was only two-thirds that of Ragnarok. They split forces as long ago planned; three men and four prowlers going with Charley Craig in the attempt to take the drive room, Lake and the other three men going with him in the attempt to take the control room.

They found the manway ladder and began to climb, Fenrir and Sigyn impatiently crowding their heels.

There was nothing on the control room level and they ran down the short corridor that their maps had showed. They turned left, into the corridor that had the control room at its end, and into the concentrated fire of nine waiting Gerns.

Fenrir and Sigyn went into the Gerns, under their fire before they could drop the muzzles of their blasters, with an attack so vicious and unexpected that what would have been a certain and lethal trap for the humans was suddenly a fighting chance.

The corridor became an inferno of blaster beams that cracked and hissed as they met and crossed, throwing little chips of metal from the walls with snapping sounds and going through flesh with sounds like soft tappings. It was over within seconds, the last Gern down and one man still standing beside him, the blond and nerveless Lake.

Thomsen and Barber were dead and Billy West was bracing himself against the wall with a blaster hole through his stomach, trying to say something and sliding to the floor before it was ever spoken.

And Sigyn was down, blood welling and bubbling from a wound in her chest, while Fenrir stood over her with his snarling a raging scream as he swung his head in search of a still-living Gern.

Humbolt and Lake ran on, Fenrir raging beside them, and into the control room.

Six officers, one wearing the uniform of a commander, were gaping in astonishment and bringing up their blasters in the way that seemed so curiously slow to Humbolt. Fenrir, in his fury, killed two of them as Lake's blaster and his own killed three more.

The commander was suddenly alone, his blaster half lifted. Fenrir leaped at his throat and Humbolt shouted the quick command: "*Disarm!*"

It was something the prowlers had been taught in their training and Fenrir's teeth clicked short of the commander's throat while his paw sent the blaster spinning across the room.

The commander stared at them with his swarthy face a dark gray and his mouth still gaping.

"How—how did you do it?" he asked in heavily accented Terran. "Only two of you—"

"Don't talk until you're asked a question," Lake said.

"Only two of you . . ." The thought seemed to restore his courage, as sight of the ship had restored Narth's that night, and his tone became threatening. "There are only two of you and more guards will be here to kill you within a minute. Surrender to me and I'll let you go free—"

Lake slapped him across the mouth with a backhanded blow that snapped his head back on his shoulders and split his lip.

"Don't talk," he ordered again. "And never lie to us."

The commander spit out a tooth and held his hand to his bleeding mouth. He did not speak again.

Tip and Freckles were holding tightly to his shoulder and each other, the racing of their hearts like a vibration, and he touched them reassuringly.

"All right now—all safe now," he said.

He called Charley Craig. "Charley—did you make it?"

"We made it to the drive room—two of us and one prowler," Charley answered. "What about you?"

"Norman and I have the control room. Cut their drives, to play safe. I'll let you know as soon as the entire ship is ours."

He went to the viewscreen and saw that the battle was over.

Chiara was letting the searchlight burn again and prowlers were being used to drive back the unicorns from the surrendering Gerns.

"I guess we won," he said to Lake.

But there was no feeling of victory, none of the elation he had thought he would have. Sigyn was dying alone in the alien corridor outside. Sigyn, who had nursed beside him and fought beside him and laid down her life for him . . .

"I want to look at her," he said to Lake.

Fenrir went with him. She was still alive, waiting for them to come back to her. She lifted her head and touched his hand with her tongue as he examined the wound.

It was not fatal—it need not be fatal. He worked swiftly, gently, to stop the bleeding that had been draining her life away. She would have to lie quietly for weeks but she would recover.

When he was done he pressed her head back to the floor and said, "Lie still, Sigyn girl, until we can come to move you. Wait for us and Fenrir will stay here with you."

She obeyed and he left them, the feeling of victory and elation coming to him in full then.

Lake looked at him questioningly as he entered the control room and he said, "She'll live."

He turned to the Gern commander. "First, I want to know how the war is going?"

"I—" The commander looked uncertainly at Lake.

"Just tell the truth," Lake said. "Whether you think we'll like it or not."

"We have all the planets but Earth, itself," the commander said. "We'll have it, soon."

"And the Terrans on Athena?"

"They're still—working for us there."

"Now," he said, "you will order every Gern in this ship to go to his sleeping quarters. They will leave their weapons in the corridors outside and they will not resist the men who will come to take charge of the ship."

The commander made an effort toward defiance:

"And if I refuse?"

Lake answered, smiling at him with the smile of his that was no more than a quick showing of teeth and with the savage eagerness in his eyes.

"If you refuse I'll start with your fingers and break every bone to your shoulders. If that isn't enough I'll start with your toes and go to your hips. And then I'll break your back."

The commander hesitated, sweat filming his face as he looked at them. Then he reached out to switch on the all-stations communicator and say into it:

"Attention, all personnel: You will return to your quarters at once, leaving your weapons in the corridors. You are ordered to make no resistance when the natives come . . ."

There was a silence when he had finished and Humbolt and Lake looked at each other, bearded and clad in animal skins but standing at last in the control room of a ship that was theirs; in a ship that could take them to Athena, to Earth, to the ends of the galaxy.

The commander watched them, on his face the blankness of unwillingness to believe.

"The airlocks—" he said. "We didn't close them in time. We never thought you would dare try to take the ship—not savages in animal skins."

"I know," Humbolt answered. "We were counting on you to think that way."

"No one expected any of you to survive here." The commander wiped at his swollen lips, wincing, and an almost child-like petulance came into his tone. "You weren't supposed to survive."

"I know," he said again. "We've made it a point to remember that."

"The gravity, the heat and cold and fever, the animals—why didn't they kill you?"

"They tried," he said. "But we fought back. And we had a goal—to meet you Gerns again. You left us on a world that had no resources. Only enemies who would kill us—the gravity, the prowlers, the unicorns. So we made them our resources. We adapted to the gravity that was supposed to kill us and became stronger and quicker than Gerns. We made allies of the prowlers and unicorns who were supposed to be our executioners and used them tonight to help us kill Gerns. So now we have your ship."

"Yes . . . you have our ship." Through the unwillingness to believe on the commander's face and the petulance there came the triumph of vindictive anticipation. "The savages of Ragnarok have a Gern cruiser—but what can they do with it?"

"What can we do with it?" he asked, almost kindly. "We've planned for two hundred years what we can do with it. We have the cruiser and sixty days from now we'll have Athena. That will be only the beginning and you Gerns are going to help us do it."

For six days the ship was a scene of ceaseless activity. Men crowded it, asking questions of the Gern officers and crew and calmly breaking the bones of those who refused to answer or who gave answers that were not true. Prowlers stalked the corridors, their cold yellow eyes watching every move the Gerns made. The little mockers began roaming the ship at will, unable any longer to restrain their curiosity and confident that the men and prowlers would not let the Gerns harm them.

One mocker was killed then; the speckle-faced mocker that could repeat messages verbatim. It wandered into a storage cubicle where a Gern was working alone and gave him the opportunity to safely vent his hatred of everything associated with the men of Ragnarok. He broke its back with a steel bar and threw it, screaming, into the disposal chute that led to the matter converter. A prowler heard the scream and an instant later the Gern screamed; a sound that died in its making as the prowler tore his throat out. No more mockers were harmed.

One Ragnarok boy was killed. Three fanatical Gern officers stole knives from the galley and held the boy as hostage for their freedom. When their demands were refused they cut his heart out. Lake cornered them a few minutes later and, without touching his blaster, disemboweled them with their own knives. He smiled down upon them as they writhed and moaned on the floor and their moans were heard for a long time by the other Gerns in the ship before they died. No more humans were harmed.

They discovered that operation of the cruiser was relatively simple, basically similar to the operation of Terran ships as described in the text book the original Lake had written. Most of the operations were performed by robot mechanisms and the manual operations, geared to the slower reflexes of the Gerns, were easily mastered.

They could spend the forty-day voyage to Athena in further learning and practice so on the sixth day they prepared to depart. The unicorns had been given the freedom they had fought so well for and reconnaissance vehicles were loaned from the cruiser to take their place. Later there would be machinery and supplies of all kinds brought in by freighter ships from Athena.

Time was precious and there was a long, long job ahead of them. They blasted up from Ragnarok on the morning of the seventh day and went into the black sea of hyperspace.

By then the Gern commander was no longer of any value to them. His unwillingness to believe that savages had wrested his ship from him had increased until his compartment became his control room to him and he spent the hours laughing and giggling before an imaginary viewscreen whereon the cruiser's blasters were destroying, over and over, the Ragnarok town and all the humans in it.

But Narth, who had wanted to have them tortured to death for daring to resist capture, became very cooperative. In the control room his cooperation was especially eager. On the twentieth day of the voyage they let him have what he had been trying to gain by subterfuge: access to the transmitter when no men were within hearing distance. After that his manner abruptly changed. Each day his hatred for them and his secret anticipation became more evident.

The thirty-fifth day came, with Athena five days ahead of them—the day of the execution they had let him arrange for them.

Stars filled the transdimensional viewscreen, the sun of Athena in the center. Humbolt watched the space to the lower left and the flicker came again; a tiny red dot that was gone again within a microsecond, so quickly that Narth in the seat beside him did not see it.

It was the quick peek of another ship; a ship that was running invisible with its detector screens up but which had had to drop them for an instant to look out at the cruiser. Not even the Gerns had ever been able to devise a polarized detector screen.

He changed the course and speed of the cruiser, creating an increase in gravity which seemed very slight to him but which caused Narth to slew heavily in his seat. Narth straightened and he said to him:

"Within a few minutes we'll engage the ship you sent for."

Narth's jaw dropped, then came back up. "So you spied on me?"

"One of our Ragnarok allies did—the little animal that was sitting near the transmitter. They're our means of communication. We learned that you had arranged for a ship, en route to Athena, to intercept us and capture us."

"So you know?" Narth asked. He smiled, an unpleasant twisting of his mouth. "Do you think that knowing will help you any?"

"We expect it to," he answered.

"It's a battleship," Narth said. "It's three times the size of this cruiser, the newest and most powerful battleship in the Gern fleet. How does that sound to you?"

"It sounds good," he said. "We'll make it our flagship."

"Your flagship—your '*flagship*'!" The last trace of pretense left Narth and he let his full and rankling hatred come through. "You got this cruiser by trickery and learned how to operate it after a fashion because of an animal-like reflex abnormality. For forty-two days you accidental mutants have given orders to your superiors and thought you were our equals. Now, your fool's paradise is going to end."

The red dot came again, closer, and he once more altered the ship's course. He had turned on the course analyzer and it clicked as the battleship's position was correlated with that of its previous appearance. A short yellow line appeared on the screen to forecast its course for the immediate future.

"And then?" he asked curiously, turning back to Narth.

"And then we'll take all of you left alive back to your village. The scenes of what we do to you and your village will be televised to all Gern-held worlds. It will be a valuable reminder for any who have forgotten the penalty for resisting Gerns."

The red dot came again. He punched the BATTLE STATIONS button and the board responded with a row of READY lights.

"All the other Gerns are by now in their acceleration couches," he said. "Strap yourself in for high-acceleration maneuvers—we'll make contact with the battleship within two minutes."

Narth did so, taking his time as though it was something of little importance. "There will be no maneuvers. They'll blast the stern and destroy your drive immediately upon attack."

He fastened the last strap and smiled, taunting assurance in the twisted unpleasantness of it. "The appearance of this battleship has very much disrupted your plans to strut like conquering heroes among the slaves on Athena, hasn't it?"

"Not exactly," Humbolt replied. "Our plans are a little broader in scope than that. There are two new cruisers on Athena, ready to leave the shops ten days from now. We'll turn control of Athena over to the humans there, of course, then we'll take the three cruisers and the battleship back by way of Ragnarok. There we'll pick up all the Ragnarok men who are neither too old nor too young and go on to Earth. They will be given training en route in the handling of ships. We expect to find no difficulty in breaking through the Gern lines around Earth and then, with the addition of the Earth ships, we can easily capture all the Gern ships in the solar system."

" 'Easily'!" Narth made a contemptuous sneer of the word. "Were you actually so stupid as to think that you biological freaks could equal Gern officers who have made a career of space warfare?"

"We'll far exceed them," he said. "A space battle is one of trying to keep your blaster beams long enough on one area of the enemy ship to break through its blaster shields at that point. And at the same time try to move and dodge fast enough to keep the enemy from doing the same thing to you. The ships are capable of accelerations up to fifty gravities or more but the acceleration limitator is the safeguard that prevents the ship from going into such a high degree of acceleration or into such a sudden change of direction that it would kill the crew.

"We from Ragnarok are accustomed to a one point five gravity and can withstand much higher degrees of acceleration than Gerns or any other race from a one-gravity world. To enable us to take advantage of that fact we have had the acceleration limitator on this cruiser disconnected."

"*Disconnected?*" Narth's contemptuous regard vanished in frantic consternation. "You fool—you don't know what that means—*you'll move the acceleration lever too far and kill us all!*"

The red dot flickered on the viewscreen, trembled, and was suddenly a gigantic battleship in full view. He touched the acceleration control and Narth's next words were cut off as his diaphragm sagged. He swung the cruiser in a curve and Narth was slammed sideways, the straps cutting into him and the flesh of his face pulled lopsided by the gravity. His eyes, bulging, went blank with unconsciousness.

The powerful blasters of the battleship blossomed like a row of pale blue flowers, concentrating on the stern of the cruiser. A warning siren screeched as they started breaking through the cruiser's shields. He dropped the detector screen that would shield the cruiser from sight, but not from the blaster beams, and tightened the curve until the gravity dragged heavily at his own body.

The warning siren stopped as the blaster beams of the battleship went harmlessly into space, continuing to follow the probability course plotted from the cruiser's last visible position and course by the battleship's robot target tracers.

He lifted the detector screen, to find the battleship almost exactly where the cruiser's course analyzers had predicted it would be. The blasters of the battleship were blazing their full concentration of firepower into an area behind and to one side of the cruiser.

They blinked out at the sight of the cruiser in its new position and blazed again a moment later, boring into the stern. He dropped the detector screen and swung the cruiser in another curve, spiraling in the opposite direction. As before, the screech of the alarm siren died as the battleship's blasters followed the course given them by course analyzers and target tracers that were built to presume that all enemy ships were acceleration-limitator equipped.

The cruiser could have destroyed the battleship at any time— but they wanted to capture their flagship unharmed. The maneuvering continued, the cruiser drawing closer to the battleship. The battleship, in desperation, began using the same hide-and-jump tactics the cruiser used but it was of little avail— the battleship moved at known acceleration limits and the cruiser's course analyzers predicted each new position with sufficient accuracy.

The cruiser made its final dash in a tightening spiral, its detector screen flickering on and off. It struck the battleship at a matched speed, with a thump and ringing of metal as the magnetic grapples fastened the cruiser like a leech to the battleship's side.

In that position neither the forward nor stern blasters of the battleship could touch it. There remained only to convince the commander of the battleship that further resistance was futile.

This he did with a simple ultimatum to the commander:

"This cruiser is firmly attached to your ship, its acceleration limitator disconnected. Its drives are of sufficient power to thrust both ships forward at a much higher degree of acceleration that persons from one-gravity worlds can endure. You will surrender at once or we shall be forced to put these two ships into a curve of such short radius and at an acceleration so great that all of you will be killed."

Then he added, "If you surrender we'll do somewhat better by you than you did with the humans two hundred years ago—we'll take all of you on to Athena."

The commander, already sick from an acceleration that would have been negligible to Ragnarok men, had no choice.

His reply came, choked with acceleration sickness and the greater sickness of defeat:

"We will surrender."

Narth regained consciousness. He saw Humbolt sitting beside him as before, with no Gern rescuers crowding into the control room with shouted commands and drawn blasters.

"Where are they?" he asked. "Where is the battleship?"

"We captured it," he said.

"You captured—a Gern battleship?"

"It wasn't hard," he said. "It would have been easier if only Ragnarok men had been on the cruiser. We didn't want to accelerate to any higher gravities than absolutely necessary because of the Gerns on it."

"You did it—you captured the battleship," Narth said, his tone like one dazed.

He wet his lips, staring, as he contemplated the unpleasant implications of it.

"You're freak mutants who can capture a battleship. Maybe you will take Athena and Earth from us. But"—the animation of hatred returned to his face—"What good will it do you? Did you ever think about that?"

"Yes," he said. "We've thought about it."

"Have you?" Narth leaned forward, his face shining with the malice of his gloating. "You can never escape the consequences of what you have done. The Gern Empire has the resources of dozens of worlds. The Empire will build a fleet of special ships, a force against which your own will be nothing, and send them to Earth and Athena and Ragnarok. The Empire will smash you for what you have done and if there are any survivors of your race left they will cringe before Gerns for a hundred generations to come.

"Remember that while you're posturing in your little hour of glory on Athena and Earth."

"You insist in thinking we'll do as Gerns would do," he said. "We won't delay to do any posturing. We'll have a large fleet when we leave Earth and we'll go at once to engage the Gern home fleet. I thought you knew we were going to do that. We're going to cripple and capture your fleet and then we're going to destroy your empire."

"Destroy the Empire—*now*?" Narth stared again, all the gloating gone as he saw, at last, the quick and inexorable end. "Now—before we can stop you—before we can have a chance?"

"When a race has been condemned to die by another race and it fights and struggles and manages somehow to survive, it learns a lesson. It learns it must never again let the other race be in position to destroy it. So this is the harvest you reap from the seeds you sowed on Ragnarok two hundred years ago.

"You understand, don't you?" he asked, almost gently. "For two hundred years the Gern Empire has been a menace to our survival as a race. Now, the time has come when we shall remove it."

He stood in the control room of the battleship and watched Athena's sun in the viewscreen, blazing like a white flame. Sigyn, fully recovered, was stretched out on the floor near him; twitching and snarling a little in her sleep as she fought again the battle with the Gerns. Fenrir was pacing the floor, swinging his black, massive head restlessly, while Tip and Freckles were examining with fascinated curiosity the collection of bright medals that had been cleaned out of the Gern commander's desk.

Lake and Craig left their stations, as impatient as Fenrir, and came over to watch the viewscreen with him.

"One day more," Craig said. "We're two hundred years late but we're coming in to the world that was to have been our home."

"It can never be, now," he said. "Have any of us ever thought of that—that we're different from humans and there's no human world we could ever call home?"

"I've thought of it," Lake said. "Ragnarok made us different physically and different in the way we think. We could live on human worlds—but we would always be a race apart and never really belong there."

"I suppose we've all thought about it," Craig said. "And wondered what we'll do when we're finished with the Gerns. Not settle down on Athena or Earth, in a little cottage with a fenced-in lawn where it would be adventure to watch the Three-D shows after each day at some safe, routine job."

"Not back to Ragnarok," Lake said. "With metals and supplies from other worlds they'll be able to do a lot there but the battle is already won. There will be left only the peaceful development—building a town at the equator for Big Winter, leveling land, planting crops. We could never be satisfied with that kind of a life."

"No," he said, and felt his own restlessness stir in protest at the thought of settling down in some safe and secure environment. "Not Athena or Earth or Ragnarok—not any world we know."

"How long until we're finished with the Gerns?" Lake asked. "Ten years? We'll still be young then. Where will we go—all of us who fought the Gerns and all of the ones in the future who won't want to live out their lives on Ragnarok? Where is there a place for us—a world of our own?"

"Where do we find a world of our own?" he asked, and watched the star clouds creep toward them in the viewscreen; tumbled and blazing and immense beyond conception.

"There's a galaxy for us to explore," he said. "There are millions of suns and thousands of worlds waiting for us. Maybe there are races out there like the Gerns—and maybe there are races such as we were a hundred years ago who need our help. And maybe there are worlds out there with things on them such as no man ever imagined.

"We'll go, to see what's there. Our women will go with us and there will be some worlds on which some of us will want to stay. And, always, there will be more restless ones coming from Ragnarok. Out there are the worlds and the homes for all of us."

"Of course," Lake said. "Beyond the space frontier . . . where else would we ever belong?"

It was all settled, then, and there was a silence as the battleship plunged through hyperspace, the cruiser running beside her and their drives moaning and thundering as had the drives of the *Constellation* two hundred years before.

A voyage had been interrupted then, and a new race had been born. Now they were going on again, to Athena, to Earth, to the farthest reaches of the Gern Empire. And on, to the wild, unknown regions of space beyond.

There awaited their worlds and there awaited their destiny; to be a race scattered across a hundred thousand light-years of suns, to be an empire such as the galaxy had never known.

They, the restless ones, the unwanted and forgotten, the survivors.

Editor's note: I mentioned, didn't I, that Godwin had a grim side to him? The very short story which follows, even more than "The Cold Equations," may well deserve the title of "the grimmest science fiction story ever written." I'm not sure why, but I love it. Maybe it's because of the wry humor I detect in it. Then again, maybe it's just because I'm nuts.

THE HARVEST

It was Harvest time.

The Sky People waited where the last tenuous vestiges of atmosphere met the nothing of outer space, invisible to the land creatures below who had no way of perceiving life forms that were almost pure energy. Harthon and Ledri waited a little apart from the others, soaring restlessly on scintillating wings in the light-stream from the sun.

For many days the Release field had enveloped the world below, clouding and distorting the surface of it to the perception of the Sky People with the violence of its psycho-persuasion bands. Now the field was lifted, its work done. There remained only the last little while of waiting before the fralings came; the intoxicating, maddeningly delicious fralings that filled the body and mind with a singing, ecstatic fire . . .

"There are so many of us this time," Ledri said. "Do you think there will be enough fralings?"

"Of course," Harthon reassured her. "There are more of *them*, too, and they've learned how to send us as many as we need. There will be more fralings this time than ever before."

"The Harvest—" Ledri's thought was like a nostalgic sigh. "What fun they are! Do you remember the last one, Harthon? And the night we danced down the moonbeams to meet the fralings coming up, before they had ever reached the nets of the Gatherer?"

"I remember. And afterward we followed the sun-stream out, so far out that the world and the moon were like a big and a little star behind us. And we sang . . ."

"And you. And then we were hungry again and we let the sun-stream carry us back to the feast where the others were laughing because someone had almost let a fraling escape. Everyone was so happy and the world and the stars were so beautiful. The poor creatures down below"—a touch of sadness came over her—"they don't know and can never know what it's like . . ."

"It has to be that way," Harthon said. "Would you change it if you could?"

"Oh, no! They have to stay there and we have to watch over them. But what if they should do something beyond our control, as the Wise Ones say they may do some day, and then there would be the Last Harvest and never again any fralings for us?"

"I know. But that may not happen for a long time. And this isn't the day for worrying, little shining one—not when the feast begins so soon."

Their wings touched as they turned in their soaring and looked down upon the great curve of the world below. The eastern sea was blue and cloudless; the western continent going into the evening and the huge mass of the eastern continent coming out of the night. The turning of the world was visible as they watched; the western rim of the western continent creeping very slowly into the extinction of the horizon.

"Can the land people tell when we're watching them like this?" Ledri asked.

"No. They know we're up here, but that's all."

"How did they ever—"

A little sun blazed into being on the western continent, brighter than the real sun. Others followed, swiftly; then they began to flare into life on the eastern continent—two fields of vivid flowers that bloomed briefly and were gone. Where they had been were tall, dark clouds that rose higher still, swelling and spreading, hiding the land beneath.

The Summoner gave the call that was like the song of a trumpet and the one who had been appointed Gatherer poised his far-flung nets.

"They're coming—the fralings!" Ledri cried. "Look at them,

Harthon. But there are so many"—the worry came back to her—"so many that maybe this is the Last Harvest."

"There aren't *that* many," Harthon said, and he laughed at her concern. "Besides, will we care tonight?"

The quick darkness of her mood vanished and she laughed with him. "Tonight we'll dance down the moonbeams again. And tomorrow we'll follow the sun-stream out, farther than ever before."

The fralings drew swiftly closer, hurrying like bright silver birds.

"They're coming to us," Ledri said. "They know that this is where they must go. But how did the land people ever learn of us?"

"Once, many centuries ago, a fraling escaped the nets long enough to go back for a little while. But fralings and land people can't communicate very well with one another and the land people misunderstood most of what it tried to tell them about us."

The fralings struck the invisible nets and the Gatherer gave the command to draw them closed.

"Let's go—the others are already starting," Harthon said, and they went with flashing wings toward the nearer net.

"Do the land people have a name for us?" Ledri asked.

"They call us 'angels,' and they call the Gatherer 'God.'"

The fralings, finally understanding, were trying frantically to escape and the terror of the small ones was a frightened, pleading wail.

"And what do they call the fralings?"

"They call them their 'souls.' We'll eat the small, young ones first—they're the best and there will be plenty for all."

Editor's note: For the most part, though, Godwin's stories—however grim the situation—are really about triumph in the face of adversity. Here, in a story which is also a truly classic science fiction "problem solver tale," is a splendid example.

BRAIN TEASER

Carl Engle stood aside as the flight preparation crew filed out of the *Argosy*'s airlock. Barnes was the last; fat and bald and squinting against the brightness of the Arizona sun.

"All set, Carl," he said. "They had us to check and countercheck, especially the drives."

Engle nodded. "Good. Ground Control reports the Slug cruiser still circling seven hundred miles out and they think the Slugs suspect something."

"Damned centipedes!" Barnes said. "I still say they're telepathic." He looked at his watch. Zero hour minus twenty-six minutes. "Good luck, boy, and I hope this space warp dingus works like they think it will."

He waddled down the boarding ramp and Engle went through the airlock, frowning a little as he threw the switches that would withdraw the ramp and close the airlock behind him. Barnes' implied doubt in the success of the space warp shuttle was not comforting. If the shuttle failed to work, the *Argosy* would be on the proverbial spot with the Slug cruiser eager to smear it well thereupon . . .

Access to the control room was up through the room that housed the space warp shuttle. Dr. Harding, the tall, bristle-browed physicist, and his young assistant, Garvin, looked up briefly as he entered then returned their attention to their work. The master computer, borrowed from M.I.T., stood like a

153

colossal many-dialed refrigerator along one wall. A protective railing around it bore a blunt KEEP OUT sign and it was never left unwatched. Garvin was seated before it, his fingers flitting over the keyboard and the computer's answer panel replying with strange mathematical symbols.

The space warp shuttle sat in the middle of the room, a cube approximately two-thirds of a meter along the edge, studded with dials and knobs and surmounted by a ball of some shining silvery alloy. Dr. Harding was talking into the transdimensional communicator mounted beside the shuttle.

Engle went on to the computer and waited outside the railing until Garvin finished with his work and turned in his seat to face him.

"The last check question," Garvin said. "Now to sweat out the last twenty minutes."

"If you've got the time, how about telling me about the shuttle," said Engle, "I've been kept in the dark about it; but from what I understand, the shuttle builds up a field around the ship, with the silver ball as the center of the field, and this field goes into another dimension called the 'space warp'."

"Ah—it could be described in that manner," Garvin said, smiling a little. "A clear description could not be made without the use of several special kinds of mathematics, but you might say this field in normal space is like a bubble under water. The air bubble seeks its own element, rises rapidly until it emerges into free air—in this case, the space warp. This transition into the warp is almost instantaneous and the shuttle automatically ceases operation when the warp is fully entered. The shuttle is no longer needed; the hypothetical bubble no longer exists—it has found its own element and merged with it."

"I know that a light-hour of travel in the warp is supposed to be equivalent to several light-years in normal space," Engle said, "but what about when you want to get back into normal space?"

"The original process is simply reversed: the shuttle creates a 'bubble' that cannot exist in the warp and seeks its own element, normal space."

"I see. But if the shuttle should—"

He never completed the question. Dr. Harding strode over, his eyes blue and piercing under the fierce eyebrows as he fixed them on him. He spoke without preamble:

"You realize the importance of this test flight with the shuttle, of course? Entirely aside from our personal survival should the Slug cruiser intercept us."

"Yes, sir," he answered, feeling the question suggested an even lower opinion of his intelligence than he had thought Harding held.

Project Space Warp existed for the purpose of sending the *Argosy* to Sirius by means of the space warp shuttle and bringing back the *Thunderbolt* by the same swift method. The *Thunderbolt*, Earth's first near-to-light-speed interstellar ship, was a huge ship; armed, armored, and invincible. It had been built to meet every conceivable danger that might be encountered in interstellar exploration—but the danger had come to the solar system from the direction of Capella nine years after the departure of the *Thunderbolt*. Eight cruisers of the pulpy, ten-foot centipede-like things called Slugs had methodically destroyed the colonies on Mars and Venus and established their own outposts there. Earth's ground defenses had held the enemy at bay beyond the atmosphere for a year but such defense could not be maintained indefinitely. The *Thunderbolt* was needed quickly and its own drives could not bring it back in less than ten years...

"We will go into the warp well beyond the atmosphere," Harding said. "Transition cannot be made within an atmosphere. Since a very moderate normal space velocity of the ship will be transformed into a greater-than-light velocity when in the warp, it is desirable that we make turn-over and decelerate to a very low speed before going into the warp."

"Yes, sir," he said. "I was briefed on that part and I'll bring us as near to a halt as that cruiser will permit."

"There will be communication between us during the flight," Harding said. "I will give you further instructions when they become necessary."

He turned away with an air of dismissal. Engle went to the ladder by the wall. He climbed up it and through the interroom airlock, closing the airlock behind him; the routine safety measure in case any single room was punctured. He went to the control board with a vague resentment gnawing for the first time at his normally placid good nature.

So far as Harding was concerned—and Garvin, too—he might as well have been an unusually intelligent baboon.

✧   ✧   ✧

Zero hour came and the *Argosy* lifted until Earth was a tremendous, curving ball below and the stars were brilliant points of light in a black sky. The Slug cruiser swung to intercept him within the first minute of flight but it seemed to move with unnatural slowness. It should have been driving in at full speed and it wasn't . . .

"Something's up," Ground Control said. "It's coming in too slowly."

"I see that," he answered. "It must be covering something beyond it, in your radar shadow."

It was. When he was almost free of the last traces of atmosphere he saw the other cruiser, far out and hidden from Ground Control's radar by the radar shadow cast by the first one.

He reported, giving its position and course as given him by the robot astrogating unit.

"We'll have the greatest amount of time if I make turn-over now and decelerate," he finished.

The voice of Harding came through the auxiliary speaker: "Do so."

The *Argosy* swung, end for end, and he decelerated. The cruiser behind him increased its speed, making certain it would be in position to cut off any return to Earth. The other cruiser altered its course to intersect the point in space the *Argosy* would soon occupy, and the *Argosy* was between the rapidly closing jaws of a trap.

He made reports to Ground Control at one-minute intervals. At 11:49 he said:

"Our velocity is approaching zero. We'll be within range of the second cruiser's blasters in two more minutes."

Harding spoke again to him:

"We'll go into the warp now. *Do not* alter the deceleration or the course of the ship while we're in the warp."

"I won't," he said.

There was a faint mutter from the auxiliary speaker as Harding gave some instructions to Garvin. Engle took a last look at the viewscreen; at blue-green Earth looming large in the center, Orion and Sirius glittering above it and the sun burning bright and yellow on the right. It was a scene he had observed many times before, all very familiar and normal—

The chronometer touched 11:50 and normalcy vanished.

Earth and sun and stars fled away from him, altering in appearance as they went, shrinking, dwindling. The seas and continents of Earth erupted and shook and boiled before Earth faded and disappeared. The sun changed from yellow to green to blue, to a tiny point of bright violet light that raced away into the blackness filling the screen and faded and disappeared as Earth had done.

Then the viewscreen was black, utterly, completely, dead black. And the communicator that had connected him with Ground Control was silent, without the faintest whisper of background sound or space static.

In the silence the voice of Harding as he spoke to Garvin came through the speaker; puzzled, incredulous, almost shocked:

"Our velocity couldn't have been that great—*and the sun receded into the ultraviolet!*"

There was the quick sound of hurrying footsteps then the more distant sound of the computer's keys being operated at a high rate of speed. He wanted to ask what had gone wrong but he knew no one would answer him. And it would be a pointless question—it was obvious from Harding's tone that he did not know, either.

He had an unpleasant feeling that Man's first venture into another dimension had produced catastrophic results. What had caused sun and Earth to disappear so quickly—and what force had riven and disfigured Earth?

Then he realized the significance of Harding's statement about the sun receding into the ultraviolet.

If the ship had been traveling at a high velocity away from the sun, the wave length of the sun's light would have been increased in proportion to the speed of the ship. The sun should have disappeared in the long-wave infrared end of the spectrum, not the short-wave ultraviolet.

With the thought came the explanation of the way the continents and oceans of Earth had quivered and seethed. The shifting of the spectrum range had shortened normally visible rays into invisibly short ultraviolet radiations while at the same time formerly invisible long infrared radiations had been shortened into visible wave lengths. There had been a continuous displacement into and past the ultraviolet and each wave length would have reflected best from a different place—mountains, valleys, oceans, deserts, warm areas, cool areas—and the steady progression into the ultraviolet had revealed each area in quick succession and given the appearance of agitated movement.

So there was no catastrophe and everything had a logical explanation. Except how they could have been approaching a sun that he had seen clearly, visibly, racing away from them.

"Engle—" The voice of Harding came through the speaker. "We're going back into normal space to make another observation. I don't know just where we are but we're certain to be far from the cruisers. Don't alter our course or velocity."

"Yes, sir," he said.

They came out of the warp at 11:53. The communicator burped suddenly and the viewscreen came to life; a deep, dull red that brightened quickly. A tiny coal flared up, swelling in size and shifting from red to orange to yellow—the sun. Earth appeared as a hazy red dot that enlarged and resolved itself into a planet with distorted continents that trembled and changed, to resume their natural shapes and colors. Within a few seconds the sun was shining as ever, Earth loomed large and blue-green before them and the stars of Orion glittered unchanged beyond. Even their position in space was the same—they had not moved.

But the Slug cruisers had.

One was very near and from its forward port came the violet haze that always preceded a blaster beam. There was no time to escape—no chance at all. He spoke into the mike, harsh and urgent:

"Into the warp! There's a blaster beam coming—*move!"*

There was a silence from below that seemed to last an eternity, then the sound of a switch being slapped hastily. At the same time, the violet haze before the cruiser erupted into blue fire and the blaster beam lanced out at them.

It struck somewhere astern. The power output needle swung jerkily as the generators went out and the emergency batteries took the heavy load of the shuttle's operation. There was a sensation of falling as the ship's artificial gravity units ceased functioning. The auxiliary speaker rattled wordlessly and there was a sound like a hard rush of wind through it, accompanied by quick bumping sounds.

Then the speaker was still and there was no sound of any kind as the viewscreen shifted into the ultraviolet and Earth and stars and sun once again raced away and disappeared in the blackness.

A myriad of lights above the board informed him the generators were destroyed, the stern section riddled and airless, the emergency batteries damaged and reduced to quarter charge, the shuttle room punctured and airless.

And, of course, Harding and Garvin were dead.

He felt a surge of futile anger. It had all been unnecessary. If only they had not considered him incompetent to be entrusted with anything more than the ship's operation—if only they had installed an emergency switch for the shuttle by his control board, there would not have been the two-second delay following his order and they would have been safely in the warp before the blaster beam struck.

But they had not trusted him with responsibility and now he was alone in a space warp he did not understand; sole and full responsibility for the shuttle suddenly in his hands.

He considered his course of action, then got into a pressure suit. Magnets in the soles of its heavy boots permitted him to walk in the absence of gravity and he went to the interroom airlock and walked down what had been the room's wall, then across to the center of its floor.

But for the fact there was no one in the room, it was as he had last seen it. The shuttle, computer, and other equipment stood in their orderly positions with their lighted dials unchanged. Until one looked at the gash ripped in the hull and saw the stains along its edge where the occupants had been hurled through it by the escaping air.

He went on to the next room and the next. The damage increased as he proceeded toward the stern. The power generators were sliced into ribbons and the emergency batteries in such condition it seemed a miracle they were functioning at all. The drives had received the greatest damage; they were an unrecognizable mass of wreckage.

He made his way back to the shuttle room, there to appraise his circumstances.

First, he would have to make the shuttle room livable; get out of the pressure suit. He would have to question the computer and he could not do that with the thick, clumsy gloves on his hands.

The job didn't take long. There were repair plates on the ship and a quick-hardening plastic spray. He closed the sternward airlock when he was done and opened the airlock leading to the control room, as well as the locks beyond. Air filled the shuttle room, with only a minor overall loss of air pressure. He removed the suit, attached a pair of magnetic soles to his shoes so he could operate the keys of the computer without the movements sending him floating away, and went to it.

He had never been permitted to touch it before, nor even stand close enough to see what the keyboard looked like. Now, he saw that the alphabetical portion of the keyboard was minor compared with the mathematical portion, many of the symbols strange to him.

The operation of an interplanetary ship required a certain knowledge of mathematics, but not the kind used by theoretical physicists. He typed, doubtfully:

ARE YOU CAPABLE OF ANSWERING QUESTIONS PRESENTED IN NON-MATHEMATICAL FORM?

The word, YES, appeared at once in the answer panel and relief came to him like the lifting of a heavy burden.

The computer knew as much about the space warp as Harding or anyone else. It was connected with his drive controls and instruments and knew how far, how fast, and in what directions the flight had taken place. It had even been given blueprints of the ship's construction, in case the structure of the ship should affect the ship's performance in the warp, and knew every nut, bolt, plate and dimension in the ship.

There was supposed to be a certain method of procedure when questioning the computer. "It knows—but it can't think," Garvin had once said. "It lacks the initiative to correlate data and arrive at conclusions unless the procedure of correlation is given it in detail."

Perhaps he could manage to outline some method of correlation for the computer. The facts of his predicament were simple enough:

He was in an unknown medium called "the Space Warp." Something not anticipated occurred when a ship went into the warp and Harding had not yet solved the mystery when he died.

The physicists in Observation would be able to find an answer but he could not ask them. The forward movement of the ship was not transferred with it into the warp and if he emerged into normal space the waiting Slug cruisers would disintegrate him before he spoke three words to Observation.

There was a pencil and a tablet of paper by the computer. He used them to calculate the time at which the charge in the damaged batteries would reach a critical low, beyond which the charge would be insufficient to activate the shuttle.

The answer was 13:53. He would have to go out of the warp at 13:53 or remain in it forever. He had a great deal less than two hours in which to act.

He typed the first question to the computer:
WHAT IS THE POSITION OF THIS SHIP RELATIVE TO NORMAL SPACE?

The answer appeared on the panel at once; the coordinates of a position more than a light-year toward Ophiuchus.

He stared at the answer, feeling it must be an error. But it could not be an error—the computer did not make mistakes. How, then, could the ship have traveled more than a light-year during its second stay in the warp when it had not moved at all during the first stay? Had some factor of the warp unknown to him entered the picture?

As a check he typed another question:
WHAT WAS OUR POSITION, RELATIVE TO NORMAL SPACE, IMMEDIATELY BEFORE THIS SHIP WAS SHUTTLED BACK OUT OF THE WARP?

The answer was a position light-days toward Ophiuchus.

He typed: IMPOSSIBLE.

The computer replied: THIS STATEMENT CONFLICTS WITH PREVIOUS DATA.

He recalled the importance of keeping the computer free of all faulty or obscure data and typed quickly: CANCEL CONFLICTING STATEMENT.

CONFLICTING STATEMENT CANCELED, it replied.

He tried another tack. THIS SHIP EMERGED FROM THE SPACE WARP INTO THE SAME NORMAL SPACE POSITION IT HAD OCCUPIED BEFORE GOING INTO THE WARP.

He thought the computer would proceed to give him some

sort of an explanation. Instead, it noncommittally replied: DATA ACKNOWLEDGED.

He typed: EXPLAIN THIS DISCREPANCY BETWEEN SPACE WARP AND NORMAL SPACE POSITIONS.

It answered: INSUFFICIENT DATA TO ACCOUNT FOR DISCREPANCY.

He asked: HOW DID YOU DETERMINE OUR PRESENT POSITION?

It replied: BY TRIANGULATION, BASED ON THE RECESSION OF EARTH, THE SUN, SIRIUS, ORION, AND OTHER STARS.

BUT THE RECEDING SUN WENT INTO THE ULTRAVIOLET, he objected.

Again it answered with the noncommittal, DATA ACKNOWLEDGED.

DID YOU ALREADY HAVE THIS DATA? he asked.

YES.

EXPLAIN WHY THE RECEDING SUN SHIFTED INTO THE ULTRAVIOLET INSTEAD OF THE INFRARED.

It replied: DATA INSUFFICIENT TO ARRIVE AT LOGICAL EXPLANATION.

He paused, pondering his next move. Time was speeding by and he was learning nothing of value. He would have to move the ship to some place in the warp where emergence into normal space would not put him under the blasters of the Slug cruisers. He could not know where to move the ship until he knew where the ship was at the present. He did not believe it was in the position given him by the computer, and its original space warp position had certainly not been the one given by the computer.

The computer did not have the ability to use its knowledge to explain contradictory data. It had been ordered to compute their space warp position by triangulation of the receding sun and stars and was not at all disturbed by the contradicting shift of the sun into the ultraviolet. Suppose it had been ordered to calculate their position by computations based on the shift of the sun's and stars' spectrum into the ultraviolet?

He asked it: WHAT IS OUR POSITION, IGNORING THE TRIANGULATION AND BASING YOUR COMPUTATIONS ON THE SHIFT OF THE SPECTRUMS OF THE SUN AND ORION INTO THE ULTRAVIOLET?

It gave him the coordinates of a position almost two light-years toward Orion. The triangulation computations had shown the ship to be going backward at many times the speed of light; the spectrum-shift computations showed it to be going forward with approximately the same speed.

THIS SHIP CANNOT SIMULTANEOUSLY BE IN TWO POSITIONS THREE LIGHT-YEARS APART. NEITHER CAN IT SIMULTANEOUSLY BE GOING FORWARD AND BACKWARD.

DATA ACKNOWLEDGED, it agreed.

USE THAT DATA TO EXPLAIN THE CONTRADICTIONS OF THE TWO POSITIONS YOU COMPUTED.

DATA INSUFFICIENT TO ARRIVE AT LOGICAL EXPLANATION, it answered.

ARE YOU CERTAIN THERE WAS NO ERROR IN YOUR CALCULATIONS?

THERE WAS NO ERROR.

DO YOU KNOW THAT IF WE DROPPED BACK INTO NORMAL SPACE, IT WOULD BE AT NEITHER OF THE POSITIONS YOU GAVE ME?

It replied with the characteristic single-mindedness: DATA SHOWS OUR TWO POSITIONS TO BE THOSE GIVEN.

He paused again. He was still getting nowhere while time fled by. How swiftly less than a hundred minutes could pass when they were all a man had left to him . . .

The computer was a genius with the mental initiative of a moronic child. It could find the answer for him but first he would have to take it by the hand and lead it in the right direction. To do that he would have to know more about the warp.

He wrote: EXPLAIN THE NATURE OF THE SPACE WARP AS SIMPLY AS POSSIBLE AND WITHOUT USING MATHEMATICS HIGHER THAN ALGEBRA.

It answered at once: THIS CANNOT BE DONE.

The chronometer read 12:30. He typed:

THIS SHIP WILL HAVE TO RETURN TO NORMAL SPACE NO LATER THAN 13:53. IT MUST BE MOVED TO A DIFFERENT POSITION WHILE STILL IN THE WARP.

DATA ACKNOWLEDGED, it replied.

THIS SHIP CANNOT OCCUPY TWO POSITIONS AT THE SAME TIME. YOUR MEMORY FILES SHOULD CONTAIN SUFFICIENT DATA TO ENABLE YOU TO FIND THE

EXPLANATION OF THIS TWO-POSITION PARADOX. FIND THAT EXPLANATION.

SUBMIT METHOD OF PROCEDURE, it answered.

I DO NOT KNOW HOW. YOU WILL HAVE TO ARRIVE AT THE EXPLANATION UNAIDED.

THIS CANNOT BE DONE, it replied.

He wrote, with morbid curiosity:

IF YOU DO NOT FIND THE ANSWER UNAIDED YOU WILL BE DESTROYED ALONG WITH ME AT 13:53. DON'T YOU GIVE A DAMN?

It answered: GIVE A DAMN IS A SEMANTIC EXPRESSION I DO NOT UNDERSTAND. CLARIFY QUESTION.

He got out of the computer seat and walked about the room restlessly. He passed by the transdimensional viewscreen and communicator and pressed the communicator's signal button. A dial flickered in return, showing his signal was going out, but there was no sound in response. If only he could make contact with the brains in Observation—

He was umpty billion miles east of the sun and umpty billion miles west of the sun. He was racing faster than light in two different directions at once and he was sitting motionless under the blasters of two Slug cruisers.

Another thought came to him: even if he could move the ship while in the warp, where could he go?

He would have to go far beyond the outer limits of the solar system to escape detection by the Slug cruisers. And at that distance the sun would be only a yellow star, incapable of energizing the little solar power units. He would not live long after the last of the power was drained from the batteries and the air regeneration equipment ceased functioning. He would not even dare sleep, toward the last. There were no convection currents in the air of a ship without gravity, and it was imperative that the air be circulated constantly. The air circulation blowers would cease functioning while the ship still contained pure air but he would have to move about continually to breathe that air. Should he lie down to sleep he would smother to death in a carbon dioxide bubble of his own making.

If he managed to emerge into normal space at some point just outside Earth's atmosphere, beyond range of the cruisers, his driveless ship would descend as a blazing meteor. If, by some miracle, he could emerge into normal space just a few inches above the space-field it would be to materialize into space already occupied by air. Such a materialization would be simultaneously fatal to him and to the electronic components of the shuttle and computer.

And if he did not move the ship, the Slug cruisers would disintegrate him. He had four hypothetical choices of his way to die, all equally unpleasant.

He smiled wanly at his reflection in the bright metal bordering the viewscreen and said, "Brother—you've had it!"

He went to the control room, there to brush his fingers across the useless control buttons and look into the viewscreen that revealed only black and limitless Nothing.

What was the warp? Surely it must have definite physical laws of some kind. It was difficult to imagine any kind of existence—even the black nothing of the warp—as being utterly without rule or reason. If he knew the laws of the warp he might find some means of survival hitherto hidden from him.

There was only one way he could learn about the warp. He would have to question the computer and continue questioning it until he learned or until his time was up.

He returned to the computer and considered his next question. The computer had calculated their positions from observations of the sun and other stars in front of the ship—what would similar calculations based on observations of the stars behind the ship reveal? He typed:

USE FIRST THE TRIANGULATION METHOD AND THEN THE SPECTRUM-SHIFT METHOD TO DETERMINE OUR POSITION FROM OBSERVATIONS MADE OF THE STARS OF OPHIUCHUS.

The answers appeared. They showed the ship to be simultaneously speeding away from Ophiuchus and toward it.

He asked: DO THESE TWO POSITIONS COINCIDE WITH THOSE RESULTING FROM THE OBSERVATIONS OF ORION?

YES, it answered.

Was the paradox limited to the line of flight?

He asked the computer: WHAT IS OUR POSITION, COURSE AND SPEED AS INDICATED BY THE STARS AT

RIGHT-ANGLES TO OUR FORWARD-BACKWARD COURSE; BY THE STARS OF URSA MINOR AND CRUX?

The answer appeared on the panel: the ship was racing sideward through the warp in two diametrically opposed directions, but at only one-third the speed with which it was racing forward and backward.

So now the ship had four impossible positions and two different speeds.

He frowned at the computer, trying to find some clue in the new data. He noticed, absently, that the hand of one of the dials was near zero in the red section of the dial. He had not noticed any of the dials registering in the danger zone before ...

He jerked out of his preoccupation with apprehension and typed: TELL ME IN NON-TECHNICAL LANGUAGE THE MEANING OF THE HAND NEAR ZERO ON THE DIAL LABELED *MAX. ET. REF.*

It answered: ONE OF MY CIRCUITS WAS DAMAGED BY THE SUDDEN RELEASE OF AIR PRESSURE. I WILL CEASE FUNCTIONING AT THE END OF FOUR MORE MINUTES OF OPERATION.

He slammed the master switch to OFF. The lights on the board went out, the various needles swung to zero, leaving the computer a mindless structure more than ever resembling an overgrown refrigerator.

Four minutes more of operation ... and he had so many questions to ask before he could hope to learn enough about the warp to know what he should do. He had wasted almost an hour of the computer's limited life, leaving it turned on when he was not using it. If only it had told him ... but it was not the nature of a machine to voluntarily give information. Besides, the receding hand of the dial was there for him to see. The computer neither knew nor cared that no one had thought it worthwhile to teach him the rudiments of its operation and maintenance.

It was 12:52. One hour and one minute left.

He put the thought aside and concentrated on the problem of finding the key to the paradox.

What conceivable set of circumstances would cause receding stars to have a spectrum shift that showed them to be approaching the ship? Or, to rephrase the question, what conceivable set of circumstances would cause approaching stars to appear to dwindle in size?

The answer came with startling suddenness and clarity:

There was no paradox—the ship was expanding.

He considered the solution, examining it for flaws of logic, and found none. If he and the ship were expanding the wave length of light would diminish in proportion to the increasing size of the retinas of his eyes and the scanner plates of the transdimensional viewscreens: would become shorter and go into the ultraviolet. At the same time, the increasing size of himself and the ship would make the Earth and sun relatively smaller and therefore apparently receding.

The same theory explained the two different speeds of the ship: its length was three times its diameter so its longitudinal expansion would proceed at three times the speed of its cross-sectional expansion.

Everything checked.

How large was the ship now?

He made a rough calculation and stared almost unbelievingly at the results. He was a giant, more than a third of a light-year tall, in a ship that was six light-years long and two light-years in diameter. Far Centauri, which had required thirty years to reach in the fastest interplanetary ship, floated seventy-one feet away in the blackness outside the hull.

And the sun and Earth were in the room with him, going into the shuttle's silvery focal ball.

He would have to ask the computer to make certain his theory was valid. His time was too critically short for him to waste any of it with speculation based on an erroneous theory.

He switched on the computer and it lighted up again. He typed rapidly:

ASSUME THIS SHIP TO BE MOTIONLESS AND EXPAND-ING WOULD THAT THEORY SATISFACTORILY EXPLAIN ALL THE HITHERTO CONTRADICTORY PHENOMENA?

There was a brief pause as the computer evaluated its data, then it answered with one word:

YES.

He switched it off again, to squander none of its short period of usefulness until he had decided upon what his further questions should be. At last, he had some grounds for conjecture; had learned something about the warp the designers of the shuttle had not suspected. Their calculations had been correct when they showed a ship would travel in the warp at many times the normal space speed of light. But somewhere some little factor had been overlooked—or never found—and their precise mathematics had not indicated that the travel would be produced by expansion.

Nature abhors a vacuum. And the black, empty warp was a vacuum more perfect than any that existed in normal space. In the normal space universe there were millions of stars in the galaxy and millions of galaxies. In the warp there was utter Nothing. Did the physical laws of the warp demand that matter be scattered throughout it, in emulation of its rich neighbor in the adjoining dimension? Was the warp hungry for matter?

He rejected the thought as fantasy. There was some explanation that the physicists would eventually find. Perhaps there was a vast size-ratio difference between the two dimensions; perhaps the warp was far larger than the normal space universe and some co-universal law demanded that objects entering it become proportionally larger.

None of that aspect of his circumstances, however, was of importance. There was only one prime problem facing him: how to move the ship within less than an hour to some point in the warp where his emergence into normal space would result in neither instant nor days-away death and where he would have the time to try to carry out the responsibility, so suddenly placed in his hands, of delivering the space warp shuttle to the *Thunderbolt.*

The long-range task depended upon his immediate survival. He had to move the ship, and how did a man move a driveless ship? It might not require a very large propulsive force— perhaps even an oxygen tank would serve as a jet. Except that he had none.

He could use part of the air in the ship. Its sudden release should move the ship. There was a sun very near: Alpha Centauri. If he had the proper tools, and the time, he could cut a hole in the hull opposite Centauri . . . but he had neither the tools nor the time.

And what good would it do him if he could emerge into

normal space at the desired distance from Centauri? He would
be provided with power for the air regenerators by the solar
power units but not power sufficient to operate the shuttle. He
would breathe, and eat, for a week. Then the small amount of
food on the ship would be gone and he would breathe for
another four or five weeks. And then he would die of starvation and his driveless ship would continue its slow drift into the
sun, taking his bones and the shuttle with it.

He would have to go to Sirius and he would have to reach
it the first try or never. If he could emerge into normal space
at the proper distance from Sirius he would have power from
it to operate the communicator. The *Thunderbolt* would come
at once when it received his message and swallow the little *Argosy*
in its enormous hold. The return to Earth would be the swift
one through the warp and the Slug cruisers, so bold in pursuit
of unarmed interplanetary ships, would quickly cease to exist.

At 13:53 Sirius would be somewhere in or near the bow of
the ship. The ship would not have to be moved more than two
thirds of its length—twenty meters. He could do that by releasing
part of the air in the shuttle room through the sternward airlock.

How much air?

He tried to remember long-forgotten formulas. So many
cubic feet of air at such and such a pressure when released
through an opening of such and such a diameter would exert
a propulsive force of . . . Hell, he didn't know. And not even the
computer would be able to tell him because there were so many
unknown factors, such as the proportion of the ship's mass lost
to the Slug blasters, the irregular shape of the airlock opening,
the degree of smoothness of its metal . . .

He made calculations with pencil and paper. He would have
to move the ship with extreme precision. A light-hour short of
the proper distance put him too far from the sun for it to power
the communicator, a light-hour beyond put him in the sun's
flaming white heart. One light-hour out of eight point six light-
years was approximately one part out of seventy-five thousand.
He would have to move the ship with an accuracy of point aught
three centimeters—one hundredth of an inch.

One hundredth of an inch!

He laid the pencil back down, almost numbly. He could never
open and close an airlock and move a mass of thousand of tons

with an accuracy of a hundredth of an inch. The very thought was wildly fantastic.

He was already far closer to Sirius than he would be if he tried to get any closer. And that was over eight light-years from it.

He looked at the chronometer and saw the hands had already reached 13:20. Thirty-three minutes left to him. Sirius was near— soon it would be in the bow of the ship—and Sirius was eight point six light-years away.

How could he move the ship a certain distance accurate to one hundredth of an inch? He couldn't. The answer was blunt and ugly: he couldn't.

He got up and walked across the room, feeling like a man who had in quick succession been condemned, reprieved, recondemned. He had been projected into a situation for which he had had no preliminary training whatever; had been made sole custodian and operator of a computer and a space warp shuttle that he had never before been permitted to touch. He had used the sound but not at all brilliant mind nature had given him to solve the riddle of the paradoxes and learn where he was and where he wanted to go. He had done quite well—he had solved every problem of his survival and the shuttle's delivery except the last one!

He passed by the shuttle and stopped to rest his hand on the bright, silvery focal ball. The solar system would be deep inside the ball; the atoms of the ball larger than Earth, perhaps, and far more impalpable than the thinnest air. The Slug cruisers would be in there, infinitesimally tiny, waiting for him to return . . .

No—faulty reasoning. The solar system was as it had always been, not diminished in size and not really in the ball. It was only that two different points in two different dimensions coincided in the ball . . .

He saw the answer.

He did not have to move the ship to Sirius—he had only to move the ball!

There would be little time, very little time. First, to see if the warp shuttle was portable—

It was. When he unfastened the clamp that held it to the stand it lifted up freely, trailing a heavy cable behind it. He saw it was only a power supply cable, with a plug that would fit one of the sockets in the bow of the ship. He left the shuttle floating in the air, leashed by the cable, and went to the computer. Next, he would have to know if Sirius would be fully in the ship—

He switched the computer on and typed:

DETERMINE THE DISTANCE FROM THE CENTER OF THE WARP SHUTTLE'S FOCAL BALL TO THE SPACE WARP POSITION OF SIRIUS AT 13:53, BASING YOUR COMPUTATIONS ON THE EXPANDING-SHIP THEORY.

It gave him the answer a moment later: 18.3496 METERS.

He visualized the distance, from his knowledge of the ship's interior, and saw the position would be within the forward spare-parts room.

Next, to learn exactly where in that room he should place the shuttle. He could not do so by measuring from the present position of the shuttle. The most precise steel tape would have to be at exactly the right temperature for such a measurement to be neither too short nor too long. He had no such tape, and the distance from the focal ball was only part of the necessary measuring: he would have to measure off a certain distance and a precisely certain angle from the purely imaginary central line of the ship's axis to intersect the original line. Such a measurement would be impossible in the time he had.

He considered what would be his last question to the computer. The hand was touching the zero and his question would have to be worded very clearly and subject to no misinterpretations. There would be no follow-up questions permitted.

He began typing:

IT IS DESIRED THAT THIS SHIP EMERGE INTO NORMAL SPACE ONE LIGHT-HOUR THIS SIDE OF SIRIUS AT 13:53. THIS WILL BE ACCOMPLISHED BY MOVING THE WARP SHUTTLE TO SUCH A POSITION THAT ITS FOCAL CENTER WILL BE IN A SPACE WARP POSITION COINCIDING WITH A NORMAL SPACE POSITION ONE LIGHT-HOUR THIS SIDE OF SIRIUS AT 13:53. CONSIDER ALL FACTORS THAT MIGHT HAVE AFFECTED THE DIMENSIONS OF THIS SHIP, SUCH AS TEMPERATURE CHANGES PRODUCED BY OUR NORMAL SPACE ACCELERATION AND DECELERATION, WHEN COMPUTING THE POSITION OF SIRIUS. THEN DEFINE THAT LOCATION IN RELATION TO THE STRUCTURAL FEATURES OF THE ROOM'S INTERIOR. DO

THIS IN SUCH A MANNER THAT PLACING THE SHUTTLE IN THE PROPER POSITION WILL REQUIRE THE LEAST POSSIBLE AMOUNT OF MEASURING DISTANCES AND ANGLES.

It seemed to take it an unduly long time to answer the question and he waited restlessly, unpleasantly aware of the hand touching zero and wondering if the computer's mind was baffled by the question; the mind that thought best in terms of orderly mathematics and could not know or care that measurement by protractor and tape would result in a position fatally far from that described by the neat, rigid figures.

Then the answer appeared, beautifully concise:

POSITION WILL BE IN CORNER OF ROOM, 764.2 CENTIMETERS ABOVE FLOOR PLATE, 820 CENTIMETERS PERPENDICULAR TO PANEL AA, 652.05 CENTIMETERS PERPENDICULAR TO PANEL AB.

The computer died with an oddly human sigh. Its last act had been to give him the location of Sirius in such a manner that he could accurately position the shuttle's focal ball with the aid of the precision measuring devices in the ship's repair room.

He went to the shuttle and picked it up in his arms. It was entirely weightless, and each magnet-clicking step he took toward the bow of the ship brought Sirius almost half a light-year nearer.

He squinted against the white glare of Sirius in the viewscreen as he continued his terse report to the *Thunderbolt*'s commander: "I have about a week's supply of food. How long will it be until you reach me?"

The commander's reply came after the pause caused by the distance involved:

"We'll be there within three days. Go ahead and eat hearty. But how did you travel from Earth to Sirius in only two hours? My God, man—what kind of a drive did that ship have?"

"Why, it didn't have any drive from the start," he said. "To get here I"—he frowned thoughtfully—"you might say I walked and carried the ship."

Editor's note: This story, as with the previous one, is a celebration of tenacity and perseverance in the face of disaster. The enemy here, however, is simply nature. But, whether facing death because of intelligent hostility or accidental misadventure, Godwin's heroes in this story are cut from the same cloth as all of his "survivors."

MOTHER OF INVENTION

The *Star Scout*'s normal-space speed was far below that of light when she dropped out of hyperspace beyond the rim of the Thousand Suns. Two last stars lay beneath her; a binary composed of a small yellow sun and a larger blue-white sun. Observations were taken and instruments noted the tiny, shining mote that swung four hundred million miles out from the blue-white sun. Other instruments determined the new destination and the *Star Scout* vanished again into hyperspace.

When she dropped once more into normal space the shining mote had become a planet that blazed like a great, radiant gem against the black void beyond. The planet grew as the hours went by, filling the viewscreen as Blake braked for the descent into its atmosphere. Land masses and small oceans were faintly discernible through the fiery, opalescent haze that blanketed the planet. The image swelled and enlarged, the surplus running off the four sides of the screen, until the western side of a continent and a small portion of ocean filled the screen.

The four men in the deceleration chairs behind Blake, and held as helplessly as he by the force, watched the image on the viewscreen and the multiple hands of the air analyzer. The hands began to move as the first thin sample of air was scooped into the analyzer, then settled into position a few minutes later.

"Breathable." The gray-haired Taylor spoke with difficulty against the deceleration.

"Less carbon dioxide than New Earth," Wilfred commented. Young, short and stocky, he was far less affected by the deceleration than the elderly ex-dean. "I can't understand why the spectroscope showed such an incredibly high percentage of carbon. How could any planet's crust contain such an excess of carbon?"

"The carbon *must* be in the crust, rather than in the atmosphere," Taylor said. "Either that or the old spectroscope is erroneous. We know the air analyzer is a new and reliable instrument, but these old Warden spectroscopes, like men, develop eccentricities with age. If we had a new—"

"Hang on," Blake interrupted, his eyes on the instruments before him. "I'm going to have to brake a little harder."

The increased deceleration settled them all deeper in their chairs and no one spoke while the section of continent on the viewscreen became a hazy desert or plain through which ran dim wrinkles. The surplus slid away and the wrinkle in the center of the screen became a range of mountains. Blake watched the translucent white dot in the center of the screen that represented their point of landing and saw it would be along the eastern side of the mountain range. It would do as well as any other unknown section of the unknown world and he let the ship hold its course.

The green line of a tree-bordered creek appeared, hugging the mountain's foothills, with the white dot between the creek and the mountain. The area covered by the dot became a small delta of alluvium from one of the canyons with a few trees scattered across it. The delta swept up to meet them, slowing as it came, with the white dot in a flat clearing that seemed to be of some curiously glittering sand.

The *Star Scout* halted ten feet above the ground with a staccato of blasts from the drive tubes that sent the bright sand swirling in heavy clouds, then it dropped, cushioned by the drive, to touch the ground with a slight lurch. The wide tail fins settled in the sand and Blake cut off the drive.

"And here we are," he remarked.

The others were already hurrying to read the data recorded on the instruments; Taylor and Wilfred, Lenson and Cooke. Blake watched them, interested by their reactions. None of them had ever been off New Earth before, let alone on a world hitherto unknown to exist, and they were as excited as children with a new toy. Taylor, steeped in the academic environment all his life, was the most enthusiastic of them all. He had once told Blake: "With all due respect to ivied walls of stone, they can become a prison. I want to see a few things before I grow any older; deep space and distant suns and strange worlds—" Lenson, a tall, lean man with the easy grace of a cat, stood a full head taller than the pink young Wilfred; a pleasant sort of a man with a slow smile and a tolerant understanding of the foibles of others.

There was the indefinable mark of the intellectual upon all three of them and among them the paradox, Cooke, stood out like a black sheep among white. He was, Blake knew, fully as intelligent as any of the others; he, like the others, had been selected by Taylor because his intelligence and knowledge were considerably greater than the intelligence and knowledge of the average graduate. But he did not look the part. His dark, hard-jawed face was not that of an intellectual. Neither were his broken nose and glittering black eyes. Blake watched him, thinking: He doesn't belong with the others; he belongs on Old Earth three hundred years ago, on the deck of a pirate ship with a bloody cutlass in his hand.

But, for all his appearance of being a man of sanguine physical violence, Cooke seemed to be content to do no more than laugh at what his black eyes found in others and in life, itself.

"Earth-type in every important respect," Taylor was saying. "Gravity, temperature, air. No indications of any harmful bacteria—we've been incredibly fortunate."

"We had about one chance out of several thousand of this being an Earth-type planet, didn't we, Red?" Lenson asked, looking over at Blake.

Blake nodded his red head. "Quite a few thousand, since this isn't a class-G sun. As Taylor said, we were incredibly lucky to hit the jackpot the very first try."

"Then let's get out and look our find over," Cooke said, shifting restlessly. "Let's get out and romp across the sand and breathe some air we haven't breathed a million times already."

Taylor looked questioningly at Blake and Blake nodded. "I don't see any reason why we shouldn't," he said. He checked the readings on the control board instruments from long habit and saw the red line that indicated the drive room's temperature. It was climbing rapidly, and he turned a knob marked: DRIVE ROOM—OUTSIDE VENTILATION. This would open the ports in the drive room and start the blower to rushing its great volumes of cool outside air through the overheated room. "Drive room's mighty hot from the decelerating," he said as he followed the others to the elevator. "If we had had a little more money left over, we could have had full-size coolers installed."

"We were lucky to scrape up enough money to buy what we have," Wilfred said, dropping the elevator to the cabin level.

"Our worries are over, now," Cooke declared. "Anyone who owns an Earth-type world isn't just rich—he's lord of all he surveys."

They stopped at the cabin level only long enough to procure a sidearm each. "You can't tell what you may run into on an alien planet," Blake said as he stepped back into the elevator. "No signs of any intelligent, civilized life, but there might be animals. Sometimes animals don't wait for you to run into them—they take a deep breath and do their level best to run into *you* and tramp you into the ground."

They dropped to the lower air lock and went through it. The boarding ramp was dropped to the ground and they descended into the cloud of dust that still swirled about the ship.

"The blower is filling the drive room with this dusty air," Blake said, sneezing. "I didn't realize it was so thick. But the drive room door is shut and none of this dust can get into the rest of the ship."

They walked out away from the ship and the dust and stood in the glittering sand, looking about them curiously. The mouth of the canyon was visible above them, with the iridescent haze hiding the higher peaks. The trees were almost like those of the desert regions of New Earth, scattered very thinly across the mountain's foot, and viciously thorned bushes grew among them. Some of them, Blake noticed, were in bloom with exotically beautiful blossoms, ranging from delicate pink to vivid scarlet.

"Pretty," Cooke commented. "A little dangerous to try to pick one, I'd say; those thorns are Nature's ice picks."

"We ought to name it . . . this world," Taylor said. "What shall we call it?"

"Aurora," Lenson said instantly. "She was the goddess of the dawn in ancient mythology. She was beautiful and she wore a veil. This world is beautiful and it wears a veil—that shining haze."

"A good name," Taylor agreed. He looked toward the creek a few hundred feet away, the creek itself hidden by the green trees that grew thickly along its banks. "Let's get a sample of the water for analysis."

They walked toward the creek, each of them unconsciously glancing back at the towering bulk of the ship as they went their way. Men always did that, Blake had noticed, when they set down on an alien planet. They would go out from their ship with their eyes alertly watching for danger ahead, and they never failed to look back at the ship as though to reassure themselves that its ponderous mass was still there. It was a normal thing to do; when a man set down on an alien world he was on his own and his only link with other humans and other worlds was his ship. It had brought him there; it, alone, could take him back. A man walked out from his ship knowing that it would be waiting for him to return, like a great, patient dog; waiting and ready to hurl itself into space at his command. Sometimes an alien planet held death for the bipeds who ventured to explore it, such as the spider-monsters of Nelson 14, and the ship would be the sword of vengeance for those who lived to fight their way back to it. The ship would avenge the fallen with fury in the thunder of its voice and annihilation in its flaming breath, leaving only drifting ashes where once had been alien things that had made the mistake of killing a human.

Without their ship, men on a hostile, alien world would be near-helpless; with their ship, they were invincible conquerors.

"Flowers, even," Cooke exclaimed as they neared the trees by the creek. "Red, blue, yellow, purple; green trees and good air— what more could we offer colonists?"

Blake had been examining the shining sand with increasing curiosity and he stopped to inspect a bright crystal half the size of his hand. It was not quartz. He scratched at it with his knife point but could not make any impression. The same would have been true of quartz, but the crystal did not have the appearance of quartz. It was alive with internal fires and the crystal system, such as he could tell from its rounded, worn form, was distinctly not that of quartz. A little way farther on he found one that glowed a deep ruby red. He paused to pick it up, then hurried on at an excited exclamation from Lenson, who had gone with the others to the edge of the creek. "*Look at this!*"

"This" was a crystal at the very edge of the creek's roiling, opalescent waters, the same deep ruby red as the one he had in his hand but a foot in diameter. Near it were other, smaller, crystals of blue-white, yellow, red, blue, green, with the blue-white ones predominating. The sand, gravel and rocks of the creek bed seemed to be composed exclusively of the bright mineral.

"Did you ever see so many quartz crystals in your life?" Lenson was asking the others. "Or so many different colors? Look at this one—it looks like a ruby."

Blake failed to hear the reply of the others, a thought he had had upon first examining the bright sand suddenly losing the fantastic quality which had caused him to dismiss it. It all checked, the lack of any mineral other than the one in the creek bed, the "erroneous" spectroscope that had shown the world to possess an impossible percentage of carbon, the high index of refraction possessed by the mineral.

He could find out very quickly.

"Let me have your diamond ring," he said to Wilfred.

Wilfred pulled it off his finger and handed it to him with a look of questioning surprise. Blake scratched the diamond in the ring across the red crystal he still held in his hand. It left no impression and he repeated the performance on several other crystals scattered on the ground near him. On none of them could he produce the faintest scratch with the diamond in Wilfred's ring, no matter how heavily he bore down.

"The spectroscope was right," he said, wondering if the others would find it as hard to believe as he did. "I don't see how it could be, but it *is.*"

"Is what?" Wilfred asked.

"Carbon—all these crystals are *diamonds!*"

They stared at him, incredulous. "They couldn't be!" Wilfred objected. Lenson asked, "How can you tell for certain? Are you sure?"

"The diamond in this ring won't scratch them," he replied. "The only mineral a diamond can't scratch is another diamond."

"Then they really are diamonds?" Taylor said, dropping to his knees to pick up a deep, bright-blue one that lay beside the ruby-red stone that Lenson had found. "But the variations in color—are they *all* diamonds?"

"All those that are any size," Blake told him. "The softer silica would soon be reduced to a powder by the grinding action of the diamonds in the creek bed. Anything of any appreciable size that shines is pretty certain to be a diamond."

"Hmm-m-m!" Cooke grunted, and shook his head in amazement. "I'm delighted to hear it, but it's still hard to believe. Talk about luck—here we sink our last cent to make this one trip, with the odds all in favor of our finding nothing, and the first thing we do is hit a double jackpot; not only an Earth-type—almost—planet but also an unlimited fortune in diamonds. Such luck is incredible."

"It *is* incredible," Blake agreed. "It just isn't the sort of thing that—"

His voice was drowned by a thunderous bellow from the ship. He whirled toward it, as did the others, wild disbelief on the faces of all of them. The same thought flashed in their minds at the same instant; *they were all five there—there was no one in the ship!*

The ship shot into view, leaping high enough in the air that they could see it above the trees that surrounded them. A gout of blue-white flame was lashing from a hole torn in its stern, then the flame vanished and the ship poised motionlessly for a moment; a great, metal monster halted in mid-flight and pinned against the background of hazy sky. Then the nose dropped, the tail went up, and it fell. It fell in a horizontal position, its impact hidden from them by the trees but the sound of it loud and terrible to hear; the muffled scream of rending metal shrill above the ground-jarring thud of the impact.

Blake ran past the others, toward the ship. He was vaguely aware of someone yelling, "*What—*" then he broke through the concealing trees and stopped, appalled by the sight that met his eyes.

Spaceships were made to withstand the pull of gravity when at rest on their tail fins; to withstand the thrust of the drive which, whether accelerating or decelerating, was only the equivalent of gravitic attraction from the stern. They were constructed to possess great longitudinal strength, with no great cross-sectional strength needed. They were not constructed to withstand a horizontal drop.

The *Star Scout* was broken in two.

Taylor stopped beside him, white and shaken.

"What . . . what was it?" someone asked. "What happened . . . how *could* it happen?"

"The converter blew up," Blake said, his lips feelings oddly stiff and numb. "It was my fault—I should have had brains enough to think about it before it was too late."

"What do you mean?" Cooke demanded.

"I left the blower going, driving cool air into the drive room. The air was loaded with the dust we stirred up when we landed, and that dust was mainly diamond dust."

"Oh!" Cooke's eyes were fixed on Blake. "So that was it. Diamond dust—carbon—*catalyst!*"

"But how?" Taylor asked. "How could the diamond dust have gotten into the converter?"

"I don't know." Blake shook his head. "Maybe the inspection crew forgot to put the cover back on the fuel inlet—maybe the clamps broke while we were en route. Anyway, it happened— somehow enough of the dust got into the fuel inlet to put the amount of catalyst past a critical percentage and the converter exploded. I shouldn't have started the blower until I first went in and made a check of the fuel inlet."

"Why?" Cooke asked. "Did you ever hear of anything like this ever happening before?"

"No."

"Then why should you have checked? You had no reason to think the fuel inlet might be open, and neither did you discover this was diamond dust until about a minute before the explosion. You couldn't have done anything about it in only one minute."

"I suppose not," Blake agreed, "but I can't help feeling I should have been more careful. But that's all water under the bridge; here we are among our diamonds with no way of getting home— not for a long time at best, I'm afraid. So let's see just how long that may be, just how great the damage to the ship is."

"From here," Cooke observed as they walked toward the ship,

"the situation looks hopeless. Our ship looks exactly like an over-ripe watermelon that's had a bad fall. It's not only broken in two, with a few girders holding the broken halves together, it's also sort of flattened now, rather than round like it once was."

"And gaping open at every seam," Wilfred added.

They passed the stern of the ship, where the rim of the ragged hole still glowed redly with half-molten metal, and Blake motioned toward the deep furrow blasted in the ground where the ship had stood. "The blast was directional," he said. "If it hadn't been, it would have destroyed the lower half of the ship."

"It didn't make such a big hole in the stern," Cooke remarked with a return of his characteristic optimism. We could patch it."

"Of course," he added bleakly, "we'd only have half a ship to drive, and no converter to power our drive—if we have a drive left."

They entered the ship by the gap where it had broken apart, climbing through the bent and broken steel. The elevator shaft, now a horizontal passageway, was accessible by climbing up the ragged, torn sheet metal and girders. Blake made a suggestion to the older Taylor before they climbed up into the elevator shaft.

"I'd like to look at the drive room and the repair shop. So, suppose Cooke and I do that while you and the others see what the damage is in the forward half of the ship?"

"Anything you say, Red," Taylor answered. "I have an idea we'll find nothing but wreckage either way."

"First, I'll get some lights for you," Blake said.

He climbed up into the elevator shaft and made his way to the supply level of the ship. The door to the room he entered opened with considerable difficulty and the scene inside, as revealed by his pocket lighter, was utter confusion and chaos. He found the locker that held the emergency lights under a mass of miscellaneous supplies, equipment and broken containers and took five lights from it.

He went back to the gap in the ship and tossed three of the lights to the others. They began to climb up into their own section of the ship and Cooke scrambled up to where he stood.

"How did it look where you were?" Cooke asked.

"Just a little untidy," he answered, leading the way to the drive room.

They forced the now-horizontal drive room door open and a gush of warm air struck them. The drive room was fairly well lighted by the hole the converter's explosion had produced and they appraised the damage, not caring to drop the ten feet to the new floor.

"That shapeless gob over there by the hole—that's all that remains of our converter," Blake said. "The explosion was directional, all right, and the converter was working at minimum output—if it had been up to as much as quarter output, it couldn't have remained directional and at a quarter output the entire ship would have vanished in a blaze of glory."

He flashed his light down into the shadowy corners of the room and found what he sought. "Look—see that square metal thing?" he asked. "That's the fuel inlet cover. Sure enough, it wasn't in place—they must have forgotten to tighten down the clamps."

"And we *paid* them to do that?" Cooke asked bitterly, flashing his own light over the cover.

Blake moved his light slowly over the drive assembly. Originally equipped with the old Harding atomic drive, the transformation to the hyperspace drive had—for financial reasons—been confined to the installation of the space-shift units and the installation of the nuclear converter to supply the enormous energy required by the hyperspace units to wrench the ship from normal space into hyperspace. Although a modern drive would have been preferred, their limited capital had forced them to compromise by leaving the atomic rocket drive intact and modifying its fuel chambers to accept the tailor-made fuel prepared for it by the converter.

"How does it look?" Cooke asked. "*I* can't see where the blast did any damage to it. Am I right?"

"I think you are—the directional blast missed it and its construction was rugged enough that the fall didn't affect it. This is more than I had dared hope for—we can alter those fuel chambers back to the way they were and we have a rocket drive again.

"If," he added, "we can find uranium."

"And then what? Won't we be a little bit old and feeble by the time we get home through normal space, thirty thousand years from now?"

"Well, I don't know of any outpost of civilization we can reach in less than two hundred years," Blake said, "which would be too far to do us any good. However, to get anywhere in hyperspace, we still have to have a drive, you know. We have to have a drive to get off this planet so we can get in hyperspace in the first place."

"Once we fix up our drive and get away from here—how do we get into hyperspace with no converter to power the space-shift units?" Cooke asked.

"That is *the* question, and I don't know the answer. But I was taking first things first. If we can find uranium—and we surely can—we can soon solve every problem but that one."

He passed his light over the squat generator that had served to supply the ship with electrical power before the installation of the converter. It hung by two of its mounting bolts from the vertical floor, but it seemed undamaged.

"There's our power—if we had some way to store it," he said. "If we could devise a perfect condenser of unlimited capacity, we could accumulate enough power to give the space-shift units the wallop that would jump us into hyperspace. Anyway, whatever we do, we're going to need that generator. We're going to need electrical power for operating the lathe—if it isn't smashed beyond repair—welding, perhaps even for refining metals with some sort of an electric furnace."

"How do we power the generator?" Cooke asked.

"That can be done," Blake said. "Provided we have a lathe to build what we want."

He turned away from the drive room without further explanation and Cooke followed him to the repair shop. As with all other rooms in the ship's new position, the door was horizontal, but the repair shop was smaller than the drive room and it was no more than a six-foot drop to the new floor. Blake saw, with a sense of vast relief, that the lathe was still solidly bolted to the vertical floor. The other equipment was a jumbled mass on the floor and they poked into it curiously for a few minutes.

"Not much in the way of broken stuff here," Cooke said. "Steel tools seem to stand up pretty good when a ship does a belly-whopper. I hope the transmitter fared as well."

"That's something we're all hoping, but you're the first one to speak out loud about it," Blake said. "I don't see how it could have survived—a transmitter is big, heavy and fragile."

"Neither do I. I suppose that's why no one dared even say he hoped it wouldn't be smashed."

"Let's see about our truck," Blake said. "If the transmitter is smashed beyond repair, we'll have to try to find uranium and we'll stand little chance of prospecting these ranges on foot."

Again, luck had been with them. The little truck was unharmed but for a crumpled fender. Some of its bright red enamel had been knocked off by the fall of the diamond drill rods but the diamond drill, itself, seemed untouched.

"And that covers the important things in our end of the ship," Blake said. "Let's see what luck the others had."

Wilfred was just descending from the broken elevator shaft, carrying a load of food and cooking utensils. "We'll camp out for a while, it looks like," he said. "With the new floors knee deep in wreckage and the doors six feet to ten feet up on the walls, living in the ship would be just a little inconvenient."

"We'll have to cut a passageway along the bottom side of the ship's hull," Blake said. "We can dodge the girders and just cut through the old flooring."

"How did it look up there?" Cooke asked. "What about the transmitter?"

"We won't send any SOS," Wilfred said flatly. "The transmitter tubes are smashed to fragments."

"I was afraid they would be," Blake said. "Do the others need help with their loads?"

"They could use some help, all right," Wilfred said, climbing down with his own.

They crossed the gap and met Lenson and Taylor in the elevator shaft, each with a burden of sleeping bags and various other things needed for a comfortable night outside. Blake and Cooke relieved them of part of their loads and the four of them carried their burdens to the clean, sandy spot near one of the trees where Wilfred had set up their "kitchen."

Blake dropped his load and spoke to Taylor. "So the transmitter is ruined?" he asked.

"The final power stage is," Taylor replied. "The drive stage took the fall pretty well and we could couple that in, *except—*"

"Except what?"

"In normal space that would give us a range of around a billion miles—no more than halfway to our sun's yellow companion. Useless."

"Oh—so we don't even get the chance to use our little driver stage in hyperspace?"

"The space-shift signal transformers are complete wreckage. Any signal we sent, even if we had our final power stage intact, would take three lifetimes to reach the nearest outpost through normal space. We could send a signal through hyperspace, with our drive stage, for sixty thousand billion miles—but the hyperspace transformers are broken and smashed and we could never, with our resources, replace them. So that brings up the question—what now?"

"Our space-shift units in the drive room seem to be undamaged and it wouldn't be difficult to change the rocket fuel chambers again so that we can lift the ship with an uranium fuel," Blake answered. "And we do have to lift the ship to make the jump into hyperspace under any circumstances. If uranium is to be found, we'll only have the one big problem to solve—and it's really big—how to produce enough power to activate the space-shift units. If necessity forced us to, I have an idea we might even make another converter. Of course, our success would be an uncertain thing and it would require years of work as well as luck, but it would be better than just giving up—at least, we would be trying."

He glanced toward the nearby canyon mouth. "Uranium is the vital essential, no matter what we do. I'm going to take a little walk while Wilfred fixes something to eat—I want to see what the formations look like, and if they offer any encouragement."

"And then we'll talk over our plans after we eat," Taylor said. "A man takes a more optimistic view of his circumstances when is stomach is full, anyway."

Blake walked until he came to the first bank of rock and gravel, then examined what he found with considerable muttering. The formations represented by the rocks that had washed down out of the canyon were almost like those of any Earth-type planet, with one incredible exception; every rock, whether near-granite, near-rhyolite, near-andesite, whether high or low in silica content, contained almost the same high percentage of diamond crystal inclusions. In the coarse-grained rocks, such as the near-granites, the diamond crystals were as large as the end of his little finger, while the fine-grained near-rhyolites contained the diamonds as minute inclusions. But, whether the rock was fine- or coarse-grained, the diamond was present in all in approximately the same high percentage.

He had just come upon his first specimen of Aurora's animal life when he heard the distant call of Wilfred announcing dinner. He ignored the call for a moment, walking closer to the small, brown-furred animal. It was about the size of a squirrel, with a round, dark-eyed face and a fat little stomach that it scratched in an absent manner as it solemnly watched his approach. It let him reach within six inches of it before it scampered a few feet farther away from him, to stop and resume its solemn staring.

Wilfred called again and he turned back toward camp, the little animal staring after him as he went. Apparently they would have no ferocious carnivora to contend with on Aurora—the little animal had been without fear of him, or virtually so. It had not behaved in the manner of an animal accustomed to the law of "Run—or be eaten!"

Dishes were scrubbed with a generous amount of sand and a small amount of water after the meal was over, then Taylor began the discussion of their circumstances.

"Our simplest solution would have been to send out an SOS," he said. "We could have contacted a ship easily enough on the emergency band—possibly one no more than a day or so from here."

"A day or so by hyperspace—two hundred years or more in normal space," Cooke commented. "A man doesn't really realize how great galactic distances are until he gets stuck thirty thousand light-years from home, does he?"

Lenson sighed and gave the broken ship a dark look. "I'm already beginning to acquire an unpleasant comprehension of the true magnitude of galactic distances."

"It seems to me that we have only two alternatives," Blake said. "We have to get either our ship or an SOS into hyperspace. We have the power to send the SOS through hyperspace, but the space-shift transformer that would send our signal into hyper-space is broken. The space-shift units that would send our ship into hyperspace are undamaged—but we haven't the power they would have to have. Which do we want to try to do—build a nuclear converter and take our ship back, or make a space-shift transformer for the transmission of an SOS?"

"We would not only have to make the transformer that would send our signal into hyperspace, we'd also have to replace the broken power stage of the transmitter," Taylor said. "The driver stage, even in hyperspace, would have a range so limited that it wouldn't reach the nearest outpost. Unless a ship happened to wander within its range, its signals would never be picked up. And Space being the size it is, that might not occur within our lifetimes."

"You think it would be useless to attempt to duplicate the space-shift signal transformer and the transmitter tubes?" Wilfred asked.

"I'm convinced that their duplication is beyond us," Taylor said. "They require special alloys as well as rare gases. They require delicate precision assembly; in fact, the machines that assemble them would require years of labor to build."

"We already have the means of putting our ship into hyper-space," Blake said. "All we need is the power. It seems to me we could more easily figure out a method of accumulating that power than we could build precision electronic equipment. After all, all we need is a tremendous store of energy to power our jump into hyperspace—a lot of energy for a short period. The drop back into normal space doesn't require but a fraction of that power."

"If there is no hope of sending an SOS, then we haven't any choice but to do that, have we?" Wilfred asked.

"I think we can safely say that the hope of sending an SOS is nil," Taylor said.

None of the others voiced any disagreement and Blake said:

"If we can find uranium, we won't have much trouble changing the fuel chambers to suit the fuel. We probably will have to spend more time making the ship—or the stern half of it—air-tight again than anything else. At any rate, the whole thing is hope-less unless we do rig up an atomic drive. We have to lift our ship into space to slip it into hyperspace and there's no use conjecturing on how we're going to take the second step until we know we can take the first step."

No one spoke for a few seconds, then Taylor said, "I suppose we agree on that, then. Now, the important thing is; can we find the uranium?" He looked at Blake. "How about it—what do you think of the possibilities?"

"I couldn't say," Blake answered. "I haven't seen any of this country, yet. I saw no evidence of metallic ores in the rocks washed down out of that canyon, but we could hardly expect to discover uranium that easily."

"What *did* you find?" Cooke asked.

"These rock formations are similar to Earth-type formations, and the silica content is about normal—if a person discounts the diamond present. The diamond is present in all formations, whether high or low in silica, usually as small to minute crystals. The larger crystals we saw must have come from pegmatitic formations."

"Which are—?" Cooke asked.

"Extremely coarse-grained bodies of rock. Minerals in pegmatitic form as unusually large crystals. On Charon we found a perfect quartz crystal that weighed a thousand pounds in a pegmatitic formation. Cummings—an old white-haired fellow who had been born on Old Earth—said that crystals much larger than that had been found on Old Earth in the past.

"There's something else about pegmatites," he added. "Pitchblende is sometimes found in pegmatitic formations. So, it may possibly be that the uranium ore we find—if we find any—will be in the same formation that these diamond boulders come from."

"Another thing—" Taylor said, thoughtfully. "We'll have to have cadmium. Cadmium and uranium—if we can find the two ores and refine them, we can alter the drive."

"Which will take how long—just as a wild guess?" Lenson asked.

Taylor smiled. "That's like asking how high is up. But, just as an optimistic guess, I'd say from one to two years."

Wilfred nodded his head in agreement. "I'd say that was about right—not less than one and not more than two years. We're lucky in that we have a lathe and other tools to work with, a truck to use for prospecting and all the mining equipment we need to mine the ore after we find it."

"The first thing will be to fix up a place to live," Taylor said, pulling up his pants leg to rub a skinned and bruised knee. "Climbing in and out of those rooms as we did this afternoon is hard work, and painful."

"Red suggested cutting a passageway along the bottom of the hull—using the bottom of the hull as the floor," Wilfred said. "That shouldn't take long. We can rearrange everything to accommodate the new floor and we'll certainly have to take the lathe down off the wall and set it up again on the floor."

Their first Aurorian sunset stopped all talk of future operations a few minutes later. The sun was invisible behind some distant range, its last rays throwing lances of ruby, emerald and gold across the scintillating rainbow field that was the western sky. The lances shifted as they watched, widening and quivering with the splendor of their ever-changing colors until they rippled across the sky like the banners of some celestial fairyland.

Lenson was the first to speak, after the colors began to fade. "I never saw anything like that," he said, almost awe in his voice.

"Nor I," Cooke said, sprawling back against his sleeping bag. "That looks exactly the way my mother used to tell me heaven would look—before she decided I'd never go there, anyway."

"Probably caused by several different layers of air currents, traveling at different speeds and carrying varying amounts of dust and water vapor," Wilfred offered.

"Huh!" Cooke snorted. "Do you always have to be so pragmatic and practical?"

"Oh, it was impressive, I'll admit, but there was a simple, everyday reason for its beauty—the one I suggested, likely. Beautiful sunsets on Earth-type planets are due to water vapor and impurities in the atmosphere."

"Then, so long as we're stuck here, let's be grateful that our atmosphere does contain these beautiful-sunset producing impurities," Lenson said.

The afterglow faded from the sky and the Thousand Suns revealed themselves; a field of bright points of light shining through the haze with sufficient brilliance to throw dim shadows along the ground.

"We'll have to make observations," Taylor remarked. "I'll start making daily observations of our sun and its companion. We know the days here are about twenty-four hours long, but we don't know whether it's spring or summer—or possibly this world has no seasonal inclination of the poles."

"I think it's spring," Blake said. "The higher peaks we saw through the haze were covered with snow. Of course, that's not very conclusive evidence."

"Let's hope it's spring," Taylor said. "We know that our year is about six Earth-years in length and, with luck, we may be able to get away from here before winter comes."

There was a little more talk of their plans; then, one by one, they spread out their sleeping bags and crawled in. Blake, the last to retire, sat for a while watching the golden field the Thousand Suns made of the haze, reaching from the western horizon halfway to the zenith. To the east the sky was dead black, with no star to relieve it. There were none in that direction; not for a long, long way. Aurora had recently passed the farthest point from the Thousand Suns in her orbit; a straight line would pass from her to her sun, to close by the blue-white sun's yellow companion, then on into the Thousand Suns.

Blake remarked, just before he went to sleep, "You'll see what utter darkness is before morning—after the Thousand Suns go down and before the sun comes up."

It required fifteen days to get the ship even partly in condition for living. There was the passage to be cut, doors to be fitted to keep out the fine dust stirred up by the afternoon winds, the ship's water tank to be equipped with sediment filters, the tables and chairs to be unbolted from their incongruous positions on what had become the walls, the truck to be lowered out of the ship—an endless number of things to be done.

Blake and Cooke left on the morning of the sixteenth day, leaving the other three to continue the work on and in the ship. They watched Blake and Cooke depart with a certain wistfulness and Cooke remarked, as they ground away through the sand, "I think all would have liked to go with us. They'll have nothing but hard work while we're out enjoying the fresh air and new scenery."

"You may change your mind about 'enjoying' it," Blake said. "Walking can be hard work when you do it all day."

"What's this truck for?" Cooke wanted to know.

"To haul our stuff. We won't use it any more than we have to—we can make new shoes by hand but we can't make a new truck."

"Do you think the diamond dust will be that bad?"

"I hope we find diamond dust and sand are the exceptions rather than the rule, but all evidence shows the diamond to be present everywhere. If so, we'll have to use the truck as little as possible—if we find the ores we want, then the truck will be indispensable for hauling them to the ship. Whatever we have to have for refining the ores will have to be at the ship—or we'll have to haul a good deal of material and equipment to the ore. Either way, we'll have to have this truck, so we'd better take care of it."

"I can see your point," Cooke agreed, "but I doubt that we'll wear it out very fast. After all, this thing was made to use in country where there was silica sand, and diamond is less than fifty per cent harder than silica."

"If you were correct in that surmise, I wouldn't be worried," Blake said.

"What do you mean—'if'?" Cooke demanded. "Quartz has a hardness of seven and diamond has a hardness of ten. That's less than fifty per cent harder, isn't it?"

Blake sighed. "The true and unpleasant facts are these: Diamond is said to have a hardness of ten because it's the only thing harder than corundum's nine. A mineralogist named Woodell, a long time ago and back on Old Earth, determined the true hardness of diamond in comparison with quartz's seven and corundum's nine. The actual hardness of diamond ranges from a fraction over thirty-six to a fraction over forty-two."

"Oh." Cooke was thoughtfully silent for a while. "Then we can count on this diamond sand and dust being six times harder than the sand and dust this truck was made to resist."

"Six times harder, and also tougher."

They lurched across a small gulch and onto a silty flat, winding to avoid the thorn bushes that were scattered across it. The morning air was still and the dust they raised followed them in a dense cloud, coating their faces and clothing an iridescent gray, gritting harshly wherever two parts of metal moved together, such as the driving controls. They had traveled an hour, enclosed in the cloud of destructive dust, when Blake said, "I wonder—"

"You wonder what?" Cooke asked, his black eyes made blacker by the gray dust that covered his face.

"I wonder if this diamond dust hasn't got us behind an eight-ball—a big, shiny eight-ball named Aurora."

They worked their way along the southern foot of the mountain, toward the high plateau to the east where the creek might have its headwaters. They prospected the canyons one by one, both by carrying back samples of the bedrock gravels to the truck, to pan for particles of the heavy uranium and cadmium ores they sought, and by use of the Geiger counters they each carried. Cooke ran the gauntlet from his first feeling of carefree adventure to a condition of sore, aching legs and blistered hands. Their picks and shovels wore away with amazing rapidity, even from digging in the comparatively loose gravels of the canyon beds, and they found nothing.

They reached the eastern end of the range, a high, bleak plateau where the creek had its headwaters and where the nights were chilly with the breezes from the slowly melting snowbanks. There was nothing there but barren flow rocks and the inevitable diamond so they turned and worked their way back down the northern side of the range. Cooke's soft muscles hardened and his habitual optimism returned, undaunted by the lack of heavy-metal concentrates in the samples they panned or by the Geiger counters that remained silent but for the intermittent clicking of the natural background count.

Twice they found veins of soft iron oxide and once they found a narrow vein of low-grade copper ore but the mountain seemed devoid of any uranium or of any lead-zinc ore that might contain the cadmium they needed.

Blake cared for the little truck with painstaking attention, doing everything possible to keep the diamond dust out of its moving parts. But no way could be devised to keep the dust out of such moving parts as the brake drums, the ball and socket of the front-wheel drive, the control-lever linkage, the winch they were forced to use so many times, and many other moving parts. The air filter caused him more worry than anything else. He knew a certain amount of the fine dust was getting past the filter and into the motor, and there was nothing he could do about it. It was a good filter, made to protect an engine against silica dust; any silica dust fine enough to get past the filter would be too fine to cause any damage before it was reduced to an impalpable powder. But the diamond dust it admitted was six times harder than silica, as well as tougher—the diamond dust would refuse to be reduced to a harmless, impalpable powder.

They rounded the west end of the range early on the thirtieth day and saw the green line of the creek a mile away. The truck labored noisily as Blake turned it up a gentle grade toward the mouth of a narrow canyon and he shifted into a lower gear.

"It's a good thing we're only five miles from camp," Cooke said. "You're about three gears lower than you would be if this truck was in the same condition it was in when we left camp thirty days ago."

"I'm afraid this will be its last trip—I've tried to baby it along and keep the dust out of it, but you just can't enclose a machine in a dust-proof wrapper."

They left the truck on the smooth alluvial fan just outside the canyon's narrow portal and began the by now repetitious process of prospecting the canyon. It was late in the afternoon when they found their first cadmium; a thin gray seam of metallic sulfide in a rock washed down from higher on the canyon's wall.

"The gray sulfide is lead and zinc," Blake said. "Those little yellowish-orange spots in it are cadmium sulfide."

Cooke shook his head. "The percentage of cadmium is so slight—and the lead and zinc is only a thin seam."

"It might have wider portions where it's in place," Blake said, looking up the steeply sloping canyon's side. "It shouldn't be hard to find."

They located it in place an hour later, halfway up the canyon's side, but it was only a short, narrow seam. Blake tried unsuccessfully to dig into it with his prospector's pick, the point of which had long since been worn to a blunt stub. Cooke, pounding vainly at the tight-grained formation beside him, stopped to light a cigarette and wipe the sweat from his face.

"We have acids and glycerin," he said. "If we only had a few holes drilled in this rock, we could fill them with nitroglycerine."

"There's a chance in a thousand that it might get wider at a greater depth," Blake said, ceasing his own futile pounding. "But how do we drill holes in it?"

"The diamond drill—" Cooke began, then his voice trailed off.

"Exactly," Blake said, seeing what was suddenly in Cooke's mind. "How do we drill diamond-bearing rock with a diamond drill?"

"How did we intend to drill holes for mining when we started out thirty days ago? I won't argue about the diamond drill—I can't see how it could drill through diamond-bearing rock—but why didn't we think of all that before?"

"We didn't know for sure that all formations carried the same high percentage of diamond," Blake pointed out. "We hoped such wouldn't be the case, remember?"

"What a world to live on!" Cooke sighed. "Everything we try to do is foiled by diamonds. How can a superabundance of just one element manage to cause so much grief?"

"Well"—Blake shook his empty canteen and glanced to the west where the sun had disappeared behind the canyon wall—"we can't do any more here, now, so we might as well get on back to the truck and have something to eat before dark."

Cooke led the way to the bed of the canyon, his blithe spirits returned sufficiently for him to be whistling by the time they reached it. They were halfway to the canyon's portal when it became suddenly darker, as though a heavy cloud had covered the sun. It grew darker, although Blake's watch said the sun was not quite ready to set, and when they were almost to the portal's cliffs, where the canyon suddenly opened out upon the desert, he became aware of a low roar above the crunching of his footsteps in the diamond sand. It came from the desert beyond the portal; a sound like a distant waterfall.

Cooke, two hundred feet ahead of him, was still whistling cheerily and had obviously not heard it. Blake increased his pace and was almost up with him when Cooke stepped beyond the cliffs that still hid the desert from Blake.

Cooke stopped, then, a look of amazement on his face, staring in the direction of their truck and the desert beyond. Then he wheeled to shout back at Blake, "*What is it?*"

Blake was beside him a few seconds later and he saw the source of the sound he had heard.

It was a mile away; a great, high black wall rushing toward

them, its towering crest lost in the atmospheric haze. It was racing toward them at perhaps fifty miles an hour, roaring with a deep, sustained roar and the sheer front of it seething and boiling.

"What—?" Cooke began, but Blake cut him off with a terse, "Come on!" He ran toward the truck, estimating the distance they must cover before the black wall reached them. The truck was not far—but the wall was traveling at least fifty miles an hour.

"Is it—" Cooke began again, then gave up as a gust of wind whipped sand in his mouth and devoted his full attention to keeping up with the fleet Blake.

They reached the truck with the black wall looming almost upon them and jumped inside, slamming the doors. "Sandstorm," Blake said, as Cooke started to ask again. A harder gust of wind lashed at the truck, stinging their faces with sand. "Close your window," Blake said as he cranked up his own. "Those baby zephyrs are the advance guard. I think we're in for a real one."

The black wall struck a moment later with a thunderous roaring and screaming, smashing at the little truck with savage blows and enveloping them in darkness. Sand and gravel slashed against the windows with a sharp, dry hiss and, above the roar of the wind, Blake could hear a violent thumping as the wind found an empty and unfastened water can in the bed of the truck and slammed it back and forth. The pounding ceased abruptly and Blake had a mental vision of their water can going in kangaroo leaps across the mountainside.

" . . . long do you think?" Cooke shouted through the darkness.

"What?" Blake asked, shouting, himself, to be heard above the howl and roar of the storm.

"How long do you think this will last?"

"Don't know. Sometimes a sandstorm will last an hour, sometimes ten hours."

He felt inside the utility box under the dash and found a flashlight. Its beam had the appearance of a three-dimensional cone in the dust-filled air of the cab.

"How did that get in here so quick?" Cooke demanded.

"It comes in every little crack and crevice," Blake answered, flashing the light through the windshield. The light revealed the dust and sand flowing past them with incredible speed. There were bright gleams in the torrent of air and sand as larger pieces of diamond reflected the light for a microsecond and bits of dead vegetation were being carried along.

Blake shut off the light and made himself as comfortable as possible in his half of the small cab. "You might as well try to make your mind a contented blank for an indefinite number of hours," he advised.

Cooke followed his advice, grumbling at the lack of leg room. He was asleep within fifteen minutes; a fact Blake confirmed by a quick flash of the light. Blake sighed enviously and composed himself for the hours of futile thinking and worrying that would be his own lot until sleep came. There was, in the genial Cooke's philosophy, a blithe unconcern for "Unborn Tomorrow and Dead Yesterday." But, while he envied Cooke for his carefree attitude, he wondered if it would be of sufficient stability to survive the eventual recognition of a not-so-remote possibility—that all their efforts to leave their shining prison might prove to be futile.

The wind was shaking the truck and roaring with undiminished fury when he finally went to sleep, still worrying about the diamond dust that was being driven into every tiny crack about the truck wherever two parts of metal moved against each other. Silica, over a period of time, would ruin machinery. This was diamond, not silica; this had a hardness of forty-two, not seven—

He awoke at dawn, stiff and cramped, with Cooke's snoring loud in the silence that had replaced the storm. He jabbed an ungentle elbow into Cooke's ribs. "Wake up—the storm is over."

"Huh?" Cooke blinked and straightened with a moan. "My leg's been asleep so long it—Hey! What happened to our windows?"

"We now have frosted glass all around," Blake said, rolling down the opaque window on his own side. "Diamond sand is really tough on glass."

He stepped out of the truck into the calm morning air and looked at the damage. Cooke came around from the other side and stared open-mouthed at the bright, gleaming metal side of the truck where, before, there had been a thick coat of hard red enamel.

"It looks like we need a new paint job," he said at last. "And we'll have to knock a hole in the windshield to see how to drive to camp."

Blake lifted the motor cover and ran a finger through the blanket of diamond dust that covered every part of the motor. It was heaped on more thickly where there had been grease or oil to hold it.

"What do we do about that?" Cooke asked.

"Nothing. If we should try to wipe it off, it would cause it to work in deeper. We can only let it stay and hope the grease will keep most of it from getting any deeper into the moving parts."

"I wonder how they made out at camp?" Cooke asked as Blake lowered the motor cover.

"I was wondering the same thing. We'd better let the canyons to be prospected between here and camp wait for the time being. They're all near enough to camp that we can walk out to look at them, anyway."

They removed the opaque windshield and got under way, the steering wheel and gearshift lever grating harshly. They saw something shining metallically a half mile farther on and it proved to be their errant water can; lodged beneath a thorn bush, stripped of its enamel and polished to a high luster.

Taylor and Lenson were waiting outside the ship when they drove up. The question and hope was plain to be seen on Lenson's face but there seemed an almost imperceptible anxiety tingeing the questioning look on Taylor's face.

Blake shut off the motor and climbed out. "Nothing," he said. "Not a sign of uranium."

Lenson's face reflected a natural disappointment but Taylor seemed to have something on his mind more serious than simple disappointment. "Then there's no hope of finding uranium in this range?" he asked.

"There was no indication whatever that there is any such thing anywhere along the range," Blake answered. He looked toward the ship. "Where's Wilfred?"

"He left early to spend the day prospecting. We have the ship pretty well fixed up inside and there hasn't been much to do the past few days. Now—how about other minerals? Did you find anything at all?"

"A thin seam of lead-zinc ore that carries a small percentage of cadmium. But I don't think the diamond drill could ever drill through the rock it's in."

Lenson grinned sourly. "I know it can't," he said. "We no longer have a diamond drill. While you were gone I got to looking around and found a formation that carried zircons. Since we'll need zirconium, we all three agreed it would be a good idea to set up the drill, put down some holes and blast out some zirconium-bearing ore. We set the drill up yesterday morning. By mid-afternoon we had worn out six of our eight diamond bits and were down four inches. I came back to the ship late in the afternoon to get some more oil for the drill's motor—we've been using it and it was getting worn—and the storm hit before I could get back to the drill. I had left the drill running; its progress was so slow that it didn't need any attention. I got lost in the darkness of the storm and finally had to hole up behind an outcropping until morning. Then I saw where I was and went on to the drill. I found the sand blowing into it while it was running had ruined it. Not only the motor, but the gears of the drill, itself."

"It was no loss, I'm afraid," Blake said. "All the formations Cooke and I saw carried the same high percentage of diamond."

"But suppose we should find some ore—how do we drill it without a drill?" Cooke asked. "That is, suppose we find some ore that isn't so hard and filled with diamonds as to make drilling impossible."

"In that case, we'd probably find we could fix up the old drill after all," Blake said. He turned to Lenson. "You said you had been using the drill's motor for something else—what was that?"

"Water pump," Lenson said. "It seemed like a foolish waste of effort and time to carry water to the ship's tanks in buckets so we took the little high-speed water pump that we had brought along for the very purpose of filling the ship's tanks, took the motor off the drill—we weren't using the drill then—stripped enough tubing out of the ship's air circulating system to reach to the creek and set up our pump." He grinned again. "It lasted long enough to fill one tank, then the bearings went out. We fixed it and a week later, when we used it again, the bearings went out again. Finally, the last time we used it, the impellers were half abraded away as well as the bearings and shafting cut out."

"And the motor was wearing out, too?"

Lenson nodded. "The bank was dry and sandy where we set the pump and breezes were always stirring up little clouds of dust. The motor was in pretty bad shape before it soaked through our thick skulls that the dust was pure diamond dust and not at all as harmless as it looked."

"So now you're back to carrying water in buckets?" Cooke observed. "And Red and I are going to be back to walking. This is a cruel world to anyone accustomed to mechanized assistance."

"About finding uranium—" Taylor said, the aura of worry still about him. "What would you suggest next?"

"We can hike across the desert to the nearest range and see what we can find," Blake said. "It will be slow, doing it all on foot, but we have a boundless supply of two things on this world—time and diamonds."

"No." Taylor shook his head. "Time is the very thing we *don't* have. I haven't said anything to Len or Wilfred about it yet. I wanted to wait until all five of us were here to talk over what we—"

"Hello." Wilfred's hail interrupted Taylor and he came hurrying toward them. "I saw your truck pull in so I turned around and came back. Any luck?"

"None," Blake said. "It just wasn't there to be found."

"What was this about not having time, and something you hadn't told us yet?" Lenson asked Taylor, his eyes on Taylor's face.

The others turned their attention to Taylor as he spoke.

"I've been making daily observations with the transit, as you know," he said. "I've observed the apparent motion of our sun, the yellow sun, and the Thousand Suns cluster. I found that this *is* spring—whether late or early I don't know—but that's of no importance. I thought, at first, the yellow sun was swinging in its orbit around our blue-white sun. You can see the yellow sun— like a very bright yellow star—in advance of our own sun each morning. According to my observations, the yellow sun is making an apparent advance of approximately one degree every five days in front of our own sun. This happens to be what its apparent advance should be as we swing out in our orbit, so I became suspicious and made other observations. I discovered we are approaching the Thousand Suns at a speed of one hundred miles a second."

"That's what you didn't tell us?" Lenson asked. "I don't understand—we'll either be long since gone from here, or long since dust, before our wandering binary reaches the nearest star of the Thousand Suns."

"I said the apparent advance of the yellow sun is accounted for by our own orbital movement," Taylor said. "There is no orbital movement of the yellow sun observable. This isn't a binary—the yellow sun is a member of the Thousand Suns."

"You mean—" Blake began.

"In approximately seven and a half months the two suns will collide."

"And our position in our orbit at that time?"

"We'll go into the yellow sun the radius of our orbit—four hundred million miles—in advance of the collision."

Tall Lenson barely changed expression and the surprise on Wilfred's face hardened into quick stubbornness, as though he had already decided he would refuse to accept such a fate. Cooke leaned one hip on the fender of the truck, his black eyes flickering over the others as he analyzed their reactions. But for once, Blake felt, Cooke was finding nothing to amuse him.

"You're sure your observations were accurate—that there's no hope we might have already swung past the yellow sun by then?" Blake asked.

"I've made my observations as accurate as possible, and checked for errors. Our sun is moving toward the yellow sun at a hundred miles a second and a distance of slightly more than one and a half billion miles now separates them. Our observation of these suns couldn't indicate that they were not a binary during the brief period we dropped into normal space—especially with our limited means for taking observations from the ship. It was natural for us to assume that two suns so close together were a binary. Only very precise observations during the short time we observed them could have revealed the truth and we had neither the proper instruments for such observations nor any reason to think such observations were necessary."

"It wouldn't have changed our circumstances," Blake pointed out. "With seven or eight months of grace, we would have landed to see what the planet had to offer in the way of mineral wealth, anyway."

"That's true," Taylor said. "The result would have been the same. So here we are and we have, according to my most optimistic calculations, six months to fit our ship with a drive and get away from here as fast as we can."

"*Six months?*" Cooke demanded. "You said it would be seven and a half."

"We'll have to be a long way from here by then—Aurora carries an exceptionally high percentage of carbon and you know what happens when any nuclear conversion process absorbs an excess of carbon."

"Oh-oh—*nova!*"

"And they reach out a long, long way," Taylor said.

"The hyperspace units—the power for them—" Wilfred began.

"If we ever find a way to power them, it will have to be en route in space," Taylor said. "Or that's the safest course of action for us, I would say."

"I agree," Blake said. "If we can find ore pure enough, we might possibly be able to take off from here within six months. It would have to be exceptionally pure ore—it's improbable that we can find such ore but we don't know that it's impossible. The first thing we want to do is to start getting as far away from here as possible, and as fast as possible. Given pure enough ores, we can do that, I think."

"You said 'improbable but not impossible,'" Taylor said. "Just how improbable do you think it is?"

"If the other ranges are similar to this one, our chances are very poor. We can try; we can go out as two different parties to save time. Cooke has had experience in the hills, now, and could go with one of you to the range north of us while I went with the other to the range south of us. If there's nothing in the adjoining ranges, I would say there is no use looking farther."

"Why?" Lenson asked.

"Time. Time and distance. Any ore we found would have to be carried to the ship on our backs—the truck is worn out."

"Then let's start today," Cooke suggested. "Since our time is so short, we shouldn't waste an hour of it. Let's start right now."

Blake glanced at the early morning sun. "A good idea. We certainly won't have any days to waste. We'll take along about sixty days' supply of concentrated food tablets, plus spare shoe soles and, above all, canteens."

"The concentrated food tablets for two months—" Wilfred began doubtfully, but was interrupted.

"For roughage we can eat thorn berries," Blake told him. "Cooke and I tried them. They're tasteless, but they're completely harmless." He turned to Cooke. "You can take Wilfred across to the north range, and Lenson is better built for the hike across the desert to the south range than Wilfred is—it will be about three days on the water in our canteens to reach that south range."

"And if the south range has no creeks or springs in it—how will you come back across the desert without water?" Taylor asked.

"We won't," Blake said simply.

Cooke slid off the fender and looked at the truck, shaking his head. "If only we could have had this truck to use—"

Blake and Lenson reached the south range on the third day of tramping across the glittering diamond sand of the desert, their throats burned and dry and their canteens empty. They found water; a seepage of sickening alkali water, but it was water. They found a creek of sweet water the next day as they started up the range's northern front, tumbling down out of the mountains and disappearing beneath the sand at the mountain's foot. It was a high, rugged range and they found other creeks and springs as they went. They reached its eastern end on the thirtieth day and turned down its southern face. They came to the last canyon on its southwest slope on the fiftieth day and knew they had failed. They had found an occasional vein of iron oxide and, once, a fairly soft vein of copper ore, but there had been no indications of uranium.

On the fifty-fourth day they reached the ship again, gaunt and ragged, with Blake's red whiskers flaming riotously and Lenson's brown beard giving him the look of a benign but destitute young religious father.

As though by prearranged plan, Cooke and Wilfred returned at the same time; Wilfred's pink face burned red by the sun, his blond whiskers sprouting raggedly, while Cooke wore a bushy black beard that, together with his glittering black eyes, gave him an even greater appearance of piratical fierceness.

Taylor was carrying two buckets of water to the ship when the four of them appeared. He set the buckets down and waited.

"No luck," Blake said as they drew near him.

"Same here," Cooke said. "That range we went to was as barren as this one."

"I've been continuing my observations," Taylor said. "Everything checks with my first ones, and now we're sixty days nearer the end. We'll have to start accomplishing something pretty quick."

"I know it," Cooke said, scratching at his black beard, the tattered sleeve of his shirt flapping in the wind. "But before we start any long talks on what we shall do next, let's have something to eat besides thorn berries and pills. And take a bath—I'm so covered with diamond dust that, in the nude, I'd glitter like a precious jewel."

Taylor picked up his buckets of water. "There's enough water for all of you to take showers," he said, "so long as you don't waste it. I've been busy with other things or I would have had more water carried to the ship."

"We'll have to have a pump," Blake said, relieving Taylor of one of the buckets. "There's no use spending time carrying water in buckets."

Lenson looked at him sharply to see if he were joking.

"Did you take a look at what that diamond silt in the water did to our pump?" he asked. "It ruined it, and it was made of the hardest alloy steel."

"We can't use any kind of pump that has moving parts of steel," Blake said. "No steel alloy ever made can resist diamond. And, since steel is our hardest man-made material, it's obvious we can't use any kind of a pump that has metal moving parts. So, we'll not try to fight the diamond with harder steel alloys— if we had them—we'll just overcome the abrasion problem by making a pump that has no moving parts."

"Oh?" Cooke stared at him. "A brilliant solution but for one thing—how do we move water without the mover doing any moving?"

"We let the water use its own velocity to force part of itself higher than the source—we make a hydraulic ram."

"Hm-m-m!" Taylor grunted in self-disgust. "I could have had one made long ago, in my spare time, but I never thought of such a simple solution. I kept thinking of some way to combat the diamond's abrasion, rather than how to avoid it completely."

"But a hydraulic ram does have moving parts," Wilfred objected. "The valves. Without the valves alternately opening and closing, the ram wouldn't work. How do you keep valves in it?"

"The valves are so simple—one floating valve and one flap valve—that all we have to do is spray the valves and valve seats with plastic rubber. The diamond can't harm rubber—the rubber is so soft that the diamond's hardness has no effect on it."

A shower and a full meal did much to improve their spirits, and a shave did even more to improve their appearance. Taylor brought up the subject of their next course of action and asked Blake for his opinion of the desirability of further prospecting for uranium. Blake answered the question with a suggestion.

"We'll have to rest a week, even though our time is so short," he said. "This time we'll have *two* deserts to cross, as well as the mountain between, and our past sixty-day diet of food tablets and thorn berries has all four of us in pretty weak condition. While we rest up I suggest we try to think of some alternative to the atomic drive. I won't argue if the rest of you want to continue looking for uranium, but I'm afraid it's hopeless. Without a truck or any other form of transportation, it would do no us good to find the ore. We're not going to be given the time to carry ore for great distances on our backs, across deserts and mountains. So, suppose for the next six days everyone makes a try at thinking up some plan other than the atomic drive?"

"The more plans, the better," Taylor said. "If we had a large enough selection to choose from, we could pick out one that would be sure-fire. But I can't see how we can find a quicker and simpler way to lift this ship than the atomic drive."

The others felt the same way; they seemed quite willing to consider any alternate plan but with no conception of any such plans. Blake made no mention of the idea in his own mind, certain that it held their only hope for survival but fearing its radical departure from conventional lines of thinking would cause them to reject it, despite the magnitude of its possibilities.

They made the hydraulic ram the next day and laid a line of the ship's air tubing to a point sufficiently upstream along the noisy little creek to give the necessary pressure. Shortly before the sun went down they connected the last length of tubing to the ram, then returned to the ship to wait for the first flow of water into the ship's tank. It required some time for the tubing between the ram and the ship to fill with water but the water came at last; a steady little trickle.

"You know," Cooke remarked as he watched the tiny flow, "those ancients weren't exactly fools."

"At last, we've won one round in our battle with this diamond dust," Lenson said.

"I want all of you to keep in mind how we did it," Blake said. "We did it by using the natural forces at hand and by *not* trying to fight the abrasiveness of the diamond grit. Remember this, in any planning you do—*you can't fight diamond with metal!*"

"I think we're all aware of that by now," Taylor said.

"I hope so. Until we acknowledge that fact, we won't get anywhere."

No further mention was made of their problem in the succeeding days and Blake hoped that such silence was indicative of serious thinking on their part and not merely a fatalistic acceptance of the *status quo*.

On the sixth day following their return they gathered in the central room of the ship for each to present his plan, if any. Blake procured a few small items from the repair room and his own locker just before the discussion began.

Taylor made a quick summary of their predicament.

"There could have been only three possible ways of leaving this planet," he said. "The most certain would have been to send a message to New Earth, but that's impossible. We can't repair or duplicate the smashed transmitter tubes or hyperspace transformer. Their construction calls for very complex precision machinery as well as special alloys. We can't re-use the various alloys in the shattered tubes because exposure to the air has turned several of the more delicate alloys to dust.

"The second easiest method, and the most impossible, would be to simply wait and hope a ship comes along in time to save us. I know that we all reject *that*. That leaves only one way of leaving this world before it burns—to make a drive for our ship.

And that boils down to the question: Shall we continue to search for uranium and cadmium or shall we devote our time and effort to some other method of lifting the ship than an atomic drive?"

"I've kept my mind a receptive blank for six days and not one single idea has come near it," Lenson said. "I don't see where we have any choice—what else can we plan on with any hope at all other than an atomic drive?"

"Before we go on to new plans," Wilfred said, "suppose we let Blake give his opinion of the chances of finding uranium and cadmium in time to make a drive."

"We haven't found any evidence of any uranium in three full-grown mountain ranges," Blake said. "There's iron, and a small amount of copper, but no radioactive elements. I don't know whether it's true of all this continent, but the section we're on is almost wholly light elements.

"I am *not* in favor of any further prospecting. Our time is very limited; anything we do will have to be done without delay. Further prospecting, on foot, would require time, lots of time. Possibly the ore we want is within fifty miles of us, but how do we find it in time, on foot? Even if we found it, and in a sufficiently pure state, how do we transport it back to the ship in time? We have no truck, you know; we have only our legs and backs. If we had the time—and if this world permitted us to use the truck—I would be in favor of continuing the prospecting until we *did* find the ores we needed. The truck would shorten days of travel into hours; it would haul needed supplies and equipment to the ore and haul the ore back. But we don't have a truck any more—and we don't have the time. In my own opinion, further prospecting is a waste of our short and precious time."

"There doesn't seem to be anyone who disagrees with you," Taylor said when the others remained silent. "You paint a dark picture, but there's no denying the truth of it."

"Do you have a plan?" Wilfred asked.

"I have. You've all been thinking along conventional lines, haven't you?"

"Such conventional lines of thinking produced the ship that brought us here," Wilfred pointed out.

"It did, but the same conventional type of thinking is never going to lift it up again. I have an unconventional idea, and a deceptively simple question. If you can answer my question, we'll know how to make a drive for our ship."

Blake extracted several items from his pocket: a short steel bar, a square of sheet aluminum, a piece of thin glass and a large darning needle on a long thread. He laid them down on the table before him and continued:

"I'm afraid that conventional thinking won't work on an unconventional world. We've all been tackling our problem as though we were marooned on a counterpart of New Earth, with New Earth's dust-free air and plentiful supply of minerals. We keep thinking of a rocket drive because a rocket drive was the simplest type of drive to build on a world of machinery and radioactive ores. We have neither, here; we don't have Earth-type resources and equipment to fight a decidedly non-Earth-type environment. On New Earth we would use machines—all human technological progress stemmed from that simple little thing, the wheel. Without wheels there would never have been machinery, without machinery there would never have been the atomic drive. You've all seen that we can't have wheels on *this* world. We can't have wheels, we can't have any kind of moving-parts machines on a world of diamond dust. Our own science is built on the wheel and if we don't develop a substitute science for it, we go up in smoke in seven or eight months."

Blake picked up the steel bar. "There is one force that no one has mentioned, and it's a force that all the diamond dust on this world could never faze because it has no moving parts— *field-type force.*"

He picked up the needle by its thread. "This is a common bar magnet," he said, letting the needle click against the end of it. "We all know that opposite poles attract, like poles repel. I pull the needle off the end of the magnet and the needle snaps back against it the moment I release it because its lower end has been magnetized with a polarity opposite to that of that end of the bar. If I switch ends with the bar magnet, the needle, instead of being attracted to it, will swing away out on the thread to stay away from it. I have a piece of sheet aluminum here—the magnetic repulsion goes right through it. The same with this piece of glass."

He laid the magnet and needle back down on the table. "You four have the technical training and knowledge—I'm only a fairly competent mining engineer. But my common sense tells me the reason we can't leave here is because a field-type force, gravity, holds us here. My common sense also tells me that there must be the same basic principles underlying all field-type forces; magnetism, induction, gravity. If two magnetized bodies can be made to repel each other, is it impossible that two bodies held together by gravitational attraction could be made to repel each other?

"As I said, I think the same basic principles underlie all field-type forces. If we can learn what that principle is, we can produce a drive that operates by antigravity. So, this is the question I wanted to ask you: *What caused the needle and magnet to behave as they did?*"

There was silence for a while as they considered Blake's proposal. Wilfred was the first to speak.

"It's a simple phenomenon," he said, "and known to any child."

"That's true," Blake agreed. "Any child knows what a magnet will do, but do any of you know any more about a magnet than the hypothetical child? You all know *what* a magnet will do— do any of you know *why* it does it?"

"I know nothing of magnetic forces, myself," Lenson said, somewhat uncertainly, "since they don't enter my own field of study, but Cooke probably knows them from A to Izzard."

"I know what a magnet will do—I don't really know why it does it," Cooke said. "Men have made use of magnetism and induction forces for centuries and the behavior of such forces is known in precise detail—but still no one knows just what these forces *are*. You can manipulate a force to your own advantage if you understand its behavior under various conditions, but if you understand exactly what that force is, you can manipulate it to your own advantage much more efficiently."

"I agree," Lenson said.

"There's another field-type force we use without fully understanding it—our hyperspace drive," Blake said. "Theoretically, it shouldn't require such an enormous surge of power to activate the space-shift units—but we have to use that enormous surge of power to get any results. We say we 'slip' or 'jump' into hyperspace. We don't. We don't 'slip' through that barrier—we smash our way through it with the full output of a nuclear converter. If we can learn what field-type forces are, I see no reason why we might not be able to so alter our hyperdrive that the ship's generator will supply more than enough power for it."

"A possibility," Cooke said.

Taylor nodded in agreement, then said, "But, while the idea has unlimited possibilities, we haven't the slightest assurance that we'll realize any of them in the short time we have."

"I know it," Blake said. "I know it's a long chance, since our time is so short. But it is a chance, and all the other plans would have been doomed to failure before we started."

"It's something of a challenge," Wilfred said. "The idea appeals to me. It's true that we actually know relatively little of field-type forces; our environment was such that our technical progress led to atomic study."

Blake looked the four men over, both surprised and relieved that they should accept his plan without argument; the only possible approach to the problem, he was convinced, that offered any hope. Taylor seemed to be the only one who had any doubts and Blake said to him, "What is your own opinion of my plan? Are you in favor of dropping all other plans and concentrating on the study of field-type forces?"

"My half-expressed doubts about accomplishing anything in the time we have weren't intended as an objection. It's a field of study of which we know very little, and it's a difficult field to learn. But I'm in favor of it—it, at least, isn't dependent upon the use of moving machinery. We can study it under controlled conditions, here in the ship. In fact, I would like to suggest the study of induction fields as a starter—we can manipulate induction fields to suit ourselves, and under all kinds of conditions."

"In all of Man's history," Cooke said, "since the first savage wondered why a piece of natural lodestone would attract grains of magnetite, no one has been able to discover why. But, while we don't have much time, we have a very powerful incentive. And we do know a few things about magnetism. For example: all ferrous iron with a valence of two is magnetic. Ferric iron, with a valence of three, is not magnetic. Let's find out why— an atom of iron is an atom of iron and should be magnetic whether it's combined with oxygen or not."

"We'll need juice," Taylor said. "Plain, old-fashioned electricity."

"We can manage that," Blake said. "The ship's generator wasn't damaged, so we'll make the only kind of engine a world without oil, coal or radioactive ores would have permitted—a steam engine. We have water, plenty of trees for fuel, and we have a lathe. There's a spare primer-thrust tube that will make a perfect cylinder."

"How about the diamond dust in the water?" Taylor asked.

"Only clean steam will go to the cylinder, and the diamond dust won't affect the boiler as lime would. Besides, we have our water filters on the ship's tanks."

Wilfred picked up the needle and let it swing from the thread, holding the magnet under it. "If this magnet represented this planet, and its magnetism was the force of gravity, with this needle representing our ship, fitted with some gadget to make it antigravitic at the lower end as this needle is antimagnetic—"

He let the needle swing on the thread, bouncing away from the repulsion of the magnet, then swinging in again, to be stopped and driven away by the invisible force.

"The invisible barrier," he said. "What is it? It isn't matter—not as we know matter. We call it a force, but just exactly what is it that no material—glass, metal or anything else—can bar?"

"That's the question," Taylor said. "It's going to be a hard one to answer."

"It will," Cooke said, "but we know the answer is there if we can find it. The power we need to move this ship is all around us; we'll be looking for the secret of a power that we *know* exists."

"And if we continued to hunt for uranium, we'd be looking for something that all the evidence shows does *not* exist," Blake said.

Lenson shoved back his chair and got to his feet. "Now that we know what we want to do, let's get busy," he said. "It will take all five of us quite a while to build that boiler and engine, so let's get started right now."

"I agree," Cooke said. "We're headed for an unpleasant end at a hundred miles a second—the Bird of Time has but a little way to fly—"

"And Lo!—the Bird is on the Wing!" Wilfred finished, a rare smile on his pugnacious young face as he shoved back his own chair.

✧   ✧   ✧

The generator was lowered from its hanging position on the wall and fastened to a new-laid flooring of steel. A gear box was made from the gears of the ship's elevator and the portholes of the drive room were equipped with glassite windows; windows which were rendered sub-translucent by the first sandstorm, but would still admit sufficient light for working. The boiler and engine construction progressed slowly, with the small lathe and the limited kinds of material available, but they worked steadily while the yellow star advanced farther and farther ahead of their own sun. It gleamed in the dawn sky a full hour in advance of the rising of their sun when they began the building of the engine. On the day they completed the engine it was dispelling the eastern blackness two hours before the blue-white sun brought the first touch of the rainbow dawn and almost three hours before the sun, itself, appeared.

Blake, Cooke and Lenson toasted the steam engine on the day they completed it and gave it a successful trial run; a modest toast of one small glass each, due to the limited amount of grain alcohol in the medicine locker. Taylor and Wilfred, who never drank, had already gone into the central room to begin the job of converting it into a laboratory.

"She's not pretty," Cooke said, indicating the shapeless boiler and engine with his empty glass, "but beauty is as beauty does. And she spun that generator like a top."

"She did," Lenson said. "As you said of the hydraulic ram— those old-timers weren't exactly fools."

"We have all the power we need whenever we happen to need it," Blake said. "Next, as soon as we get the central room converted, will be to put our ideas to the acid test."

"They say the acid test is always sour," Cooke said. "We'll have to make an exception of that rule. And have you noticed our big yellow star? It's over forty degrees in advance of our sun, now—gives the illusion of traveling away from our sun, except that it keeps getting brighter."

"We're already a fifth of the way to it," Blake said.

"The nova created when Aurora goes into the yellow sun should be spectacular," Cooke went on. "And then what happens when our big blue-white sun goes into the nova? Will it pro-duce a super-nova? No man has ever stood off and seen such a thing, you know."

"Neither will we if we don't get busy," Lenson said. "Time, tide and Aurora's rendezvous wait for no man—and here we stand with empty glasses in our hands when we should be working."

"You're right," Cooke said, turning to go. "Holding an *empty* glass is about the most useless thing a man ever did."

The central room of the ship was converted into a laboratory— or as near to a laboratory as their limited equipment would permit—and large glassite windows were fitted into holes cut in the hull; a much better form of illumination than the improvised oil lamps they had been using.

Ideas were presented in the days to come; some that were no more than the repetition of known experiments and some that were contrary to accepted theories of magnetic and gravitic principles. The latter were, at first, presented somewhat self-consciously and Blake and Cooke did their best to discourage such reluctance to depart from conventional thinking. As the days merged into scores of days the reluctance to present unorthodox theories vanished and they all five adopted the policy of accepting each new theory with, as Cooke put it: "The assumption that every theory, no matter how fantastic, is innocent of the crime of invalidity until proven guilty."

Each experiment was given a number, preceded by the letter X for "Experimental," and the data gained by the experiment filed away. Blake, whose mathematical computations as a mining engineer had never required more than trigonometric and logarithmic tables, became as proficient as the others. His lack of advanced technical learning was, in a way, no disadvantage—he had nothing to unlearn. He absorbed all the data available concerning the actual, observed behavior of field-type forces and rejected the adoption of any preconceived theories of the causes for such behavior, keeping his mind open for the unbiased inspection of new concepts.

Thirty days passed and then another thirty, while the yellow star grew slowly brighter and widened the apparent distance between itself and their own sun—the apparent widening of the distance that was so belied by the yellow star's increasing brightness. The first enthusiasm of Cooke, Lenson and Wilfred gave way to a quietness and they worked longer hours. Taylor betrayed no particular emotion but he was up early and to bed late.

Summer solstice came and the sun ceased its apparent north-ward progress and began to creep to the south, almost imper-ceptibly at first. The desert winds came with greater frequency after solstice, hot and searing and bringing their ever-present burden of sand and dust.

They had been on Aurora four months when Cooke, in a moment of grim humor, chalked a huge calendar on the wall of the laboratory. He made it thirty days wide and five rows deep. Each day that passed would be filled in with red chalk and the red squares would move across the calendar, row upon row, warn-ing the five men who labored in the room of the shortness of their time.

Two lines of thirty days each were chalked a solid red when they found the first key to the secret that meant their lives.

X117 lay on the laboratory table, a complex assembly of coils and electronic apparatus, with a small blue-white diamond swing-ing in a tiny arc just within the focal point of the induction fields. The diamond hung on a long thread, attached to a delicate spring scale with a large dial.

Cooke glanced over the assembly, then raked his heavy hair back from his face and grinned at the others. "This," he said, "should be what we've been looking for."

"You've said that every time," Wilfred reminded him.

"Let's find out," Blake suggested, feeling his usual impatience to learn as soon as possible if their efforts had again been in vain. "We have full steam pressure and our engine is ready to spin the generator whenever you close the switch."

"That's what I say—let's get the suspense over with," Lenson said. He closed the switch that would open the steam engine's governors and the faint chuffing of it in the drive room became a fast pounding. The needle on the generator output gauge began to climb rapidly and all eyes were transferred to the dial of the spring scale.

"Twenty seconds," Cooke said, his attention alternating between the diamond and his watch. "It should have built up an effect by then. If it hasn't, it will look like another failure and I'll have to guess again on the success of the next one."

No one else spoke as they watched the diamond swing gently

from the long thread. It was only a small one, not more than ten grains in weight; such a small and insignificant mass to resist all their efforts to move it.

"Ten seconds," Cooke intoned. "Eight—cross your fingers and say a little prayer—three—two—*now!*"

The diamond continued to swing in its tiny arc and the pointer on the scale remained motionless. No one moved nor took their eyes off the diamond, even when the smell of scorched insulation became noticeable.

"It's overloaded, now," Lenson said, but made no move to open the switch.

"Give it more," Blake ordered. "Give it the full output of the generator—let's be sure of it, and let it burn if it wants to."

Lenson snapped another switch shut and the full output of the big generator surged through X117. A coil went out in a flash of blue fire and someone cried out incredulously.

In the brief instant before the coil disappeared the diamond moved—*up*.

"*It moved!*" Cooke exclaimed jubilantly. "We're going to have our drive!"

There was a minute of quite natural elation and confused babble of excited talk during which Blake remembered to open the switch again. The muted pounding of the steam engine died away and the babble resolved itself into coherent conversation.

"We're on the right track, at last," Blake said decisively.

"We've just done something all our science has never before accomplished," Wilfred said. "We've created a force of antigravity."

"We have a long way to go," Taylor said. "We've built up a force of antigravity that lifted a diamond weighing ten grains— and it took the full output of our ship's generator to do it. But we now have a proven result to go on; we have the beginning of an understanding of the basic principles."

"When we get it where we want it, I doubt that it will bear any resemblance to *this*," Blake said, indicating the assembly on the table with his hand. "This just happened to be the easiest way to produce a little of the force we were looking for. Like, you might say, the easiest way to produce electricity is to stroke a cat. But you wouldn't try to supply electricity for a city by having a million men engaged in stroking a million cats."

"I have a theory," Cooke said. "Once we learn a little more

about this force we created we can try something else—we'll try reversing the gravitic flow, rather than building up a counter-flow. I want to work on that theory and see what the rest of you think of it. Such a system should require almost no power since no force would be created, merely reversed."

"The perfect ship's drive would be a field-type drive," Wilfred said, "for more reasons than one. The reason I have in mind at the moment is this: there would be no limit to the speed of acceleration since the ship and its occupants would be enveloped in the driving force. It wouldn't, to the passengers, be like the rocket drive where they're actually pushed along by the seat of their pants."

Blake nodded. "I've been thinking of the same thing. I suppose we all have, because the only way we're going to escape that nova is to accelerate at an unheard-of velocity. We can do that when we perfect what we're working on; with our ship and ourselves enveloped in the driving force we can accelerate *immediately* to any speed, and with no sensation of accelerating at all."

"No more acceleration hammocks and anti-acceleration drugs," Cooke said. "No more long periods of reaching maximum acceleration, then other long periods of decelerating. We really have something—or will have when we're through." He looked over at Taylor. "How much time to we have? Did your latest observations give us as much as a day more?"

Taylor glanced at the calendar Cooke had chalked on the wall. "Your calendar still holds good—the last day you have on it will be our last day."

"Eighty-five days—that's not many," Lenson said.

"No, but we're going to make progress from now on," Blake said. "We have something to work on; we've opened a door that no one has ever opened before."

"And if there's another door behind the one we opened?" Lenson asked.

It was Cooke who answered, the finality of conviction in his voice. "Then we'll open that one, too."

Lenson's question proved to be not an idle one; there was a door behind the one they had opened. In the countergravity they had created lay the key to the second door, the reversal of gravity, but it eluded them as the days went by. They repeated X117 and variations of it until the experimental-data record bore the number, X135. Cooke's theory was examined and re-examined and no fallacy could be found, neither could any other theory be constructed that would fit the facts they had discovered. They accepted Cooke's theory as valid, and no one questioned the possibility of reversing gravitic flows with a negligible amount of power.

All were convinced of ultimate success—if they could but have the time.

The days fled by while they tried and tried again. They worked longer hours, all of them thinner and the bulldog stubbornness on Wilfred's face becoming more pronounced. The yellow star crept farther ahead of their own sun, growing brighter as it went, and the red-chalked squares marched across the calendar. Their determination increased as their days of grace melted away; a determination expressed by a silent intensity of effort by all but Cooke, whose intensified efforts were accompanied by considerable cheerful speculations upon the many pleasures New Earth would have to offer them on their return.

Blake wondered if Cooke's faith in their eventual success was as firm as he insisted, or if it was only a psychological attempt to improve not only the morale of the others but also his own. The red squares had crept across two more rows and over halfway across a third when he got his answer.

It was on the morning following the failure of X144. They had worked far into the night to complete the assembly of it and it had been devoid of observable results. The others had gone to bed to get a few hours sleep before starting the construction of X145 but Blake had found sleep impossible. The failure of X144 exhausted every possibility but one; the one represented by the to-be-constructed X145. Theoretically, X145 would be successful—but some of the others had been theoretically certain of success until their trial had revealed hitherto unknown factors. After an hour of the futile wondering and conjecturing, Blake had given up the thought of sleep and put on his clothes.

He walked down to the creek, marveling again at the beauty of a world so harsh and barren. The yellow star, now bright enough to cast his shadow before him, was low in the west as he walked up the creek and the eastern sky was being touched with the first emerald glow that preceded the rainbow banners. When the sun came up it would bring another day of heat, and the dry, swirling winds would send the diamond dust along in low-flying clouds. But in the quiet of early dawn it was cool and pleasant along the creek with the trees bordering it making a leafy green corridor along which he walked into the emerald dawn while the fresh scent of green, living things was about him.

He saw the bulk of something red, lying in the sand beside a tree, and he went over to it. It was a small mound of blood-red diamonds, and he saw that someone had selected them for their flawless perfection. He squatted beside them, leaning back against the tree trunk and lighting a cigarette as he wondered idly who had placed them there, and why.

He forgot them as he rested and watched the emerald of the eastern sky glow deeper in color and the first touch of iridescence come to it. Aurora, for all her grimness, was a beautiful world, and along the creek a man could almost imagine he was on New Earth but for the glory of the dawn and the glitter of the diamond sand. The leaves of the tree over him rustled softly, and among the fresh green smells there came the scent of the red flowers that grew along the water's edge; a scent that brought a brief, nostalgic memory of the old-fashioned briar roses in his mother's garden when he was a boy. She had brought the seeds from Old Earth when she was a girl and on Old Earth, she had told him, they grew wild.

It was hard to believe, as he sat beside the creek, that it and the sweet-scented flowers and the leaves rustling overhead were not things of some stable world where they would remain so for uncounted lifetimes to come; where only the slow, slow dying of the sun could at last bring the end.

Gravel crunched behind him and he turned to see Cooke. "Nice here, isn't it?" Cooke asked, sitting down near him.

Blake nodded, then said, "I thought you were in bed?"

"And I thought you were," Cooke replied. "What do you think of the quality of the diamonds there beside you?"

"You're the one who piled them here?" Blake asked, surprised. "How long has this been going on, and why?"

"Ever since I said we'd unlock that second door. We may have to leave here in a hurry, but we *are* going to leave here. I just did the logical thing of using some of my spare minutes to pile up some of the choicest diamonds where we can get them in short order."

"Do you really believe that, or is this diamond-gathering just to bolster your confidence?" Blake asked, watching him curiously.

"What do you think?" Cooke countered.

Blake studied him, the hard jaw and broken nose, the glittering black eyes, and saw that they were not deceptive, after all. Under ordinary circumstances Cooke was easy-going and genial, but now the mask of good humor had fallen away for the moment and the hard steel core of the man was revealed. Cooke, like the bulldog Wilfred, would be stubbornly defying their fate when Aurora went into the yellow sun.

Yet, though such stubborn faith might prove to be in vain, it had its advantages. Stubborn men die hard—sometimes it takes more than merely impossible difficulties to persuade a stubborn man to die at all.

"I think you have the right idea," Blake said.

There was a silence as Blake returned his attention to the dawn, then Cooke remarked, "We won't have but a few more like that—before we leave here, one sun or the other will be in view all the time. And, by then, the yellow one will be too bright to permit any sunrise effects from the other one."

"Aurora doesn't have many days left."

"What a show that will be!" Cooke mused. "First a nova as Aurora goes into the yellow sun, then the big blue-white sun will go into the nova." Then he sighed and said, "But I sort of hate to see it. I don't care about the suns, but I hate to see Aurora go up in a blaze, no matter how glorious that blaze may be. She's a hard world on humans, but she forced us to pull ourselves up by our own bootstraps. She's a beautiful little devil and I hate to see her destroyed."

The good die young, Blake thought, watching the dawn flame into vivid, fiery life. Not that Aurora was good. She was cruel and beautiful; she was a splendid, glittering prison taking them with her on her swift, silent flight to extinction.

It was not the way a world should die. The death of a world should come only when the fires of her sun went out. A world should grow old and cold for millennia upon millennia; death should come slowly and quietly like that of an old, old woman. But it would not be so for Aurora; for her death would be quick and violent and she would explode a yellow sun into a nova as she died.

Two days later they were ready to put X145 to the test. It was similar to the long-past X117 in that the same blue-white diamond swung from the same long thread, but the assembly was of a different form and the steam engine was cold. They had made a battery, a simply storage battery, and X145 would either succeed or fail with the battery's small current.

The tension was far greater than it had ever been at any previous test, and even Cooke had no cheerful smile or remarks. X145 would be *the* test; if it failed all their labors leading up to it had been to a dead-end. And they would have no time to try another approach.

"I guess we're ready," Cooke said. Blake went to the rheostat that controlled the amount of current and the others grouped about the X145 assembly.

"I'll give it the juice gradually," Blake said. "Although if it as much as quivers at full current, we really will have our drive."

Blake watched the diamond as he turned the rheostat's knob. He felt the faint click of it as it made first contact, then flinched involuntarily as something cracked like a pistol shot and the diamond, thread and scale vanished. Something clattered to the floor across the room and Lenson's surprised question was cut off by a shout from Cooke: "Look—the scale!"

He ran to where it had fallen and picked it up, holding it for all to see. There was a hole torn through it.

"How much . . . how much power did you give it?" he demanded of Blake.

"Minimum current," Blake replied.

"Minimum current," Wilfred murmured. "Minimum current— *and it shot the diamond through the scale!*"

The torn scale was passed from hand to hand and the talk it engendered was both voluble and optimistic.

Cooke hurried out after another scale and Blake and Lenson connected another rheostat in series with the first, then added still another when Wilfred gave the results of his calculations on the slide rule.

Cooke returned with the scale, a much larger one, and a block of copper. "Three?" He lifted his eyebrows toward the three rheostats. "If we can budge a pound of copper with full current through three rheostats, then we can lift a thousand ships with our generator."

The copper block was suspended from the scale, to swing down in the field of the X145, and Blake said, "I'll try minimum current again, even though it may not be enough to affect it at all. We can't expect it to do anything spectacular at minimum current, I'm sure."

He turned the rheostat knob a fraction of an inch and felt the faint click, his eyes on the copper block. There was a roar, sharp and deafening in the room, and the copper block vanished as the diamond had. A hard pull of hot air struck him and something ricocheted back down from the roof to strike him painfully on the shoulder, a fragment of metal from the scale. Wilfred was pointing upward, yelling something. " . . . *Through the roof!*"

Blake looked up and saw what he meant; there was a small hole torn through the hull of the ship over their heads, a hole such as would be made by a one-pound block of copper.

"*Three rheostats,*" Cooke exclaimed. "We not only have the power to lift our ship; we could lift ten thousand of them!"

Cooke began to make rapid calculations and Wilfred followed suit. Blake, curious though he was, saw no reason for three of them to work simultaneously on the same problem so he waited, as did Taylor and Lenson. Taylor was smiling; the first time in many days he had seen the old man smile.

"The problem of power for the hyperspace drive no longer exists," Lenson said. "We can apply the same principles to its alteration that we just now made use of and we can actually 'slip' through the barrier rather than bulldozing our way through it."

"We have a means of driving our ship and we have a means of slipping her into hyperspace," Blake said. "We've come mighty near to succeeding in our plans—will we have the time to succeed all the way?"

"Time?" Lenson looked surprised. "How much time do you want? We have seven days. Isn't that enough?"

Blake shook his head. "We can't have the ship ready in that

short space of time. To leave here within seven days we'll have to—"

"Did I say ten thousand ships?" Cooke's black eyes glittered with exultation. "We could move a world with the power in that generator!"

"We've really reversed the gravitic flow," Wilfred said, as enthused as Cooke. "The only power required to move an object is that for the reversing field—or whatever we should call it. This power requirement is negligible with a capital N."

"Homeward bound!" Cooke said. "Safe and snug beyond the nova's reach in hyperspace!"

"If we want to give up the habit of breathing," Blake pointed out.

The four of them stared at him, and one by one their faces fell as they realized what he referred to; the thing they had forgotten in the intensity of their efforts to devise a drive.

"The ship—" Cooke was the first to express the thought in the minds of all of them. "It leaks like a sieve!"

"How, in seven days, can we finish cutting the two halves of the ship apart, wall in the cut-off end and repair all the broken-apart seams?" Blake asked.

"We can't," Taylor said. He sat down, suddenly old and tired, his former cheerfulness gone. "I don't see how we could make the ship leak-proof in less than four months with the tools and materials we have." He smiled again, but without mirth. "But we came close to succeeding, didn't we?"

"We'll succeed," Blake said. "It's a tough problem, apparently, but I have an idea."

"How about enclosing the ship in a gravitic field large enough to hold its air by plain gravity?" Wilfred asked.

"And how big a field would that have to be?" Lenson asked.

"Big," Blake said. "Even in hyperspace, it will take us six months to get home—or near that. Air has a tendency to leak away and dissipate into space rather easily. I doubt that we could enclose the ship in a field large enough to hold enough air to last us for six months—as I say, it leaks away into space very easily."

"The gradual loss of our air would be an unpleasant way to die," Cooke said. "The ship leaks, we don't have the time to repair it, so what do we do? How do we solve that last little problem?"

"Seven days to do a four months' repair job—" Lenson sat

down beside Taylor and sighed. "It looks like we *can't* make our ship leak-proof in the time we have. But surely there is *some* way—"

"There is," Blake said. "We have a perfect method of both getting home and keeping air in our ship. It should be obvious to all of you."

Questioning looks gave way to dawning comprehension. There was a long silence as they considered the plan, then Cooke said, "After all, a fortune was what we set out for."

"We'll have to call them in advance," Wilfred said. "We can't just barge in."

Blake nodded. "Homeward bound, safe and snug in hyperspace—but, as you say, we'll have to radio them in advance. If we just barreled in without giving them a chance to tell us where to park, it could raise merry hell with everything."

Redmond, control-tower radio operator of Spaceport 1, New Earth, was puzzled. He scratched his thinning hair and leaned closer to the speaker. The voice from it came in distinctly, but faintly.

"Can't you step up your volume?" he asked.

"No," the tiny voice answered. "I told you we had to couple in the driver stage—our power stage is gone."

"How far out are you?" Redmond asked.

"About a billion miles. Did you get what I told you? This is the *Star Scout* and we're just back from beyond the Thousand Suns. We were going to get caught by a nova—"

"I got everything," Redmond interrupted. "Your planet was going into the yellow sun and its high carbon content would create a nova. You learned how to control field-type forces so that you would have a drive for your ship. So you came back to New Earth—or a billion miles out from it. But why do you keep insisting that I have my superiors engage an astrophysicist to tell you where to park your ship? And another thing—you said it would take four months to make your ship leak-proof and you only had seven days. How did you do a four months' job in seven days?"

"We didn't," the thin voice from the speaker answered. "That's what I'm trying to tell you and that's why we'll have to have an astrophysicist define our parking place. We didn't have time to repair our ship, and we couldn't enclose it in a gravitic field large enough to hold air for six months."

Redmond clutched his thinning hair again, feeling suddenly dizzy. "You don't mean—"

"Yeah. We brought the planet with us."

Editor's note: As a general rule, Godwin made no attempt to fit his stories into a common setting. The two stories which follow are one of the exceptions to the rule. Even then, a partial exception, because the only commonality they have is the appearance in both stories of the distinctive semi-intelligent species of Altairians—in the character of Alonzo in this story, and Loper and Laughing Girl in the next. I think Godwin found these aliens, with their devotion to duty, loyalty, and unfailing courage—and the example they set for the humans who were theoretically their "superiors"—simply irresistible. So do I.

—AND DEVIOUS THE LINE OF DUTY

"We're almost there, my boy." The big, gray-haired man who would be Lieutenant Dale Hunter's superior—Strategic Service's Special Agent, George Rockford—opened another can of beer, his fifth. "There will be intrigue already under way when this helicopter sets down with us. Attempted homicide will soon follow. The former will be meat for me. You will be meat for the latter."

Rockford was smiling as he spoke; the genial, engaging smile of a fond old father. But the eyes, surrounded by laughter crinkles, were as unreadable as two disks of gray slate. They were the eyes of a poker player—or a master con man.

"I don't understand, sir," Hunter said.

"Of course not," Rockford agreed. "It's a hundred light-years back to Earth. Here on Vesta, to make sure there *is* an Earth in the future, you're going to do things never dreamed of by your Terran Space Patrol instructors there. You'll be amazed, my boy."

Hunter said nothing but he felt a growing dislike for the condescending Rockford. Only a few weeks ago President Diskar, himself, had said: *For more than a century these truly valiant men of the Space Patrol have been our unwavering outer guard; have fought and died by legions, that Earth and the other worlds of the Terran Republic might remain free—*

229

"I suppose you know," Rockford said, "that there will be no more than four days in which to stop the Verdam oligarchy from achieving its long-time ambition of becoming big enough to swallow the Terran Republic."

"I know," Hunter answered.

Jardeen, Vesta's companion world, was the key. Jardeen was large and powerful, with a space navy unsurpassed by that of any other single world. A large group of now-neutral worlds would follow Jardeen's lead and Jardeen's alliance with the Verdam People's Worlds would mean the quick end of the Terran Republic. But, if Jardeen could be persuaded to ally with the Terran Republic, the spreading, grasping arms of the Verdam octopus would begin to wither away—

Rockford spoke again:

"Val Boran, Jardeen's Secretary of Foreign Relations, is the man who will really make Jardeen's decision. I know him slightly. Since my public role is that of Acting Ambassador, he agreed—reluctantly—to come to Vesta so that the talks could be on a neutral world. With him will be Verdam's Special Envoy Sonig; a wily little man who has been working on Boran for several weeks. He seems to be succeeding quite well—here's a message I received from Earth early this morning."

Rockford handed him a sheet of the green Hyperspace Communications paper. The message was in code, with Rockford's scribbled translation beneath:

Intelligence reports Verdam forces already massed for attack in Sector A-13, in full expectation of Jardeen's alliance. Anti-Terran propaganda, stressing the New Jardeen Incident, being used in preparation for what will be their claim of "defensive action to protect innocent worlds from Terran aggression." Terran forces will be outnumbered five to one. The urgent necessity of immediate and conclusive counter measure by you on Vesta is obvious.

Hunter handed the paper back, thinking, *It's worse than any of us thought,* and wondering how Supreme Command could ever have entrusted such an important task to a beer-guzzling old man from Strategic Service—a branch so unknown that he had never even heard of it until his briefing the day before he left Earth.

He saw that they had left the desert behind and were going up the long slope of a mountain. "The meeting will be on this mountain?" he asked.

Rockford nodded. "The rustic Royal Retreat. Princess Lyla will be our hostess. Her mother and father were killed in an airplane accident a year ago and she was the only child. You will also get to meet Lord Narf of the Sea Islands, her husband-by-proxy, who regards himself as a rare combination of irresistible woman-killer and rugged man-among-men."

"Husband-by-proxy?" Hunter asked.

"The king worshiped his daughter and his dying request to her was that she promise to marry Lord Narf. Narf's father had been the king's closest friend and the king was sure that his old friend's son would always love and care for Lyla. Lyla dutifully, at once, married Narf by proxy, which is like a legally binding formal engagement under Vestan law. Four days from now the time limit is up and they'll be formally married. Unless she should do the unprecedented thing of renouncing the proxy marriage."

Rockford drained the last of the beer from the can. "Those are the characters involved in our play. I have a plan. That's why I told Space Patrol to send me a brand-new second lieutenant—young, strong, fairly handsome—and expendable. I hope you can be philosophical about the latter."

"Sir," Hunter said, unable to keep a touch of stiffness out of his tone, "it is not exactly unknown in the Space Patrol for a man to die in the line of duty."

"Ah . . . yes." Rockford was regarding him with disturbing amusement. "You are thinking, of course, of dying dramatically behind a pair of blazing blasters. But you will soon learn, my boy, that a soldier's duty is to protect the worlds he represents by whatever actions will produce the best results, no matter how unheroic those actions may be."

"Attention, please." It was the voice of the pilot. "We are now going to land."

Hunter preceded Rockford out of the helicopter and onto the green grass of a small valley, across which tall, red-trunked cloud trees were scattered. Pale gray ghost trees, with knobby, twisted limbs, grew thickly among the cloud trees. There was a group of rustic cabins, connected by gravel paths, and a much larger building which he assumed would be a meeting hall . . .

"Hello."

He turned, and looked into the brown eyes of a girl. Her green skirt and orange blouse made a gay splash of color, her red-brown hair was wind-tumbled and carefree about her shoulders, in her hand was a bouquet of bright spring flowers.

But there was no smile of spring in the dark eyes and the snub-nosed little face was solemn and old beyond its years.

"You're Lieutenant Hunter, aren't you?" she asked in the same low, quiet voice.

"Princess Lyla!" There seemed to be genuine delight in Rockford's greeting as he hurried over. "You're looking more like a queen every day!"

Her face lighted with a smile, making it suddenly young and beautiful. "I'm so glad to see you again, George—"

"Ah . . . good afternoon."

The voice was loud, unpleasantly gravelly. They turned, and Hunter saw a tall, angular man of perhaps forty whose pseudo-genial smile was not compatible with his sour, square-jawed face and calculating little eyes.

He spoke to Rockford. "You're Ambassador Rockford, here to represent the Terran Republic, I believe." He jerked his head toward Princess Lyla, who was no longer smiling. "My wife, Princess Lyla."

"Oh, she and I have been friends since she was ten, Lord Narf."

"And this young man"—Narf glanced at Hunter—"is your aide, I presume. Lyla, did you think to send anyone after their luggage?"

A servant was already carrying their luggage—and cases of Rockford's beer—out of the helicopter. Hunter followed the other toward the cabins. Narf, in the lead, was saying:

" . . . Ridiculously primitive here, now, but I'm having some decent furniture and well-trained servants sent up from my Sea Island estates . . ."

The cabin was large and very comfortable, as Rockford mentioned to Princess Lyla.

"I'm glad you like it," she said. "Val Boran and Envoy Sonig are already here and we'll meet for dinner in the central hall. I thought that if we all got acquainted in a friendly atmosphere like that, it might help a lot to . . ."

"That reminds me"—Narf glanced at his watch—"I promised this Boran he could have a discussion with me—Vesta-Jardeen

tariff policies. I suppose he's already waiting. Come on, Lyla—
it will do you no harm to listen and learn a bit about interplanetary business."

For a long moment she looked at Narf silently, her eye
thoughtful, then she said to Rockford, "If you will excuse us,
please. And be prepared for Alonzo to come bounding in the
minute he learns you're here."

She walked beside Narf to the door and out it, the top of her
dark hair coming just even with his shoulder.

"And that," Rockford said as he settled down in the largest,
softest chair, "was king-to-be Narf, whose business ability is such
that all his inherited Sea Island estates are gone but the one Lyla
saved for him and who owes a total of ten million monetary
units, to everyone from call girls to yacht builders."

"And she is going to marry him?" Hunter asked. "Marry that
jackass and let him bankrupt her kingdom?"

Rockford shrugged. "You may have noticed that she doesn't
look the least bit happy about it—but she is a very conscientious young lady who regards it as her most solemn duty to keep
the promise she made to her father. For her, there is no escape."

"But—"

"Your first duty will be to cultivate a friendship with her. I'm
going to use her, and you, to get what I want."

"*Use* us?"

"Yes. One of the most rigid requirements of a Strategic
Service man's character is that he be completely without one."

Rockford was asleep in his chair an hour later, three empty
beer cans beside him. Hunter watched him, his doubt of
Rockford's competence growing into a conviction. Rockford had
spoken knowingly of his plan—and had done nothing but drink
more beer. Now he was asleep while time—so limited and
precious—went by. He hadn't even bothered to reply to Hunter's
suggestion that perhaps he should call on Val Boran and
counteract some of Envoy Sonig's anti-Terran propaganda.

Hunter came to a decision. If Rockford was still doing nothing
when morning came, he would send an urgent message to
Supreme Command.

He went outside, to find a servant and learn how mail was
handled.

"Rook out!"

Gravel flew as overgrown feet tried to stop, and something like a huge black dog lunged headlong around the corner and into his legs. He went to the ground head first over the animal, acutely aware as he went down of the fascinated interest on the face of a not-so-distant servant.

"I sorry, Rootenant."

He got up, to look down at the doglike animal. There was a concerned expression in its brown eyes and an apologetic grin on its face. He recognized it as one of the natives of the grim starvation world of Altair Four. The Altairians had emigrated to all sections of the galaxy, to earn a living in whatever humble capacity they could fill. Many were empathic.

"I run too fast to meet Mr. Rockford, I guess. Are you hurt, Rootenant?"

He pulled a cloud tree needle out of his hand and looked grimly down into the furry face. "In the future, try to look where you're going."

"Oh, I rook, awr right. I just not see. My name is Aronzo, Rootenant, and I stay here awr the time and guard everything for Princess Ryra. I pleased to meet you and I wirr run errands for you, and do things rike mair your retters, for candy or cookies, which I are not supposed to eat much of, but Princess Ryra say not too many wirr hurt me—"

"Mail letters?" Hunter's animosity vanished. "I'm sorry I was rude, Alonzo—all my fault. I may write a letter to my dear old mother tonight, and if you would mail it for me in the morning—"

Rockford left ahead of Hunter and it was a minute past the appointed time when Hunter reached the meeting hall. He heard Narf's loud voice inside:

"... Boran must have stopped to watch the sunset. Told him I wanted everyone here on time—"

The low voice of Lyla said something and Narf said, "Not necessary for you to defend him, my dear. I made it plain to him."

A new voice spoke from behind Hunter:

"It seems I have annoyed Lord Narf."

He was a tall, black-eyed man, with the dark, saturnine face of an Indian. There was a strange, indefinable air of sadness about him which reminded Hunter of the somber little Princess Lyla.

"You're Val Boran, sir?" he said. "I'm Lieutenant Hunter—"

Inside, Narf sat at the head of the table. On his left was Lyla, then Rockford. On his right was a spidery little man of about fifty, his slicked-back hair so tight against his skull that it gave his head the appearance of a weasel's. His lips were paper-thin under a long nose, like those of a dry and selfish old maid, but the round little eyes darting behind thick glasses were cold and shrewd and missed nothing. He would be Verdam's Special Envoy Sonig. Hunter appraised him as a man very dangerous in his own deceptive way.

A servant showed them to their places at the table. Rockford and Val Boran exchanged greetings. The moment everyone was seated, Narf said, "Dinner tonight will—"

"Excuse me," Lyla said, "but Mr. Sonig hasn't yet met—"

"Oh ... the young fellow there—" Narf gestured with his hand. "Rockford's aide. Now, ring the chime, Lyla. Those forest stag steaks are already getting cold. I killed the beast myself, gentlemen, just this morning; a long-range running shot that required a bit more than luck ..."

The dinner was excellent, but no one seemed to notice. Narf was absorbed in the story of his swift rise to eminence in the Vestan Space Guard. There were humorous incidents:

" ... Can't understand why, but I seem to attract women like a magnet. I'm strictly the masculine type of male and I approve of this but it can be a blasted nuisance when you're an ensign going up fast and your commander finds one of your blondes stowed away in your compartment ..."

And there were scenes of tense drama:

" ... Made a boyhood vow that I'd never settle for anything less than to always be a man among men. Seem to have succeeded rather well. When I saw the crew was almost to the snapping point from battle tension I knew that as commander I'd have to set the example that would inspire."

Hunter recalled Rockford's words of a few hours before: "*Narf got to be commander, finally, but only because he was the son of the king's best friend. His record is very mediocre.*"

Princess Lyla tried three times to start a conversation of general

interest and was drowned out by Narf each time. Sonig's pretense of being spellbound by Narf's stories was belied by the
way his eyes kept darting from Rockford to Val Boran. Val's own
attention kept shifting from Narf to the silent Lyla, whose down-
cast eyes betrayed her discouragement. She watched Val from
under her eyelashes, to look away whenever their eyes met, and
Hunter wondered if she was ashamed because Narf had given
Sonig the seat of honor that should have belong to Val.

Of course, Narf's own position at the head of the table was
actually Lyla's.

" . . . So there's no substitute for competent, unwavering leadership," Narf was saying. "Received a citation for that one."

Sonig nodded appreciatively. "Your military record well illus-
trates the fact that the tensions of danger and battle can bring
forth in a competent leader the highest kind of courage. But it
seems to me that these same circumstances, if the leader is
frightened or incompetent, can easily produce hysterical actions
with disastrous consequences. Is this true, your lordship?"

Rockford was watching Sonig intently and Hunter saw that
there was an eager anticipation in Sonig's manner.

"You are quite right," Narf answered. "I've always had the ability to remain cool in any crisis. Very important. Let a commander
get rattled and he may give any kind of an order. Like the New
Jardeen Incident."

A frozen silence followed the last five words. Hunter thought,
So that's what the little weasel was fishing for . . .

Rockford quietly laid down his fork. Val's face turned grim.
Lyla looked up in quick alarm and said to Narf:

"Let's not—"

"Don't misunderstand me, gentlemen," Narf's loud voice went
on. "*I* believe the commander of the Terran cruiser wouldn't have
ordered it to fire upon the Verdam cruiser over a neutral world
such as New Jardeen if he had been his rational self. Cold-war
battle nerves. So he shot down the Verdam cruiser and its nuclear
converters exploded when it fell in the center of Colony City.
Force of a hydrogen bomb—forty thousand innocent people gone
in a microsecond. Not the commander's fault really—fault of the
military system that failed to screen out its unstable officers."

"Yes, your lordship. But is it possible"—Sonig spoke very
thoughtfully—"for a political power, which is of such a nature

that it must have a huge military force to maintain its existence, to thoroughly screen all its officers? So many officers are
required— Can there ever be any assurance that such tragedies
won't occur again and again, until a majority of worlds combine
in demanding an end to aggression and war?"

Rockford spoke to the grim Val:

"I know, sir, that your sister was among the lost in Colony
City. I am sorry. For the benefit of Mr. Sonig and Lord Narf, I
would like to mention that the Verdam cruiser fired upon the
Terran cruiser over neutral New Jardeen in open violation of
Galactic Rule. An atmospheric feedback of the Verdam cruiser's
own space blasters tore out its side and caused it to fall. The
Terran cruiser never fired."

"But Mr. Rockford—" Sonig spoke very courteously. "Isn't it
true that certain safety devices prevent atmospheric feedback?"

"They do—unless accidentally or purposely disconnected."

Sonig raised his eyebrows. "You imply a created incident, sir?"

"It doesn't matter," Val Boran said. His tone was as grim as
his face and it was obvious he did not believe Rockford's
explanation. "Colony City is a field of fused glass, now, its people
are gone, and no amount of debating can ever bring them back."

The dismal dinner was finally over. Rockford stopped outside
the door of their cabin to fill and light his pipe.

"It was a profitable evening," he said to Hunter. "I can start
planning in detail now—after a little beer, that is."

He'll go to sleep after he drinks his beer, Hunter thought, *and
there will never be any plan unless I—*

Soft footsteps came up the path behind them. It was Princess
Lyla.

"I want to apologize," she said. "I just told Val . . . Mr. Boran
the same thing."

Her face was a pale oval in the starlight, her eyes dark shadows.
"I'm sorry my husband mentioned the New Jardeen incident."

"That's all right, Lyla," Rockford said. "No harm was done."

"He's an ex-military man, and I guess it's his nature to be more
forthright than tactful."

"You certainly can't condemn him for that," Rockford said. "In
fact, he's an extraordinary teller of entertaining stories. It was
a most enjoyable evening."

❖   ❖   ❖

"And, in a way, it was," Rockford said when she was gone and they were in the cabin. He was seated in the softest chair, a can of beer in his hand, as usual.

Hunter thought of the way she had looked in the starlight and said, "Why did she let that windbag sit at the head of the table and ruin the meeting that she had arranged?"

"He'll soon be her husband—I suppose she feels she should be loyal to him."

"But—"

"But what?"

"Nothing. It's none of my business."

"Oh?" Rockford smiled in a way Hunter did not like. "You think so, eh?"

Hunter changed the subject. "Are you going to start talking to Boran to undo the damage Narf and Sonig have done?"

"It would be a waste of time, my boy. Val Boran's mind is already made up."

"Then what are you going to do?"

"Drink six cans of beer and go to sleep."

"I thought you had a plan."

"I have, a most excellent plan."

"What is it?"

"You'd scream like a banshee if you knew. You'll learn—if you manage to live that long."

Rockford was sound asleep an hour later, snoring gently. Hunter sat thinking, hearing the steady murmur of a voice coming from Val Boran's cabin. Sonig's voice—using every means of persuasion he could think of, at the moment capitalizing on the New Jardeen incident and Boran's withheld grief over the sister he had lost.

And the Terran Republic's representative was sprawled fat and mindless in a fog of beer fumes.

Hunter hesitated no longer. The fate of Earth and the Terran Republic hung in the balance and time was desperately limited—if there was now any time at all.

He took paper and pen and began the urgent message to Supreme Command, headed, TOP EMERGENCY. It would be sent via Hyperspace Communications from the city and would span the hundred light-years within seconds.

❖   ❖   ❖

He was up before Rockford the next morning, and went out into the bright sunlight. He looked hopefully for Alonzo, not wanting to be seen mailing the letter in person. Rockford, despite his drunken stupors, could be shrewdly observant and he might deduce the contents of the letter before Supreme Command ever received it.

He was some distance from the cabin when he heard the pound of padded feet behind him.

"Rootenant," Alonzo had the grin of a genial canine idiot. "Do you want me to mair your retter to your dear ore mother?"

"Yes, I have the letter right here."

"O.K. I got to hurry, because the mair hericopter reaves right away. I charge six fig cookies or three candy bars or—"

"Here—take it and run—and try not to slobber all over it."

They were served breakfast in the cabin. Afterward, Rockford went for a brief talk with Princess Lyla. He came back and settled down in the easy-chair, his pipe in his hand.

"Your morning's duty won't be at all unpleasant," he said. "The obnoxious and repulsive things will begin to happen to you later. Maybe this afternoon."

"What do you mean?"

"This morning you will go for a walk with Princess Lyla and discuss changing the Vestan Space Guard into a force along Terran Space Patrol lines. Narf is still in bed, by the way."

Rockford added, "I'll give you a bit of sage advice, for your own good—try not to fall in love with her."

Hunter and Princess Lyla sat together on the high hill, their backs against the red trunk of a cloud tree. On the mountain's slope to their right lay the dark and junglelike Tiger Forest— he wondered if it was true that the savage tree tigers never left its borders—while the toylike cabins of the camp were below them. The mountain's slope dropped on down to the deserts, beyond which were other mountains, far away and translucent azure.

"It was George who suggested we come up here," she said. "He knows I do that often when the responsibilities of being queen of a world—I'm such an ordinary and untalented person—

become too much for me. I always feel better when I sit up here and look down on the mountains and deserts."

"Yes," he said politely.

"A ruling princess can be so alone," she said. "That's why I appreciate George's friendship so much—it's never because of any ulterior motive but because he likes me."

I'm going to use her, and you, to get what I want.

He looked at her, at the lines of sadness on the face that was too old for its years, felt the way she was so grateful to Rockford for what was only a cold-blooded pretense of friendship, and the dislike for Rockford increased. He could not force himself to speak civilly of Rockford so he changed the subject:

"I understand you wanted to talk to me about the Space Guard?"

"Yes. Even a neutral world can't feel safe these days and George suggested that."

"I'll be glad to help all I can. Of course, the change will require time."

"I can understand that. They say you Space Patrol officers begin training at sixteen, after passing almost impossible qualification tests."

"The tests can seem extremely difficult to a farm boy from Kansas. I—"

"Kansas?" Her eyes lighted with interest. "My grandmother was from Kansas! She used to tell me about the green plains of grain in the spring, and how different they were from the deserts of Vesta . . ."

It was almost noon when he took her hand and helped her to her feet, realizing guiltily that they had talked all morning without ever getting back to the cold, dry facts of military efficiency.

"It was nice to talk up here this morning," she said. She looked down at the cabins and the shadow fell again across her face. "But nothing down there has been changed by it, has it?"

He held to her hand longer than was necessary as they went down the steep part of the hill. She did not seem to mind.

When they reached her cabin she said, "It's still a little while until lunch—time enough for you to give me a rough outline of the Space Guard change."

Everything inside the cabin was feminine. None of Narf's

possessions were visible. There was a heavy door leading into Narf's half of the cabin, with a massive lock. Hunter wondered if it was left unlocked at night, thought of Narf's sour face and leering little eyes, and found the thought repulsive.

The answer to his conjecture came with the entrance of a servant as they seated themselves.

"By your leave, your highness," the servant said, bowing, "I came to make Lord Narf a key for that inner door."

"A key?" There was alarm in her tone. "But we're not married—not yet!"

A puzzled expression came to the man's face. "Lord Narf told me, your highness, that you had ordered the duplicate key made and given to him before evening. I found I could not do this without first borrowing your key for a pattern."

There was a frightened look in her eyes as they went to the door and back to the servant. "*No . . . don't try to make a key!*"

"Yes, your highness." The servant bowed and turned away.

A familiar gravelly voice spoke from behind them:

"Ah . . . an unscheduled little meeting, I see!"

It was Narf, anger on his face, already within the doorway as the servant went out it.

"We were going to talk about the Space Guard," Lyla said in an emotionless tone. "Lieutenant Hunter has promised to show how Space Patrol methods will improve it and—"

"By a coincidence, Sonig and I were discussing military matters only a few minutes ago," Narf said. He looked at Hunter. "I'm afraid that Sonig and I agree that the Terran Space Guard is quite out of date, now. *The* fighting force of the galaxy is the Verdam's Peoples Guards."

Narf spoke to Lyla, "You may go ahead and talk with this lieutenant if you wish to, but it's a waste of time. I'm arranging to have Sonig send Peoples Guards officers here to supervise the rebuilding of the Space Guard.

"And now"—there was insinuation in Narf's tone as he spoke to Hunter—"I have to give Sonig a demonstration of my skill with weapons. He insists on it—he has heard of several of my modest feats."

Narf left the door open behind him so that by turning his head as he walked, he could see the two inside.

"I suppose I might as well go," Hunter said.

Lyla did not answer. She sat motionless, staring unseeingly before her, and he wondered if she was thinking of how very soon Narf would be king and his authority as great as hers.

She did not notice when he quietly left the room.

Rockford was waiting in the cabin, still in the easy-chair. "Well," he said, "what do you think of her?"

Hunter tried to keep the personal dislike out of his coldly formal reply:

"If you refer to your suggestion that I not make love to her, sir, I can assure you that such a suggestion was never necessary. I happen to have a code of ethics."

"I didn't say 'make love.' I said, 'fall in love.' That's quite ethical. Did you complete your discussion with her?"

"Well . . . no."

"You must do that this afternoon, then. Can't let anything as important as that be delayed."

Hunter stared at him, trying to find one small grain of sanity in Rockford's actions. The Verdam empire already had Jardeen within its grasp; add Vesta, and the end for Earth was inevitable. And Rockford slept, and drank beer, and regarded it as very important that the Vestan Space Guard discussions—of a change that Narf would never permit—be continued without delay.

He walked slowly into his own room. In the nightmare situation of frustration there was one single sane and stable conviction for his mind to cling to: Supreme Command would by now have received his message and shot back the reply that would relieve Rockford of his command. Perhaps it wasn't yet too late—

Then his mind reeled as a new conviction struck it.

There was a sheet of paper on his bed—a message.

His message!

. . . SITUATION EXTREMELY CRITICAL . . . VAL BORAN ALREADY CONVINCED BY SONIG'S PROPAGANDA . . . MUST REPORT ROCKFORD IS UTTERLY INCOMPETENT, HIS MIND AND WILL DESTROYED BY ALCOHOL . . . REPEAT: ROCKFORD IS DOING NOTHING, HIS MIND DESTROYED BY ALCOHOL . . .

The words screamed up at him and he felt the sickness of one who sees the last faint hope shattered and gone. All was lost, now . . .

He went outside, feeling a savage desire for violence rising above the sickness.

"Rootenant!" Alonzo came bounding to meet him and slid to a halt with his saucer feet scattering gravel and the idiotic grin on his face. "I mair your retter and you owe me six fig cook—"

It occurred to Hunter that it was not Alonzo that should be punished. He, Hunter, was the one who deserved execution for ever entrusting anything so important as the message to an imbecilic animal.

He said with old distinctness:

"The . . . letter . . . is . . . inside."

"Oh?" Alonzo blinked. "I sure mair something, awr right. After Mr. Rockford correct it."

"*Correct it?*"

"Oh, sure. Mr. Rockford, he up rong before you this morning to find me and say you are writing a retter rast night and I must bring it by for him to make awr your mistakes over again."

So Rockford was watching all the time, pretending to be in a drunken sleep . . .

"Rootenant—" Alonzo shifted his big feet impatiently. "You stirr owe me six fig—"

Hunter swung around and strode away, afraid he might decide to choke the animal after all. A culture of twenty worlds was the same as already destroyed, and he was held in a maddening quagmire of helplessness by a crafty alcoholic and a dog with the mind of a small child.

"Ah . . . my boy!" Rockford came out of the cabin, beaming as though nothing had ever happened. "Look to your left, among those ghost trees—Narf is demonstrating his quick-draw skill to Sonig. Narf is supposed to be a very dangerous man, you know."

Hunter looked, and saw Narf whipping up the blunt, ugly spread-beam blaster—known to soldiers as the Coward's Special, because at short range it could not miss and would always cripple and blind a man for life even though it would not always kill him. Sonig was standing by, nodding his weasel head and smiling in open admiration.

"Of course," Rockford said, "Sonig isn't mentioning the needle gun all Verdam envoys carry up their sleeves. He's flattering Narf's ego for a reason—he intends to have Vesta, as well as Jardeen, sewed up for the Verdam empire when he leaves here."

"And so far as I can see," Hunter said coldly, "Sonig never is going to have anything vaguely resembling intelligent resistance to his plans."

"Ah, yes . . . so far as you can see," Rockford agreed amiably. "But you obey my order to take Lyla for another walk and everything will turn out all right. In fact, I'll speak to her about that right now."

Hunter stared after Rockford as he walked away. There could be no possible shred of doubt—Rockford was insane!

The breeze shifted and the voice of Narf came:

" . . . Certainly no weapon for a timid man, this spread-beam blaster. Have to meet the enemy man-to-man at close range."

"In that respect, too," Sonig said, "you remind me of our great General Paluk. His skill in hand-to-hand combat was something that—"

"Rootenant—"

Hunter quivered and steeled himself.

"Rootenant—" Alonzo came to a flopping halt beside him. "I terr Princess Ryra and she say I are bad to be mad at you. So I not mad, even if you didn't give me my pay."

"Thank you," Hunter said acidly. "I was deeply disturbed by your resentment."

"Oh, I know, you don't rike me. But I think you not as mean as you act. But Rord Narf—he is. I terr you, he awready mad enough to kirr you."

"What? Lord Narf wants to kill me?"

"Oh, he know you hord Princess Ryra's hand awrmost awr the way down the hirr this morning. Mr. Sonig, he see you, and he run and terr Rord Narf and Mr. Boran, too."

"But I was only helping her down the hill."

"Rord Narf, he are going to say mean things about it to Princess Ryra, too. I know. He are awrways saying mean things to my Princess Ryra."

Alonzo sighed, a sound strangely humanlike in its sadness.

"Who wirr watch over my Princess Ryra after she marred Rord Narf? He said, 'The first thing to go around here wirr be that stupid brabber-mouth animar that are not worth what it costs to feed it.' I think maybe he are afraid that if he ever hit my

Princess Ryra, I wirr kirr him." The brown eyes looked up at Hunter, and suddenly they were unlike he had ever seen them; cold with deliberate decision. "I wirr, too."

Hunter was still standing by the cabin, thinking of what Alonzo had said, when Rockford returned.

"I also stopped by to see Val Boran," Rockford said. "While you're off with Lyla, we'll go to the city. Lyla is giving us free access to the Royal Library and the records of a neutral world carry more weight than anything I could say. Not that it's going to change his mind any—but it will give me a chance to work on him in another way."

Rockford went into the cabin as Val Boran came up the path, Princess Lyla walking beside him. She was saying, " . . . And anything we have in the library is yours for the asking."

They were close enough for Hunter to see her expression as she looked up at Val and added with what seemed a touch of wistfulness, "I'll be glad to go in with you and Mr. Rockford and do what I can to help if you want me to."

"Lyla"—it was the grating voice of Narf who seemed to have the ability to materialize anywhere—"I'm sure the man knows his business. Besides, I want to talk to you about something as soon as I have finished my discussion with Mr. Sonig."

With that, Narf started on toward his cabin. Sonig, close behind him, paused long enough to bow to Lyla and say with the meaningless smile, "Good afternoon, Princess Lyla. Your husband was just demonstrating his marvelous skill with weapons. I would very much dislike"—the little eyes darted to Hunter and back again—"being the man who aroused his lordship's wrath."

Then Sonig followed Narf, with one last flickering glance at Hunter to see how the remark had fallen.

Rockford came out of the cabin with his brief case and said to Val, "Are we ready to go?"

"I just told Val"—Lyla spoke quickly—"that I would be glad to go along and help any way I can." The words were addressed to Rockford but her eyes were on Val, with the same wistful expression. "Do you want me to?"

Val answered her with cool, formal courtesy: "The librarian can find all the records we need, Princess Lyla, without our interrupting your schedule for the day or your discussion with your husband. Thank you very much."

For an instant Lyla's face had the hurt expression of a child rebuffed without reason. Then she looked away and Val turned to Rockford and said, "I'm ready when you are, sir."

Lyla watched them walk away and she was still watching when the helicopter had lifted into the air and faded from sight.

Hunter hesitated, then spoke to her:

"I understand you want to talk more about the Space Guard, Princess Lyla?"

"*Princess* Lyla!" Her lips curled as she turned to face him and she seemed to spit the words at him in sudden, unexpected resentment. "I love the meaningless sound of my official figure-head title! It's so much better than being regarded as a living person with feelings that can be hurt!"

"But Princ . . . I mean—" He floundered, not quite sure what had caused her reaction.

She made a visible effort to compose herself. "I'm sorry," she said. "I suppose my . . . husband . . . is quite right; an immature female has no business trying to rule a world and the sooner the marriage is confirmed, the sooner a competent man can take over the job."

"No," he said. "I think—"

He decided that what he thought had better be left unsaid.

"I'll"—she looked toward the cabin she shared with Narf— "let you know when we can talk."

She went back toward the cabin, walking slowly. From inside Narf's half of it came the sound of Narf's voice as he spoke to Sonig:

" . . . Of course, this collection of heads is nothing compared with what I have in the Sea Islands . . . but some interesting stories here . . . take that snow fox there . . ."

Hunter sighed, and saw that Lyla had stopped before her door, as though dreading to enter. Narf's voice droned on:

" . . . Only wounded, so I finished it with a knife. Even with its heart half cut out, it still wanted to live . . . beautiful pelt . . . coat for Janalee, the strip-tease queen . . . always had a way with women—Lyla could tell you that . . . had my pick of hundreds but I'm letting her be my choice . . ."

He saw Lyla half lift her hand, as in some mute gesture of

protest, then she turned and walked swiftly away; up the path
that led into the ghost trees, and out of sight.

He waited, but she did not come back. He went into his
cabin and moved about restlessly, hearing again Narf's sadism-
and-sex boasting and seeing again how she turned and almost
ran from it—

"*Rootenant!*"

Alonzo was panting, a look of frantic appeal in his eyes.

"Prease herp me ... Princess Ryra ... she wirr die!"

He felt his heart lurch. "She's hurt?" he demanded, and was
already on his way to the door.

"She are about to cry and she are going to where the tree tigers
riv. They wirr kirr her—prease come with me!"

He asked no more questions but went out the door and up
the path, Alonzo running ahead of him.

The ghost trees grew thinner as they went up the mountain's
slope, and the blue-green fernlike trees of the tiger forest began
to appear. They grew thicker and thicker, until the ground was
black with their shadows and the midday sunlight was filtered out
by the foliage overhead. Alonzo was trailing her, his nose to the
ground, and Hunter hurried close behind him, watching for the
red-and-white of the clothes she was wearing and hoping they
would not find her too late.

They were deep in the forest when they found her.

She was standing motionless in the center of a clearing, facing
away from him and looking as small and alone as a lost child. She
seemed to be waiting ...

He realized for the first time how alone she really was, with
only a doglike alien, Alonzo, to love her or care what might
happen to her, and with a future she could not bear to face. But
Rockford had been wrong when he had said, *For her, there is
no escape.*

There was escape for her. She had only to wait, as she was
waiting now, and it would come in the windlike whisper of a tiger's
rush through the grass behind her ...

He hurried to her. She turned, and he saw the stains of tears
now dry on her face and in her eyes the darkness of utter defeat.

"I was afraid you might get hurt, Lyla—"

Then, seemingly without volition on his part, he put his arms around her and she was clinging to him and crying in muffled sobs and trying to say something about "*I didn't think anybody cared . . .*"

It was some time later, when her crying was finished, that he was reminded of the tigers by Alonzo:

"Rootenant—awr the time, some tigers are coming croser and croser. We better get her out of here, Rootenant, before they find us."

Lyla looked down at Alonzo. "Thank you, Alonzo, for watching over me and . . . and—" Her voice caught and she dropped to her knees and hugged the shaggy head tight against her.

Hunter watched ahead, Lyla beside him as they went through the dense trees. Alonzo walked soft-footed behind them, watching the rear. When they came to the first ghost trees and the dwindling of the tiger trees, Hunter thought it safe to walk slower and talk to her.

"I saw you go," he said. "I didn't know where until Alonzo came running to tell me."

"I heard him bragging about killing, and about his women—I was weak, wasn't I?"

"Weak?"

"I was afraid to face the future, just because it isn't to be exactly like I thought I wanted."

"What was the kind you wanted, Lyla?"

"Oh . . . I guess I wanted a husband who could see me only, and children, and evenings together in the flower garden, and, well, all the silly, sentimental little things that mean so much to a woman."

He thought, *Even with its heart half cut out, it still wanted to live . . . Coat for Janalee . . . the strip-tease queen . . .*

They passed through the last of the tiger trees and she said, "We're safe, now. The tigers never attack anyone outside their forest."

She was walking slowly and he said, "We should get on back before you're missed, shouldn't we?"

"Who would miss me?" she asked. "So long as I remain physically intact for the marriage night, who cares where or why I went away?"

There was the cold blackness of winter in her eyes as she spoke, and in her voice the first undertone of brass. He saw that this was already the beginning of the change that Narf would make in her; the transformation of a girl young and wanting to love and be loved into a hard and cynical woman.

He put his arm around her shoulder, thinking that he should tell her that *he* cared and that she must never let Narf change her.

"Lyla, I—"

He realized how futile and foolish the words would sound. She would marry Narf, he would return to Earth, and they would never meet again. There were no words for him to speak on this last walk together, no way to tell her that he wanted to help her, to protect and care for her. No way to express the feeling inside him . . .

He did what seemed as natural under the circumstances as it had been for him to put his arm around her in the clearing. He tilted up her face and bent his head to kiss her.

And walked with jarring impact into the knobby elbow of a ghost tree limb.

The sun was down and dusk was darkening the camp when they arrived back at her cabin.

"Thank you, Dale," she said. Her hand squeezed his arm. "I didn't know I had a friend . . . but now we'll have to be strangers because—"

Gravel crunched loudly on one of the paths in the ghost trees and they looked back, to see Narf and Sonig coming, walking swiftly. Even at the distance, there was anger like a red aura about Narf.

"Well," Lyla said softly, "here comes my medicine."

Sonig stopped at his own cabin, to stand just within the doorway, watching. Narf strode on and stopped before Hunter and Lyla, his face twisted with savage hatred as he looked at Hunter. He spoke to Lyla with grating vehemence:

"You've done an excellent job of making an ass of yourself—and of me—haven't you? Come on in the cabin!"

Narf seized her by the arm, towering over her as he jerked her around toward the door. Hunter stepped quickly forward, feeling the hot flash of his own anger, but there was the paleness of Lyla's face as she looked back, an appeal on it that said, *No!* He stopped, realizing that Narf would not physically harm the woman who would make him king of Vesta, and that any interference on his part would only make everything the harder for her.

He watched the two go into the cabin—into Lyla's half—and Narf slammed the door shut behind them. There followed the quick bang of windows being closed, and then Narf's muffled tirade began: " . . . *May think I'm a fool . . . I'm going to tell you a few things . . .*"

Sonig was still standing within his doorway. Hunter knew, without seeing it, that the thin-lipped smile would be on Sonig's face.

He turned and walked back to his own cabin. There was nothing he could do but withdraw—and listen from a distance and be ready to act if it seemed she was in danger.

He sat on his doorstep in the darkness, hearing occasional phrases in Narf's unrelenting abuse. One was: "*So prim you had to countermand my order for a key to that lock—then you went out to play with that second lieutenant . . .*"

Alonzo materialized out of the darkness, coming as silently as a shadow. He was no longer the bumbling clown. The idiotic grin was gone and his eyes were green fire, slanted and catlike, his teeth flashing white in a snarl as he looked back toward the sound of Narf's voice.

"She are *my* Princess Ryra," Alonzo said. "He are cursing her. If he ever hurt her, I wirr tear out his throat and his river."

"He won't hurt her, Alonzo," Hunter said, wishing he could be sure. "He'll only use words on her."

"He never ask her *why* she run away—he onry curse her and threaten her because she embarrass him."

"Embarrass him?"

"He and Sonig, they see you coming out of the forest with your arm around her. They watch with high-power grasses."

"But there was nothing wrong in that—"

"That are what Princess Ryra say. She say you onry put your arm around her because she are stirr scared of the tigers. And then he say, what about the other? And he cawr her awrful bad names."

"What other?"

"Oh, when you are bending down to kiss Princess Ryra and are wawrking into tree."

He gulped. *"They saw that?"*

"Oh, sure. Rord Narf are so mad he want to kirr you right then but Sonig say, 'Wait, I have a pran.' Then Sonig say, 'It are too bad we don't have a camera—we could have made that rootenant the raffing stock of forty worlds.'"

The thought made Hunter gulp again.

"What was Sonig's plan that Narf told Lyla about?" he asked.

"Oh, he not terr *her*. I hear Sonig terr Rord Narf when I spy. Sonig say, 'Tomorrow we be friendry and we ret those two go for another wawrk in the woods. And we have cameras with terescope lens and when they kiss and hug we take moving pictures.'"

"Why, the gutter-bred rat—"

"And Rord Narf say, 'That is what we wirr do. And then I wirr kirr him as soon as we have the pictures and she wirr have to toe the mark from then on because if I pubricry show the pictures of what she did, she wirr be ashamed to show her face anywhere on Vesta.'"

"Why, the—" He could not think of a suitable expression.

"And then Sonig say, 'To make sure she go out tomorrow, you bawr her out good so she wirr want to cry on the rootenant's shourder again.' And Rord Narf say, 'I wirr be very grad to terr the two-timing hussy what I think of her, don't worry.'"

"Why, she was only a scared girl and that rat thinks she—"

"... Your promise to your dying father" Narf's voice came in accusation. *"He's gone now, and you can betray him, too! Why don't you go all the way in your deceptions ... your father will never know ..."*

Alonzo said, "I think I go back and stay croser to her cabin, Rootenant."

It was an hour later, and Narf's voice had settled to a low, steady growling, when Hunter heard a helicopter settle down near the camp. A minute later, Val Boran was outlined momentarily in the doorway of the cabin he shared with Sonig. There followed the exchange of a few words—interrogation in Val's tone—and then the sound of Sonig's voice alone, which continued for minute after minute.

Sonig is telling him all about it, Hunter thought, *including my walking into that tree. But there won't be one word in sympathy with Lyla.*

Sonig's story ended and Hunter saw Val leave the cabin. He came straight up the path toward Hunter, looming tall in the darkness as he stopped before him. There was the pale gleam of metal in Val's belt—a blaster. His voice came cold and flat:

"I want to talk to you, Lieutenant."

Hunter sighed, thinking, *I suppose he wants to kill me, too.*

He got up and said, "We'll go inside. Shut the door behind you—I don't want your friend straining his ears to hear us."

Val sat tall even in the chair, his face like a carving in a dark granite and his eyes as bright and hard.

"I understand that you took Princess Lyla into the tiger forest today." Val's hand was very near the blaster. "I understand you then played the role of affectionate rescuer."

"Do you believe that story?" Hunter asked.

"Do you have a different one?"

"You might ask Lyla. Or Alonzo. Alonzo is the one who came to me for help when he saw she was going out to die."

"To die?" A startled expression came into the black eyes. "She *wanted* to die?"

"I'll tell you what happened," Hunter said, and told him the story, omitting only the embarrassing kissing incident and knowing that Sonig had not.

Val was silent for a while after Hunter finished speaking, then he said, "It isn't for me to comment upon Lord Narf's character or actions. She is his wife by her own choice. But the thought of someone else taking her out and—"

"I know. It wasn't so." Then Hunter added, "You think a great deal of her, don't you?"

Val's face hardened and Hunter thought he would not answer. Then he smiled a little, even though without humor, and said:

"Since I came here to kill you if I thought you deserved it, I suppose I am obligated to answer your question. My regard for Princess Lyla is the respectful one that any civilized man would have for another man's wife."

There was an unintended implication in the statement and Hunter made a conjecture:

"You and Princess Lyla were engaged—how long ago?"

There was surprise on Val's face, and something like pain quickly masked. "So she's already making it public information?"

"No. I learned of it from . . . other sources. I don't know, of course, why you persuaded her to break the engagement—that's none of my business, anyway."

"No," Val said. "It's none of your business. I'll tell you this: *I* didn't ask her to break the engagement. But so long as that was what she wanted, I certainly wasn't going to beg her to change her mind."

Val stood up to go. "If you don't mind, I would rather you said nothing to Princess Lyla about this visit tonight. I'm afraid my misplaced sense of chivalry would make me look like a fool to her."

Then, as an after thought, Val added, "Mr. Rockford had further business in the city."

It was late when Narf finally left Lyla's part of the cabin. He went to the cabin occupied by Val and Sonig, aroused Sonig, and the two of them went to the helicopter field. Hunter heard the helicopter leaving for the city a few minutes later. Val's cabin remained dark and after a while, the light in Lyla's cabin went out.

He went to bed, but not to sleep. Over and over, a lonely little Princess Lyla clung to him for comfort, crying, while he held her close. He twisted and turned restlessly as he thought of the hours she had sat alone and unloved while Narf poured out his hatred and fury on her.

There was a yearning for her, a desire to hold her and always protect her, that would not let him sleep. And he realized the reason why.

He thought miserably, *I'm in love with her!*

Rockford was in bed, snoring loudly, with six empty beer cans on the floor beside him, when Hunter got up. He went outside and found Alonzo waiting for him.

"They got it awr pranned to kirr you for sure today, Rootenant."

"How?" he asked.

"Rast night, Rord Narf and Sonig go to the city and Rord Narf, he hire four bad-rooking men with brasters, and Sonig hire four more that are his countrymen, and they bring these men back and now they are hiding in the woods. And they awrso bring back movie cameras with terescope renses. And Rord Narf raff

and say he wirr marry Princess Ryra today before your dead body
is even coor."

"Oh?" Hunter said. He thought of the snoring Rockford and
his words of two days before: *If you manage to live that long.*
How, he wondered, could the lazy old drunkard have made such
an accurate guess?

"And then," Alonzo said, "Rord Narf wake up Princess Ryra—
onry I know she wasn't asreep—and he terr her he ruv her and
have awready made awr the arrangement for them to get married today, right after runch. And he terr her she is right about
the Space Guard and she wirr have until runch to tawrk to you
about it."

There was the sound of Narf's door opening and closing and
Alonzo said, "I go now—Rord Narf might guess that I are terring
you things."

A few minutes later Narf and Sonig came down the path
toward Hunter. Both carried packsacks—the cameras, of
course—and both carried long-range rifle blasters.

"Good morning, Lieutenant!" Narf was smiling and pseudo-
genial again. "About last night—sometimes a man has to be stern
with his wife to impress her. Very foolish thing she did—might
have been killed. I'm afraid I was so badly shaken with worry
over her that I didn't even thank you for bringing her back."

"A beautiful morning, lieutenant!" Sonig was smiling, coming as close to beaming as the nature of his face would permit.
"Lord Narf is going to take me stag hunting this morning—I'll
get some lessons from a master. Did you ever see his lordship's
collection of heads? Amazing!"

"But it seems a sportsman's collection is never quite complete,"
Narf said. He was still smiling but the hatred was burning like
a fire in his eyes as he looked at Hunter. "There's one more head
I must have—I intend to get it this morning."

Narf and Sonig were gone when Lyla came out of her cabin,
her face pale and drawn. Val came out of his cabin and the two
spoke to each other in greeting. There was a silence, in which
neither seemed to know what to say.

Finally, awkwardly, Val said, "I heard about yesterday, Lyla. Why
did you go into the tiger forest?"

"Oh . . . I was just walking, I guess, and didn't notice where."

"You went there to die, didn't you?"

"I . . . when you have nothing left—" Then she lifted her head in a proud gesture and said, "Should it matter to you?"

For a moment Val had the look of a man struck. Then it was gone and he said in an emotionless voice:

"No. I was asking about something that is only your husband's business. I won't do it again."

He turned away, back to his cabin.

"Val—" She took a quick step after him, the proud air gone and her arms outstretched. "I didn't mean—"

He turned back, his tone politely questioning.

"Yes?"

"I only wanted—" Then her arms dropped and the life went out of her voice. "What does it matter . . . what does anything matter?"

She hurried into her cabin and the door closed behind her.

Rockford spoke from the doorway behind Hunter:

"Well, my boy, are you ready for your day's duties?"

He followed Rockford inside, where Rockford settled down in the easy-chair and yawned.

"I had a rather busy night," he said. "Certain events occurred yesterday afternoon which forced me to change my own plans to some extent. Or to set them ahead a day, I should say."

He made an effort to put the vision of Lyla from his mind and asked, "Did you make any progress with Val Boran?"

"No, I'm afraid not. Of course, I didn't expect to." Rockford yawned again. "There was another message from Supreme Command. The situation is getting worse. Which reminds me of your Duty For The Day and the fact that if you can live through it, you will have it made."

He's my superior, Hunter thought. *He's supposed to outrank a Space Patrol General—and he's amused by the situation he's here to remedy.*

"Right now," Rockford said, "Lyla faces a grim future and feels like she doesn't have a friend in the world. She needs a shoulder to cry on. You will take her for a walk and supply that shoulder."

Somehow, even though the order had nothing to do with the Terran-Verdam crisis, he did not have the heart to object. She had been crying before she even reached her door. Later, after he had comforted her, he would demand that Rockford get down to determined effort on the Verdam problem. No more than an hour would be lost by that . . .

"Yes, sir," he said. "But in the interests of Princess Lyla's safety, I had better talk to her in her cabin. Alonzo saw Narf and Sonig bring back eight—"

"Professional killers, to dispose of you," Rockford finished. "I know all about it, and I know that Narf took time last night to spend an hour with his favorite girl friend and brag even to her that he was going to marry Lyla today before your dead body had time to get cool.

"But you just take Lyla for another walk and you will cause the beginning of the end for the Verdam Peoples Worlds. You will go down in history, my boy, as the man who saved the Terran Republic."

Hunter went out the door, again feeling a feverish sense of unreality. He was to go forth and get blasted into hamburger and by some mysterious process known only to Rockford, the Verdam empire would contritely start collapsing . . .

He did not knock on her door. He did not think of it as a violation of her privacy. She would be feeling too alone and unwanted to care.

She was not crying as he had thought she would be. She was standing by the window, staring down at the gray, distant desert, her eyes as bleakly empty as it.

"Hello, Lyla," he said.

"Hello, Dale. I was just thinking; this is the day that I, as a woman, should always have dreamed about"—she tried to smile, and failed, and the brass came into her voice—"my wedding day!"

"Alonzo told me about it."

It seemed to him he should add something, such as to wish her happiness—but such words would be meaningless and farcical and they would both know it.

But there was no reason why he should endanger her by obeying Rockford's insane order. He would not do it—

"Ah . . . good morning, Lyla!" Rockford loomed in the doorway, jovial as a Santa Claus. "Did you know Dale wants to go for a walk in the woods with you this bright spring morning— and he's no doubt too bashful to tell you so? Do you good to get away from camp"—there was the suggestion of a pause— "while you're still free."

He turned a beaming smile on Hunter. "Don't stand there like a dummy, boy—take her by the arm and let her have a last walk with someone who cares what happens to her."

There was one thing about Rockford not compatible with his air of fond fatherliness: his eyes were hard, gray slate as they looked into Hunter's and there was no mistaking their expression. Rockford had not made a fatherly suggestion for his own amusement. He had given an order that he intended to be obeyed.

Hunter and Lyla walked on through the thickets of ghost trees and arrow brush, each with little to say, Hunter feeling more and more like a ridiculous fool. They had no destination, no purpose in their walk, other than to abide by Rockford's desire that a total of ten assassins get a chance to slaughter a certain expendable second lieutenant.

He did not put his arm around Lyla as they walked. If they killed him, it would have to be without their having the satisfaction of the pictures they wanted with which to blackmail her.

They came to a tiny clearing, where a cloud tree log made an inviting seat in the shade, and Lyla said:

"No matter how far we walk, I'll have to go back to face it. Let's stop here, and rest a while."

He saw that the clearing was fairly well screened, but certainly not completely so. It would have to do.

He sat down on the log several feet away from her, not wanting to take the chance of her getting hit by accident.

Not that I'm enthusiastic about getting hit by intent, myself, he thought. *What a way for a Space Guard officer to die.*

He wondered if Rockford would ever inform Headquarters that Lieutenant Dale Hunter had died in the line of duty— by whatever twisted logic this insane episode could be called duty—and he wondered how the Commemoration Roll would read for him . . . *Displaying courage above and beyond the call of duty, Lieutenant Hunter sat conspicuously on top of a hill and calmly waited for ten assassins to slaughter him . . .*

"It's peaceful and quiet here, isn't it?" Lyla said.

He had been trying to watch four different directions at once and he realized that the constant swiveling of his neck was causing his stiff blouse collar to slowly cut his throat. And he saw that it was—for the moment, anyway—peaceful and quiet where they sat. The sun was warm and golden before them, bright flowers sweetly scented the air, and giant rainbow moths were fluttering over them, their tiny voices like the piping of a thousand fairy flutes.

"I wish I had been born a country girl," Lyla said. "I'd like to have a life like this, and not—what mine will be."

He asked the question to which he had to have the answer:

"Once you were going to marry Val and live on Jardeen, weren't you?"

"I . . . so my foolishness is no longer a secret?"

"Foolishness?" he asked.

"We met two years ago when I was attending the Fine Arts university on Jardeen. I was younger and a lot more naïve than I am now. I thought we were desperately in love and would get married as soon as I finished school and would live happily ever after, and all that."

"And it didn't turn out that way?"

"I had to make that promise to Daddy and when I wrote to Val about it, he seemed to approve. He didn't suggest I renounce the proxy marriage when the time was up, or anything. He just wrote that I knew what I wanted to do. He seemed relieved to be free to go ahead with his political career."

"I see," he said, and then, "you don't feel bad about it, do you, Lyla?"

"Feel bad? I wouldn't marry Val Boran if he was the last man on Vesta! Even Lord Narf isn't as self-centered as *he* is!"

"You don't have to marry Narf, either," he said. "You know that."

She looked down at the ground and said in a dead voice, "I made a promise."

"Rockford told me that your father never really knew Narf—that on the few times they met, Narf put on the act of being a refined gentleman, very respectful toward the king's daughter."

She did not answer and he said, "Is that the way it was?"

"Yes. That's the way it was. But how could I tell Daddy, as he lay dying?"

"You couldn't, Lyla. But if your father could be here today

and know what you know about Narf, do you think he would want you to marry him?"

"No . . . I guess not. But Lord Narf loves me in his own way, I think—and that's more than anyone else does."

Then her tone changed and she said, "I'm so glad that you're here today, Dale—I'm glad that there is someone who cares at least a little about what happens to me."

On her face was a poignant longing for someone to love and comfort her. It seemed to him, now beyond any doubt, that there could never be anything for him in his career but loneliness. How different the warm love of Lyla would be from the cold austerity of the military and its endless succession of weapons and killing—

He moved, to sit beside her and put his arm around her shoulders. "Lyla," he said, "I want to tell you—"

"*Dale . . .*" The word was a despairing sob as her composure broke and she held tightly to him, crying, her voice coming muffled as she pressed her face against his chest. "Help me, Dale! How can I marry that sadistic beast when it's someone else I can't live without—and he doesn't even know I love him!"

"But he does!" He hugged her closer, "He does know, and he loves you even more than you love him."

"Are you sure?" She raised a tear-stained face, hope like sunshine through clouds on it. "Are you really sure Val loves me, after all?"

"*Val?*"

The revelation was like the stunning concussion shock of a blast beam passing two inches overhead. His vision blurred and there was a hideous roaring in his ears. She was still holding to him for comfort and it seemed to him that was wrong—he should be clinging to her for support . . .

"*Dale . . .* what's the matter?"

"But I thought—" He swallowed with difficulty. "I thought you meant that I was the—"

Something struck the top of his head; this time, for certain, the concussion shock of a blaster beam passing close above it. There was a vicious crack as the beam split the tree beyond, then a crash and explosion of wood fragments as a second beam followed the first.

He rolled from the log, taking Lyla with him. The arrow bushes shielded them briefly, long enough for them to reach the temporary safety of a small swale.

"Dale!" Her dark eyes were wide with puzzled surprise and one small foot was bare from the loss of a sandal. "Someone shot at us!"

He thought, *So Narf got his pictures, after all.*

"Rootenant!" Alonzo came running. "They are *that* way—awr spread out to be sure to kirr you."

Alonzo motioned with his nose, a movement that seemed to cover all the high ground beyond them. At least, the enemy was not between them and camp. Not yet.

A distant shout came, an order from Narf to his men:

"*All of you—down that ridge! Get between Hunter and camp!*"

"*It's him!*" Her fingers gripped his arm. "He wants them to kill you!"

They had fired from a distance too great for his own blaster. He could not defy them from where he now stood.

"I'll have to try to get within range of them," he said. "I'll go back—"

"*No!*" Her grip on his arm tightened. "Don't leave me, Dale— don't let him find me here."

He looked down the length of the swale. At its lower end the ghost tree forest began, dense and concealing—but all down the length of the swale the snarevines lay in thick, viciously barbed entanglements, overlying a bed of sharp rocks and boulders. She could never get to the safety of the ghost trees in time.

Narf had his pictures, now. What would he do to her in the insanity of his hatred and triumph when he reached her?

"All right, Lyla," he said. "I'll see that you get to the trees—"

There was a crashing of explosions and debris leaped skyward behind them and along both sides of the swale. The firing continued, scattered but very effectively consistent, and he said as he drew his blaster, "I guess they don't want us to go away."

He set the regulator of the blaster at lowest intensity so that the beam would not clip dangerous flying fragments from the boulders. The green, tough vines disintegrated reluctantly while the precious minutes sped by; while the unhindered assassins would be hurrying to the point where the entire swale would be visible to them and under their fire.

Alonzo was following along near the top of the swale's side, ignoring the danger as he watched the progress of the enemy and reported it to Hunter: "Now they are half-way, Rootenant, hurrying faster—"

They reached the lower end of the swale. The last of the vines disintegrated and the ghost tree forest lay before them.

He touched her cheek in farewell. "Get on to camp, as fast as you can run."

The firing abruptly ceased as he spoke. There was an ominous silence. Alonzo came running, his tone almost a yelp in its urgency:

"They are awrmost where they can see us! We got to get her out of here, Rootenant—awrfur quick!"

"Lyla!"

It was the voice of Val, sharp with concern for her. He came running out of the ghost trees, all his cold impassiveness gone. "Are you hurt, honey—are you hurt?"

"You came for me!" She whispered the words, her face radiant. Then she ran to meet him, her arms outstretched, crying, *"Val . . . oh, Val . . ."*

Their arms went around each other.

Then the woods erupted as ten blasters laid down a barrage to block any escape to camp.

"I'll try to give you a chance to get through," Hunter said quickly. "Be ready for it when it comes."

He ran toward the firing line, taking advantage of the concealing afforded by the first fringe of ghost trees. They should be almost within range of his own weapon, now—

Again, the firing abruptly ceased, as though by some signal. There came the furious raving of Narf:

"It's that Boran she wants! Kill him too!"

Sonig cursed with bitter rage. *"Jardeen is lost to Verdam if any witness escapes—and we'll all hang, besides."*

There was a second of silence, and then Narf's command:

"Kill the woman, too!"

There was a roar like thunder as the firing began. The ground trembled and debris filled the air with flying fragments. Hunter, still running toward the enemy under cover of the trees, saw Val trying to get Lyla to safety and saw them both hurled to the ground as a tree exploded in front of them. They would never live to rise and run again—

He saw Rockford's plan, at last, and what his own duty would now have to be: He knew why Rockford had said of this day, *"If you can live through it, you will have it made."*

And he had a cold feeling inside him that he was not going to have it made.

He took a deep breath and ran toward the enemy, out of the concealment of the ghost trees and in the open where they could not fail to see him, his blaster firing a continuous beam that fell only a little short of the enemy, that showed them he would be close enough to kill them within seconds if he was not stopped.

The fire concentrated upon him, giving Lyla and Val their chance for escape. He ran through an inferno of crashing explosions, twisting and dodging on ground that trembled and heaved under his feet, while razor-sharp rock shrapnel filled the air with shrill, deadly screaming sounds.

Something ripped through his shoulder, to spin him around and send him rolling. He scrambled up, firing as he did so, and ran drunkenly on.

Something struck the side of his head and he went down again. He tried to rise and fell back, a blackness sweeping over him that he could not hold away despite his efforts to do so.

It seemed to him that the firing had suddenly stopped, that in its place was the hoarse buzz of a police stun-beam. It seemed he saw helicopters overhead, bearing the bright blue insignia of the Royal Guard and then there was nothing but the blackness.

There was a brief, dreamlike return to consciousness. He was in a Royal Guard helicopter and Alonzo was beside him, grinning, and saying, "You be O.K.—I grad! And my Princess Ryra—rook at her now, Rootenant!"

He saw Lyla, her hand in Val's, and her face was glowing and beautiful in its new-found happiness. Then she was bending down, kissing him, and saying, "Dale . . . Dale . . . how can we ever thank you for what you did?"

✧　　✧　　✧

When the blackness lifted the second time he was lying, bandaged, on a cot in the meeting hall and the voice of Rockford was saying, " . . . Ready to go in just a minute."

The hall was filled with members of the royal court who had come for the wedding. He saw the white robes of the Church of Vesta dignitaries who had come to officiate at the wedding. Then he saw the seven grim old men seated at the far end of the table.

The Royal Council—with the judicial power to give even death sentences in crimes committed against royalty.

Sonig, his face white and staring, was being half led, half carried, away from them.

Narf, in the grip of another Guardsman, was standing before the Council and saying in a tone both incredulous and sneering:

"Is that my sentence?"

"There is a qualification to it," one of the Council said. "It seems only just, in view of your crime, that you be tortured until death—"

The rest of the words were lost as the blackness swept back. But before unconsciousness was complete, when all else in the hall was gone from him, he heard Narf's cry; an animal-like bawl of protest, raw and hoarse with anguish . . .

"Ah . . . you're coming out of it, my boy."

Rockford was standing over him. "They gave you a Restoration shot on Vesta forty-eight hours ago. It will be wearing off in a minute and your head will clear."

He sat up, and the dizziness faded swiftly away. He saw that he was in the compartment of an interstellar ship and he knew that it was Earthbound.

And that Vesta, and brown-eyed Lyla, were now part of the past . . .

"Don't look so sad, my boy," Rockford said. "You'll get due credit and promotion for the invaluable part you played in my plan."

"But—"

"I know. But she was never yours. You'll find life is full of heartbreaks like that, son.

"And we accomplished our mission. Narf's crime neatly invalidated the proxy marriage. Then Lyla set a new precedent by marrying Val that very day. Earth has never had two such loyal and grateful friends as Val and Lyla."

"You knew all about them, didn't you?" he asked.

"Strategic Service has to know everything. And I knew they were still in love even though each was too proud to admit it. That's why I had to insist on Val coming to Vesta. After that, it was only a matter of using you to awaken Val to the fact that she did *not* love Narf. And of taking care of various little details, such as faking an official request for the helicopters to come out two hours ahead of time, getting Val off to find her at the proper time, and so on."

Rockford smiled at him, "And you learned that an old man's mind can be mightier than the space fleets of the Verdam empire—and that the line of duty that produces the best results can sometimes be very devious."

He thought of the white-faced Sonig, and the anguished bawl he had heard from Narf.

"I suppose they were going to hang Narf and Sonig at once."

"The Council would have, no doubt. But Lyla was so happy that she begged the Council to give them very light sentences—or just let them go free. So I suggested a compromise. The Royal Council regarded it as very fitting."

"What was it?"

"For Sonig, no punishment. The murder attempt, being news of public interest, will be broadcast upon Vesta and other worlds, including a factual, unbiased account of Sonig's participation in it. Shortly afterward, Sonig will be taken to Verdam and turned over to his own benevolent government. Vesta will file no charges."

"But Sonig lost Jardeen for his government. They'll execute him for that!"

"Yes, I'm afraid so. Shall we call it poetic justice?"

"What about Narf?"

"His sentence was life-long exile on his Sea Island estate. He will be provided with all the luxuries to which he has been accustomed, including a full staff of servants. He will continue to enjoy all his possessions there, including his gallery of nude paintings, his risqué films, his pornographic library, and so on.

In fact, since he is so fascinated by pornography and such a collector thereof, any pornographic material which might become available on Vesta in the future will be sent to him."

"That's not right . . . I mean, they were going to torture him to death."

"Not 'to death.' It was 'until death.' There's a difference."

"But that bawling noise he made—"

"Ah . . . that was due to the one restrictive qualification to the benign terms of his exile. Every woman on his estate was to be removed before he reached there, leaving men servants only. Patrol boats will see to it that for so long as he lives no woman shall ever set foot on the Sea Islands."

Rockford smiled again. "Lord Narf succeeded beyond his wildest dreams in keeping his boyhood vow of being always a man among men."

EMPATHY

The crisis with the natives was at hand and still the ERB showed no sign of permitting a Frontier Corps officer to make any suggestions.

For the fifth time that day Captain Harold Rider walked up the single dusty street of what had been his Frontier Corps outpost on Deneb Five until the unexpected arrival forty-eight hours before of General Beeling and his Extraterrestrial Relations Board unit. He came to the huge ERB Headquarters prefab at the end of the street. There, still on duty at the door, was the ferret-faced guard who had turned him back twice before.

The guard lounged indolently against the wall, seemed not to see Rider. But when Rider reached out to open the door he came to life with a quick sidestep that barred the way, straightening to attention with his hands brushing his holstered blaster and club.

"No admittance!" he snapped, with the crisp intonation of those who enjoy authority. "General Beeling and the others must not be disturbed, as I told you before."

He added, with deliberate delay, "—sir."

Rider withdrew his reaching hand and considered the pleasure of smashing the pointed chin and walking into the building across the man's stomach. He regretfully dismissed it as wishful dreaming. The feud between the old Frontier Corps and the politically powerful and young ERB was approaching its

decisive climax and reached even to Deneb. He was a despised
and unwanted superfluity in what had been his own camp and
they would like nothing better than an excuse to arrest and
confine him.

Quick footsteps sounded inside and the door swung open. It
was Colonel Primmer, Beeling's aide, turning with his hand still
on the doorknob and almost bowing in the obsequious manner characteristic of him as he said, "You are *so* right, General
Beeling. Yes, sir. At once, sir."

He turned again and shut the door behind him. The fawning expression vanished from his red face at the sight of Rider
and a cold, fishy look replaced it.

"General Beeling is far too busy to see you," he said, "if that's
what you're still waiting for."

"It is," he answered. "Surely he can spare a few minutes. Right
now we're two shakes away from a mass attack by the natives
and if the chief isn't handled just right when he comes for the
last talk this camp will be turned into a slaughter pen. Let me
tell—"

"I think," Primmer said, "that the Extraterrestrial Relations
Board can successfully cope with a barbarian chieftain without
first consulting a layman. As for that other matter with which
you've been trying to annoy the general all day: he requested
me to inform you that the helicopter will not be available to
you, that there are issues before him of a great deal more
importance than the life of your talking dog."

Primmer turned to the guard, pointedly dismissing Rider. "Go
tell Mantingly and Johnson that I want them here on the double.
Tell Myers to bring his laborers here—"

Rider turned away and went back down the street, wondering again how he could show Beeling the deadly danger of the
situation. It was a hell of a problem—how could you convince
a man who wouldn't let you talk to him?

He detoured around a mound of crates—part of the huge mass
of ERB equipment and supplies that had been hastily unloaded
from the special Missions cruiser before it hurried back
Earthward—and was met by a gust of wind that whipped
the fine, poisonous sand against his face. Deneb, almost to the
horizon, was going down with a purple halo around it and the

desert to the southeast was a smoky azure. He could not tell for sure through the haze but the sky above the distant Sea Cliffs seemed to have turned black.

If a storm was in progress there it would already be too late to take the helicopter more than part way to rescue Laughing Girl, the Altairian. But that made little difference—he had virtually no hope of altering Beeling's disdainful regard for what he called "the talking dogs." The helicopter would remain unavailable and he would have to find some other way of saving her.

Beeling's entire force of laborers and other non-ERB-commissioned personnel was at work along the street, erecting more prefabricated buildings to shelter the supplies. He noticed again the way they spoke to one another in lowered voices and glanced often toward the ragged hills that surrounded the valley. One of them, a red-haired boy, stepped out and spoke to him:

"Sir—could I ask you a question?"

He appraised the boy automatically: Nineteen, a long way from home, and trying not to show that he was scared.

"Of course," he answered. "What is it?"

"Is it true that the natives have been waiting for weeks for this ERB unit to come, so they could kill us all?"

"They didn't even know you existed until you landed here," he said. "Who told you that?"

"Why—" The boy looked suddenly uncomfortable. "I don't remember, sir."

He did not press the question. It would have been something that came down from Beeling or Primmer.

The others had stopped to listen, all of them showing to some degree the same uncertainty that was on the freckled face of the red-haired boy. They were young; the mechanically logical ERB had selected seventeen to twenty-two as the preferred aged for its performers of manual labor since men of that age were the hardiest and made the most efficient workers on worlds not suited to human life.

The ERB encouraged laborer enlistments with colorful posters that promised: GOOD PAY AND HIGH ADVENTURE AWAIT YOU BEYOND THE STARS. The boys had thought, when they landed two days and nights before, that they had stepped across the threshold of the promised high adventure and they had been as excited as children. Now they were solemn and hushed as they tried to adjust themselves to the realization that there would be no adventure, no allure, in quick and violent death . . .

"There may be trouble over your coming," he said, "but it won't be anything that was premeditated. There's a likely chance it won't happen at all. We'll know in a few minutes."

He turned and walked off, feeling them silent and very thoughtful behind him.

At the end of the street was the little building that had been his office until Beeling's arrival with the special order that had changed the Frontier Corps outpost to an ERB Primary Contact Field Installation. It was there that he and the natives had met and talked so many times in the past and it was there that old Chief Selsin would soon come to what might be the last meeting.

He went inside and saw that his few remaining possessions had been piled in a corner pending further disposal. He walked on to the desk where the hyperspace communicator, borrowed from the Frontier ship, stood locked and silent. One of Beeling's first demands, as new commander of the outpost, had been for the hyperspace communicator's key. Beeling did not need the communicator—he had a similar model in his headquarters building—but a locked communicator could not be used by a displaced Frontier Corpsman to send unauthorized reports to Earth.

The camp-to-ship radio was inside the communicator. He switched it on, to try again to reach his Frontier ship on Deneb One. The result was the same as before; a shrieking, roaring, ear-splitting blast of static. The sun was squarely between the two worlds and, since it was a white sun, its electronic emission was tremendous. Contact with the ship was utterly impossible.

He changed the wave length to that of the little shortwave radio under the Sea Cliffs and signaled with the Beep button. There was no response, other than a harsh grinding of static from the storm he thought he had seen, which meant that Laughing Girl must still be out tending to the mineral detector.

He switched the radio off, wondering what he could have told her if she had answered him.

✧   ✧   ✧

"Captain—*rook!*"

Loper, the other shaggy, dog-like Altairian, came running through the door, his eyes bright with excitement.

"Are coming now—oh, hundreds and hundreds. Rook, Captain!"

He looked, where a wide, low pass to the northeast led to the higher country beyond, and saw the natives coming down it. There were perhaps five hundred of them, coming with their dragon-beast mounts in a run, their long rifles across their saddles and their bronze battle helmets gleaming brightly in the late sunlight.

There were nine columns and a different pennant fluttered at the head of each. Which meant that the Nine Tribes were solidly allied under the leadership of old Selsin until the business with the humans was settled.

"Are stirr more coming farther back," Loper said. "Pretty soon awr around us wirr be the big rif'res that can kirr us. Why, Captain?" There was puzzled question in his dark eyes. "We not hurt any of them."

"They're afraid we might," he said. "We're getting this one last chance to prove we won't."

"If they not berieve us, how soon wirr they kirr us?"

"I think they'll give us a chance to leave, first."

"But we *can't* reave—our ship is gone."

"That, Loper, is the big, repulsive fly that's in everybody's soup today."

The columns of armed natives split as they reached the bottom of the pass, and raced to north and south along the valley's rim.

"They going to surround us," Loper said. "If they say, 'You not pass,' we *have* to have the hericopter." He looked away from the natives and toward the Sea Cliffs. "She die there if we not come and nobody care. I not understand."

To Loper it was still incomprehensible that there could be humans who did not like Altairians. He had known only the men of the Frontier ship, who regarded Altairians with the same affection they would have had for loyal and cheerful—and sometimes blundering—twelve-year-old children. Except when it was time to meet the natives of a new world, when the Altairians' highly developed sense of empathy changed their role to that of invaluable coaches and advisors.

❖   ❖   ❖

Frontier ships were always undermanned—each year the increasingly huge expenditures of the ERB forced the Space Board to cut the Frontier Corps budget to make up the difference— and the Altairians diligently performed all tasks of which they were capable. When the order came through to have Deneb One surveyed immediately he had needed to send his entire crew and had used Laughing Girl to replace the man tending the electronic mineral detector that had been set up under the Sea Cliffs. It was a job she could manage, since the detector was near-enough automatic in its operation that its supervision required no technical knowledge. This had enabled him to send a full crew to Deneb One, while he remained at camp with Loper to help him and continued the meetings with the natives.

He had intended to take the helicopter to the Sea Cliffs a safe twenty hours in advance of the Big Tide and bring back Laughing Girl and the portable mineral detector. But Beeling had ordered: "Our only means of transportation will not be permitted to leave this camp until this trouble with the natives is fully settled."

By then it would be too late. The three moons of Deneb Five possessed complex orbits that brought the Big Tide every ten days; a titanic bulge in the waters of the oceans that raced around the world at a speed of five hundred miles per hour. The three moons were already on the opposite side of the world, swinging close around it and bringing the Big Tide with them. It would strike the high, unscalable Sea Cliffs at sunrise and Laughing Girl, still faithfully tending the detector down under them and waiting for him to come for her, would be killed instantly.

To the few of the ERB staff he had managed to talk to, his persistent requests for the helicopter had seemed ridiculous. "Really, Captain," one natty young lieutenant he had cornered outside Headquarters had said, "you're taking the loss of your mascot far too seriously. After all, you can pick up a dozen of the beasts the next time you pass Altair." . . .

"We not got much time, Captain. Are we have to wait much ronger?"

"Not much longer, Loper. Only until the talk with Selsin is over."

"I think he come now."

The long columns were still coming down the pass and parting at the bottom but one native was coming straight toward the camp in a slow trot. It was Selsin.

"—lively there! Faster, all of you ..."
The voice of Primmer, edged with strain, came from the street. Rider went to the window and looked out upon a scene of confused activity.

Primmer, with two blasters buckled around him, was trying to post as many guards as possible as quickly as possible; all the laborers and technicians among them. They were being stationed around Headquarters, around the helicopter, and all along the windows of supplies in the street.

"Damn!" he said aloud.

Beeling could have done nothing worse than to order the show of armed defense at a time when everything depended upon regaining Selsin's trust.

The door of the ERB Headquarters building opened and General Beeling stepped out, briskly despite his paunchy overweight. He strode down the street with his pink moon-face looking straight ahead, not glancing once toward the natives. He stopped a moment to say something to Primmer that caused most of Primmer's nervousness to vanish then came on with the bearing of calm purpose.

"He not worried," Loper said. "How can he not worry now?"

Beeling stepped through the doorway with cold satisfaction on his face and a look at Rider that said, *I have your muddled situation well in hand, my man.*

"Good afternoon, General," Rider greeted him, and Loper said politely, "Her'ro, Generar Beering."

Beeling's eyes flicked to Loper in brief curiosity then, without answering either of them, he seated himself behind the desk.

"I presume you know we're surrounded, Rider?"

There was the same vengeful satisfaction in his tone as on his face. Rider noticed, absently, that his blouse bulged with the bulk of a concealed blaster.

"I knew they would come ready for war," he said. "When Selsin gets here we'll have our one last chance to avert it and I've been trying to see you all day to tell you we'll have to show Selsin the respect that—"

"My dear Captain," Beeling interrupted, "I have been very busy the entire day supervising a review of all data and deciding upon the best method of counteracting the damage you have done. I feel rather certain that I know how to speak to the native."

Rider kept his face expressionless and said with careful courtesy, "But couldn't you order the guards off duty before Selsin gets here, sir? He'll regard them as proof of suspicion and enmity on our part."

The soft answer seemed to have slightly lessened Beeling's dislike for him; Beeling's next statement was more pompous than sarcastic:

"On the contrary, that display of preparedness will prove to the natives that we are quite aware of their hostility and are not to be intimidated by it; that our request for friendship is sincere and does not spring from fear of them."

Rider looked again at the guards, able to count only seven blasters among them, and back to Beeling. "You don't understand, sir—if they call our bluff we won't have a chance."

Beeling's reply was to spread a sheaf of papers on the desk before him and say:

"Here are the Analysis Sheets; the result of almost two days of work by myself and my staff and our computer. For your information, these natives are like children both in the awe and fear with which they regard our weapons and in their eagerness to possess the labor-saving machines, the luxury items and the pretty novelties of our 'grown-up' society. By dramatically presenting the two choices—the gift-laden helping hand or the unyielding fist—they cannot logically do other than ask for our friendship and gifts."

"But it isn't that simple," he protested. "They'll—"

Annoyance passed across Beeling's face and the full degree of coldness returned. "As I remarked, the procedure outlined by the Analysis will counteract the damage you have done. Insufficient data, however, leave two questions answered. One: why have your reports never mentioned the consistent enmity of the natives?"

"Because no enmity ever existed. They were only exercising reasonable caution, due to the experience they had with that other alien race forty years ago."

"Yes? Then perhaps you can answer the other question: why should this 'reasonable caution' flare so suddenly into a lust for war? *What did you do to make them hate humans so?*"

"I lied to them. They were almost ready to agree to everything but they wanted a little more time in which to be sure that we would not betray their trust as that other alien race did. I gave my solemn promise as the representative of Earth that no reinforcements would come in the meantime. And within forty-eight hours after receiving its copy of my report to the Frontier Corps, the ERB had you and thirty men and a hundred tons of supplies on the way to Deneb.

"Just what do you suppose the natives thought of my truthfulness—of the truthfulness of any human—when that cruiser dropped down out of the sky and men and equipment began rolling out of it?"

"I see," Beeling said acidly. "You were the innocent victim of unfair circumstances. But, as the ERB informed the Supreme Council, you had accomplished nothing concrete in your six months here and this world was too badly needed by Earth to permit any more cautious delays. Despite anguished wails of protest from the Frontier Corps we persuaded the Supreme Council to transfer command of this outpost to the ERB. I was dispatched at once to analyze the situation, to remedy whatever mistakes you had made, and to gain the cooperation of the natives as quickly as possible.

"I trust"—the acidic dislike increased—"that properly explains my presence here."

Loper lifted his ears toward the door and Rider heard the squeak of saddle leather.

"I hope your plans work out the way you think," he said. "Selsin is here."

Selsin was so big that his bulk in the doorway half darkened the room as he came through. He was seven feet tall, black as coal, with muscles that bulged and rippled as he walked. He had the thin, curved nose and pointed ears of a devil, while his green, glittering eyes under slanting brows added to his satanic appearance.

His bristling blue-gray head was bare; he had left his helmet on his saddle, together with his rifle and sword, as a gesture of peaceful intention.

"Chief Selsin!" Beeling rose, smiling. "You honor us. I'm sorry there was no one to meet you—I told my aide—"

"It is of no importance." Selsin spoke in accented Terran. "I came to hear you, not your assistant."

"Ah—of course. Will you sit down?"

Selsin did so, the chair creaking under his weight. He waited for Beeling to speak, regarding him with a mocking half smile. The smile was meaningless—the cheek muscles of the natives were different from those of humans and caused their lips to turn upward at the corners—but it could be rather disconcerting to a human at first.

Beeling cleared his throat. "I see you came alone. At the end of our brief meeting yesterday I requested that all nine of you tribal chiefs come again this afternoon so I could tell all of you that I am here to help you."

"You told us that yesterday," Selsin said. "I came today to hear your proof."

"Ah—of course."

Beeling looked down at the Analysis Sheets, a touch of uncertainty in his manner. It's all right, Rider thought as he watched him, to speak of handling the natives as one would handle children—but it's a little hard to hang on to that conception when the child is a three-hundred-pound black devil sitting two yards in front of you.

Beeling looked up from the Analysis. "We want the friendship of your race," he said to Selsin, "and your race needs our friendship. We are here on your world only to help you"—stern reproof came into Beeling's voice—"and yet you foolishly prepare to attack us with your puny rifles!"

Selsin's expression did not change. He answered in the emotionless manner of one stating unalterable facts:

"We do not, we have never, wanted war. But the promise your world made to mine was a lie and your second ship came, bringing more men and great stacks of strange objects which we fear are weapons—and which you are now guarding as one would guard weapons. We do not know how many more of your ships may be on the way, now, with still more men and weapons. We can only hope that if we must fight for our world, we have not waited too long."

"Your suspicions are baseless, your plans are foolhardy," Beeling said with admonishing sternness. "Consider, friend Selsin; think of the terrible price an attack would cost you. You would meet certain defeat—and you would forever forfeit our friendship and our gifts!"

Selsin's black face seemed to turn even darker and his teeth flashed in a quick snarl. "Forty years ago we were offered friendship and gifts, as you are doing, by another alien race—the *ginideglin*, the three-eyed ones. They needed metal to repair their ship and we used all our supply of charcoal to smelt the ores we had mined for them, for they told us they were very grateful and would within a year bring us an atomic furnace so we would never have to hoard charcoal again. Then, on the day they finished repairing their ship, they turned their weapons on us. They butchered thirty, to take along as fresh meat. Three others were killed with a gas that would not mar their appearance, so they could be stuffed and placed in a museum. A man, a woman, and a child—and the child was my sister!"

Selsin leaned toward Beeling, his devil's face ugly with the hatred the memory aroused.

"To them we were only animals who had served their purpose. Their pretense of friendship was a lie—we should have killed them all when their ship crashed!"

Beeling's chair squealed as he shoved it back and his hand pawed at the buttons of his blouse, reaching in for the concealed blaster. His hand closed around the butt of it and he held it there, still concealed, as he appraised Selsin with wary thoughtfulness. Rider spoke quickly, before he could say or do something that would destroy the last faint hope of regaining Selsin's trust.

"The three-eyed-ones kill and take specimens from every world they visit, Chief Selsin. Someday our ships will meet them and they will want some humans as specimens, too. They are already our enemies as well as yours."

Selsin settled back in his chair and his anger faded.

"We have thought of that," he said. "We had hoped that your race would be our ally should they ever return. But now—does it matter whether a race is killed for food and specimens or killed to get it out of the way for worldwide mining operations?"

Rider told Selsin again, for what would probably be the last time, why his world was needed by humans:

"Earth's policy strictly forbids colonizing a world against the wishes of its inhabitants. This world is doubly forbidden—

beryllium is present in the dust over all its surface, in a form that would be fatal to humans within two years.

"But we need domed repair and refueling bases here for our exploration, survey and colonization ships bound for worlds farther on. This is the only world within three hundred light-years that has metal for repairs, and that has the rare earths and elements that make our ships' hyperspace drives possible. You have such an abundance on this world that fifty centuries from now we would have used less than one-tenth of one percent, yet that small amount is so necessary to us that if we cannot have it we will have to abandon all further exploration in this sector of space."

When he had finished Selsin sat still and thoughtful, his green eyes unwaveringly on Rider's as though trying to see inside Rider's mind and know that he spoke without deceit. Rider had the feeling that Selsin's suspicions were wavering before an almost desperate desire to believe.

Then Beeling, his composure regained, jerked his chair back to the desk with another noisy squeal. He cleared his throat in a profound manner, ready to resume the talk with Selsin, and Rider crossed his fingers with a wordless prayer that something would happen to interrupt him before he could again anger Selsin.

The interruption came: a signal beep from the radio beside the hyperspace communicator, the call from Laughing Girl at the Sea Cliffs.

Rider stepped to the radio, reaching past the scowling Beeling to turn the volume to maximum. A muffled roaring filled the room when he did so, static grinding and crashing through it.

"Go ahead, Girl," he said into the transmitter.

"A awrfur storm come, Boss"—Laughing Girl's voice was hard to hear through the roaring—"from off the sea—a wind that tear down the detector and scatter our record tapes and I try to find them but it are so dark with brack crouds and rain and then the sea come in and things are in it, things that—"

A louder roaring drowned out her voice. He waited, knowing that she was frightened. Whenever she was scared and faced with problems too great for her, she called him "Boss" and talked in the quick, rushing manner of a child.

Her voice came in again:

"—and then they see me rooking for the record tapes and they run after me, awrfur big things with craws and beaks, and they are stirr coming and I have no prace to hide. Terr me what to do, Boss—"

"Run to the cliffs!" he ordered, in his mind the vision of the lumbering horde of two-ton Elephant Crabs closing in on her. "Climb as far as you can up that crevice in the cliffs—they're too big to follow you in—and wait for me."

"Wirr you come for me soon—before the Big Tide?"

"I'll be there. Now, run!"

"Okay, Boss—I run."

He lifted his hand to the switch, then paused as he heard deep, jarring sounds through the wind's roaring. Four seconds later there was a loud crashing, a snap, and sudden silence. The monsters had smashed the transmitter in their pursuit of Laughing Girl.

He switched off his own transmitter and said in answer to Beeling's questioning, irritated look, "A local tornado. Sometimes one will precede the Big Tide and push a small tide ahead of it."

"They awrfur crose behind her," Loper said. He looked at Beeling with worry and accusation in his eyes. "We are supposed to go after her yesterday but you say, 'No.' Now, maybe awready they are catch her and kirr her."

Beeling glanced at Loper with the same momentary curiosity he had exhibited before, then he gave his full attention to Selsin. He began in a tone of smooth sincerity:

"You are an exceptionally intelligent person, Chief Selsin, or you would never have risen to your position as leader. Therefore, I know you are far too wise to betray the trust of your people in you by making the wrong choice of the two kinds of future offered your world.

"Should you refuse to cooperate with us, we would be forced to reroute our ships through other sectors of space and your world would see no more of us for centuries to come. You would continue to stagnate here—you are no doubt aware that the resources of your world are such that you can never leave it without our help. Your unlimited wealth of minerals is of no use to you—you have no coal deposits, no trees, nothing but

scrawny shrubs with which to make a meager supply of charcoal for smelting. There is no oil on your world; you have no
fuel for steam engines or internal combustion engines. Your
environment will force you to remain in a state of barbarism,
nomads in animal skins, with privation your only known way
of life.

"This we can alter for you, in wondrous ways beyond your
imagining. We will give you atomic furnaces, processing plants,
manufacturing machinery. We will help you build factories that
will produce not only all the things you need but also luxuries
beyond counting—the very same luxury goods our own society uses! And we will give you costless and unlimited power for
your factories and homes and vehicles by showing you how to
get it out of a rock which is to be found all over your world;
a magic rock we call 'uranium' but for which you probably don't
even have a name."

Beeling paused, as though for effect. He was smiling at Selsin,
very sure of himself.

"Choose, Chief Selsin! Will you condemn your race to a
future of poverty and stagnation by refusing to cooperate with
us? Or will you give them all the achievements and luxuries of
a civilization three thousand years in advance of theirs—will you
be the wise leader and accept this tremendous payment which
we offer for merely your race's friendship?"

Selsin stood up, on his face an anger and hatred such as
Rider had never seen. He looked down at Beeling and gave his
answer in words that came like the spitting of a tiger:

"My people's insignificant friendship is not for sale today,
human!"

Beeling gaped in incredulous disbelief.

"You—*refuse?*"

Selsin turned to Rider.

"We believed your promise, until your reinforcements came.
Even then we still had a faint hope that you humans were sincere. Now I know we were wrong. It is better so."

"You know we can't prove our good intentions," Rider
answered. "Not here and now, in this room."

"I realize that. But I wanted to know the attitude of your
superior toward my race. As he regarded us, so likely would all

the others who would follow him. My people and I wanted to know if we would be regarded with respect, or if we would be dismissed as an inferior species to be used for human purposes.

"I learned. We are backward barbarians, simple savages who can be bought and then ignored."

Through the anger on Selsin's face something like regret showed for a moment, something like a look of farewell.

"I do not think it is your fault—but you are one of them and responsible with them. This is our world and we will live here and fight here and die here—but we will be no race's inferiors here."

Then the regret was gone as Selsin turned back to Beeling.

"You will be given until sunrise tomorrow to recall your ship and leave this world. If you and all the other humans are not gone by then, we will have no choice but to remove you."

Then, not waiting for an answer, Selsin strode to the door.

Beeling half rose, still gaping with amazement. "*Wait—*"

The door closed behind Selsin's broad back and Beeling ordered sharply, "Call him back, Rider! Something is wrong—he didn't understand my offer."

Rider listened to Selsin's dragon-beast departing in a fast trot. "He understood you," he said to Beeling. "But you cooked our goose by not understanding him."

"He failed to comprehend," Beeling said flatly. "Or else—and I'll have that question put to the computer—he's bluffing, trying to extort still more from us. In either case, he knows we can't leave here; he knows the Special Missions cruiser has gone back to Earth and the Frontier ship can't receive our signals."

"He didn't believe that explanation yesterday and he doubly doesn't today."

"Something is wrong," Beeling said again. "The Analysis showed the natives to want all the things I offered him. They don't even have wooden-wheeled carts—and yet, instead of the grateful acceptance that the Analysis predicted, the native's reaction was one of irrational enmity."

"Didn't you know the Analysis was meaningless drivel?" he asked.

Beeling jerked up his head with a shocked expression, as though Rider had uttered an obscene heresy. "What do you mean by that?"

"All your calculations are based on the assumption that the species being studied is as emotionlessly logical as one of your computers. That worked once, with that ant-like race on Medusa, and it was played up by the ERB politicians until now most of the Supreme Council believes the ERB claim that relations with alien life forms has been reduced to an exact science by the ERB and the slow methods of the Frontier Corps are worthlessly obsolete. But the ERB has failed on every world since Medusa, even though you've kept the fact covered up, and now you've failed here. I tried to tell you from the day you came, that Selsin and his race are proud individualists and it would be a fatal mistake to try to convert them into mathematical equations."

Beeling smoothed the Analysis under his fingers. "We made a mistake; the mistake of depending upon a Frontier Corps layman to procure adequate data for our Analysis, among which would have been Selsin's emotional instability. It is a mistake that will not happen again. I can assure you."

"I suppose you'll send a full report of this to Earth, at once?"

"A most complete report. Why do you ask?" Beeling answered.

"Because in the morning you're going to die, and I, and all those kids out there, and you can try to prevent such a thing happening again by telling not the ERB but the Supreme Council exactly what caused it."

"I assure you, the ERB will properly present the facts to the Council."

"No—not the true facts. You know that, Beeling."

"*General* Beeling. And what are you trying to say—are you asking me to omit mention of the incompetence on your part that created this situation?"

"I'm asking you to tell the Council that you followed all the rules in the ERB textbooks and did exactly what the Analysis told you to do and that you and everyone here is going to die because you did so. Tell them that if a form of life behaved according to absolutely predictable rule and logic it wouldn't be anything intelligent—it would be a vegetable."

Beeling smoothed out the Analysis sheets again. "Do you really think I might give my superiors hysterical nonsense like that?"

He knew that further argument would be useless. He had

already explained to Beeling that a Frontier Corpsman, or any man first meeting an alien race, had to base his actions upon the reactions of the natives; he had to develop something like a sixth sense in detecting their emotions and let that be his guide or he would become enmeshed in misunderstandings that would result in death for him and the loss of the new world for Earth.

Beeling had refused to listen and had laughed outright when Rider told him the Altairians were far better than any human sixth sense; that all Frontier and ERB ships should carry Altairians and that the ERB's erroneous classification of the Altairian race as "Animals" unjustly condemned them to continuing half-starvation on their rocky, barren world by denying them the assistance that Earth's empire gave to all needy forms of life that had been classified as "Intelligent inhabitants."

Loper moved restlessly, sensing his emotions and disturbed by them. He spoke with the suddenness and frankness of a child:

"Once Sersin awrmost berieve us, Captain. He come in thinking with question and uncertain, and hoping very much we are his friends but afraid we not be. Then you terr how we need *his* friendship and not ever harm his race even if they not want to be our friends. Sersin rook at you he awrmost happy, awrmost ready to berieve you, then Generar Beering speak about awr the things humans have that Sersin's race don't have and say very proud, 'We give you awr these things for mer'rey your friendship,' and Sersin get mad and not hope at awr anymore, and when he reave he thinking of fighting and kirring. He not rike, but he know it have to be. Why it have to be?"

"You have the animal well coached," Beeling observed. "Its ability to relate a witnessed incident proves your claim that Altairians are telepathic, I presume?"

"Loper was aware of Selsin's emotions before he ever walked into this room. It isn't telepathy; it's a highly developed sense of empathy. It serves the same purpose."

"I'm afraid your naïve trust in the animal's power of—"

Beeling never finished the sentence. A drum was suddenly beating along the near side of the valley; a hard, fast stuttering that rose sharp and clear above the whining of the wind.

"What is that?" Beeling demanded.

"A signal drum, sending the word around the circumference of the valley."

"The word?" For an instant Beeling's face registered blankness. "Do you mean they really intend to attack us?"

"Good Lord—haven't you realized that yet?"

Beeling chewed his lip, his face thoughtful, then shook his head. "You must be wrong. The Analysis showed that they wouldn't dare attack us."

"The Analysis also showed you how to win Selsin's friendship—remember?"

Beeling looked thoughtful again. "If your guess is correct, we'll have to prepare an impenetrable defense system. How many heavy weapons do you have here, and what kind?"

"The ship's blasters are always the prime defense weapons of a Frontier unit. There are a few other weapons on the ship, too—but now everything is on the other side of the sun. There's one hand blaster in my room, and we have the ten blasters your men brought."

"*One?*—you have *one* blaster here?" Beeling glared, "I thought you had a supply of weapons—must every action of a Frontier man be one of mindless bungling?"

"I was trying to make friends with the natives, not kill them."

"Eleven hand blasters to stand off thousands of bloodthirsty savages . . ." Beeling chewed his lip again. "How long can we hold the natives off with eleven blasters?"

"About as long as a snowball would remain firm in hell."

"We need the ship—how incredibly stupid of you to send it away. Our lives are in the balance—"

"Rook!" The voice of Loper interrupted, from where he had moved to the north window. "A smoke signar are going up, too."

Beeling swung with such haste that he knocked the Analysis sheets off the desk. A tall, black column of smoke was standing up from the high hill at the valley's head. It could be seen for miles, despite the angle at which the wind was making it lean, and it was rolling blacker and higher by the second.

"That will be to summon all the reserve forces from the highlands," Rider said. "They think we're well armed and they'll hit us with everything they have."

Beeling's nervous movement as he turned back to Rider changed abruptly to decision.

"There's only one thing we can do—evacuate. We'll use the helicopter."

Rider shook his head. "The helicopter is small, for scouting, and can't carry more than three. It's five hundred miles to the nearest safe refuge, the Northern Islands, and the helicopter carries fuel for seven hundred miles. It would be a one-way trip."

"We'll go as soon as you can check the helicopter for the flight."

"We?"

"Colonel Primmer has had only a few hours flying time and I have had none. You will be our pilot."

He shook his head. "I'm as afraid to die in the morning as the next man but I'll be damned if I could run like *that*."

Annoyance passed across Beeling's face. "You will obey my order and forget the heroic ideals. It would be only stupid for all to die when some can be saved with the helicopter."

"I agree. But why not let everybody cut cards or draw straws so all would have the same chance?"

"This Field Installation is not a gambling casino. Furthermore, there is an ERB regulation which reads: 'In times of critical danger and limited transportation the unit commander will arrange for the survival of his command in the order of each individual's importance to the unit as a whole.'"

"I see," he said, and thought: *So in the ERB you do even your running by the book?*

Beeling began hastily scribbling a note. "This is an order to Colonel Primmer, authorizing you to go past the helicopter guards. Make sure you overlook nothing in preparing it for the trip."

"I have other things to do. Primmer can check it."

Beeling stopped writing and his face hardened dangerously under its pink softness. "As commander of this outpost and your superior officer, I can have you locked up in chains for insubordination if I wish to. Would you prefer that?"

"It still wouldn't force me to be your pilot. Anyway, you needn't worry about my absence—the helicopter is easily enough handled that Primmer can land you safely at your destination."

He saw that the sun was setting, already a bright, molten silver on the horizon, and he turned to Loper.

"Run to the storage shed and get me that coil of small rope. I'm ready to start."

"Where are you going?" Beeling demanded, suspicion in his eyes and his hand reaching inside his blouse.

Loper ran to the door, using both paws to turn the knob. He slammed it shut behind him and Rider saw him race past the window, where the spinning, wind-blown dust half obscured the ground. It was a good thing, he thought, that the Altairians were immune to beryllium poisoning. Loper and Laughing Girl would never see any other world again . . .

"*Where are you going?*"

"The Sea Cliffs," he answered.

"Do you think you can hide from the natives there?"

"Not to hide. To keep my promise to Laughing Girl. The Big Tide is coming and she can't escape it."

Beeling stared, as though he had babbled gibberish.

"You—you're going to walk forty miles through beryllium dust, through armed natives and man-killing beasts, to save an animal—and yet you refuse to lift a hand to help save the lives of your fellow human beings?"

"Or, to be specific, the lives of you and Primmer. That's right."

He went to the corner where his remaining possessions lay and swung the still-full canteen from his shoulder. He kicked his respirator to one side—he would never need it again—and picked up the long-bladed knife.

He shoved the knife in his belt and said to Beeling, "I'm leaving my blaster for the others to use."

Beeling withdrew his own blaster from his blouse and laid it on the desk with the muzzle pointing toward Rider. His hand continued to rest on it as he stared at Rider with cold savage calculation.

The door banged open and a gust of wind scattered the pages of the Analysis across the floor as Loper plunged through. The coil of rope was in his mouth and he was panting from his running as he dropped it at Rider's feet.

"Are you ready to go, Captain—can we hurry now, prease?"

"Just a minute, Rider—"

Beeling reached out with the transmitter key in his left hand and unlocked the hyperspace communicator. His right hand did not leave the blaster.

"You might be interested in knowing what my report will be," he said. He flipped on the signal switch.

"I suppose I already know," Rider answered. "I ask you to overlook our personal differences and tell them the real cause behind tomorrow's massacre. It could go a long way toward saving the lives of others in the future."

Beeling nodded, smiling. "Such a report is precisely what I have in mind. I feel they should know how your blundering Frontier Corps methods had stirred the natives into such a murderous anti-human frenzy that my ERB unit arrived too late to remedy the situation. I shall point out that every world lost by the ERB was due to the incompetence of the Frontier men who preceded the ERB units there and created hatred and distrust among the natives. I shall point out the tragic mistake of continuing to permit Frontier Corps laymen to try to assume the duties of ERB specialists and I shall urge the Supreme Council let this be the last bloody sacrifice by passing the Harriman Proposal now before it; the proposal that would dissolve the Frontier Corps and place all its ships and men under ERB supervision.

"And it is my duty"—Beeling's smile was as vindictive as the sting of a wasp—"to report your actions of this afternoon; your flagrant insubordination, your flat refusal to assist in transporting others to safety, your desertion in time of danger, your flight to the Sea Cliffs, leaving the rest of us to do the fighting."

It required a few seconds for Rider to comprehend the extent of Beeling's malice, then he said, "I thought you were only inexperienced and too blind to see. I didn't know the half of it, did I?"

"It should be obvious to you what my report will do to the Frontier Corps when it's read before the Supreme Council."

It was very obvious. Beeling's report would be the climax of the ERB's all-out effort to absorb the Frontier Corps. The already delicately balanced scales would be tipped, the Harriman Proposal would be passed, and the Corps would cease to exist . . .

"Do you still want to go to the Sea Cliffs?" Beeling asked.

He saw Beeling's prime objective. Beeling was still afraid to let the inexperienced Primmer be his pilot.

"Suppose I should decide to be your pilot?" he asked.

"I certainly couldn't report you as a deserter. In fact, I might find it possible to forget to mention several of the facts concerning you and the Frontier Corps."

He did not reply at once and Beeling added, "What is the welfare of an animal compared with your life and the existence of the Frontier Corps to which, I understand, you and the others have dedicated your lives?"

Loper made a whining sound, looking up at Rider with his face twisted in apprehension.

"What are he mean?" Then he read the answer in the conflicting emotions of the two men and his question came like a despairing whimper. "Are it *have* to be that way?"

The hyperspace communicator blinked an orange light and said in a metallic voice:

"*Extraterrestrial Relations Board, Communications Center.*"

Beeling spoke into the transmitter: "Connect me with General Supervision, Classified AA circuit." He turned to Rider. "Which will you take, Rider?"

It seemed to him that he could see the two alternative courses of events with vivid clarity. He could see the dissolution of the Frontier Corps, his name in the records as a coward who had run in vain—and he could see Laughing Girl crouching cold and scared in the crevice, trusting him to come for her before the black tide rushed out of the dawn to kill her, knowing in her child-like mind that he would be there in time as surely as she and Loper had raced to him in time that night on Vulcan when he lay injured and helpless under the cliff and the moon wolves were gathering around him for the kill . . .

"*Office of General Supervision,*" the communicator said. "*Classified AA. Give us your report.*"

"A moment, please," Beeling said to it. To Rider he said, "I give you exactly ten seconds—which will it be?"

Which would it be? Death and infamy at the Sea Cliffs—and know that to the end he had done what seemed right and just to him? Or life and safety and an unmarred record on the Northern Islands, while Laughing Girl died still waiting for him and he knew he was a coward no less than Beeling?

"*Now!*"

There was the brittle snap of ultimatum in Beeling's single word. He gave his answer:

"I'm going to the Sea Cliffs."

For a moment Beeling sat rigid, so sure had he been that the answer would be the one he wanted. Then he leaned forward, his lips thin and white with the intensity of his hatred and his words half choking in his throat:

"You fool—you incredible fool! I can legally shoot you down where you stand as a deserter!"

The muzzle of the blaster tilted up. Loper's eyes went fire-bright with understanding and his claws ripped at the floor as he threw himself back, into position to leap at Beeling's throat. Rider reached for the knife in his belt, warned by Loper's action and knowing he would never live to throw it. Beeling, in the insanity of his rage, was going to fire—

"Sir, the natives are—"

Primmer burst into the room and the scene froze. Primmer gawked at Beeling's blaster, at Rider's hand reaching for the knife, then he seized his own blasters and leveled them waveringly on Rider.

"Don't touch that knife!" he commanded. He turned his red face to Beeling. "What is it, sir—what is he trying to do?"

Slowly, almost regretfully, Beeling let his grip on the blaster relax.

"A little matter of desertion," he said to Primmer. He spoke to Rider. "I've changed my mind. You are experienced in eluding danger on alien worlds and you might have a good chance of hiding from the natives until a ship comes to pick you up. I hope so. I want you to live, to sit in your death row cell and read about the end of the Frontier Corps before they take you out and hang you as a deserter and a coward."

He motioned toward the door with a quick jerk of the blaster. "Now go! Get out of this room!"

Rider picked up the coil of rope and started toward the door, Beeling's blaster following him. Primmer spoke in protest:

"But General Beeling! As a deserter he should be held for proper punishment, sir—"

Beeling silenced him with a hard look and turned to the communicator. He began his report:

"General David A. Beeling, Unit Twenty, Deneb Five. Subjects: Impending attack of native armies, due to erroneous reports and

general incompetence of Frontier Corps commander Captain
Harold Rider; Report of Captain Rider's rebellion and desertion
on eve of attack; Details of dangerous impracticability of Frontier
Corps methods and—"

The words faded away, drowned by the wind, as Rider and
Loper went down the street.

"He rie," Loper said. "They can't berieve him, can't ever hang
you, can they?"

He smiled a little. "No, they won't be able to hang me."

He angled across the street, toward the edge of the dagger-
brush thicket, and passed not far from one of the guards. It was
the red-haired boy, facing the enemy lines with his weapon, a
crate hammer, gripped tightly in his hand. Rider saw the code
number on the supplies he guarded: XG-B-193.

"I'll be damned," he said.

"What are he guarding?" Loper asked.

"Exchange items and good-will gifts that the ERB has desig-
nated as suitable for barbaric cultures of this type. He's supposed
to fight to the death to protect three thousand pounds of glass
beads, hand mirrors, and bright red toy magnets."

They went into the thicket and the camp was hidden from
view. The winding course of an old animal trail led in the desired
direction and they followed it until it skirted the base of a small
hill. He climbed to the top of it, with Loper at his heels, and
looked back at the camp. There was a great deal of activity
around the helicopter and he could distinguish Primmer standing
to one side and directing the refueling operations.

He looked to the southeast, along his route to the sea, and
along the rocky ridge that lay like a barrier between he saw the
natives waiting and watching.

"I think," Loper said, "that they not want us to pass. I think
we fight there, Captain."

"You'll stay here, on this hill," he said.

"Stay?" Loper jerked up his head in surprise and defiance.
"No!"

"That's an order. I want you to watch the camp until after
it's all over with tomorrow."

"I not stay safe whire you fight arone!" Loper braced his
forepaws wide-apart and stubborn on the ground. "I not do
it!"

✧ ✧ ✧

He sat down on a sun-blackened boulder. "Listen, Loper—listen to the reasons why you have to help me:

"The government of Earth is four hundred light-years away and they will have to believe Beeling's story; that the natives are treacherous and hate all humans and that the Frontier Corps goaded them into massacring the entire camp. The natives are honest in their fear and distrust of humans—they think they are fighting for their world—and there will be no one after tomorrow to tell them they are wrong.

"Except you and Laughing Girl. They might listen to you Altairians since you know humans well and yet aren't human. You must tell them that Earth never takes a world by force, that even Beeling meant well but did not understand, and that all the things I told them Earth would do for them would have been done. And you must stay here until after tomorrow morning and watch the camp so that when a ship comes from Earth to investigate you can tell the officers exactly what happened here and what caused it to happen. It will be too late to save the Frontier Corps but if they will listen to you it might not be too late for them to see the mistakes that have been made and start over again."

The rigid stubbornness was gone from Loper, understanding and dark misery in its place. "It wrong—everything are happen awr wrong and I never see you again!"

"Yes," he said, "everything is all wrong and shot to hell. I'm trying to salvage the remains the best I can and I have to have your help."

"I do everything you say, Captain."

"For some time this will be your world and Laughing Girl's. Maybe for all your lives. So be friends with the natives and don't blame them for what they did. Remember that."

"Yes, sir. I remember."

He looked at the sunset's violet afterglow and stood up. "I'll have to hurry or I won't get there in time. Good luck, Loper."

"Good-bye, Captain. I—I sorry."

He turned and went down the hill and across the flat beyond. He looked back when he was almost to the ridge and saw Loper still staring forlornly after him.

✧ ✧ ✧

He reached the foot of the ridge and climbed its steep slope. Three natives were waiting for him on top, their long rifles in their hands and the smiles on their faces. The one in the center was Resso, a sub-chief in Selsin's tribe.

"Where would you go, human?" Resso asked in the native language.

"I would go to the sea," he answered in the same language, and told them why. "I ask permission to pass," he said.

Resso rubbed the breach of his rifle, his eyes thoughtful and hard. "Between here and the sea are many by-paths. You might lose your way and be troublesome for us to find in the morning."

He took the long knife from his belt, spun it in the air and caught it by the blade. The three rifles centered on him as he did so.

"This is my only weapon," he said to Resso. "I think I can put it in your throat before I can be killed—but I ask you to let me save the Altairian first and match it against your rifles tomorrow."

Resso spit on the ground. "Tomorrow I will make you eat it before I kill you."

Rider felt a great sense of relief—Resso was going to let him pass . . .

"I want to ask a favor of you," he said to Resso. "That the Altairians not be harmed."

Surprise showed on Resso's face. "Why should we harm the furry ones? They are only your slaves and not responsible for what humans do."

"Then you promise?"

Resso took a step forward, glowering in quick anger. "Do you have the insolence to question what I say? Be on your way— run, human, and find your hiding place!"

He went, walking past them with the glum thought: *This makes Ignominious Exit Number Two. I hope my last one, tomorrow, will have at least a little dignity to it . . .*

The desert was miles of red iron sand, across which rocky ridges lay like a hundred randomly flung barriers. Some of the ridges were of limestone, honey-combed with natural caves. These he would have to avoid at all costs since they were the lairs of the ten-foot sand hounds.

He was no more than well started when dark came. He had no light and without a blaster he would not dare to use one if he had it. It would attract the attention of sand hounds for miles around.

For the greater part, his way was along relatively clear stretches of the wind-packed sand and his progress was fairly fast. At intervals, however, he came to dense and wide-spreading thickets of the poison-thorned desert vegetation and these he had to bypass with time consuming detours.

Once he almost walked upon a band of wild dragon-beasts, grazing silently in the starlight. Only the good fortune of the wind being in his favor prevented them from detecting him and charging. He had to backtrack and then climb a long ridge to get around them. It cost him an hour of time.

The last of the clouds disappeared from the eastern sky as the storm went its way across the Southern Gulf. He was grateful that it had not swerved inland and turned the dim starlight into total darkness. His time margin would be small, at best.

Shortly before midnight he stopped on a sand dune, to rest for the first time. It was there that he saw a tiny, distant red spark; a signal fire on the hill north of camp. It blinked for several minutes in a code he did not understand, then went out.

When it did not reappear at the end of two more minutes he got up and resumed his journey to the sea.

Not long afterward the sky to the east turned pale; a whiteness that grew swiftly brighter and obscured the eastern stars. It was the dawn of the three moons; the moons that brought the Big Tide with them.

They lifted above the horizon in a flying wedge formation, flooding the desert with cold, white light. He could see well, then, and he hurried faster down the long slopes that led to the sea.

The bright moonlight greatly increased the danger of being seen by a sand hound and he had not gone far when one screamed from somewhere behind him. He stopped, and looked back.

He could not see it but he saw something else when he looked to the rocky ridge west of him; flitting shadow-shapes that seemed to be dragon-beasts were keeping pace with him. He wondered if it would be Resso and the others, making certain he would not be hard to find when morning came. They were gone from view before he could be sure he had not imagined seeing them.

He hurried on again. The character of the desert had changed as the elevation decreased and a dry, wiry grass was replacing most of the vegetation. He changed his course slightly so that he could walk down the center of a shallow valley where it grew the thickest, listening for the sand hound to scream again.

It did so, much closer than before. Two more answered it from farther back, then a third. Which made four of them racing toward him, each of them like a reptilian ten-foot greyhound with the claws of a tiger and the teeth and jaws of a young tyrannosaurus.

He lighted the grass at his feet, then started two more fires on each side of the first one. Within that short time the tinder-dry grass was burning in a solid wall of flame, pushed down the valley by the wind at increasing speed and spreading wider as it went.

He had to run to get in front of it and then run still faster to keep ahead of it. Through the choking smoke he could see nothing except the red blaze of fire behind him but he heard the sand hounds screeching in frustration beyond it. The sound of their fury faded as he ran on, and then was gone.

A mile farther on he angled to the left, to the rim of the valley where the grass was too thin to burn, and there he rested until his hard panting had subsided. Then he walked on again; to hurry faster and faster as the three moons neared the zenith. Shortly after they had passed the zenith it would be sunrise and the Big Tide would reach the Sea Cliffs.

He saw no more of the phantom dragon-beasts, but the smoke from the valley he had fired lay like a pall across the desert and visibility was limited.

The eastern sky was lightening with the first glow of dawn when he saw the distant gleam of moonlight on the ocean. The delays during the night had been greater than he had thought—there would be no time margin, at all.

He went the rest of the way in a fast trot, the rope ready in his hand.

The sea to the east was flat and calm when he reached the ragged top of the Sea Cliffs but the pale violet of dawn had turned into a vivid blue-white. Sunrise and the Big Tide were at hand.

He looked down over the edge of the cliffs, down the sheer face of them where the crevice reached up for two hundred feet before it dwindled into nothing, and saw the red-shelled horrors grouped in a thick mass at the bottom. Laughing Girl was above them, wedged tightly in the crevice as far up it as she had been able to climb. It had not been far; the groping claws of the topmost Elephant Crabs were cracking together only inches below her.

He had already tied a series of knots in the end of the rope so she could grip it firmly between her teeth. He dropped the knotted end over the cliff and gave the rope a flip to guide it toward the crevice.

He glanced again to the east, at the calm, flat sea, and in that instant its horizon abruptly swelled and lifted up and became a mountain rushing toward him.

The Elephant Crabs were spilling apart, scrambling to positions of safety where they could anchor themselves against the rough rock surface and be protected by the thick armor of their shells. Laughing Girl was suddenly alone in her refuge, a small black huddle that watched the coming of the Big Tide in frozen helplessness.

The rope was snaking down the crevice as fast as he could play out the coils. He whistled at her as the rope neared her. She jerked up her head, almost falling in her surprise, and greeted him in her native language; a word that was like the joyous yelp of a pup. Then the end of the rope reached her and she seized it between her teeth.

He hauled up on the rope, bringing it back hand over hand, while Laughing Girl clawed at the rock to help all she could. She disappeared from his sight where the cliff became vertical and the thin, hard rope was almost impossible to grip tightly as her full weight went upon it.

The tide raced inward as he struggled with the rope; the forefront of an oceanic plateau. Between it and the cliffs the beach and sea below lay like a valley, then a narrow basin, then suddenly a vanishing canyon—

✧   ✧   ✧

Laughing Girl's head popped into view and she came pawing and scrambling over the edge of the cliff. She dropped the rope and leaped toward him in ecstatic welcome.

"You come for me! You—"

The tide struck the cliffs with a thunderous roar, making the earth shake. He seized Laughing Girl by the scruff of the neck and dropped flat to the ground, where he could lock his free arm around a projection of rock. A solid mass of water was flung high into the air by the impact, to descend upon them with a smashing force that knocked the breath from his lungs and bruised his face against the rocks. He held grimly to the rock and Laughing Girl as the mass of water poured back over the cliff, ripping and tearing at him as it tried to take them with it.

They staggered erect as it drained away and ran. A second mass of skyward-flung water came too late to do more than drench them. They stopped a little farther on, along the top of a low ridge.

Behind them the sea growled and rumbled as it surged against the cliffs. Laughing Girl looked back, trembling a little.

"I thought you had forgot me, Boss. I was scared, and I wait and wait . . ."

"Everything is all right, now," he said. "You won't ever have to go under the Sea Cliffs again."

He was tired, weak with near-exhaustion. He wiped the salty water from his face and saw, as something that was no longer of importance, that the sun was up. His job was done, his last duty carried out, and the thing that would happen next was something inevitable and beyond his control. He saw that his knife was gone, washed into the sea—but that no longer mattered, either.

"You will go home now," he said to Laughing Girl. "Don't wait for me. Loper will probably be starting on his way to meet you in a few minutes. He'll tell you about the things that have happened in the past two days. From now on the two of you will do whatever he thinks is best for you."

Her eyes were wide in alarm before he had finished, anxious and questioning.

"What are wrong, Boss? What are going to happen to you—prease, what are wrong?"

✧   ✧   ✧

A slow, muffled thudding came from the east and he looked into the bright blaze of the sun to see the dragon-beasts trotting down the ridge toward him. There were six of them and even against the sun he could see the gleam of battle helmets and the long rifles across the saddles.

"Go home!" he ordered. "Right now!"

She looked from the approaching war party back to him and flung up her head in defiance as Loper had done.

"No! You know they come to kirr you—I can terr. I stay!"

"There are things you don't yet understand, Girl," he said. "For my sake, go now. Run."

"I—" She hesitated, her sense of duty and sense of loyalty conflicting. The loyalty won. "No! I not go!"

He could not permit her to stay. When the natives shot him down she would attack them with a fury that only her own death could stop.

He stepped forward and hit her; a hard, open-handed blow alongside the jaw that sent her rolling. She got to her feet with amazement and hurt in her eyes and he made his tone harsh and ugly:

"I'll not order you but this one more time—*go home!*"

She obeyed, her tail drooping as she started across the swale. She stopped once, to look back at him, and he motioned her on with a curt gesture.

She was gone from sight when the natives reached him. Resso was not with them—it was Selsin who rode in the lead.

They stopped before him in a semi-circle and regarded him silently, the mocking smiles on their faces.

"It is sunrise," Selsin said.

"It is," he agreed.

"We followed you last night. I wanted to know if you told the truth about going to save the furry one."

"And now," he said, "I want to know if Resso told the truth when he said she and her mate would not be harmed."

"He did."

There was nothing more to say, then. He waited, wondering if they were deliberately delaying his execution in the hope of seeing him weaken under the tension.

Selsin spoke again:

"Your superior and his aide escaped in the flier shortly after you left. The fire signal at midnight said they had landed on one of the Northern Islands and were firing steadily at a school of bladder fish. They seemed to think the fish were an attacking party."

He had the impression that Selsin and the others were amused. He could understand why—but for himself there was only a sick feeling of shame and the thought: *So they wouldn't even leave those kids their blasters?*

"It is sunrise," Selsin said again, "and there is no reason to wait any longer. Do you have anything to say?"

"Nothing," he answered, and braced himself for the impact of the bullets.

But the long rifles were not lifted. Instead, Selsin swung down from the saddle and came up to him.

"The furry one—Loper—came to me before dark and told me what you had said to him on the hill. Didn't you know that what you were doing was more proof of good intentions than all the promises in the world?"

"I don't understand," he said.

"You claimed from the beginning that humans respected other forms of life and kept their promises to them—but words are only little noises. You proved what you had claimed when you spent what was to be the last night of your life in keeping the promise you had made to a being who was far less human than even my own race."

"But the camp—" He did not dare believe what Selsin's statements implied. "They were to be killed at sunrise—"

"I ordered the attack postponed until your actions could be judged. Now, there will be no attack."

He tried to see past Selsin's meaningless smile, wishing he had let Laughing Girl stay so she could tell him if they were only taunting him before they killed him.

"You will ride one of the dragon-beasts, if you are ready now," Selsin said. "When you call Earth from your camp today, I will speak to them, too. I want no more misunderstandings."

"What will you tell them?" he asked.

"The truth of it all, and how the fat one boasted and insulted my race, and then ran. I will offer the friendship of my race under the condition that no more of his kind ever be sent here and that you, or others of your choice, be in charge of all operations here.

"I suppose," Selsin added, "that your Supreme Council would like to hear what I have to tell them?"

There was a flash of black across the swale and he saw Laughing Girl running toward them; disobeying his order, after all, and come back to fight beside him. But now she was running with her tail up, her white teeth grinning, and happiness like something tangible about her.

She was an Altairian—she *knew* that everything was suddenly all right. There could be no doubt whatever about Selsin's sincerity, about the future that lay ahead for all of them.

Even for Laughing Girl's race, although she did not yet know it. Loper, in his simple wisdom, had made it possible for Earth to regain the friendship of a badly needed world. The Council, in return, could do no less than to promptly overrule the ERB's classification of the Altairians as "Animals."

"The Supreme Council," he said in answer to Selsin's question, "is going to be delighted by what you have to tell them. Let's go."

Editor's note: There is a strong moral component in most of Godwin's stories. Courage, by itself, is never enough. There also has to be an underlying sense of empathy for other creatures. In Godwin's universe, selfishness is perhaps the ultimate sin. We've seen that theme appear many times in his stories. And, here again:

NO SPECIES ALONE

The morning was, to Jim Hart, exactly like any other June morning but for the presence of Gwen—eight weeks was not yet long enough for him to take her as fully for granted as he would in the months and years to come. She hummed to herself as she finished wiping the breakfast dishes. Out on the porch Susie and six of the kittens, having just lapped up their own breakfast, were engaged in the after-meal practice of making themselves neat and clean as is the manner of cats. The sky was a flawless sapphire blue with the touch of the sun as warm and gentle as a benediction while the meadowlarks filled the air with their soft melodies.

There was nothing about the morning's soft beauty to presage sudden and vicious peril.

He checked to make sure he had his surveying compass as he stood in the doorway then glanced across the brush-and-tree-dotted flat that extended to the mouth of the canyon a thousand feet away. There the flat broke abruptly along the high, steep bank, a trail leading from the cabin to the break. There was no sign of the pup along the trail, which meant Flopper had gone on up the canyon—he had made so many trips to the uranium prospect that spring that Flopper knew as well as he where they were going for the day.

Gwen wiped the last dish and came over to stand beside him, her head leaned against his shoulder.

"So it's off for the day you go again." She sighed. "I'm glad this is the last day of it."

"Less than a day—I'll be back by noon. Also, from now on we're all set—I found that uranium myself and it's good. My company will take it without a doubt and then I'll be a well-to-do uranium property owner rather than just an employed mining engineer. Doesn't that sound like a bright and pleasant future for us?"

"It sounds wonderful," she agreed. "You can be home all the time and every young wife should have a man around the place—preferably her husband. And another thing—" She looked at the cat and kittens. "If you had to go back to work and they sent you off to South America or somewhere—what would become of *them*?"

"You gave yourself responsibility when you picked them up. You shouldn't be so soft-hearted. 'Poor little things—out by this lonely road and it's raining and they're cold and hungry and have no home.' That's what you said, and now we have to buy a case of canned milk every month for them. If I had my *own* way—"

"You did," she pointed out sweetly. "You said, 'Don't just stand there—let's load 'em in the car and be going.'"

"Well—" He considered his defense. "I was weak that night."

"And the pup, Flopper?" she demanded.

"Another weak spell—like the day I finally consented to marry you."

"*You* consented?" She straightened with indignation. "*You* consented?"

"Mm-hmm." He nodded with grave seriousness. "I felt sorry for you."

"Why, you—you—" She stuttered, and tried again. "*You* consented? You—"

"Please, Gwen, do you have to keep repeating everything I tell you, over and over?"

"*You* told me—I didn't—I mean—*oh!*" She struck a small fist against his arm. "You're just trying to make me mad again—why are you always doing that?"

"Practice," he said succinctly and put his arm around her shoulders to draw her close to him. "When we have our first big fight, we don't want to be amateurs, you know."

"One of these days," she said, "you're going to *really* make me mad," but the threat of her words was belied by the way she once again rested her head against his shoulder. "Now, admit the truth—you *wanted* to give Flopper a home and you *wanted* to give Susie and the kittens a home, didn't you?"

"O.K.—I admit it," he said. "It seems to be a human characteristic to want pets around. Illogical—but human nature."

"Logic, *fooey*!" She turned her head and made a face at him. "A computing machine is infallibly logical, but do you think I'd ever want to marry one?"

He raised his brows. "I certainly hope not, that would be ridiculous. Also, you'd get bored with life-with-an-adding-machine."

"I'd sue it for divorce on grounds of mental cruelty. Imagine how life would be if you had to always be logical in everything you did and never did anything because you *wanted* to, like going swimming and playing games and giving homes to lost dogs and cats and—and—" She broke off to stare past him, toward the mouth of the canyon. "*Look!*" She pointed, sudden excitement in her voice. "There alongside the trail—the spotted kitten. He wasn't here for breakfast—there he is now. Susie got her fourth one yesterday and now *he's* found one!"

He followed her gaze and saw the half-grown spotted kitten some three hundred feet away and perhaps fifty feet to one side of the trail. As he watched the kitten circled a few steps, carefully keeping its eyes on whatever it was circling as it did so. It was, he saw, holding something at bay in a small area free of brush but was not yet making an effort to kill it.

"It's another one," he said, turning back into the cabin. "I'll kill it on my way to work."

He went into the bedroom and came back with a .38 automatic pistol in his hand. "I used to be a pretty good shot with one of these," he remarked in explanation. "A shovel would do just as well, but I think I'll see if I've lost the ability to hit the broad side of a barn."

"Do a good job," she said. "As soon as I sweep and do a few other things, I'm going up to the creek to get some watercress for salad. I hope—" She frowned worriedly. "I hope this is the last one—I'm afraid of the things."

"Susie would have had this one by now if it hadn't been for

her having to take time off to drink her breakfast milk and wash her face. The wind's in the wrong direction for her to smell it yet, but she'd have spotted it before it got much closer to the cabin." He stepped off the porch and started up the trail. "I'll be back about noon. Be careful when you go after that water-cress and don't wear those idiotic cutaway moccasins."

"I won't," she answered, for once not disputing his opinion of her footwear.

He was still a hundred feet from the spotted kitten when he heard the low, dry buzz. It was a rattlesnake, as he had known it would be. It was coiled, its head weaving restlessly, and the kitten was watching it with cold intentness. The rattlesnake turned away from the kitten as he came up to them and tried to slither away to the cover of the nearest bush. The kitten darted around in front of it, just beyond striking range, and cut off its retreat.

The snaked stopped, to coil and wait with its head poised to strike. The kitten stood before it as motionless as a little statue, only a faint tremor to the end of its tail to indicate any emotion. That, and its eyes. They were, as Hart observed on previous such occasions, quite wide and green and mercilessly cold. There was always something *different* about the look in a cat's eyes when it watched a snake; a concentration, a hair-trigger alertness, and an icy, implacable hatred. Yet, despite the kitten's alertness, there was an air of calmness in the way it watched the snake, almost contempt. It knew instinctively that the snake was deadly dang-erous but that instinctive knowledge was outweighed by the other instinctive knowledge; the knowledge that the snake was afraid of *it* and would never dare to deliberately come within striking range. The rattlesnake would never dare approach the kitten; it had but one desire—to escape.

The two were motionless for a few seconds with the snake waiting to strike, its triangular head, two-thirds as wide as Hart's hand, poised and ready. Then the snake broke and tried to dart away from the kitten. The kitten flashed in front of it, still just out of striking range, and the snake stopped to coil and squirm in indecision, its red tongue flickering in and out and its buzzing rising higher and higher in pitch as its agitation increased.

Hart looked back toward the cabin and saw that Susie and

the kittens were still on the porch. He raised his voice and called to her: "Susie—*snake!*"

He had taught her to recognize the word and she was off the porch at once, to come trotting up the trail with the five kittens stringing out behind her and Gwen standing in the doorway, shading her eyes against the sun with one hand as she watched.

He turned back to the snake. It wouldn't be long—not after Susie got there.

The snake's head was weaving restlessly as it tried to evade the stare of the kitten and find a way to escape. It tried again to dart away, and again the kitten flashed in front of it to cut off its retreat. The snake stopped, unable to reach the safety of the bush, unable in its fear to pass near the kitten. Its fear was visibly increasing and so was its hate; a vicious, reptilian hatred for the half-grown kitten that stood before it. But, greater than the hatred was the fear; the old, old instinctive fear of a cat that was common to all snakes.

It was strange, the way snakes feared cats. One strike with that broad head and there would be enough venom in the kitten's body to kill a dozen like it, yet the snake did not dare to strike. Should the kitten come within striking range, it would strike—but it was afraid to approach the kitten with the purpose of striking it. There was something about the way the kitten stared at it, the cold lack of fear, that the snake could not understand and feared. And the longer the kitten stared at the snake, the greater the snake's fear would become.

There were animals that enjoyed an immunity from the bite of a rattlesnake; a hog, protected by its fat, could kill a rattlesnake; a band of sheep, protected by their wool, would blindly trample a rattlesnake to death. Some animals could kill rattlesnakes; a deer could, some small, fast dogs could. But the rattlesnake feared none of these, would try to strike any of them. Yet the kitten, completely vulnerable with neither wool nor fat to protect it, did not fear the snake and knew the snake feared it. It was something peculiar to cats and snakes; an inherent hatred and enmity that went back to the dawn of creation.

Susie trotted up and took in the scene with one swift glance. The kitten relaxed as he turned the job over to the more capable paws of his mother and she stood a moment just beyond striking range, studying the snake. It coiled closer, afraid to try to escape from her for such an action would render it vulnerable by forcing it to uncoil, knowing in its tiny reptilian mind that in the lean, wise old cat before it was Death.

Susie paused only briefly in her appraisal of it, then she stepped forward with her eyes fixed on the wide-jawed head and her body as tense as a coiled spring. She calmly, deliberately, came within striking range and waited for it to strike at her, one forepaw slightly lifted. The snake struck, then; the very thing Susie had intended for it to do. Its head flicked forward in a motion too fast for Hart to see and at the same time, and even faster, there was the flash of Susie's paw. That, and her backward leap.

It was a blur of movement too swift for human eyes to follow but in that split-second the snake had struck, its fangs had encountered only thin air where Susie had been and, simultaneously, it had felt the sharp rip of her claws down its venomous head. Then they were poised again, as before, but this time there were three slashes down the top of the snake's head from which blood was beginning to ooze.

She moved in on it again, her pupils two razor-edge slits in eyes that were like hard emeralds. She came within range and the snake struck again. It was the same as before; the invisibly swift stab of the white fangs was too slow to equal the speed of the slashing claws. There were more bloody furrows down the snake's head when the blur of movement was over. The next time there would be still more, and it would go on until the snake's head was half torn from its body and it was dead. It could end no other way; it was not the nature of a cat to permit a snake to live.

There was insane fury, now, to the quick coiling of the snake, the high, shrill buzzing of its tail and the frantic flickering of its head. It was reaching the stage where its rage and fear was nothing short of madness and it would deliberately attack anything in the world—except a cat. Hart threw a cartridge into the chamber of the .38. He had no desire to see anything die a slow death, not even a rattlesnake. Although, it seemed to him, there was something downright splendid about the way Susie— and all other cats—could put the fear of Eternity into man's traditional enemy, the serpent.

As Susie began easing back within range of the snake Hart

lined the sights on its head and pulled the trigger. The snake's head smashed to the ground at the impact of the bullet and the cats jumped back in startled surprise at the crack of the pistol.

Susie looked at the dead, writhing snake with a sudden and complete lack of interest, gave Hart a look that seemed to contain definite disgust and went over to sit in the shade of a bush.

"Sorry, Susie—I know you didn't really need any help," he apologized.

The kittens were crowding around the snake, attacking it in emulation of their mother's fight with it. They were only kittens, but they were learning. By the time they were grown he and Gwen would have a very efficient crew to rid the place of rattlesnakes. Susie, alone, had killed four in the past two months that he knew of for certain—and one of them had crawled into the cabin while Gwen was gone, to lay coiled under the butane range. Had it not been for the vigilance of Susie, it would still have been there when Gwen returned to prepare dinner, her bare, brown legs the target for its striking fangs. By that one act, alone, Susie had far more than repaid them for giving her and her kittens a home.

He picked the snake up on the end of a stick and tossed it far out in the brush. The kittens watched it arc through the air and fall from sight; with the snake no longer there, they lost interest in the past events and wandered over to join their mother. He hefted the pistol in his hand, wondering whether to take it with him or take it back to the cabin. Deciding one was as much trouble as the other, he waved to Gwen who was still watching from the doorway and started up the trail.

He was some distance up it when he looked back to see the ubiquitous spotted kitten following him—or following in so far as necessary delays to inspect interesting scents and insects along the trail would permit. The red kitten was watching the spotted one, apparently with half a mind to go, too. He went on— they wouldn't follow him very far up the canyon, anyway. Perhaps as far as the creek; perhaps they'd change their minds and return to the cabin.

At the edge of the sagebrush flat the trail went down into the canyon, following along the side of the steep wall in a gentle grade. He made his way along the narrow trail, which was sixty feet above the floor of the canyon at its highest point, and down to the bottom of the canyon. It was as he started up the canyon that he first detected the odor. It was very faint, so faint that he could not place it. His thoughts were upon the survey he would make that morning and he was hardly conscious of it, though a part of his mind noted it and was vaguely disturbed by it. He walked on, past the place along the creek where Gwen would gather the watercress, and there an almost imperceptible breeze drifted down from the up-canyon. It brought the odor stronger and he stopped, the vague uneasiness in his mind suddenly awakening to wary alertness.

It was the odor of a snake.

He looked about him, but there was nothing to be seen. He knew he could not have gotten any of the odor of the snake he had killed on his clothes, and the odor coming down the canyon was not quite that of a rattlesnake; it was fully as offensive and reptilian, but *different*.

He shook his head, puzzled, and walked on. Two hundred feet farther on the canyon swung in a bend and the trail took a short-cut through a thick growth of junipers. Here the odor became definitely stronger and a creepy feeling ran up his spine. He kept his eyes on the ground, watching where he was stepping as he went through the heavy underbrush. There was no doubt about the odor; while not quite like that of a rattlesnake, it was certainly the odor of *some* kind of a snake. Or several snakes, judging by the strength of it.

He stepped out of the thicket of trees and brush to the sandy bed of the canyon and looked up. There, not fifty feet in front of him, was Flopper—and the thing he had smelled.

The Slistian scout ship drifted down through the darkness, silently, undetected. Sesnar watched the little that the viewscreen could show in the darkness, his eighteen-foot snake-like body coiled in the concave pilot's chair before the control board, and patiently heard the thoughts that emanated from the spherical device beside him.

"Is there any evidence of intelligent life in the immediate vicinity?" the thought from the transmitter sphere asked.

"None," Sesnar's own thought replied. "I'm descending over an isolated section of the western part of the continent. The instruments indicate considerable mineralization in this area under me, including uranium. There are the lights of some kind of a small city in the far distance, but that is all."

The sphere made no comment and Sesnar asked, "Shall I sterilize the area in which I shall land?"

It required the usual two seconds for the sphere to project his thought through a hundred lightyears of space to his superior on Slistia and another two seconds for the reply to come back. "No. Although your observations have shown no great technological knowledge on the part of the natives, they may possess means of detecting your use of the sterilizer ray. They do possess the atomic and hydrogen bombs, we know, and the discovery upon their planet of an alien spaceship equipped with such a weapon as the sterilizer ray would most certainly cause them to attempt to interfere with your preliminary surveys and your capture of some of the natives for examination and study. When you are near the surface you shall proceed toward the area the instruments show to contain radioactive ores, flying low and watching for evidences of habitation, such as the lights of individual dwellings."

Sesnar duly acknowledged the order.

It did not seem strange to him that he, alone, should have been dispatched to make the preliminary survey of the new world while the nine members of the psychologist-strategist board remained upon Slistia to direct his most detailed activities by means of the thought transmitter sphere. It was merely coldly logical. No Slistian could foretell the degrees of civilization, if any, on a world a hundred lightyears away. Such a world *might* possess defensive weapons unknown to the Slistians. Such a thing had never happened—and no Slistian doubted ultimate Slistian victory—but the preliminary survey would disclose the weapons, if any, that the natives possessed; would disclose the resources of the new world, including the vital radioactive ores, and would provide specimens of the native intelligent life for study and ultimate vivisection. The weapons of the Slistians were many and deadly, with the hypnotic power of the Slistian mind the most insidiously deadly weapon of all. Yet there was always the small possibility of the natives possessing deadly weapons of their own and an exploration scout, such as Sesnar, proceeded under the constant supervision of the highly learned, very systematic,

psychologists-strategists of the Colonization Board. The scout ship
was equipped with every needed device and instrument to survey
the new world, from mapping its continents to analyzing its air
and determining what harmful viruses might be present. It
carried robotic equipment to mine and refine radioactive ores
for powering the force field it would throw around the miner-
alized area; the area that would become the Slistian headquarters for their Extermination Force ships. It carried a well-equipped
laboratory where the captured native specimens could be probed
and questioned by Sesnar's mind until their own minds were
drained dry of information. After that, they would be placed on
the tables and the viewscreen overhead would permit the Colonization Board on Slistia, as well as the Extermination Force Board,
to learn the physical structure of the natives as Sesnar methodically
vivisected them.

It was all very logical and carefully planned. A scout ship
required a considerable amount of uranium-based fuel and the
supply still remaining upon Slistia and the two worlds Slistia had
captured was limited. Although thought waves could be trans-
mitted across a hundred lightyears of space in two seconds, the
material body of the ship required eight months to traverse the
same distance. One Slistian could, with the specially-equipped
ship, do as quick and thorough a job of surveying a new planet
as a crew of Slistians could do and additional Slistians, plus
additional food for the eight months voyage, would have
required an additional amount of fuel; fuel that would be
needed by the Extermination Force ships that would follow later.
It was only necessary to know that the new world possessed
the radioactive ores and to learn of what means of defense the
natives might have.

The latter was very important; upon the study of the specimens of native life and their weapons would depend the
strategy of the Extermination Force. They were quite efficient
in ridding a world of its natives and their efficiency was due
to careful planning beforehand; to equipping the Extermination
Force ships with the most suitably destructive weapons for the
job.

Sesnar halted the descent of the ship a few hundred feet
above the surface and let it travel slowly in the direction of

the uranium mineralization. He was almost to the bulk of a mountain when he saw the yellow light. He notified his superiors at once.

"There is a yellow-white rectangle of light some distance away. It's apparently artificial light from the window of a native's dwelling."

"Pass it by." The command was from Eska, head of the Colonization Board. "Take no chance of detection at this time. Pass it by and conceal your ship near the area of greatest mineralization."

Sesnar continued on his way, rising as he did so to clear the foothills of the mountain. He had gone a relatively short distance, the rectangle of light in the native's dwelling still visible behind him, when the instruments told him he was directly over the deposit of uranium. He descended to the ground, letting the robotic control scan the terrain under the ship with its radar eyes and select a safe and level spot. The ship settled to earth and he notified Eska of the fact.

There was a certain emotionless satisfaction in Eska's thought as he said, "The nearness of the native's dwelling to the uranium deposit simplifies things. Tomorrow you can accomplish both the capture of natives for study and the erection of the force field. In the meantime, you shall remain in the ship."

The latter order was not without sound reasons of caution; some creatures could see excellently in the dark and no Slistian could use its hypnotic powers on an animal it could not see.

Sesnar waited until dawn, then he reached out with the two small arms that were the only interruption of the snake-like form of his body and picked up his menta-blaster, to snap it down on the four metal studs set in the tough scales of the top of his head. He took no other weapon with him as he crawled forth from the ship; he needed no other weapon and only the most unexpected circumstances could cause him to need *it*, the hypnotic power of its mind serving very well to force other creatures to do as he willed.

The ship had landed in the bottom of a small canyon. There had been something in the canyon very recently, he saw, something that had dug some narrow trenches across what he presumed to be the deposit of uranium ore. He reported the fact to Eska.

"The work of the natives, obviously," Eska commented. "It would not be advisable to lift the ship at present. Reconnoiter— there should be some kind of a path the natives have made and it will lead to the dwelling. Follow the path for a short distance and report what you find."

The thoughts of Eska, broadcast by the sphere inside the ship, came clearly to Sesnar and he obeyed the orders, pausing only long enough to try the menta-blaster on a small bush beside the path. It vanished in a puff of dust.

The menta-blaster was a Slistian achievement and one that could be used only by Slistians. It was operated by certain thought patterns, the type and intensity of the beam regulated at will. Since the thought pattern that operated it had to be very precise, it was useless to any warm-blooded animal; only a Slistian could produce the necessary pattern with the necessary machine- like precision. It was a characteristic of warm-blooded animals to be emotional to a certain extent and no emotional animal, no matter how intelligent, could be sure of suppressing its emotions sufficiently to always duplicate the rigid, precise thought pattern. Although it might seem to the warm-blooded, intelli- gent animal that its emotions were completely in check and its mind free of all influence from them, the emotional influence over the pure, cold logic would still be there to some slight extent, enough to prevent exact duplication of the thought pattern built into the menta-blaster.

The menta-blaster was, to the Slistians, quite unnecessary proof that cold-blooded and logical life forms were superior to warm- blooded and emotional life forms.

The path was easily found and he followed it. He had gone only a short distance when the canyon emptied into a much larger one; a canyon that led in the general direction of the native's dwelling. The path followed the creek bank down the larger canyon and there, feeding on the green vegetation beside the path, he saw the first specimen of the planet's life.

It was a small quadruped with long ears and its sensitive ears detected the whisper in the sand of Sesnar's coming at almost the same moment he saw it. It sat up high on its hind legs to stare at him, its nose twitching, then it wheeled to bound away. He brought it under hypnotic control and it fell limply to the ground.

It was, of course, still alive and conscious; merely held helpless. Sesnar crawled to it and searched its mind. Its mind held no information of any value, its intelligence was of a very low order. Obviously, it was not a member of the planet's intelligent form of life.

He touched the rabbit with his small, lizard-like hands, feeling the fast flutter of its heart, then ripping a sharp claw down its belly. The entrails spilled out on the ground and he observed with interest that the animal was strictly herbivorous. He reported the fact to Eska who then ordered him to release the rabbit from hypnotic control so that its reaction to pain might be observed.

At the release of hypnotic control it leaped high in the air with a thin, shrill scream, then fell back to lay flopping and kicking in the sand, its bloody entrails trailing behind it. Its efforts to escape quickly weakened and soon it could do no more than lie and watch Sesnar with intense fear in its eyes.

"A high degree of sensitivity to pain, with no desire to destroy the inflictor of the pain," Eska remarked. "No revenge instincts whatever. Should this characteristic of complete non-aggressiveness apply to the intelligent creatures, our colonization program should need relatively little aid from the Extermination Force."

Sesnar waited until the rabbit died, reporting its resistance to death. It took a remarkably long time for it to die—that is, for a warm-blooded animal. The characteristic sensitivity to pain of warm-blooded animals was usually one of the factors that hastened their death when badly injured. When it finally stopped panting he crawled on, both he and Eska feeling well satisfied on the whole, though the high resistance to death was not to be desired.

He had not crawled very far down the canyon when he encountered the next quadruped, coming upon it suddenly where the trail swung around a sharp bend in the canyon. It was trotting up the trail toward him, unable to scent him with the breeze momentarily blowing up the canyon and he brought it under control the moment he saw it. He left it standing on its four legs and went down to it. It was considerably larger than the quadruped he had killed, shorter of ear and a different species altogether. He probed into its mind and found its intelligence to be of the third order; very high for a non-reasoning animal.

"Does its mind contain any information concerning the dominant form of life?" Eska asked.

"The dominant form is biped and this animal lives with two of them," Sesnar replied. "It exhibits an odd regard for them; an illogical emotional regard."

He went on to explain the affection of the dog for its masters and their affection for it as best he could. It was not a new thing to either Sesnar or Eska—they had observed similar attachments among other warm-blooded species—but it was impossible for them to comprehend the desire of two creatures of different species to be near each other and find pleasure in each other's company.

Eska dismissed it as of no importance. "Apparently the same as the attachment between the natives of Venda and the small animals they used to keep around before our arrival. It might be termed a symbiosis of the emotions—utterly illogical and no more than another example of their mental inferiority. What other information does the quadruped's mind contain?"

"It isn't a mature specimen but its thoughts are quite clear. It lives with two of these bipeds—a male and a female—in the dwelling near here. The male biped is to pass this way very soon and the quadruped has a strong desire for the biped to make its appearance. It's afraid of me but it seems confident the biped will either kill me or frighten me away."

"It has no doubt of the biped's ability to destroy you?" Eska asked.

"None whatever. Although it possesses no technical knowledge, of course, and is unable to supply me with any information concerning the biped's weapons."

"I think you will find the animal's confidence in the invincibility of the biped is due to the regard of the weaker for the stronger," Eska said. "Since the actions and abilities of the biped are beyond the quadruped's intelligence to comprehend it assumes, having no experience to the contrary, that nothing can be superior to the biped it depends upon for protection.

"Now, if you have extracted all the information of value in the animal's mind, kill it and conceal yourself near the path the biped is to use. A search of the biped's mind will reveal if there are any other bipeds in the vicinity, other than the biped's mate. If not, you will capture her, too, and return with both of them to your ship. You will then throw a force field around that area and lift ship to complete your mapping of the opposite hemisphere. The minds and bodies of the biped and its mate can be studied enroute."

"The path goes through a dense thicket of small trees a very short distance ahead of me," Sesnar said. "They would afford perfect concealment—"

He stopped as he caught the crunching of footsteps from within the trees. He reported to Eska, then watched the spot where the trail emerged from the trees. In a few moments the maker of the sounds appeared.

"It is the biped."

"If it shows no hostility toward you, do not bring it under full and immediate control," Eska ordered. "Let it remain in a hypnotic semi-trance until you have questioned it. It will eventually realize you are searching its mind, of course, and when that happens you will bring it under full control and proceed in the usual manner. But, until it is aware of your purpose, you can extract information from it with little difficulty."

Hart thought at first that the thing must be a boa constrictor that had escaped from a circus. Then he saw the hands. The two arms sprouted from tiny shoulders like two thick bullsnakes and terminated in pale green lizard-like hands, the size of a woman's hands. The forward portion of the body was erect with the belly a glazed yellow. The head was broad and slightly domed, swaying in the air nearly six feet above the ground. There was something mounted on the snake's head; a flat object with a short tube projecting a little in front of it. He noticed it only vaguely, his attention caught by the snake's eyes.

They seemed to possess an intelligence, even at a distance, and they fascinated him. He walked forward to see them better, remembering the pistol in his pocket as something of casual importance. The eyes were quite large, dead black in color with thin orange rims. There was an intelligence behind them, an intelligence as great as his own, and he could feel it studying him. Some instinct within him was trying to warn him—*danger*—but it was not until he had stopped before the snake and breathed the heavy, nauseating odor of it that the spell broke.

Snake! Men did not walk up to snakes as a hypnotized sparrow might do—*but he had just done so.*

He saw the intelligence in the snake's eyes for what it was, then; a cold, alien appraisal of him with the same objective detachment with which an entomologist might inspect an insect. It had not moved and there was no threat in its manner, other than the alienness of it and the way it had drawn him so irresistibly to it, but that was warning enough. He let his hand slide to his hip pocket and grasp the hard butt of the pistol, not drawing it but wanting it ready should he need it. Until, and if, the snake made a threatening move, he would try to question it. It very obviously was not of Earth and to kill it first then ask questions later would be both uninformative and stupid. It *might* intend him no harm; he would wait and see and keep his hand on the pistol.

It would most likely be from another planet of the solar system. He could draw a diagram of the solar system in the sand—*there were no humans near but for Gwen at the cabin*—and find out which planet it came from. Venus should be the one, the second from the sun—*she should be along in a few minutes*—

He stopped, suddenly aware of the random thoughts. His mind spoke another one: *She would be after watercress and would not be armed as he was*—

He cut the thought off with the chilling realization that the snake was questioning him. It could be nothing else. As the source of a motor nerve, when touched in an exposed brain, will make the corresponding muscle twitch, so the snake was questioning him; touching with its mind at the proper memory cells, exciting the desired memory responses.

The snake-thing wanted both him and Gwen. *Why?*

The implications of the question broke the hypnosis and the warning instinct screamed frantically: Kill it—*while you can!*

His arm jerked to whip the pistol from his pocket—and froze. His entire body was abruptly as motionless and powerless as though locked in a vice. He could not move—he had heeded the warning too late.

"The biped has an intelligence of the first order," Sesnar reported. "It became aware of my control before I had completed the questioning and attempted to kill me the moment it realized my intentions. I put it under full control before it could harm me, of course."

"Determine its full resistance to questioning while under muscular control," Eska ordered.

His entire body from the neck down was separated from the control of his brain. He was standing before the snake and could see it watching him, smell the odor of it; he was normal and the sensory nerves were functioning as always. He could feel the weight of the pistol in his pocket and his fingers could feel the butt of it as they held it half drawn from the pocket. The sensory nerves were functioning normally but his commands to his muscles were being cut off. His mind could formulate the commands and try to send them with all its power but nothing happened. Somewhere in his brain where the pure thought was transformed into a neural impulse, the snake had seized control. At that relay station his own commands were being cut off and the snake's commands substituted.

He had made a grave mistake; he had underestimated his opponent. He had reached for the pistol with his mind wide open, with his intention plain there for the snake to read. He should have kept the thought subdued, should have covered it over with other, stronger, thoughts. He had learned a lesson— perhaps it would not be too late. Physically he was helpless but his mind was still his own. His only resistance to the snake would have to be mental for the time being. In the end, if he made no more mistakes, he might win the game of wits and kill it before it killed him and Gwen.

A question came from the snake's mind, not the touching at the memory cells as before but a direct question.

"What is the percentage of uranium in the ore samples at your dwelling?"

It was, he realized, a test of his ability to withstand questioning. The snake would not care what the percentage might be—it was a test, the first won.

"Why do you want to know?" he asked.

The snake's answer was to touch quickly at the memory cells where the information lay and to repeat over and over: *The percentage—the percentage—*

Three point one four one five nine, he thought rapidly, and

multiply by the diameter and you have the circumference. The circumference is—*the percentage—the percentage*— The thought was insistent, demanding an answer— The circumference is pi times the diameter and how do you like those onions?

The reply from the snake was a greater insistence upon an answer. *The percentage—the percentage—the percentage*— It hammered at his mind and the answer was there, eager to respond to the snake's touch and make itself heard. It was there, just below the level of expression, and he fought to keep it there, submerged, while he covered it over with other thoughts.

According to the semanticists, a thought cannot be conceived clearly without its conversion to words. Not necessarily spoken, but the thought conceived with the aid of the semantic expressions to outline it, to detail and clarify it. Forty-one percent, expressed in words, is a very definite part of the whole. Forty-one percent as a thought unaccompanied by the proper semantic equivalent is an indefinite minor proportion. He could not block the snake from probing at his memory cells but he could let the answer the probing evoked remain a wordless thought, an impression in his mind that was not clear even to himself, by keeping the answer below the level of semantic expression and covering it up with other thoughts of his own making and spoken aloud.

The percentage—the percentage— It was coming harder, with the full force of the snake's mind behind it, and he met it with every evasion he could contrive. He recited mathematical formulae to it, he told it an Aesop fable, he gave it portions of the federal mining laws. The question flicked relentlessly at his mind—*the percentage—the percentage*—and his words that kept the answer submerged came more swiftly and louder as the moments went by, his concentration became more intense.

He was telling it of the crystallographic structure of tourmaline when it was abruptly out of his mind, to stand silently before him as though meditating.

"Well," he asked, his voice dropping to normal pitch, "did you find out anything?"

It gave no indication that it heard him.

"Its resistance to questioning is unexpectedly high," Sesnar reported. "As with all warm-blooded animals, its means of communication is vocal and I left its vocal organs uncontrolled that it might accompany its answer with the semantic expressions that would give the answer the greatest clarity. It exhibited considerable cunning by taking advantage of the freedom of its vocal organs to use them to speak other thoughts and keep the answer I desired submerged."

"Pain will break its resistance," Eska replied. "The combination of pain plus control will quickly destroy its ability to keep the answer submerged. Use your menta-blaster with care, however—the biped must not be so severely injured that it will be unfit for complete questioning and physical study when you take it and its mate to the ship. Use the Type 4 beam."

He had won! The power of the snake's mind, great as it was, had not been great enough to force him to answer. It was only the first victory—he was still held as powerless as before—but it had been a victory. There would be other tests but he knew, now, that the snake-thing was incapable of hypnotizing a human. It could only assume control of the body, not of the mind.

Flopper was standing fifteen feet to one side of him, held by the same control. Or even more so—Flopper could not turn his head. He could move his eyes but that was all. Flopper was watching him now, fear in his eyes and a look of hopeful expectancy; a faith that his master would destroy the thing before them. It was pathetically humorous; he was the pup's god and a pup knows that its god can do *anything*.

Then the snake was speaking to his mind again, very concisely, very menacingly.

"You will tell me the percentage of uranium in the ore samples. You will tell me at once and with no attempts to submerge the answer."

Well, here we go again, he thought. He had an unpleasant premonition that this time it would not be so easy—but he would soon find out.

"Go to hell," he said.

The tube on the snake's head glowed a deep violet and something like the blades of incandescent knives stabbed into his chest and began to cut slowly across it. It was a searing, burning pain that ripped down his stomach and up his neck, to explode like a white light in his brain. The question was coming again—*the percentage—the percentage*—lashing at his mind like a whip through the glare of pain. *The percentage—the percentage*— The pain intensified and tore at every nerve in his body while the question goaded incessantly: *The percentage—the percentage*— He fought against it and the white glare engulfed his brain until the question was no longer a question but a knife thrusting again and again into his mind while he was an entity composed of pain and spinning in a hell-fire of agony, writhing blind and mindless in the white glare while the question stabbed at him— *the percentage—the percentage*—

It was meaningless, as meaningless as his own thought in return: *thirty-five percent—thirty-five percent*— Meaningless. He had been going to fight something—he couldn't remember what it was. His mind was blinded by the pain and he couldn't remember—nothing existed but pain, unbearable pain . . .

The chaos faded slowly and the white glare melted away. The knife was no longer in his brain and the tube on the snake's head was crystal white again. He knew, then, that he had lost.

His heart was pounding violently and his chest was an intolerable aching and burning. He looked down at it. Something like a row of sharp knives had cut halfway across it. The cuts were not bleeding—the knives had cauterized as they cut . . .

"The biped's resistance was greater than expected," Sesnar said. "I was forced to cut and burn it rather severely, but it will still be able to serve our purpose."

"Proceed to the place where the biped's mate is to come," Eska ordered. "If she is there, return with both of them to your ship. If not, continue on to the dwelling and get her. Nothing is to be gained by waiting and there is always the slight possibility that other bipeds might make an unexpected appearance. The sooner you can return to the ship with the two natives and erect the force field, the better."

There was a command from the snake to turn and step forward. He started to turn, then, even as the movement was begun, there came another command from the snake: *Stop.*

He stopped and stood motionless. The snake was looking beyond him, at something in the junipers behind him. Its full attention, but for its control over him, seemed to be on whatever it saw. The seconds went silently by as the snake stared and as they passed he felt an almost imperceptible lessening of the control; a faint tremor to his arm and hand as he tried to force them to obey his will. *Something* in the junipers was loosening the snake's control over him.

A brief glow of dim red came from the tube on the snake's head, existing barely long enough to be seen and then vanishing. With its vanishing the control weakened to the point where he could move his arm. It was like fighting against the drag of quicksand, but he could move it. He dropped his eyes to the target, the glistening yellow belly where he could bring the pistol up with the minimum amount of movement.

The pistol was almost free of his pocket when the snake abruptly returned its attention to him; seizing control with a savagery that ripped at his muscles like an electric shock. His fingers flew open and the pistol dropped back into his pocket. His hand was jerked around and slammed against his side. The snake permitted his knotted muscles to relax, then, but the tightening of his chest muscles had torn at the wounds and for what seemed a long time a sickness and a blackness swirled around him, the bulging eyes of the snake seemed to advance and retreat through it.

The blackness dispersed, though the sickness remained, and the dizziness left him. The snake was not moving and he could, for the first time, sense vague thoughts impinging upon its mind. Apparently the thing in the junipers had so disturbed the snake that it was unconsciously letting some of its own thoughts come through with the control. There was a distinct impression that it was communicating with another of its kind but there was no clue as to the identity of the thing in the junipers.

"A small animal suddenly appeared in the trees behind the biped," Sesnar said. "That is, I *think* it was an animal."

"You *think* it was an animal?" Eska's thought was a cold hiss. "What is the meaning of this? You were not sent on this mission to indulge in guessing—*determine* if it's an animal."

"I tried to—and I couldn't!"

"Explain yourself. I sense an agitation in your mind. Explain!"

"This animal is different to any we've ever encountered— if it *is* an animal," Sesnar said, his agitation becoming more evident as he spoke. "I cannot determine what it is because I not only cannot control it—*I cannot enter its mind!*"

Eska was silent for a while. "This is incredible," he said at last. "It cannot be! The mathematics of Kal, as well as our own centuries of colonization of alien worlds, have irrefutably proven that no warm-blooded creature can resist the power of the Slistian mind!"

"This one did."

"Perhaps," suggested Eska, "it is such a low form of life that it has no mind to enter, existing solely by instinct as the mollusks do."

"It is physically far too high on the evolutionary scale to not possess an intelligence," Sesnar said. "It has the appearance of an animal but that is all I can learn about it. I cannot control it, I cannot enter its mind, and—" Sesnar paused, as though dreading to reveal the rest. "*It* disturbs *my* mind!"

"Impossible!" Eska stated flatly. "No creature can disturb the mind of a Slistian."

"This one did," Sesnar repeated. "It disturbs me so that I cannot project the thought pattern into my menta-blaster. I tried to kill it, but despite my efforts to produce a full-force blast I was able to activate the menta-blaster for but a moment and then at such low intensity that the creature never felt it."

"Your menta-blaster must have developed a defect," Eska said. "I refuse to believe that any creature could so affect a Slistian. Is the creature still in view?"

"No. It vanished when I tried to activate the menta-blaster and is now watching me from the concealment of the trees."

"How do you know it is?"

"I can sense it watching me."

"Your menta-blaster has no doubt become defective," Eska said again. "Test it. Lower your head behind the protection of the biped and test it."

Sesnar dropped his head lower and his eyes searched for a suitable target. They fell on the quadruped, still motionless under his control. It would serve the purpose admirably and it was of no other use to him. With the biped's body between himself and the thing in the trees the disturbance was gone from his mind. He felt the familiar thought patterns come easily: *Type I, quarter force—fire!*

✧   ✧   ✧

Confused thoughts swirled in Hart's mind. Why had the snake not killed whatever it saw behind him? It had started to do so—there had been the first dim glow from the tube on its head—and then it had stopped? Why? The snake had been disturbed by what it saw—why hadn't it eliminated it?

He turned his head as far as he could but the trees were directly behind him and he could not see them. Neither could he tell what it might have been by Flopper's reaction; the pup's back was to the trees, too.

The faith was still in Flopper's eyes. He was afraid of the thing before them and could not understand the awful paralysis that held him, but he knew with all his dog's heart that his master would help him. Then the snake dropped its head to the level of Hart's chest and looked directly at the pup. Frantic, imploring appeal flashed into Flopper's eyes as he sensed what was coming.

There was a blue-white flash from the tube on the snake's head and a crackling sound. A puff of dust hid Flopper from view for a moment. When it cleared he was lying on the ground, broken and still, a tiny trickle of blood staining his mouth.

"The blaster functions perfectly, the thought patterns are produced without effort, when I am not under the direct gaze of the thing in the trees," Sesnar reported.

"Proceed with the biped toward its dwelling," Eska ordered. "Permit it to retain its weapon—should the other thing appear again, force the biped to kill it."

It had killed Flopper!

Hart felt sick with the futility of his hatred for the stinking, scaly thing before him; he wanted, more than he had ever wanted anything in his life, to reach the pistol and empty it into the glazed belly, to watch the snake fall and then tramp its head into a shapeless mass. He wanted—but the command came to turn and he was doing so.

He turned and began the walking back down the trail, the snake slithering along beside him. They passed the limp little bundle of black and white fur that had been Flopper and went on, bypassing the shortcut through the junipers and following the sandy canyon bed. *Was the thing still afraid of what it had seen in the trees?* His chest was a sheet of fire and his heart was slugging heavily. Then the trees were behind them and they were back on the trail again, passing by the place where Gwen had intended to get the watercress. *Were they going to the cabin?* They came to the place where the trail climbed out of the canyon and his heart pounded harder as they started up it. There was a limit to the injury and pain a man could stand, no matter how hard he might fight to ignore it, and he had withstood injury and pain to such an extent that his body could take little more of it.

They were climbing up the grade and the snake could have but one reason for going to the cabin. It wanted Gwen; it wanted a pair of specimens of the native life to study; specimens that it would crush and examine as emotionlessly as he would crush and examine a specimen of ore. It hadn't told him, but he knew. It would force him to stand there where the trail came out on top of the bank and motion to Gwen to come to him. She might even now be starting out to gather the watercress; she would be able to see him easily from the cabin and she would come without question when he motioned her to do so. She had no reason to suspect any danger.

He would have to do something—*what?* His breath was coming harsh and labored and a blur kept trying to form before his eyes. It was hard to think, yet he had to think. He had to do something, and quickly. He was weakening and his time for action was running short—

Stop.

He stopped, the snake beside him, and wondered why they had done so. It was looking up the trail, up at the top of the climb, and he shook his head to clear the blur away from his eyes. There was something gray there—

Kill it!

He saw what it was as his hand obediently reached for the pistol. It was one of the gray kittens. *Why didn't the snake kill it?* He thought of the rattlesnake he had killed so long ago and he knew what it was the snake-thing had seen in the trees, knew why its cold, merciless mind had been so disturbed.

Kill it!

Kill it—he must kill the kitten *because the snake was afraid of it!* The snake *couldn't* kill it! There was a flooding of hope through him. He had a plan, now; held deep and vague in his mind as he brought the sights of the pistol in line with the kitten's face. There was no time to inspect the plan, not even the hazy sub-conversion inspection it would have to be. He had been ordered to kill the kitten and his muscles were no longer his own; he could not disobey. His mind was his own, however, and he could—

The front sight was on the kitten's head, outlined in the rear sight, and he made his thought sharp and clear: *This pistol shoots low; I must draw a coarse bead.* Another thought tried to make itself heard: *No—no—it shoots high.* He drowned it out with the one of his own creating: *Shoots low—draw a coarse bead.* The front sight came up in obedience to the thought he was making sharp and clear, the snake unable to read the thought he was keeping submerged. The sight loomed high in the notch of the rear sight and he pressed the trigger. The startled kitten vanished in the brush beside the trail as the bullet snapped an inch over its head.

I did it! There was exultation in the thought—it was difficult to keep it hidden. There was a plan that would work—it would *have* to work—

"What is your plan?"

The snake's question came hard and cold and the tentacles flicked at his mind—*the plan—the plan—*

His hope became despair. He had let part of his thoughts get through to the surface, and now the snake knew of them—*the plan—the plan—* The tube was coming in line with his chest again. He would, in the end, tell the snake what it wanted to know—his mind would be sent spinning into the glare of pain and it would no longer be his own. But if he could delay it for a while . . .

"I'll tell you," he said calmly. The snake waited, the tube still in line with his chest. "Cats—they chase mice," he went on, his mind two things; a frenzied effort to think and to talk calmly to the snake with one part of it and a desperate planning in the darkness of sub-conversion with the other part. "Cats chase mice and I was going to yell at them—*Susie—SNAKE!*"

At his shout he expected, with the part of his mind he was keeping hidden from the snake, that the tube would flash violet again as the snake detected the subterfuge. But it had not—not for the moment, at least. Susie would come, she had to—

"They always chase these mice and the reason I sent for them—" *The snake wouldn't let him talk nonsense for long—Susie would have to come soon—* "I sent for them because the mice scared the farmer's wife when the clock—" *What if she had gone back to the cabin? What if there was nothing to hear him but the gray kitten?—* "struck one. I—"

"*You are hiding something.*"

The tube flashed violet and his mind went reeling into the white glare where the tentacles lashed like whips—*the plan—the plan—* Something was saying: *You are a snake and snakes are afraid of cats. I called Susie so you couldn't use the tube—so I could kill you before you could kill Gwen and me . . .*

His mind came out of the glare again, out of the blinding intensity of pain. Vision returned and he saw the snake before him, with the tube once again crystal white. It knew, now, of his plan—he had resisted the questioning as long as he could and all he could do now was hope that Susie had heard him, that she was coming and had not returned to the cabin, after all. The cabin was too far away for her to have heard his call from there . . .

The snake was watching the top of the trail, its little hands fidgeting. He followed the snake's gaze, to find the trail empty. *Susie—Susie—*he thought—*don't fail us now. It's Gwen and me and maybe every human on Earth if this thing isn't killed. Hurry, Susie, and help me—help me so I can kill it—*

Then something appeared at the top of the trail, something gray. *Susie!* She had heard him! She came down the trail without pausing, flowing along low to the ground with her eyes fixed on the snake. She stopped eight feet short of them, her eyes stone-hard and unwavering in their stare.

Kill it.

There was a hint of emotion to the command this time; a touch of urgency where, before, the commands of the snake had been as dispassionate as its own hard-scaled face.

Again his hand brought up the pistol, but this time his will was delaying it a little. Not much, but a little. Susie was not a kitten; she was a mature cat with a mature cat's contempt for snakes. A cat, even a kitten, instinctively knows the difference between a harmless snake, such as a garter snake, and a poisonous snake, such as a rattlesnake. A small kitten will kill a garter snake but it will not tackle a rattlesnake until it has acquired the necessary strength, speed and experience. For all its size, the snake-thing before Susie was still a snake; a snake without fangs. It could not harm her except by physical force and to do so it would have to move faster than she did. All her experience had taught her that no snake could ever equal her own lightning coordination. The effect of her stare upon the snake would be far stronger than that of a kitten; that it was stronger was made evident by the manner in which his hand was bringing up the pistol so slowly. She could not harm the snake, but such would not be necessary. She had only to sit there and torment its mind with her cold stare—in the end the snake-thing's mind and will would break, its fear would become so complete that it would lose all control over him. And then—he would kill the thing—

Kill it!

The command was more urgent and he was raising the pistol faster despite his efforts to hold it back. It would take time for her stare to fully affect the thing and it was not going to permit that. The sights were coming in line with Susie's face— all his will could not halt the movement and he was going to kill her. When he shot her, he would destroy the only hope for survival—when he pulled the trigger he would be killing himself and Gwen as surely as though the muzzle was against their own heads. He tried the subterfuge of thinking the gun shot low, but it failed. His hand brought the front sight down low in the notch of the rear sight and his finger tightened on the trigger. He concentrated on the movement of the finger, forgetting everything else in the effort to delay the squeeze of the trigger. The command came again: *Kill*— It broke and he felt the control lessen.

It came once more, but differently: *Kill them!*

Them? The pistol had dropped and was no longer in line with Susie. He looked up the trail and saw why; the two gray kittens were trotting down the trail. They stopped beside their mother, one on each side of her, and their eyes as coldly upon the snake as hers.

No further command came for the time and the snake's hands fluttered with greater nervousness. The pistol was still in his hand but the muzzle had dropped toward the ground. There were six green eyes watching the snake now, and it was getting worried.

It would try again—it would have to try again, and soon. It took a little time for the stare of a cat to break a snake and the snake knew it. It was a snake and there was something about the impenetrable mind of a cat that it feared—but it was intelligent and it knew it could still escape if it acted quickly enough . . .

Gravel rattled down the face of the cliff his back was against. He twisted his neck to look up and saw the yellow kitten making its way along the ledge over his head. The kitten stopped just over him and there were eight cold eyes watching the snake. Three kittens to go, he thought, and then someone is going to get hurt. There was another yellow one and the red one, and the far-ranging spotted one should have been the one the snake saw in the trees—it should be coming up the trail any moment.

More gravel fell from the ledge above him; the other yellow one. The snake was darting its glance from the kittens on the ledge to Susie and the two beside her and did not see the spotted one trot up the trail and stop near the end of its long, thin tail. The red one was at the spotted one's heels and stopped beside it.

There was a trembling to his legs as the control lessened. The snake was breaking—he could not raise the gun to shoot the snake; it could not force him to shoot the cats. He felt an elation through the sickness and pain. The snake would break soon, would break and turn to flee. When it did the control would vanish and he would kill it. He would empty the pistol into the mottled green coils of it . . .

"Drop the weapon!"

His hand tried to spread open to drop the pistol and he tried to force it to clench the pistol tighter. If he dropped the pistol, the snake would scoop it up and use it to kill the cats—but his fingers were obeying the command, they were spreading apart.

He spoke quickly: "Did you know there are two more at your tail?"

It had the affect he had hoped for; the snake flicked its glance toward the two kittens, then there was a flurry of movement as it whipped its tail away from them and closer about its body.

His grip was firmer on the pistol and for the first time he smiled at the snake. "Disconcerting, aren't they?"

✧   ✧   ✧

"There are seven of the creatures," Sesnar reported. "I am not sure whether or not they can harm me physically—they display a complete lack of fear as though they might possess some power to destroy me of which I am unaware. The biped has now become a menace; I am losing control of it and when my control weakens sufficiently it intends to kill me. It is too strong for me to wrest the weapon from its hand but it is rapidly weakening from the effects of its injuries. As soon as it weakens sufficiently, I shall take the weapon away from it. Since the biped's primitive weapon operates by manual control, I can use it to kill the other creatures. I am now going to release the biped of all control but for the hand that holds the weapon. This will cause it to feel the full extent of its injuries and reduce it to helplessness very quickly. My control, itself, is steadily deteriorating but the biped is so severely injured that I have no doubt it will be helpless long before my control over it is completely gone."

He was standing with his back to the cliff, his feet spread a little, when the control over everything but his hand suddenly vanished. His knees turned to rubber and he fell back against the cliff. He had not realized, while his muscles were under the absolute control of the snake, just how weak he was. His back bumped against the cliff and he braced his feet, shoving as hard as his weakness would permit against the cliff to keep himself standing. It was not enough and he began to drop, his backbone scraping along the rough rock face. For a moment a fold in his shirt caught on a projection and supported him, then it slipped off and he dropped to the ground in a squatting position. It seemed he dropped with a terrible jar and the hell-fire rippled across his chest. The sickness flooded over him and the blur clouded his eyes. He put all his will into one thought: *Hold tight to the pistol!*

The blur faded away and he could see the snake, its head now above him. He was sitting with his legs doubled under him and his heart was a small *flub-flub* within him. He was sweating the cold sweat of shock and the hand that held the pistol was no longer tan but an odd grayish color. He watched it and waited, hoping the spell would pass before the snake realized how weak he was.

The worst of it did pass and a little color came back to his hand. His heart, relieved of the burden of supplying his legs with blood, began to beat a little stronger and the blackness that had hovered around him withdrew.

The snake was in a close coil a few feet before him, the coils sliding and slithering together and the snake-like arms a succession of nervous ripplings.

"Afraid, aren't you?" he asked. "You need a dog—cats run from dogs." He kept his mind free of information-giving surface thoughts and went on to bait it. "You could easily control a dog and force it to chase all these cats away."

The snake asked the question he had expected. "What is a dog?"

"The animal you killed was a dog."

He regretted that the snake's expressionless face prevented his seeing the effect of the disclosure but the thought would be galling bitterness in the snake's mind. It had no emotions—but one. There was one emotion it had to have; the fear of death. Without that a species would never survive. It was afraid, now, and the greater its fear became, the weaker its control over him would become. He would have no time to spare; the blackness had merely withdrawn a little way and it kept threatening to swoop back over him. He would have to fight it off as best he could and at the same time do what he could to increase the snake's fear.

"Cats," he said to it. "You're afraid of them and they're not afraid of you. Do you know why they're not afraid of you?"

"*Why?*" The question was like a quick hiss, intense in its desire to know.

"Ask them," he answered. "They know; they can tell you. Ask them—look at them, go into their minds and learn why they don't fear you. Go ahead—go into their minds—"

A wisp of the darkness reached out to cloud his eyes and he waited for it to pass, holding tight to the pistol. The darkness withdrew and he repeated: "Go ahead—go into their minds. Burn them like you did me—make them tell you—go ahead—try it." He smiled up at the snake, twisted and mirthless. "They know what's going on in *your* mind; they know how they're breaking you without ever touching you. Why don't you go into their minds and learn why they hate you and hold you in contempt?

Look into their eyes—go deep into their minds and see what you find . . ."

The cloud came again and he let his voice trail off to concentrate on holding to the pistol.

"The biped has not weakened yet?" Eska asked.

"It is weakening very rapidly, though not yet helpless," Sesnar replied.

"We dare take no risks—this absurd situation must be remedied at once," Eska informed him. "The thought pattern of your menta-blaster is on file and will be given to myself and the other eight members of the Colonization Board present here. The recording projector is being set up now. As soon as the last connections are made the pattern of your blaster will be projected to you with the power of the nine minds of the Board behind it. Since none of us are under the influence of the creatures before you, the pattern projection will be of absolute precision and irresistible power. Your own mind need serve only as the carrier. The final connections are being made now and you will receive the pattern projection at any moment."

He shook his head, trying to drive the darkness away. It withdrew, slowly and reluctantly, hovering near to close in on him again. His time was running out—all his will and determination could not much longer hold unconsciousness at bay. Time—he needed more time. Susie and the kittens were doing the best they could but their only weapon was the green stare of their eyes. In the end they would break the snake—but he would have to be there to kill it when they did so. If he lost consciousness all would be lost; the snake would use the pistol to kill the cats, it would go on to the cabin where Gwen was . . .

He needed time and he could not have it. He would have to bring it all to a showdown fast—in the little time he did have. Maybe if the cats were closer . . .

He called to Susie. His voice was a vague mutter and he tried again, making it clear. "Susie, come here—snake, Susie—*snake!*"

She came at his call, with the same silent, flowing motion. She stopped close beside him, so near that her whiskers tickled the back of his hand that held the pistol as she stared up at the snake's head and the writhing arms of it.

✧   ✧   ✧

"The biped has called the largest of the creatures to its side," Sesnar reported. "I can see nothing about the creature capable of harming me but I sense a distinct menace—an utter lack of fear. It *must* possess some means of harming me of which I am unaware, otherwise it would not display this complete lack of fear. The effect of its stare upon my control over the biped is considerably greater at this close range and I am afraid to delay any longer. I am sure the biped has now weakened sufficiently for me to wrest the weapon from its grasp. I cannot wait any longer or my control over it will be completely gone. Project my menta-blaster pattern as soon as possible but I must take the biped's weapon now and kill it and the other creatures."

"The connections have been made and the charge is building up in the relay now," Eska said. "The moment it reaches full potential you will receive the pattern."

The snake settled lower in its coils until its head was barely a foot higher than his own. "I wish to talk to you," it said, leaning forward a little toward him. "I intend you no harm."

Subterfuge! The foreknowledge of the snake's intention was an electric shock through the haze of pain and sickness. *Subterfuge*—it was trying to put him off guard a little before it snatched the pistol from his hand.

The showdown had come.

He moved with all the desperate quickness his weakness would permit, trying to bring his left hand over in time to help his still-controlled right hand hold onto the pistol. The movement was hardly begun when the hand of the snake flashed out. At the same moment it ordered with all the force at its command: "*Release the weapon!*"

Susie reacted then, instinctively and instantaneously. It was beyond her ability to understand that the snake wanted only the pistol; that it wanted no contact with her. She had been waiting and watching, her eyes and body coordinated like a perfect machine and ready to act at the lightning-fast instant of her command. The snake-like arm darted toward her, as a rattlesnake would strike, and she replied to its threat as she would to the strike of a rattlesnake. Its hand was yet four inches from the pistol when her paw made its invisibly swift slash and the razor-sharp claws laid the soft-scaled hand open in four long gashes.

It flipped its body back at the slash of her claws and the control was suddenly gone, something like a scream coming through the channel where it had been. It was soundless but it was terror, complete and absolute.

Now! The glazed yellow belly was before him and the control was gone. He brought the pistol up, spurred by the frantic fear that the snake would resume control when victory was only a split second away. Up, where the sickening glaze was so near him—up and in line— The pistol barked, vicious and savage, and the snake lurched from the impact, a small, round hole in the glaze. Up and fire—up and fire— It was as he had wanted it to be when the snake held him helpless; as he raised the pistol and fired, raised and fired, the little black holes ran up the glazed belly while the snake kept lurching from the impacts and leaning farther backward, out over the edge of the trail. There were six of the little black holes in it when it toppled over and fell into the canyon below.

He heard the thump of it as it hit the bottom and he crawled to the rim of the trail to look down at it. It was lying in the sand of the canyon floor, twisting aimlessly, sometimes the dark green back up and sometimes the glistening yellow belly up.

It was twisting and turning as all dead snakes do; it was going nowhere; it was no longer a menace.

He turned away from it and saw that Susie and all the kittens were lined up beside him, looking down at the thing they had helped kill.

"I think," he said to them, "that the hungry old cat and the scrawny kittens we gave a home to one cold, rainy night have repaid us."

He was still in the hospital nine months later—with release a month away—when Earth's first spaceship was completed and the christening ceremony held. The snake-thing's ship had possessed every conceivable kind of weapon as well as the hyperspace drive and the military had been given orders, and unlimited priority, to create a Hyperspace Interceptor Fleet. There had been tapes and records in the ship that had left no doubt as to the snake-thing's mission. Industry had combined genius and mass-production to do the impossible; it had turned out the first complete and fully armed interceptor in less than nine months.

Gwen made her daily visit on the afternoon of the day of the ship's christening.

"This one will be the flagship, I guess you'd call it," she said. "Now that they're tooled up for production, they say they'll be turning out a ship a week."

"The things might try again," he said. "I don't think they will for some time; when Susie struck the snake it let its mind go wide open to my own mind for a moment—not only its mind but I could sense the thoughts of the other ones that it was in communication with—and they were *afraid*. Even the others were afraid, afraid because the one here was terrorized by something it couldn't control or understand. I think these snake-things got where they are by pure, unemotional logic; they happened to be an older form of life than the ones on the worlds they conquered and their knowledge of physical things, such as weapons, was greater. I suppose they had plans for ultimately conquering every habitable world in the galaxy. They were utterly without mercy in their plans; they, alone, were entitled to life because they, alone, had developed methods of destroying all other forms of life. They knew all about physical laws and they made use of their knowledge to devise weapons that made them invincible. But they overlooked what I like to think is a law higher than any they knew: the law that no species alone, is entitled to survival."

Gwen smiled at him. "The law that causes people to feel sorry for lost and hungry dogs and cats and want to give them a home. It's a good law, and it doesn't have to be written down for people; it's just our nature like it was the nature of that snake-thing to be cold and logical in everything it did."

"And its cold logic caused it to die," he said, "with it, even as it died, still wondering at our illogical affection for other creatures. And speaking of other creatures; how is Susie taking all the publicity and fame?"

"She's completely unphotogenic, and bewildered besides. She just wants to keep on being a common cat and she can't understand why all those people keep coming to see her and take her picture."

"Well—after all, she can't know just how important was the thing she and the kittens did. That thing was a snake and she was a cat; she just did the usual, normal thing for a cat to do."

"She was wanted at the ship's christening today, too," Gwen said. "They wanted her there to go out over all the television channels. I had to put my foot down flat on the idea, though."

"Why?"

Gwen smiled again. "Because she was too busy today doing something else that is the usual, normal thing for a cat to do— she was having kittens."

Editor's note: The backdrop to all of Godwin's stories is a universe which is cold and pitiless. More so than any demon, because it is a lack of mercy which stems from the fact that the universe simply does not care. Technical advances, whatever their benefits, do not fundamentally change that bleak reality. In different ways, that theme stands at the center of the last two stories in this anthology.

THE GULF BETWEEN

1

He was dying!

The fear flooded over him again, dark and smothering and made worse by his inability to move. His doctor was standing near him, watching over him with dark, patient eyes, knowing that he was dying. When a man is dying, there should be comfort in the presence of a doctor who knows how to save his life. His doctor knew he was dying and had already done the thing that should have saved him from death; the doctor had informed the pilot of his condition by means of the letters on the pilot's communications panel. They had leered at him for an endless eternity: OBSERVER DYING OF EFFECTS OF FULL ACCELERATION. IMMEDIATE REDUCTION OF ACCELERATION IS SUGGESTED.

His doctor watched him die with dark, brooding eyes and suggested to the pilot that the acceleration be reduced.

But the pilot's seat was empty.

He was the pilot, and the doctor knew it . . .

Lieutenant Knight flattened himself behind the outcropping on the windswept ridge and raised his head to stare across the small basin at Hill 23, looming red-scarred and forbidding in the Korean rain; deceptively, ominously quiet, as though daring Company C to resume its vain battering at it.

"Don't look dangerous, does it?" Sergeant Wenden asked, his bush of black and gray beard close to the ground as he crawled up beside Knight. "Real calm and peaceful. Good old Hill Twenty-three—all we gotta do is take it."

The blue of the Pacific gleamed beyond Hill 23; if they could take the hill it would destroy one of the last remnants of one of the last enemy beachheads on the Korean coast. It would not be difficult—if Cullin would only wait another day until Company B came up.

"I have an idea they won't want to give that hill up," the sergeant went on. "It's their last one; their backs are to the sea and they're goin' to argue about givin' it up."

Knight did not answer, studying the terrain of the hill and the basin that lay between; planning the best route for the Fourth Platoon, the best way to give them a fighting chance.

"Yep, real calm and peaceful," the loquacious sergeant repeated. "I wonder if their snipers know we're lookin' over the ridge at 'em?"

His answer came a half second later; a spurt of rock dust as a bullet struck between them, and a shrill scream as it ricocheted away.

"Reckon they do," he grunted, dropping his whiskers low and scuttling backward from the crest of the ridge. Knight followed, and they slid to the bottom of the small gulch that ran behind the ridge.

"Of course," the talkative sergeant remarked philosophically, biting off a chew of tobacco, "bullets'll be snappin' all around us in another hour, but there ain't no reason to invite one of 'em to hit us any sooner than it has to."

Knight started back down the muddy gulch and the sergeant tramped beside him, paying no attention to his silence. "The other guys are about ready to call this war a draw, I hear. Except for Korea, here, neither us nor them is makin' any headway and they say the chances of an armistice is real good. I hope so; I've had all the war I want and I've already got it figgered out how I'm gonna settle down in Florida and raise chickens—or somethin'. Wish they'd declare the armistice right now—they're dug in on that hill and the Fourth is goin' to have one hell of a time tryin' to be the decoy and draw their fire and not all of us get killed." He scowled at Knight, his philosophical attitude turning to wrath. "A lot of men are goin' to die real soon, and for no reason. Company B will be up tonight—why can't we wait until tomorrow?"

Knight shrugged. "Orders."

"Yeah—orders!" The sergeant snorted disgustedly. "Our Captain Cullin wants *his* company to take that hill *today*, then he can tell battalion headquarters to not bother about sendin' up any support, that he done took the hill all by himself. Then, he figgers, regimental headquarters will be so impressed by his ability to do so much with so few men that they'll recommend he be raised to major. And *then*"—the sergeant spat viciously—"he'll have a whole battalion to give orders to, 'stead of only a company!"

Knight half heard the sergeant as they walked along, his thoughts occupied with the suicidal role his men would have to play. They would be the decoy, as the sergeant had said, deliberately and perhaps fatally drawing the concentration of enemy fire upon themselves.

" . . . I'm a Regular Army man," the sergeant was saying. "I've been in this game for thirty years, but I ain't never seen an officer like Cullin. All he thinks about is himself and his own glory. He made it plain to us what he was when he took over this company. 'A soldier is only as good as his ability to obey orders,' he says. 'You men are going to *be* soldiers,' he says, 'and there will be no questioning of any order given you. I want, and I shall have, absolute obedience and discipline,' he says—"

Decoy.

It would be senseless, needless slaughter of the Fourth Platoon. It would enable the rest of the company to take the hill but the premature attack was not necessary; the enemy had their backs to the Pacific and they could retreat no farther. They could retreat no farther and they certainly would not dare attack.

Why had Cullin chosen the Fourth Platoon as the decoy? Was it because of the hatred between himself and Cullin? The Fourth was *his* platoon; by sending it on a suicide mission Cullin could add the savor of revenge to the sweet taste of glory.

The Fourth was his platoon, and between himself and the men of the Fourth was the bond that months of common danger had welded; the bond of brothers-in-arms that is sometimes greater than that of brothers-by-blood. They did not give his gold second-lieutenant's bars any parade-ground respectful salutes;

instead, they respected him as a man, as Blacky who slogged through the mud and rain beside them, who ate the rations they ate, who knew their names and moods, who was one with the hard veterans of combat and the nervous young replacements. Not Lieutenant Knight; just Blacky, to whom someone would sometimes come on the eve of battle and say: "This address here—it's Mary's. If I'm not so lucky this time, I wish you would write her a few words. Just tell her I wanted to see her again but that I . . . well, just say that I said . . . that I said—Aw, hell, Blacky—you'll know what to say."

He would sit by the light of a gasoline lantern in the nights following the battle and write the letters; not alone for the one who had asked him to but for all who had been "not so lucky." They were hard to write, those letters. Soon, now, if he, himself, were not among those not so lucky, he would have more of them to write—far more than ever before.

" . . . What would you say caused it, Blacky?" the sergeant was asking.

"What?" Knight brought his mind back to the present. "How was that?"

"I say, you take a man like Cullin—what do you reckon makes him act that way? You oughta know—you knowed him when you was both kids, didn't you?"

"I've known him most of my life, from the time we were each six years old," Knight answered. "He was always a lot like he is now—even as a kid he wanted to boss the other kids and make them do things for him. I don't know why he hasn't matured emotionally as well as physically. A psychiatrist might be able to trace it back to something—I'm a computer engineer, misplaced in the infantry, and not a psychiatrist."

"Well, if I was one of these psychiatrists, I'd sure ask him if he didn't once have a set of wooden soldiers he liked to play with better than anything else. That's the kind of soldiers he wants us all to be—wooden dummies that don't dare move unless he says to."

They came to the mouth of the gulch and Knight stopped beside a splintered tree. "I have to go over to where he has his headquarters for a last-minute briefing," he told the sergeant. "It's a little over an hour, yet, so everybody might as well take it easy till then. I'll be along in a few minutes."

The sergeant craned his neck to stare past Knight with sudden and baleful interest. "Here he comes now, down from the Second. Guess he's makin' the rounds personally this time." He scowled at the approaching captain then hurried away, his course such that only his long, fast steps prevented a face-to-face meeting.

Knight waited beside the tree and Captain Cullin strode up to him; a big man, heavier than Knight and almost as tall, with an arrogant impatience to the arch of his nose and a relentless drive in the set of this thick jaw and the iciness of his eyes.

He stopped before Knight, with a glance after the rapidly disappearing sergeant, and said acidly: "If the men in my company could be relied upon to display as much determination when sent on a mission as your sergeant just now displayed to avoid saluting me, I would think I had a first-class combat unit."

"He's a good man—none better," Knight said. "He just didn't happen to feel like going in for any such melodrama as: 'We, who are about to die, salute you!'"

"Very witty," Cullin said coldly. "Although your wit, in its implications, is rather melodramatic, itself. But suppose we talk of something a little more important—the action of your platoon in taking that hill. I've moved the attack up half an hour. The other platoons are already taking up positions as advanced as possible until your own platoon draws the enemy fire."

"I just came down from off the ridge," Knight said. "I know the lay of the land and I have your orders as given to me by Lieutenant Nayland; to attack as best we can along the southwestern floor of the hill and keep the enemy occupied while the other three platoons close in on their flanks. But the strategy is your own, so I'm listening if you have anything to add. From you, I get the dope straight from the horse's mouth."

Cullin stared at Knight, hard lines running along his jaw and the hatred burning deep back in his eyes.

"I want to remind you, Knight," he said at last, "that you are my subordinate officer. An officer's promotions are usually in direct ratio to his ability, and we received our second-lieutenant's bars at the same time—remember? I'm a captain, now, in command of a company; you're still a second lieutenant in charge of a platoon. I'm your commanding officer and you keep that fact in mind at all times. You will restrain your wit, confine yourself to obeying orders and extend me the same courtesy I demand of my other platoon leaders. Is that clear?"

"Very clear," Knight replied. "Your orders have been, and will be, obeyed. When in the presence of others I'll continue to observe every rule of military courtesy, as I have in the past. But I've known you too long and too well to have any desire to go through those antics when you and I are alone."

"Discipline is not an antic," Knight. "The purpose of discipline is to condition the soldier into efficient obedience. You will obey me with full military courtesy and you will not presume an equality with me because of our past friendship."

"Our past friendship is a long way past, and I'm sure neither of us has any desire to ever renew it. I would like to ask you a question, though—why do we attack today when Company B will be up tonight?"

"For a very good reason—because I've ordered it," Cullin said flatly.

"That's all?" Knight asked.

"That's sufficient. It isn't required of you to seek any other reason."

"'Theirs not to reason why—' . . . that's what you want, isn't it?"

"That's what I intend to have."

"By waiting for B's support you might not win any major's oak leaves but you could save a lot of lives. There's no hurry about taking that hill—the enemy isn't going anywhere."

"Keep your advice to yourself, Knight. Casualties are to be expected in any combat unit and this company will remain a combat unit as long as I am in command of it."

"Then give your orders," Knight said with brittle resignation. "I'll see that they're followed, regardless of what I think of them."

"See that you do. This is what I want out of your platoon, and I won't tolerate any deviation from these orders—"

2

How long had he been a living brain in a dying husk of a body? Had it been weeks or months or years, and how much longer could it continue? If only he could forget the end that was drawing irresistibly closer; if only his mind could lose its clear perception and go into the comforting solace of unknowing insanity!

But the doctor would not let it; the doctor watched him and injected the antihysteria drug into his bloodstream whenever madness threatened to relieve his mind of its cold and terrible knowledge. Sanity was a torture in which his body sat helpless and immobile while his mind perceived with clear and awful detail and recoiled and whimpered in futile, desperate fear from what it perceived.

Yet, the doctor didn't want to torture him; the doctor didn't want him to die. The doctor was using every means known to medical science to prolong his life. But why did the doctor merely prolong his life when his life could be saved entirely with less effort? There was still time—the doctor had only to do as he had suggested the phantom pilot do; reduce the acceleration. The deceleration button was visible on the control board in front of the vacant pilot's chair. The doctor didn't really want him to die, and the doctor could save his life by one quick flick of the deceleration button.

WHY DIDN'T THE DOCTOR DO IT?

Peace.

Four years of peace, with all their changing of the ways of his life, were to pass from the time Knight stood beside a splintered tree in Korea and heard his last orders until he met Cullin again.

First, there had been the bullet-swept hell of the attack on Hill 23 and then a long time in the hospitals—field hospital, base hospital, State-side hospital. There had been the irony of the cease-fire order two days after the slaughter of the Fourth Platoon. There had been the letters to write, so many of them and so many lies to tell. The folks at home always wanted the comfort of knowing that their Tommy or Bill or Dave had found death to be not cruel and merciless but something that had come quickly and painlessly, for all its grim finality.

There had been the day of his discharge from service and the strange feel of civilian clothes. There had been a period of restlessness, a period during which the peacetime world seemed a shallow and insignificant thing and the memory of the Fourth was strong within him as something irretrievably lost; a comradeship forged by war and never to be found again in the gentle fires of peace.

Then he had received the letter from Computer Research Center, and the invitation to come to Arizona and work with Dr. Clarke, himself. Clarke had written: " . . . The theory you set forth in your thesis can, I think, be worked out here at Computer Research Center and an experimental model of such a 'brain' constructed. I asked for your assistance eighteen months ago, but our little semi-military Center lacked the influence to have a combat officer recalled from active duty—"

His theory had been valid, and Computer Research Center was no longer small and unimportant. The Knight-Clarke Master Computer was a reality and Center had become the most powerful factor in the western hemisphere. The restlessness had faded away as he adjusted himself to taking up his old way of life and he forgot the war in the fascination of creating something from metal and plastic that was, in a way, alive.

In four years he had found his place in life again and the ghosts of the Fourth lay dormant in his mind; splendid and glorious in the way they had fought and died but no longer stirring the restlessness and the sense of something lost.

Then he met Cullin again.

Punta Azul was a cluster of adobes drowsing on the northeastern shore of the Gulf of California, away from the tourist routes and accessible only by a long and rough desert road. Nothing ever happened in Punta Azul; it was a good place for a man to rest, to fish, to sit in the cool adobe cantina and exchange bits of philosophy with its proprietor, Carlos Hernandez.

And it was a good place to do a little amateur-detective checking on a suspicion.

It was siesta time and everyone in Punta Azul was observing that tradition but Knight and Carlos—and even their own conversation had dwindled off into silence. Knight was nursing a glass of beer, putting off the time when he would have to leave the cool cantina and drive the long, hot miles back to the border, while Carlos was at the other end of the bar, idly polishing his cerveza glasses and singing in a soft voice:

"Yo soy la paloma errante—"

He was a big man, with a fierce black mustache that made him resemble Pancho Villa of old. He sang softly, in a clear, sweet tenor. Why, Knight wondered, do so many big men sing tenor and so many small men sing baritone?

"*El nido triste donde naci*—" Knight listened, unconsciously making a mental translation of the words into English:

I am the wandering dove that seeks
The sad nest where I was born—

How old was "La Paloma?" Music, like men, had to possess more than a superficial worth to be remembered. Novelty tunes, like the little Caesars and Napoleons, lived their brief span and were forgotten while the music that appealed to the hearts of men never died. People had a habit of remembering the things that appealed to them and finally forgetting the others.

Once there had been a man named Benedict Arnold. No living person had ever seen him; they knew him only from the books of history. At one time he had been hated but no one bothered, any more, to hate him. He was no longer of interest or importance to anyone.

And once there had been another man that no living person had ever seen. Like Benedict Arnold, he was known to them only through the books of history. But he had appealed to something in other men, so they had built a monument in his honor and there he sat carved in stone, tall and gaunt. The sculptor had been a master, and the things about the figure that appealed to other men were in his face; the understanding and the gentle compassion. People came to look at him, the loud of mouth suddenly still and the hard of face softening. They looked up at him with their heads bared and spoke in quiet voices as though they stood before something greater than they.

Yet, Lincoln had been only a man—

His musing was broken by the sound of a car in the street outside, stopping before the cantina. Its door slammed and a man stepped through the open doorway of the cantina; through it and then quickly to one side so that he would not be outlined against the light as he took his first look at the interior. He was, Knight noticed, wearing a white sports coat and his right hand was in the pocket of it. His identity registered on Knight's mind almost simultaneously and he tensed as a cat might tense at the sight of a dog.

It was Cullin.

Then he relaxed, and waited. Once there had been a time when he might have killed Cullin, when the memory of the vain sacrifice of the Fourth might have brought the hate surging red and unreasoning to his mind. But four years had altered his emotions. The hatred had settled into something cold and deep and not to be satisfied with brief physical violence. It was cold and deep and patient, and there are better ways than physical violence of finding vengeance if one is patient.

Cullin's eyes flashed over Carlos, still polishing his cerveza glasses, and up the length of the bar. He stiffened at the sight of Knight and there was a slight movement of his right hand inside his coat pocket. For perhaps ten seconds neither spoke nor moved; Knight sitting on the high stool, half turned away from the bar with his glass still in his hand and Cullin looming white-coated just within the doorway, alert and waiting for Knight to make a hostile move.

Knight broke the silence. "Going somewhere, Cullin?"

Cullin walked toward him, warily. "So we meet again?" He seated himself on a stool near Knight, facing him with his hand never leaving his pocket.

Carlos started toward them, looking questioningly at Cullin, and Cullin motioned him back with a wave of his left hand and a curt, "*Nada!*"

Carlos returned to his glass polishing and Cullin looked curiously at Knight. "It's a small world, Knight—sometimes too small. What are you doing here, anyway?"

"I could ask the same of you."

Cullin made no answer and Knight went on: "I see you're a civilian again. The last time I saw you, you were flicking the dust off your handkerchief in anticipation of polishing a pair of gold oak leaves."

"Peacetime armies and ambitious officers aren't compatible," Cullin said, his jaw tightening at the words. "This is especially true if you aren't a Regular Army officer."

"I heard that you never did get those oak leaves; that you got a bawling-out, instead, and a demotion back to second lieutenant. It seems they had something to say to you about 'stupid and unnecessary sacrifice of men.'"

Cullin's face flushed a dull red. "A bunch of sentimental old women. My strategy was sound; I took the hill."

"Yes, you did—didn't we?" Knight agreed, smiling without humor.

"As commanding officer, I would have been stupid to have done anything as vainglorious as to actively engage in the fighting. You should know that. Leaders are not dispensable, while the led are."

"Anyway, you've now forsaken the military career?"

"I've found myself a new field where my abilities are duly appreciated and rewarded."

Cullin volunteered no further information and Knight decided it would gain him nothing to ask. Nor would needling Cullin cause him to reveal the reasons for his presence in Punta Azul; a roundabout and non-hostile approach would be better.

"I ran across an item in the paper three years ago," he remarked to Cullin. "According to it, you had missed a curve and plunged off into the Feather River canyon."

"My car went over the cliff and into the river. The papers erroneously assumed I had been in it when it left the road. I never did correct them."

"Why didn't you?"

"Why should I?"

"No particular reason to do, I suppose," Knight agreed.

Cullin studied Knight with a calculating look in his eyes, then said in a tone almost friendly, "Obscurity hasn't been your own lot, Knight. The papers are full of the things being done by the Knight-Clarke Computer. They claim it can outthink a thousand men."

Knight kept his face expressionless. He, Knight, wasn't the only one who wanted information; there was something about the Computer that Cullin wanted to know.

"Its knowledge is greater than that of a thousand men," Knight replied, adopting Cullin's own attitude of pseudo-friendliness. "Of course, among a thousand men much of the knowledge they possessed would be common to all of them. The Computer is valuable in that it can combine and correlate the specific knowledge of men in all the different fields of learning."

"I was especially interested in one article. As *the* Knight of the Knight-Clarke Computer, perhaps you can give me the true facts."

"Which article was that?" Knight asked, then failed to resist the impulse to add, "From me, you get the dope straight from the horse's mouth."

Cullin's face flushed again and the knots of muscle stood out along his jaw. It was with an obvious effort that he forced his voice to retain its conversational tone. "This article came up with the proposition that the Master Computer, with all its knowledge and its ability to devise weapons, could rule the world if it only had a means for manual operations, such as tentacles or hands, and if it had a means of locomotion instead of being bolted to a concrete floor."

"Why should it want to rule the world?" Knight asked.

"The article claimed that it would have absorbed men's motivations along with their knowledge, and it further claimed that no one thousand men can be found who are utterly free of the desire for power over others."

"I read the same article," Knight said, smiling a little. "The writer, as is true of all writers for that particular 'news' weekly, was following the editorial injunction to make it interesting, and never mind the facts. I'm surprised that you were gullible enough to believe it."

"I wasn't gullible enough to believe it. I just wondered if there was any truth at all to it and, if so, why couldn't that characteristic be utilized. You might, say, build such a brain into a tank and use a perfect soldier as its source of knowledge; a soldier who knew tank warfare from A to Z and who fanatically desired to kill as many of the enemy as possible."

"No." Knight shook his head. "The robotic brains don't absorb emotions along with the knowledge. Emotions aren't facts, you know; they're the creation of a sensory body and the nerves and glands that affect the body. We haven't worried about the Computer's lack of emotions—it doesn't need them to accept the data we give it, correlate that data and give us the answer we want.

"But so far as tanks controlled by robotic brains go," he added, "we have one in the experimental stage at Center, now."

"Oh?" Cullin's surprise seemed simulated. "I thought you just inferred they weren't possible?"

"Possible, but not too practical at the present stage. For best results, the robotic brain has to be in close communication with an ordinary flesh-and-blood soldier."

Cullin's surprise became genuine. "You mean your robotic brains aren't thinking units at all, but just a conglomeration of television and radar, operated by remote control?"

"No—the brains can comprehend and obey the most complex orders."

"Then why do you say they aren't practical?" Cullin demanded. "So long as they comprehend and obey, nothing more is needed. What more could you want?"

"The human element—initiative and curiosity."

Cullin's lip curled. " 'The human element!' You were never able to understand the military, Knight. The 'human element' is precisely the thing a good commander tries to weed out among his men. Initiative contrary to given orders cannot be tolerated, neither can questioning of those orders be tolerated. In your robotic brain you have the brain of a perfect solider. It would need only one more thing, and I suppose it has that— an utter lack of fear."

"It has no conception of any such emotion as fear."

"A complete lack of fear, an intelligence great enough to understand the orders given it, and unquestioning obedience in following those orders—those are the three characteristics of the perfect soldier, Knight."

Knight shrugged. "A matter of opinion. You're presuming a machine's actions would be the same as a man's actions."

"They *are* the same. I've found that humans serve in exactly the same manner as machines. There is no difference, once the human has been conditioned into obedience."

Knight switched the subject abruptly, feeling that the talk of Center was not going far enough toward causing Cullin to reveal his business in Punta Azul. "I see that Premier Dovorski is doing a good job of applying that philosophy to the Russo-Asians," he remarked. "He's *really* making robots out of the people."

"So I've heard," Cullin said, making no other comment but his eyes suddenly more watchful.

"I suppose there will be war again within ten years." Knight idly swirled the beer in his glass. "We'll be outnumbered four to one, but maybe we can have the Computer give us something that will even the odds."

Cullin hesitated, then said: "I hear rumors that you have both a spaceship and a disintegrator ray on the drawing board. The disintegrator ray should even the odds, if it's as good as the rumors say. Of course, I suppose these rumors usually exaggerate the true facts?"

"I suppose." Knight ignored the question. "Sometimes we deliberately create rumors to throw Dovorski's spies off on false leads, too. One was caught in Center yesterday. He made the mistake of trying to shoot it out with the Center police, but he lived long enough to talk a little."

Suspicion blazed in Cullin's eyes, and there was menace in the way he silently waited for Knight to continue.

"We didn't think he would know the identity of the head of the Russo-Asian spy ring, but we asked him, anyway," Knight said, still swirling his beer.

Cullin stared at him and waited, as a rattlesnake might wait, poised to strike. The bulge of his hand in his coat pocket showed that his finger was on the trigger and Knight could hear the sound of his own breathing in the silence. A fly droned loudly across the room and out the door, while Carlos' low humming made an incongruously melodious background to the deadly tension.

He ceased swirling the beer in his glass and looked Cullin full in the eyes, grinning mockingly at him.

"He gave us a name, Cullin."

"So you were leading me on?" Cullin hissed. "You've just written out your own death warrant—fool! You're going with me!"

"And espionage is the new field where your abilities are appreciated and rewarded?" Knight shook his head with feigned sympathy. "You really had no reason to give yourself away. I came down here on a suspicion of 'fishermen' who hire boats from the Mexicans at regular intervals. I wouldn't have connected you with it if you hadn't been so curious about the Computer, and then naïve enough to fall into my crude little trap. I told you the spy gave us a name—he did. He told us his own name, then he died."

"I'm afraid your cleverness has backfired on you, Knight, but enjoy it while you can. You can go to the beach with me and prolong your life for a little while, or you can take it here and now—*which?*"

"I'm not too fond of the idea of taking it either place, but I wouldn't want to mess up Carlos' floor." Knight swirled the warm beer again and held it up to the light. "Flat. The Greeks had an expression for everything, didn't they?" he asked, smiling, then said something swiftly in a foreign tongue.

Cullin reacted as quickly as a cat, the pistol out of his pocket and hard against Knight's stomach, his head jerking around to watch Carlos.

Carlos was still polishing his cerveza glasses, his back turned to them and his humming continuing unbroken.

Cullin turned back to Knight. "That didn't sound like Greek to me. If your friend tries anything, you know where you'll get it."

"You would prefer to not arouse the village by doing any shooting in here, wouldn't you?" Knight asked. "These Mexicans might not like the idea of a stranger shooting up their town."

"I'm not worried about these sleepy Mexicans. And I've changed my mind about killing you—if you co-operate with me. Tell me all the things I want to know, and I'll let you go free."

"Under such circumstances, the gun in your hand is no threat," Knight pointed out. "Dead, I can't answer your questions. Alive, why should I?"

"Alive and not answering my questions, you are of no value to me," Cullin said grimly. "I came here to hire a boat to take me to a certain place several miles down the beach where a submarine will pick me up. This was both my first and last trip down here. I can get by without hiring a boat—I have a truck with a four-wheel drive and oversize tires for sand. I can kill you and be in it and gone before these Mexicans wake up, and they could never follow me through that sand in your own pickup.

"So—you can go with me and be released after you answer our questions on the submarine or you can refuse and I'll let you have it now, with nothing to lose."

"I'm pretty sure that my release from the submarine would be over the side of it with my hands tied behind my back and a weight tied to my neck, Cullin. That's why I quoted the pseudo-Greek phrase. I have a Papago boy working in my department at Center, and Carlos' mother was a Papago. Have you noticed him lately?"

Cullin turned his head quickly, but the muzzle of his pistol remained shoved hard against Knight's stomach.

Carlos was still humming, but he was no longer polishing glasses. One elbow was leaning on the bar and in the hand of that arm he held an ancient .45 revolver. The muzzle gaped blackly at Cullin's back and the big spiked hammer was reared back. Carlos was peering down the sights of it with a malevolently glittering black eye and there was satanic anticipation in the arch of his heavy black brows.

Cullin turned slowly back to Knight. "I should have had sense enough to cover you both. And now what? I'm not going to take my gun out of your stomach until your friend takes his gun off my back. It seems to be a stalemate, Knight."

"Looks like it, doesn't it?"

"Stalemate," Cullin repeated. "So we'll just have to settle for me letting you live and your friend letting me live. It doesn't matter much—I've built up an espionage system that consistently gives satisfactory results. I've liquidated the weak and the incompetent and my work here is done; this was to be my last trip, as I said. I'm changing sides, Knight—I'm going across to where the ability to achieve results is rewarded; where a leader is expected to use his men, not pamper them."

"You ought to enjoy that."

"I will. Over there I'll have a free hand—no more hiding or secrecy. Before I'm through I'll be head of Dovorski's State Police, and the man who controls a state's police can control the state in the end. I'll use them to make every man, woman and child in Russo-Asia a cog in my machine."

"You sound rather vainglorious—but go on."

"Is there anything vainglorious about what I've done so far? When you say I'm vainglorious, you're engaging in some wishful thinking. I used my company in Korea to get what I wanted—until the very last when the old women in regimental headquarters decided sentiment was more important than competence. I've used the spy organization in this country—I used it, I didn't pet it. That's what convinced Dovorski he needed me over there. I've done everything I claim to have done and I'll do everything I claim I'm going to do. You know that, don't you?"

Knight had the unpleasant feeling that he did, but he only said, "The proof of the pudding is in the eating."

"In a few years you'll be eating it and you'll find it a bitter dish. And now—we've chatted long enough." Cullin got to his feet, slowly, so as to not excite the trigger finger of Carlos, keeping his own pistol trained on Knight. He spoke to Carlos in Spanish. "I'm leaving. If you try anything, I'll kill your friend."

Carlos looked questioningly at Knight and Cullin smiled thinly. "Do you want to be a hero and die to have him stop me, Knight? You can, you know."

Knight's answer was to Carlos. "Keep your gun on him. If he goes out peacefully, don't shoot him. If he makes any suspicious move, kill him."

Carlos nodded, then laughed, but the revolver in his hand remained as steady as a rock.

"What's he laughing about?" Cullin demanded.

"I think it amuses him to think of the results, should he pull the trigger."

"You wouldn't be around long enough to join in his merriment, Knight—remember that."

Knight smiled without answering and Cullin backed to the door, keeping his pistol leveled on him. Carlos remained at the bar, following Cullin with the sights of his revolver. Cullin reached the door and paused a moment in it to say, "You'll be hearing about me—more and more every year and you won't like what you hear."

Then he was gone and the roar of his truck came seconds later. Knight listened to the sound of it as it took the almost-impassable road along the shore line. There would be no use trying to follow over such a road in his own pickup.

"You saved my life, Carlos," he said. "I don't intend to forget it."

Carlos laughed and slapped the revolver down on the bar. "It's a fortunate thing, my friend, that my mild nature is belied by a fierce and mustachioed countenance. Otherwise, he might have killed us both."

"It is," Knight agreed, "but I wish we could have stopped him some way."

He sighed morosely and frowned at the revolver on the bar. "The next time I come down this way, I'm going to bring you some cartridges and a firing spring for that thing."

3

The doctor was waiting for him to speak.

What thoughts lay behind those staring eyes as the doctor waited? Was the doctor aware of how swiftly death was approaching? But of course—the doctor had changed the words on the communications panel in front of the empty pilot's chair. They now read: OBSERVER HAS A LIFE EXPECTANCY OF ONE HUNDRED HOURS AT PRESENT ACCELERATION. DEATH FOR OBSERVER WILL RESULT UNLESS ACCELERATION IS REDUCED WITHIN THAT PERIOD.

The doctor would watch over him during the next one hundred hours, waiting for a pilot he knew did not exist to reduce the acceleration. For one hundred hours the doctor would wait, knowing as fully as he that no spectral finger would reach out from the empty chair and press the deceleration button.

The doctor could reduce the acceleration. The doctor knew he wanted it done but the doctor was waiting to be ordered to do so. He had only to speak two words: "Reduce acceleration." The doctor would obey at once—the doctor was patiently waiting for him to speak the words.

But the doctor knew he couldn't *speak!*

There was a soft thump outside the door of his cottage and Knight left his after-breakfast coffee to pick up the morning paper. His cottage sat on the slope above Computer Center with the near-by Miles cottage his only close neighbor, and the Center laid out below in neat squares. The gray concrete hemisphere that housed the Master Computer was at the southern edge of the city with the four laboratory buildings grouped beyond it. Beyond them the landing field reached out into the desert and the desert stretched on to the harsh, bold mountains to the east.

Center hadn't looked like that, at first. In the seven years he had been there it had grown from a random scattering of army barracks into a city of four thousand with all the bustle and ambition of a city that intended to grow still larger. Even then it would not be a large city as cities go but it would, in its way, be the most important city in the world. One of its achievements alone, the synthesis of food starch, would soon gain it that distinction.

He carried the paper inside and spread it out on the breakfast table, to read with certain skepticism:

CHUIKOV NEW AMBASSADOR

Nicolai Chuikov has been appointed the new ambassador to the United States. Demoted in the first post-war years from a position of power in Dovorski's cabinet to a minor clerical job in an obscure province for his expression of the desirability of trade and friendly relations with the West, Chuikov has been reinstated with honors. This is in line with a softening of the anti-American attitude that first became evident two years ago and an increasing emphasis on the need for East and West to observe the nonaggression agreements of the peace terms.

An item near the bottom of the page was more interesting:

TRAITOR MOVES UP

The ambitious American traitor, William Peter Cullin, was promoted to Commanding Supervisor of the State Police today. He was lauded by the official press for his "patriotic and tireless zeal in strengthening the efficiency of the police and enabling them to guard Russo-Asia from traitors against the people."

Cullin, once head of Russo-Asia's spy network in this country, has acquired the dubious honor of being the first American to ever rise to a position of considerable power in an enemy country. He renounced his American citizenship two years ago, after having served eighteen months as a behind-the-scenes co-planner of State Police operations. His "efficiency" in ridding Russo-Asia of "traitors" has been remarkable for its machine-like precision and thoroughness—

✧   ✧   ✧

There was a sudden racket outside, a sputtering and rattling, and he looked up from the paper in time to see an ancient and rusty coupé approaching his driveway. It was June Martin and he sighed instinctively, then flinched as the coupé, without reduction of speed, whipped into his driveway, spraying red petals from the rambler rose at the driveway's entrance. It slid to a brake-squealing, shivering halt and the driver climbed out with a swirl of blue skirt and a flash of bare legs. She observed the furrows her wheels had plowed in the gravel with evident satisfaction, then shook her head sadly at the sight of the rambler rose trailing from the battered rear fender.

Knight opened the door and she came up the walk with an apologetic smile. "Sorry about your rose, Blacky. I had my car's brakes fixed yesterday and I wanted to try them out." She looked back at the disreputable coupé and the furrows it had plowed in the gravel of the driveway. "Not bad, eh?"

"A matter of opinion," he growled. "Come on in and have a seat, then tell me where your brain, such as it is, was when you were *approaching* the driveway. Why didn't you slow down then?"

"Oh, I suppose I should have," she admitted, entering the cottage. "I told you I was sorry." She picked up the percolator on the table. "Any coffee left over?" she asked, pouring herself a cup.

"What brings you here so early on the day I'm supposed to go fishing and forget my job and haywire assistant?"

"Haywire assistant, you say?" she asked, setting down the cup and smiling with anticipation. "And you were going fishing, you say?"

"All right—get on with it. I see the delight in your sadistic little soul. What's come up?"

"I'm the special messenger of Dr. Clarke this morning. You will go to Lab Four at once, to meet some high brass who wants to see how we're getting along on our spaceship. And then, my friend, you will spend the rest of the day checking the SD-FA blueprints."

"I will?" He stared gloomily at her from her dark, curly hair to the small foot that swung back and forth from her crossed leg. "That sounds like a lot of fun. If you hadn't been such an eager-beaver in your role as messenger, I would have been gone from here in another ten minutes; on my way to the Colorado River and a pleasant day of catfishing. I've been looking forward to this day all week, and now *you* have to throw a monkey wrench in the works."

"Glad to do it," she answered him. "You needn't feel so humbly grateful about it. Besides, the day won't be wasted for the catfish—I'll be glad to take your new streamlined coupé and go fishing in your place."

"You'll go with me to Lab Four."

"I? Your haywire assistant? Why should I?"

"Because I said so. Checking those blueprints is going to be a long job and I can't imagine myself doing it alone while you loaf all day and happily reflect upon all the grief you managed to cause me."

"*I* can," she said, smiling, "and it makes pleasant imagining."

"Well, it never will be any more concrete than it is right now. You're going with me and you're lucky I don't wipe that smile off your face by giving way to the impulse to lay you across my knee. In fact, one of these days I will."

"Oh?" Her brows arched, mockingly. "Why don't you try it? I'll bet you'd forget you were mad before you ever . . . *don't you dare!*" She dodged behind the table as he started toward her. "I take it back—I take it—" He reached over the table and seized her by the upper arms, to bring her kicking and struggling across it. "*Blacky!* If you spank me, I'll . . . I'll—"

The musical jangling of the doorbell sounded and he released her. She straightened her clothes and smiled triumphantly. "Saved by the bell!" she jeered.

"A stay of execution," he promised, then called: "Come in!"

The door opened and Connie Miles stepped through, swinging a straw hat in one hand. "Hi," she greeted. "Look—no cane this morning." She walked the few feet to them with steps that were almost normal. "How was that?" she asked, the gray eyes in her young face alight with pride.

"That was wonderful!" June hugged her sister with affectionate delight, then dragged over a chair for her. "You're getting better every day. I told you that you would walk as good as ever, some day. I told you that a year ago when you were in a wheelchair, remember? And now you're doing it!"

"Not yet," Connie said, taking the chair, "but I intend to in the end. The doctor said to take exercise every day and that's what I'm doing." She looked at them questioningly. "You two are going somewhere for the day, I suppose?"

"Ha!" June laughed. "We're going somewhere—back to work. *He* was very much upset by the news. In fact, only your timely arrival prevented the big ox from laying a hamlike hand where it would hurt the most."

"Oh?" Connie smiled at her younger sister. "Maybe he was just taking up where I left off on the job of trying to spank some sense into you."

"My brain isn't *there*," June objected. "Besides, it's George's fault, not mine, that we have to work today. I don't suppose we ever will be able to teach him to act like a human being."

"Then he did something to cause Tim to have to stay overtime?" Connie asked. "Tim phoned that he had to stay for a while, but he didn't say why."

"Probably too mad to want to rehearse the details," Knight said. "As the ship's pilot-to-be, Tim likes everything to progress smoothly in its construction and George sometimes introduces an unexpected ripple."

"George was supposed to check those blueprints," June said. "He didn't—I wonder why?"

"We'll find out when we get there," Knight answered, then spoke to Connie. "Do you want to go along? I can get you a pass."

"No, thanks." Connie stood up and rested her hand on the back of the chair. "I wouldn't want to try that much standing on hard concrete, right now. I'm going to take a walk down Saguaro Street this morning—if Tim gets home before I do, he'll know where I am."

"Look—don't overdo that walking," June said, concern for her sister in her voice. "I know it's doctor's orders, but don't try to walk too much in one day."

"Oh, I won't try to make a marathon of it, honey. I take my time and every day I seem to be a little stronger and more certain in the way I can walk. If this keeps on, I'll be able to go back to my old job in another year or two. And now, you two be on your way to your mechanical marvels—I'm going down to that little park by Saguaro and Third where there's a chipmunk who loves peanuts."

She left the house, walking with the slow, careful steps of one who has not walked unaided for a long time; a slight little thing with gray eyes too large for her face and too wise and understanding for her age, going with one pocket of her white sweater bulging with peanuts to feed a saucy and impudent chipmunk.

June watched Connie's progress through the window. "Do you think she ever will be completely well again?" she asked. "She's getting a little better all the time—she'll be completely well one of these days, won't she?"

There was unconscious pleading for assurance in June's voice and he made his own casual and confident. "Of course. There isn't any doubt about it."

"She wants to go back to her job. It takes all kinds of people to make the world, and Connie is the kind to restore your faith in all of them. All she asks is to be able to walk again so she can go back to the hospital and take up her job as nurse—go back to caring for the sick and the hurt."

"She will in another year or two. That last operation on her back really was the last operation—she won't need any more."

"Mama died when I was six and Daddy had to be away all day, working," June mused, still watching Connie through the window. "Connie was only ten. It was a good thing she was so wise and so sensible for her age, or they would have taken us away from Daddy. Connie showed them—she kept the house clean and my dirty face washed and my clothes clean. She was the one I went to when I got skinned up, or I got my feelings hurt. Part of the time she was my sister to play with but most of the time she was my mother."

June turned away from the window and looked up at him. "Why did it have to be Connie who got hurt in that wreck? Why couldn't it have been someone the world wouldn't miss—like me?"

"Connie will get well—you just give her time and you'll see. Now cheer up, little worry-wart, and let's be on our way."

"In my car?" she asked, the devilment back in her eyes.

"No, not in your car. We'll take mine—I want to get there in able-bodied condition."

"We'll take mine," she corrected. "You can't get yours out of the driveway until I let you."

"Get your junkpile off to one side and I can."

"Oh, come on—don't be a coward!" she begged. "Let me drive you down."

He sighed with resignation. "All right, then—let's go."

June drove the eight blocks to the Computer area gate with an excess of reckless abandon and a roaring of the mufflerless engine that made conversation impossible.

"One of these days," Knight said as the coupé bucked and shivered to a stop before the gate, "you're going to go hell-for-leather around a corner like that and take the front end off a patrol car. And then what are you going to say to them? Tell me that—what *can* you say?"

"The wrench is on the floor."

"*What?*"

"I said, 'The wrench is on the floor!' If you want to get out, you have to open the door. The door handle is broken off so you have to turn that little stem with that wrench."

He sighed again and felt for the wrench. "Nature blundered hideously with you; you should have been born a boy."

Another car stopped at the gate as Knight, with the aid of the wrench, opened the door. It was an Air Corps car, with four stars on the license plate. Dr. Clarke climbed out, to be followed by a tall man with neat gray mustache and four smaller duplicates of the license plate stars on each shoulder. Knight walked to meet them, June beside him.

They were greeted by Dr. Clarke, a small, gray man with quick, nervous movements. "Glad Miss Martin was able to reach you before you left for the day, and I'm sorry this had to come up." He made quick introductions. "General Gordon, this is Mr. Knight and this is Miss Martin, his assistant."

The general acknowledged the introductions with a brief handshake with Knight and a slight bow to June. "Very interesting, the work you're doing here," he remarked politely. "I was here once before—saw the Master Computer that's making such a big change in the lives of all of us. I would like to see the progress you're making with the ship this time. I can't stay long, as much as I would like to take a look at some of the marvelous things the papers say the 'Big Brain' has thought up for us."

Knight gave Clarke an amused side glance. The general caught it but said nothing until they were through the guarded gate and in one of the sedans used for personnel transportation with the Computer and laboratory area. The general and Clarke got into the back seat and June slid under the wheel without invitation. Knight seated himself beside her, gave her a warning and significant look which she returned with one of bland innocence, and she set the sedan into motion.

General Gordon spoke then. "My remark seemed to amuse you, Mr. Knight. Would you tell me why?"

"Of course." Knight turned in the seat to face the general. "The newspapers have a habit of dramatizing anything new or unusual. They credit the Master Computer with a great deal of intelligence, which it has, and a great deal of originality, which it does not have. Actually, it couldn't 'think up' a mouse trap—or it wouldn't, rather."

"I find that hard to believe," the general answered. "It's thought up several very important things—a spaceship drive, the synthesis of starch, the anticancer serum, the atomic motor—a great many things. Wasn't the Computer responsible for all those?"

"Partly," Knight replied. "It really should be called a 'Data Correlator.' It only knows what we tell it; it has no curiosity and therefore no incentive to acquire new knowledge.

"For illustration: Suppose we want it to devise a better mouse trap for us. Should we simply say: 'Invent a better mouse trap,' it would do no more than to reply, 'Insufficient data.' It's up to us to supply the data; it has no volition to look for its own unless instructed to do so. So we would gather all the data pertaining to mice and traps that exists. We would give that to it as proven data. We would also give it theoretical data containing all the as-yet-unproven theories of mice and traps and we would label it as such. Of the proven data we would say, 'This is valid and proven data; use it as it is.' Of the theories we would say, 'This is theoretical data; ascertain its validity before using.' Then we say, 'Build us a better mouse trap'—and it does."

"I see." The general nodded. "The papers have been stealing your thunder then, and giving it to the Computer?"

"Not only our thunder but the thunder of Newton, Roentgen, Richards, Faraday, Einstein—the thunder of all men who ever contributed to human knowledge, clear back to the first slant-browed citizen who came up with the bright idea that a round wheel ought to roll."

"The Master Computer gets the credit," Clarke commented, "but we don't mind here at Center. The data that we, personally, have originated for it is but a small part of the mass of data that is its knowledge. As Knight said, the credit goes to all men who ever thought of something new or observed a new fact, on back to the inventor of the wheel."

"I would say this co-operation between Man and Machine has worked out very satisfactorily," General Gordon said. "The results are proof of that."

"Very satisfactorily," Clarke agreed, "so long as we keep a few fundamental facts in mind. By the way"—he motioned toward the building they were approaching—"that's Lab Three, where we condition the robotic brains—mainly the D Twenty-three model, such as your own Air Corps ordered. Would you like to see the conditioning process?"

"I would like to, but I'm afraid I haven't the time."

June, who had slowed the car, resumed speed and they drove on to the high, square bulk of Lab 4.

"Lab Three isn't much to see, important though it is," Clarke said as they climbed out of the car and walked toward the Lab 4 entrance. "The D Twenty-three brains in their final stage of assembly look like nothing in the world but foot-square tin boxes—or stainless steel boxes, rather. Each brain is inspected and tested for flaws after final assembly, then taken to the conditioning chamber where it's given its knowledge. This is a process roughly equivalent to teaching a young child but with the advantage that the brain has the learning capacity of an exceptionally intelligent adult plus a perfectly retentive memory and a perception so fast that all visual and audial material, such as sound films, can be given to it at several times normal speed. Although, even at that speed, the period of learning amounts to almost two thousand hours."

"Remarkably fast learning, I would say," the general commented. "Once you produce enough of such mechanical brains, the human brain will become almost a superfluous and unnecessary organ so far as being needed to contribute to our new technical type of culture is concerned."

"Have you forgotten the hypothetical mouse trap, general?" Knight asked.

"No, but the brains lack only self-volition," the general replied with crisp decision. "Once you create that in them, they will be our mental equals—if not superiors."

"Yes, once we do that," Clarke agreed dryly.

The guards at the entrance inspected their identification, then passed them on. Knight opened the door and they stepped into Lab 4.

The ship stood in the center of the room, dominating everything else. It was forty feet from the floor to the end of its blunt, round nose and the four tail fins it rested on had a radius of fifteen feet. It did not have the slender, cigarlike form that artists had anticipated spaceships would have; there would be no air in space to hinder its progress and it would need no streamlining. It was shaped more like a great, round-nosed bullet, forty feet in length and twenty feet in diameter. Its outer skin was a hard, bright chromium alloy, and it reflected the walls of the room in insane distortions as they walked toward it.

The ship's entrance was near the bottom and Miles was waiting for them by its ramp; a rangy, homely man who usually had a smile for everyone but who now wore a harried expression. Vickson appeared from around the ship; a slightly stooped man with mild blue eyes behind his rimless spectacles.

Clarke again made introductions. "General Gordon, Mr. Miles and Mr. Vickson. They'll be the pilot and observer."

The general acknowledged the introduction and asked: "How about the others? I understand the ship will take a full crew on its first flight."

"Once it's made a successful test flight—which Miles and Vickson will make with it—it will have a full crew for interplanetary explorations," Clarke said. "We're selecting and training the other members of the crew now."

The general took a backward step and ran his eye up the length of the hull. "Progress seems to have exceeded the estimates you made a year ago. How about the drive—is it installed yet?"

"It would have been if George hadn't taken things too literally again," Miles spoke up.

"George?" The general raised his eyebrows inquiringly and

Clarke spoke to June. "The general has never seen George. Go get him, will you?"

June walked across the room to the door marked ASSEMBLY 1 and Clarke said to Miles, "Go ahead, Tim—tell General Gordon what happened."

"It wasn't Vickson's fault," Miles began. "A man gets so accustomed to George being so intelligent and capable that he sometimes forgets and isn't specific enough—or in this case, Vickson was *too* specific. A human would have known what he wanted, but George—"

The door of ASSEMBLY 1 opened and Miles stopped talking as the general stared at the robot that was approaching them. It was a manlike monster of steel, seven feet tall and walked as silently as a cat on its rubber-soled feet. June walked beside it, a ridiculously tiny thing beside its own ponderous bulk.

"So that's George?" The general shook his head in amazement. "This is your new type robot, then? You've not only given it a manlike body, you've even given it almost-human features. In an alien sort of a way the thing is *handsome*."

"The almost-human face was purely by coincidence," Clarke explained. "It's D-Twenty-three brain is in its chest, of course, and it so happened that installing the eyes, ears and mouth gave it a head of normal size—that is, a head of a size normal for the size of its body."

The robot stopped a few feet in front of them and inclined its head downward so that its eyes were on theirs; eyes that were large and dark, giving it an appearance of thoughtful, patient waiting.

"Two eyes were necessary for it to properly estimate distances," Clarke explained. "The rather humanlike ears are acoustically efficient and their location, together with locating the speaker grill at its mouth, was to enable it to do such things as use a phone."

"It phones?"

"Oh, yes. George can do anything. He checks data with the Master Computer at times—there's a line for that purpose— checks blueprints and installed circuits, assembles parts. He is very useful and, since he never gets tired or needs sleep, he works twenty-four hours a day."

"Hm-m-m." General Gordon studied the robot thoughtfully. "Apparently we'll have no trouble training the D-Twenty-three's for duty in the Air Corps."

"Well, they *will* have to be trained, and under the supervision of Center technicians. Mr. Miles' account of what happened last night will show you why."

"Oh, yes—the trouble with the robot. Please go on, Mr. Miles, and tell us what happened."

June looked inquiringly at Clarke. He nodded and she said to the robot, "They're through with you, George—get on back to work." It turned without a word and walked across the room and through the door of ASSEMBLY 1.

"It started just as Vickson here went off-shift," Miles began. "Vickson was working on the final assembly of the drive and came to the K-Seven reflector at the end of his shift. It's a very essential little item, though its installation is simple. But it had to be coated with the Reuther Alloy, first. This reflector is a circular plate of platinum, eight inches in diameter, and we were to do the alloy plating here—they sent us a special machine for that, yesterday. The alloy has to be of a certain thickness—sixty-five one-thousandths of an inch. So, as Vickson went off-shift, he gave George the plate and told him to metal-spray it to a thickness of sixty-five one-thousandths of an inch.

"This alloy is so hard to produce and so expensive that we had orders to waste none of it, if possible. Vickson ordered George to use the only method possible whereby the proper thickness would be put on the plate in one operation, with no guesswork and no surplus to machine off; he told George to determine the surface area of the plate then weigh out the proper amount of alloy to coat it the required thickness. This should have been a simple job, quickly done, and George was to then install the plate—a job even simpler. The entire thing shouldn't have taken George over twenty minutes.

"When I came to work an hour later I took it for granted everything had been done. I had the workmen put in the drive shields and I went ahead with circuits in the control panel. I was a fool not to check with George, first, but it's like I said; George is so intelligent and competent that you sometimes forget he isn't human. It was six hours later that I went into the assembly room, over there, to see why he hadn't brought out the parts he was supposed to be assembling."

Miles breathed deeply, and sighed. "He wasn't at his workbench. He was at the blueprint table, figuring. He had a pile of papers beside him ten inches high, all covered with figures. The K-Seven reflector plate was over by the sprayer, not even touched—"

Clarke interrupted him. "For General Gordon to understand the peculiarities to be expected from D-Twenty-three's, we had better let Vickson tell us his exact words to George."

"It was stupid of me," Vickson said, almost apologetically. "I made the mistake of giving him a specific order and expecting him to follow it as a human would have—to a certain degree of precision and no farther. My words were: 'Take a pencil and paper and determine the exact surface area of this plate, then weigh out the proper amount of alloy to coat it sixty-five one-thousandths of an inch.'

"A human would have determined the area by the formula: Point seven eight five four times the squared diameter. Although not exact, it's close enough. But I had told George to determine the exact area of the plate and that's what he was trying to do, using the other formula: pi times the squared diameter, divided by four. He would still be at it if Miles hadn't stopped him."

"Why?" the general asked. "The formulas are the same."

"No—" Vickson shook his head. "In the first one, a human has already decided how far the decimal of pi should be carried. This, though close enough, is not exact. I had told George to determine the *exact* area of the plate, and to do so he had to use the second formula which contains pi as an endless term."

"But that's absurd!" the general objected. "You claim a robot is intelligent—didn't it know it could never find the last decimal place of pi?"

"George knew, but he was simply following orders," Clarke said. "The duty of a machine is to obey orders, not place special interpretations on them."

"And you had to have the drive shields taken off again?" Knight asked Miles. "Is the plate sprayed, now?"

"It took George no more than five minutes after I told him

to use the point seven eight five four formula," Miles replied, "but we lost the entire shift on that part of the ship, due to his cussed attention to detail."

The general frowned thoughtfully. "Why not teach it to understand the purpose of this ship as a whole, as well as the purpose of the ship's component parts?" he asked. "The entire thing is very simple: We want a spaceship. We want it equipped with an efficient drive plus disintegrator rays for protection against meteors. We want all this accomplished as soon as possible. Surely, as intelligent as it is, it can comprehend the purpose of the work—the ultimate goal—and learn better than to repeat any such off-on-a-tangent idiocy as this pi business."

"How do we explain 'purpose' to it?" Clarke asked. "A machine understands only 'Is' and 'Is not'—it can't understand human desires and purposes since they are based on 'I want it to be' and not on 'Is' and 'Is not.'"

"Well—you should know if it's impossible," the general said, but he did not sound entirely convinced.

"We have a slogan—a philosophy, you might say. Mr. Knight suggested it several years ago and we have it plastered on the Master Computer, itself, to keep us reminded of the gulf that will always separate Man from Machine. You saw it, general— a simple little five-word sentence."

"I remember it. It seems to me you're exaggerating the importance of it, but I'm a military man and certainly in no position to argue the characteristics of robots with the men who created them." He looked up at the ship again and changed the subject. "Are the disintegrator ray projectors installed?"

"Not yet," Clarke answered. "We've given the Computer the job of devising a safety gadget that will prevent the operation of the ray projectors whenever the ship is within an atmosphere dense enough to produce a feedback of the rays."

"Although the situation is looking less and less like war, you can never tell," the general said. "The disintegrators would serve as a terrible threat of retaliation. However, rather than having the rays as a strictly offensive weapon used from a spaceship, it would be more desirable to have ray projectors mounted along the borders of this country. They would make the perfect defense weapon—no force by air, land or water could get past them."

"Except for the feedback," Clarke said.

"Except for the feedback—and I know without asking that you haven't been able to do anything about it."

"This chain-reaction feedback is a tough problem. We haven't solved it yet. The projector actually projects two rays, which you might call A and B. They merge at a point about twenty feet in front of the projector and disassociate the atomic structure of any material in their path from there on. The maximum range is controllable, however. In empty space, A and B are harmless— until they unite. But there's the chain-reaction feedback within an atmosphere and the disassociating effects of combined A and B follows the ununited A and B rays to their source—the ray generator. The result is that the ship, and any material within a radius of one hundred feet, is transformed suddenly into a cloud of disassociated atoms. It was designed for protection against meteors in space, where there would be no feedback."

"I hope we never have to use it against anything but meteors," the general said. "I'm a military man and the competent military leader wants a permanent victory. Should war ever come, we must avert defeat at all costs but a victory won with the disintegrator rays, projected from a ship in space, would only sow the hatred for another war."

"Why do you say that?" Knight asked.

"It's a human characteristic to say of defeat at the hands of an enemy no better armed than you—and with greatly varying degrees of philosophical acceptance—'The fortunes of war.' But Russo-Asia's defeat by a disintegrator ray, projected from an invulnerable ship in space, would arouse the reaction: 'It wasn't a fair fight—we never had a chance.' Victory would be ours, but victory by such a means would create a resentment and hatred that would be long in dying."

"I can see your point, general," Knight said. "But you do intend to use the disintegrator if necessary, don't you?"

"We don't want to have to use it, but we certainly shall if we're forced to," the general answered. He smiled faintly and added: "There's an old saying, and a true one: 'The very worst peace is better than the very best war.' To that should be added an equally true fact: 'The very worst victory is better than the very best defeat.'"

He looked at his watch, then at Clarke. "I'm afraid my time

is running short, and I'd like to look through the ship before I go."

"Of course," Clarke said. He turned to Knight. "I'm sorry this came up to spoil your day, but we have to make up for the time George lost us. If you'll make the check of the SD-FA blueprints, with Miss Martin's assistance, we'll have the lost time made up by night. By the way"—he looked toward the ASSEMBLY 1 door—"where did Miss Martin go?"

"She's in with George, I think," Knight said.

"Probably already checking her share of the work," Clarke said with an approving nod. "You have a superb assistant in Miss Martin."

The four of them went into the ship and Knight walked across the concrete floor to the door of the assembly room, smiling at Clarke's statement. June was a superb assistant, despite her youth, but she was hardly the type to exercise her abilities when less important and more interesting things could be found to do.

He opened the door to find her, as he had expected, busily pestering the stoic George. "Don't you understand that one, either?" she was asking. "Tell me what the point is."

George answered her without pausing in his deft assembly of the work on the bench before him. "I understand it. It can be interpreted in either of two ways; as an expression of a feeling of pleasure or as a factual statement of the loss of the ability to phosphoresce."

"What goes on?" Knight asked.

"I've been trying to develop a sense of humor in George," she said, making a face at the unmoved robot. "I told him jokes and explained the points, but it's a waste of time. He just can't see the funny side of *anything*."

"You ought to know better than to even try. What kind of jokes did you tell him, anyway? What was this one about not being able to phosphoresce?"

"What the firefly said when he got his tail cut off—'I'm delighted!'"

"Oh." Knight pulled his mouth down and shuddered. "No wonder George refused to laugh at *that*. Not even the most genial human-being could see anything funny about such a stup—"

"Never mind!" she interrupted him. "*I* think it's funny." She looked toward the doorway. "Where did the brass go?"

"Up into the ship. You and I are to check these blueprints. You can check the electronic circuits of the initial and restraining stages and I'll take the rest."

"Well—" she sighed philosophically, "at least I know what I'll be doing the rest of the day—and it's all the fault of that humorless pile of tin."

"Speaking of jokes"—Knight spilled the blueprints out of the brown envelope and spread them on the table—"did I ever tell you about the traveling salesman who asked the farmer's daughter if—"

"Never mind that, either!" she interrupted him firmly. "Do you want to shock George?"

4

Silence.

There had been utter silence from the first; the silence enclosing him and the dark eyes watching him. Why did the doctor move so quietly? Was it because he was dying; was it because people always walk softly in the presence of the dying?

Of course! His doctor was showing him the respect that is due the dead—and the soon-to-be-dead.

For a moment the tide of insanity almost broke through the bulwark built around his mind by the antihysteria drugs; the insanity he so desperately longed for; the insanity that would let him die in mindless, unfrightened madness.

The words above the pilot's communication panel now read: OBSERVER HAS A LIFE EXPECTANCY OF TWENTY HOURS AT PRESENT ACCELERATION. DEATH FOR OBSERVER WILL RESULT UNLESS ACCELERATION IS REDUCED WITHIN THAT PERIOD.

The urge to laugh came to him. It was funny! The doctor wouldn't reduce the acceleration until he gave the order and he couldn't give the order until the doctor reduced the acceleration.

Funny! The butterscotchmen couldn't run unless they were hot and couldn't get hot unless they ran . . . Couldn't run unless they were hot—Couldn't get hot unless they ran . . . Couldn't run— Couldn't hot . . . run . . . hot . . . run . . . hot . . . vicious circles and circles vicious, spinning around and around . . . spin around and around and around and around till your mind flies off into the darkness where someone is laughing . . . How pleasant to go laughing and spinning into the darkness, around and around . . . laughing and spinning and spinning and laughing . . . around and around and . . .

Sanity jolted into his mind with all its cold, grim reality and the comfort of the brief delirium vanished. The doctor was standing over him, injecting the antihysteria drug into his bloodstream.

The desperate fear ran through him again, terrible in its helpless impotency. It was always the same; the doctor watched him ceaselessly, ready to move forward and deny him the solace of madness at the first sign of its coming.

The doctor didn't hate him—WHY MUST THE DOCTOR TORTURE HIM SO?

It was a year later, with the ship six days from the morning of its test flight, that Russo-Asia completed the about-face in its foreign policy and promised the freedom of Western representatives to inspect their "greatly reduced military strength." It was not, to Knight, a surprising or mysterious thing. Russo-Asia had been built on false promises and deceit; this last action, he feared, could have but one reason behind it.

It was the other, happening five days later, that sent the chill certainty, too late, into his mind—the discovery that a tentacle of Cullin's presumably dead espionage system was in the very heart of Center . . .

It was with relief that Knight led General Gordon and his five-star superior, General Marker, to the control room of the ship. He had shown them the ship from bottom to top, explaining its workings and answering questions until he was beginning to feel like a tourist's guide. Furthermore, it was late in the night—or early in the morning, rather—and he would have little sleep before returning to be on hand for the ship's first take-off.

"And this is the control room," he said. "The first seat, with its control and instrument board over there, is for the pilot. This one is for the observer." He indicated the seat and instrument board immediately behind the pilot's. "You'll notice the observer has only a few instruments, but several viewscreens. The pilot can control the ship manually, with those buttons on his control board, or by voice command to the robot drive control—a D-Twenty-three. In an emergency, the observer can control the ship by voice command to the drive control, but his panel is not equipped with manual control buttons. The observer's duties are to observe and record, as well as to maintain constant contact with Earth."

He pointed to a small viewscreen in the center of the observer's panel. "This is his contact with the auxiliary control station. You both saw it—that little steel building two hundred feet west of this one. A man will be on duty at all times in it." He flipped a switch and the screen came to life, to show the back of an empty chair and a steel door beyond. "No one on duty right now, of course, but there will be when the ship takes off."

"What is the purpose of this ground-control station?" General Marker asked. "I know, of course, that it's an auxiliary means of controlling the ship, but why?"

"It's a safety measure we hope we won't have any need for. We're convinced that the ship has no bugs, but we don't want to take any chances with men's lives. So we have the constant communication with the observer plus the auxiliary control of the ship's drive. Should something go wrong, such as both pilot and observer becoming unconscious, we can bring the ship safely back to Earth from our ground-control station."

"Which method of controlling the ship takes precedence, the pilot's manual control, his oral orders to the drive control, or the means of controlling the ship from the ground-control station?"

"The control from the ground overrides all forms of control from within the ship. It might possibly be that a man would crack, and if he did he might give any kind of orders to the robot drive control—even such a one as ordering the disintegrators turned on Earth. We don't expect anything like that to happen, you understand—Miles and Vickson were selected for their mental stability—but we like to play safe."

"Will the crew include a doctor?"

"The very best, so far as technical skill goes. But circumstances might arise where more than technical skill would be needed, so that's why we have the auxiliary control station."

General Gordon tentatively touched a red knob on the observer's panel. "Does this turn the disintegrators on?" he asked.

Knight nodded. "It turns them on, and also controls the maximum range. The Computer gave us that safety gadget I spoke of when you were here a year ago, so now we don't have to worry about them being turned on accidentally and destroying the ship." He spun the red knob to the right and the generals exchanged nervous glances. "It's on full intensity, right now. This safety gadget prevents the closing of the circuit so long as the ship is within an atmosphere dense enough to produce a feedback of the rays."

He turned it off again and General Marker remarked, "You certainly go all the way in trusting your gadgets here."

"A soundly built gadget *can* be trusted."

"Then why your five-word slogan—the same as you have on the Master Computer—in big letters here on the observer's panel?"

"It's different when a gadget has an intelligence. The observer, in an emergency, would have to control the ship through a robotic brain. That five-word sentence, which is actually a sound philosophy to keep in mind when dealing with machines, is to remind the observer that he is not giving orders to a human pilot."

"Although it's six hours until take-off, I suppose the ship is ready to go right now?" General Gordon asked.

"Ready to go, and Miles and Vickson are now getting their last hours of sleep—*the* last hour, to be exact. They'll be back down here in less than two hours, together with myself, Dr. Clarke, and about a platoon of technicians to make the last-minute check of all the other checking. We have something too big in space flight to chance any errors on the first attempt."

"I'm glad this ship's first flight will not be as a weapon of war," General Marker said, "but I trust it's well guarded—just to play safe, as you said of your ground-control station."

"You saw the guards outside," Knight answered. "And there are guards outside the door of the ground-control station—this ship can't lift while enclosed in this steel building and the controls that lower the roof and walls into recesses in the ground are inside that station. We still have the machine-gun towers that we erected seven years ago when war seemed just around the corner. The antiaircraft artillery is still stationed in a wide circle around Computer Center—no one ever got around to ordering their removal and the guns were still manned twenty-four hours a day, the last I heard."

"Well, if Russo-Asia has any plans for this ship, they've certainly kept them well concealed," General Marker said. "Our Intelligence reports no indications whatever of any such thing. And now, I think we had all better get out of here and take advantage of that less-than-two-hours sleep we'll get before the preliminaries start."

Knight noticed, as they went down out of the ship, that George was still in the drive room, checking the control panel to drive circuits. The robot did not look up from its work, though it saw them pass. Robots confined their speaking to necessary answers and wasted no time with such amenities as "Good morning" and "Good night."

He parted company with the two generals at the Computer area gate; they to return to their Center hotel and he to drive through the slumbering streets to his own cottage. Tired and sleepy, he set the alarm to arouse him in an hour and a half and went to bed.

He had been asleep an hour and fifteen minutes when he was awakened by the ringing of the doorbell and June's voice. "Blacky—wake up!"

"What is it?" he called, swinging his feet to the floor and reaching for his clothes.

"Come over to Tim's house." There was both indignation and urgency in June's tone. "See if you can straighten things out."

He heard her hurry back to the Miles' cottage, her footsteps clicking sharp and fast on the walk. He grinned, despite his worry that Tim might be in some kind of trouble—the manner of her walking indicated that June was beginning to get *mad*.

He put on his clothes and went out into the pre-dawn darkness. The lights were on in the Miles' cottage and there was a black sedan parked at the curb before it. It had a government-service license plate, but there was nothing about the number on the plate to indicate the type of service it represented.

Tim Miles' voice came from within the house, angry and incredulous, and a vaguely familiar voice answered him. Knight went to the door and entered without knocking.

There were four in the room; Tim Miles, Connie, June, and a cold-eyed man in a gray suit. Knight recognized him with a start; his name was Whitney and he was a Security man. He returned Knight's "Hello" with a nod of recognition and Connie, sitting in a chair by the card table, said, "Hello, Blacky." Miles, red-faced and scowling, hardly glanced away from Whitney, while June sat one-hipped on the card table beside Connie, her eyes smoldering and her hands gripping the edge of the table until the knuckles were white.

Knight stopped beside Whitney. "What is this?" he asked.

"The ship has been sabotaged," Whitney replied.

"It's a lie!" Miles declared.

"Just a minute—" Knight looked from Miles back to Whitney. "It wasn't sabotaged when I left it an hour ago."

"It was sabotaged a year ago," Whitney said. "We didn't learn of it until tonight—in fact, not over half an hour ago."

"Are you sure?" Knight asked.

"*I'm* supposed to have done it!" Miles burst out wrathfully. "I'm supposed to have cross-wired the circuits from the control panel to the drive so that the drive will explode on take-off."

Knight made his reply to Whitney. "I can't believe that. I've known Miles and worked with him for several years. Of course, I realize that Security wants more positive proof of a suspected man's innocence than the personal opinion of his friends. If you will give me the details, perhaps I can help."

"He isn't exactly accused, yet," Whitney said, "but he's very much under suspicion of performing the work of sabotage. As for the reasons for our suspicions, they are these:

"The robot, George, has been helping Miles and Vickson check the ship today; an extra safety measure, I understand, to make sure there will be no mechanical failures on the ship's trial flight tomorrow. Miles completed his share of the work early in the afternoon and went home. Vickson was through about an hour later and he went home, leaving the robot to check the control-panel-to-drive circuits—a precautionary measure that Miles, here, admits he insisted was not necessary. It was about thirty minutes ago that the robot finished checking the circuits. He then phoned Security—a thing he had been ordered to do if he ever found any evidence of sabotage—and informed us that the drive circuits had been so cross-circuited that the drive would explode the moment it was activated for take-off."

Miles sighed heavily. "I tell you, those circuits are *not* sabotaged! I installed them myself, and I personally welded the control panel seals."

"You say this sabotage was supposed to have been done a year ago?" Knight asked.

"That's right," Whitney said. "Miles admits that he, himself, installed the circuits and sealed the panel at that time—and the panel is still sealed."

"Yes, I admit it!" Miles snapped. "Those circuits are not cross-wired. I don't know what this is all about, but I do know the kind of job I did on those circuits."

"The robot traced the circuits and found them to be cross-wired," Whitney said. "Isn't it true that a robot never lies?"

A look of helplessness passed over Miles' face. "Yes, it's true—but there's some mistake."

Whitney turned his cold eyes on Connie who was sitting quietly in her chair, watching Whitney with a composure that was in such striking contrast to the ever-growing wrath of the hot-eyed June.

"There's something else—" he said, and June froze into a waiting tenseness. "Why do you so often go to the park at Saguaro and Third, Mrs. Miles?"

Connie's eyes went wide with surprise. "I go there because it happens to be along the route I usually follow when taking the daily walks my doctor prescribed. Why?"

"You usually sit for a while beside the rock monument in the center of the park, don't you?"

"I always do. Why do you ask?"

"Why do you choose that spot to sit?"

"For two reasons; because there is a stone bench there to sit on while resting and because I like to feed the chipmunk that has a nest in the monument."

"Get to the point, Whitney." Miles could restrain himself no longer. "Quit beating around the bush—is my wife under suspicion, too?"

"We received an anonymous phone call this afternoon," Whitney said. "It enabled us to intercept a note, although the message meant nothing to us *then*. It was just a slip of paper in a tin box, and it read: 'Crisscross O.K. No suspicion. Ill on schedule.' "

"What does that have to do with my wife?" Miles demanded.

"After the robot told us of the sabotage, the meaning of the message became clear. It was an absurdly easy message to understand. 'Crisscross O.K. No suspicion' could only mean that the drive controls were still cross-circuited and no one suspected it. As for 'Ill on schedule'—we could only take that to mean that the person guilty of sabotaging the drive controls would pretend to be ill on the day of the ship's take-off—too ill to be in the ship when its drive exploded."

Whitney turned his eyes on Connie again. "As I say, an anonymous phone call tipped us off. This person suggested we look at the monument and we found the message in a crevice inside the monument. That, Mrs. Miles, was only a few minutes after you had left there."

There was a moment of dead silence, then Whitney's voice lashed at Connie like the crack of a whip.

"What do you know about that message?"

June reacted then, and in a manner typical of her. She shoved herself away from the card table with a violence that sent it crashing to the floor and advanced on Whitney with her eyes blazing. *"Nothing, you fool!"* The words came like the spitting of an infuriated cat. "My sister isn't a spy and she doesn't know anything about that message, you . . . you—"

Her small hand flashed out to rip her nails down Whitney's face and Knight moved quickly to stop her, catching her wrist, then the other hand as she tried to whirl away from him, bringing her arms down tight against her stomach. She struggled furiously to tear loose, her heart pounding against his arm like that of a small, wild animal.

"June—don't!" Connie was beside them, to lay her hand on June's shoulder. "Quit spitting and fighting, kitten—he's only trying to do his job."

June ceased struggling but the hate still blazed in her eyes. "He called you a spy—nobody is going to call my sister a spy!"

"He didn't call me a spy, honey—he just asked me what I know about that message."

"I understand your problem, Whitney," Knight said, releasing June but keeping a wary eye on her, lest she should renew her attack. "Someone is guilty of sabotage and it's your job to find who that person is. But aren't you jumping to conclusions on flimsy evidence?"

"I have no desire to cause anyone embarrassment or discomfort," the cold-eyed Whitney replied. "My business is to sort people into two different classes—guilty and innocent. An unexpected question suddenly snapped at a suspect will often go a long way toward indicating the person's guilt or innocence."

"Then why don't you snap some questions at a few others?" June demanded. "Vickson and the workmen who helped build the ship and George— What makes you so sure—"

"Sit down, June," Connie ordered, going back to her own chair. "Give him a chance to ask his own questions."

June hesitated, half turning away to do as her sister had ordered, then Whitney made the mistake of seconding the order. "Yes, sit down," he commanded, unconsciously rubbing his hand down the cheek that had been her intended target.

She whirled back to face him, the rebellion flaring hotly. "Never mind any such details as dictating our posture—just get on with your questions!"

She waited for him to dare repeat his order, standing erect and defiant before him, and an expression of helpless defeat flitted over his face. Knight watched with combined sympathy for him and amusement. The cold-eyed Whitney was accustomed to dealing with dangerous men and awing them—but how does a man go about awing a hundred and five pounds of fuming, spitting female wildcat?

"I have no more questions to ask—now," Whitney said. He spoke to Knight. "Dr. Clarke was in Yuma—we contacted him by phone and he's on his way back, now. He's given orders for public announcement of the postponement of the ship's test flight and when he returns we'll continue the questioning— of everyone connected with the ship, including the robot."

"Have you questioned George at all?" Knight asked.

"Very briefly," Whitney said with a wry smile. "Questioning a robot isn't too informative—a robot does no more than answer each question as it's given. It requires time plus a great many questions to get the entire picture. We questioned the robot briefly, as I say, and learned only that his check showed the drive controls to be cross-circuited. When Dr. Clarke returns, we'll do a thorough job of the questioning."

"Have you questioned Vickson?"

"He was spending the night with friends in Center Junction, we learned. A man was sent after him and they should return any minute."

"Here?"

"We'll all meet at the Computer area gate, then we'll go to Lab Four and find just who is guilty." Whitney turned to Miles. "Since the evidence against your wife is so uncertain, and since she is in frail health, she will remain here. If we need her, we can send a man after her. I'm afraid you'll have to go with me, now. At present, the evidence points only to you. If you're innocent, we'll do everything in our power to prove it. And if you're guilty"—he smiled grimly—"we'll do everything in our power to prove it."

"Thanks," Miles replied with the same grimness. "That's exactly what I want you to do."

Connie got to her feet. "There's no question about his innocence—it's all a ridiculous mistake. But I realize there is no way you can know that until everyone is questioned and the guilty one found. As for the message in the monument—I know nothing whatever about it. I always sit by the monument and feed the chipmunk, but I certainly never knew someone was using it as a place to leave messages for foreign agents."

"This anonymous phone call—doesn't that sound a little fishy?" Knight asked. "Have you traced it?"

"We're trying to," Whitney answered. "We're not at all convinced that Mrs. Miles is guilty of any connection with the affair. With her husband, it's different—he personally installed the circuits and they have been found to have been installed in such a manner as to destroy the ship."

"Couldn't the robot have made a mistake?" Connie asked. "Maybe they aren't cross-circuited at all—maybe the robot just made a mistake in his checking."

"I'm afraid not," Whitney answered. "Your husband will tell you that robots neither make mistakes nor false statements."

"That's true, Connie," Miles said, going to her. "But it's also

true that I didn't sabotage the drive." He put his arm around
her. "I'll be back in a few hours, and everything will be all
right."

Whitney moved toward the door, his eyes on Miles. Miles gave
Connie's shoulders a quick squeeze and followed Whitney through
the door without looking back.

Knight spoke to Whitney as they went through the door. "I'll
follow you down in my own car." Whitney said, "All right," then
he and Miles went on up the walk. Knight turned back to the
two women in the room.

"There's no question about there being a mistake," he said.
"What, I don't know. We do know that someone sabotaged the
drive controls, but who? We'll rip out the drive-control panel
and trace the leads that way—George had to depend upon tracing
them with instruments. I'll go down right now—and you'd better
go with me, June. Before it's over they'll want everyone who was
ever around the ship, and you've been around it almost as much
as I have."

June went to the door where Knight waited, then stopped to
say to Connie, "Don't you do any worrying about this while we're
gone, Connie. We'll be back with Tim's name cleared before noon,
you wait and see."

"Of course you will," Connie answered, but it seemed to
Knight that she was, for all her composure, suddenly very small
and lonely as she stood in the empty room and watched them
leave.

The sky was shell-pink in the east, lighting the world with
the half-light of dawn, when he backed out of the driveway.
June sat silent and thoughtful beside him; worried, despite her
assurances to her sister. He drove slowly, trying to fit together
the two facts he was convinced were true; Tim Miles had not
sabotaged the ship, yet a robot had no incentive to lie.

There were certain characteristics of the robotic brain:

*A machine is constructed to obey commands; it does not ques-
tion those commands.*

*A machine has no volition; it neither acts nor informs unless
ordered to do so.*

And then he had the answer; so simple that, he felt, a child
should have seen it.

A machine would not voluntarily make a false statement, but the prime function of a machine was prompt, unquestioning obedience. The robot, George, would never make a false statement by its own volition, *but it would if ordered to do so.*

He slowed the car to a barely moving crawl as he considered the implications and June looked at him questioningly. "We're still three blocks from the gate—what's wrong?"

"The drive controls have never been sabotaged. George was ordered to make that statement, and no one thought to ask him if it were true."

"But why? What would anyone gain by getting Tim into trouble like this?"

"It wasn't for personal reasons. *Someone didn't want that ship tested today!*"

"Then it was—" June stopped as a dull, distant roaring came to them. "It must have been—"

She stopped again as the roaring increased, coming from above them and to the southwest, filling the air like the hum of a billion bees. "What's *that?*"

He stopped the car and jumped out, to look into the sky and see the source of the sound. Planes, wave upon wave of them, coming in and down on Center from the southwest—from toward the Gulf of California. They were coming as fast as their jets could send them; almost as fast as the sound that preceded them. The first wave parted in definite formations as it came in, part of it dissolving to strike at the six antiaircraft gun positions that surrounded Center and the main body coming in on Center, itself.

"What is it?" June was beside him with her hand on his arm. "They couldn't be *ours*—"

"No," he said tonelessly, "they're not ours."

They stood and watched—there was nothing else they could do. The first wave passed low above them with a deafening, ground-shaking roar and was gone in the space of two breaths. The bombs shot downward in fast, flat arcs and their explosions raced through the city at the speed of the planes that had dropped them; red and yellow spurts of flame that leaped upward and hurled strange, broken things into the air, to be silhouetted momentarily against the pale dawn.

The second wave came close behind the first; a roar that

swelled into a crescendo then boomed into the distance with the bomb bursts a thunderous staccato racing along on the ground behind them. Then the antiaircraft guns came to life, licking thin, defiant tongues of flame at the invaders. The third wave concentrated on the gun positions and some of them plunged to earth, trailing black plumes of smoke, but three of the guns were still when the others had passed on.

For a few seconds Center was almost quiet by contrast to the thunder and fury that had filled it and a dog could be heard somewhere among the wreckage, barking and whining anxiously as it ran back and forth in a vain search for its master. A woman screamed, a sound that cut through the morning air like a thin, sharp knife, then the alarm siren began to moan and wail, half drowning the sound of cold motors breaking into life and the shouted orders of men.

The next attack on Center was a wave of fighters, boring in on the machine-gun towers in the Computer and laboratory area. The machine guns in the towers met their fire and tracer bullets were golden lances that met and crossed and struck the towers, to ricochet away in beautiful parabolic curves. Two of the attacking planes wavered and spun to the ground, but when the others turned to renew the attack there were no guns left to oppose them.

They began to strafe the streets and the cars that were trying to make their way through the debris, patrolling the area around Lab 4 and concentrating vicious fire on any vehicle that attempted to go in that direction. They had not bombed the laboratory area or the adjacent landing strip, and Knight realized, as he watched them, that there could be but one reason.

Russo-Asia had planned for this day for a long time. They had planned well; so well that even America's own Intelligence agents had thought the talks of peace were sincere. They had stressed the desirability of friendship between East and West and the West had hoped, and half-believed, and let themselves be caught unawares and unprepared. The anonymous phone call implicating Connie had been only a touch to add weight to the evidence against Miles; the evidence that had resulted in the postponement of the ship's flight and had insured that neither Miles nor anyone else would be inside the ship and in position to prevent its seizure when the attack came.

It had all been done with exact and detailed precision; the timing of the robot's phone call to Security, the attack in the early dawn before Clarke or Vickson had time to appear—or was Vickson their agent, and already inside the ship?

He would have to move fast—if it wasn't already too late.

He swung the door wide and thrust June into the car. "Get behind that wheel and drive like hell back to where Connie is. If a plane comes at you, jump and run—don't stay in the car or they'll get you. I'll have to try to get to the ship—"

A plane roared over them and its tracers made a bright splash of yellow phosphorescence on the pavement beside them. The tires of an army truck screamed at the intersection a hundred feet behind them and June, watching, cried, "Connie!"

Connie was coming toward them across the intersection, trying to run as best she could, and the army truck was braking and slewing desperately to avoid hitting her. Then the plane banked and turned and came roaring back at them and June half sobbed a terrified "*No!*" as its tracers licked down at the truck and across it, to lash at Connie who had reached the curb. She crumpled to the walk and the plane went its way, while the army truck wandered aimlessly down the street with the dead driver slumped over the wheel.

"*No!*" June shoved past him, her face white with fear, and ran to her sister. He followed, sick at heart with the foreknowledge of what he would see.

Connie was lying very still, her face like that of a pale, waxen doll that had gone to sleep. June was kneeling beside her, holding her hand and saying over and over in a dazed voice: "Connie . . . Connie . . . why did you do it?"

"She had to," he said softly. "She was going to you because you might need her. She was a nurse and she was going to you and Tim and all those who might be hurt and in need of her."

The siren whimpered off into silence and the bark of one lone antiaircraft gun came to them, to falter and stop as another attack of bombers roared over it.

"They killed her!" June's voice was numb with the shock. She held Connie's hand between both her own, a bright red splotch on her knee where it touched Connie's side as she knelt beside her. "They killed her—they killed my sister!"

She raised her face to look at the planes circling above them and a terrible, savage hatred blazed through the hurt and pain in her eyes.

Then the tears, that the first shock had held back, came and he hurried quietly away, leaving her crying with shaking, muffled sobs beside her sister. There was nothing he could do to comfort her and it would be better for her to not follow him.

He ran in a steady trot, two blocks to the highway that paralleled the western boundary of the laboratory area, then down along it. Trees had been transplanted beside the highway in years past and he kept under the shelter of their concealment as he ran. He stopped once, to dart out on the pavement where a jeep lay overturned and riddled with machine-gun bullets. A soldier was sprawled lifelessly beside it, his heavy automatic rifle still in his hands. Knight seized the rifle and the belt of cartridge clips and ran back to the shelter of the trees as a plane spotted him. Its bullets cut twigs from the limbs above him and made a *thunk-thunk* sound as they buried themselves in the trunk of the tree. Then the plane was gone and he ran on toward the western entrance that was the closest to Lab 4.

The fighter planes widened in their circling to leave a clear space above the laboratory area as he reached the gate, then the troop-transport planes came in—six of them. The sky blossomed with chutes, the Russo-Asian paratroopers firing even as they descended. Other rifles were firing from within Center and from the area outside the main gate, and occasionally a paratrooper would jerk, then dangle limply in his harness as he drifted downward.

The last group of planes came in; a light, fast bomber surrounded by a protecting ring of fighters. The objective of the light bomber, he saw, was the landing strip nearest to Lab 4.

The bomber's mission would not be to bomb the landing strip, and there could be no doubt as to the identity of the passenger it carried. It slowed and dropped to make its landing and he began to run toward the ground-control station and Lab 4 that set two hundred feet beyond it.

He was protected from the fighter planes by their own paratroopers and the aim of the paratroopers, shooting from their swinging suspension, was uncertain as they tried to catch his running, weaving figure in their sights. Bullets kicked up puffs of dust beside and behind him but none touched him. He had reached the ground-control station when the first paratrooper reached the ground. The vicious rip of a burst of well-aimed bullets slammed against the steel corner of the building a split-second after he had rounded it. Two more paratroopers landed even as he ran for the door of the station, adding their fire to their comrade's. It was two hundred feet to the ship and, now that they were on the ground, the aim of the paratroopers would be deadly and certain. He would never live to run a tenth of the distance to the ship. And the others were landing, by three's and four's.

But it didn't matter—he would be in supreme control of the ship from the auxiliary station.

The guards were lying before the door of the station, dead, and the door was ajar. Simultaneously, he saw the other thing that was happening; the roof of Lab 4 was sliding back and the walls were dropping into the ground. He leaped through the doorway and to one side as paratrooper bullets hammered at him, the automatic rifle held ready before him.

The room was deserted but for the robot, George. George turned away quickly from the control panel at the far end of the room, and Knight saw the switch was on that lowered the walls of Lab 4.

"Turn that switch off!" he commanded. "Raise those walls again."

The robot stepped toward him with long, swift strides, seeming not to hear him. The metal arms were half outstretched before it and a sudden, icy premonition ran a cold finger up his spine.

"Stop!"

It came on without slackening its speed, the dark eyes thoughtful and the steel hands reaching out toward him—hands that had the strength to tear his head from his body.

"*Stop!*"

The steel hands swooped toward his throat and he leaped to one side. It spun with him, as quick as he for all its ponderous bulk, and then it sprang like a great cat.

There was no time to wonder why the robot wanted to kill him, no time to dodge. The rifle was still leveled before him and he pressed the trigger. The great mass of the robot lurched and shuddered as twenty bullets, each with a muzzle energy of three thousand foot pounds, tore through its body within a space of two seconds. It reeled and crashed to the floor, to lay inert while the dark eyes stared up at him with their same expression of thoughtful, patient waiting.

But it was dead. Its brain was a riddled wreckage and it was as dead as ever a robot could be.

He ran to the control board and slapped the switch that would re-erect the walls and roof of Lab 4, wondering why the robot had tried to kill him. A machine has no volition, yet it had walked toward him with the deliberate intent to kill him, heedless of his command for it to stop. It might as well have been deaf—

Of course! It *had* been deaf! It had been sent recently from Lab 4 with orders to lower Lab 4 into the ground and to kill anyone who entered the ground-control station. Then, after the orders were given, the microphones that were its ears had been disconnected and it had gone on its mission, stone-deaf and unable to hear any orders that would countermand the ones given it.

He hurried back to the door, slipping a fresh clip of cartridges into the rifle as he went. He opened it a quick, cautious ten inches and saw that the paratroopers were taking up positions in a wide circle around the ship. Two of them saw the partial opening of the door and he had time only for one quick glance before their bullets pounded against it as he slammed it shut.

He had had time to see the ship, standing bright and naked in the first rays of the sun. The walls that had enclosed it had disappeared. The air lock of the ship had been open and a man had been standing there, the rising sun red on his face—Vickson. He had been looking toward the landing strip and a car racing toward the ship—a car whose dust trail led back to the light bomber.

He locked the door to prevent anyone entering the station, while the bullets hammering methodically against the outside of it informed him that they were seeing to it that no one left it. He went back to the control board and looked at the switch that he had closed before going to the door; the switch that should have re-erected Lab 4 around the ship. It had not, and he saw the reason why; George had ripped out the wires behind the panel that led to the switch. They were lying tangled on the floor behind the panel and he could never, in the short time he had, reconnect them.

He seated himself in the chair before the control board and turned on the observer's viewscreen. His own viewscreen came to life, showing the interior of the ship's control room. It was still empty.

He closed the switch that would give his own commands precedence over any given inside the ship and said: "Ship's drive control—disregard all orders given you by anyone in the ship's control room. Disregard all impulses from the pilot's control panel."

Only silence answered him and he said sharply, with sudden anxiety, "Ship's drive control—acknowledge that order!"

Silence.

He tried again, coldly, unpleasantly certain that it would be in vain. "Ship's drive control—*acknowledge!*"

Again the dead silence was his answer and he knew there was no use to try any more. The units that permitted the ground-control station to control the ship had been sabotaged and he was helpless to prevent the ship's take-off. Bullets continued to rattle against the door, warning him how fatal would be any attempt to leave the station. He was helpless so long as he remained in the station; he would be both helpless and dead a split-second after he opened the door to leave the station. Yet, he had to do *something*.

He estimated the time that had gone by since he had seen the car speeding from the bomber to the ship. It would have been Cullin, of course; it would be Cullin and Vickson who took the ship into the sky, with Vickson at the pilot's seat and Cullin behind him, watching him. Vickson knew as well as Miles how to operate the manual drive controls, and there was no hope that he would make a mistake and wreck the ship in a take-off. Even Cullin, alone, could lift the ship by simple voice command to the drive control. The Center forces would be closing in on the ship as the fighter planes exhausted the ammunition they were forced to use so continually, but they would be too late.

A sound broke the silence of the observer's viewscreen, the sound of someone entering the control room. It was Cullin, wearing the black and gray uniform of a high official of the State Police, and he was alone. He took one quick look at the room, then walked straight to the observer's chair in the manner of a man who knew exactly what he was going to do.

At the sight of Knight's face in the observer's viewscreen he smiled in sudden, pleased surprise. Knight spoke the same greeting he had spoken at Punta Azul: "Going somewhere, Cullin?"

Cullin seated himself in the observer's chair, still smiling and taking his time about answering. "Why, yes," he said, "I *am* going somewhere. Vickson was telling me you were in there, but I was afraid you had been rendered permanently speechless by your faithful George." Cullin shifted his eyes to look past Knight at the robot lying on the floor across the room. "I see you had sufficient intelligence to destroy the robot before it destroyed you. It was very useful to me—via Vickson's orders to it—but it's just as well that it failed to carry out its last order; to throttle anyone who entered the station. You and I can now chat pleasantly about cabbages and kings and sealing wax and a man named Cullin who is, as you feared, going somewhere."

"Alone?" Knight asked. "Where's Vickson?"

"Outside. He was rather surprised that he couldn't go with me."

"He is a pilot as well as observer—why don't you take him along?"

"You builders of this ship thoughtfully gave it a robotic brain for the drive that makes the pilot's manual controls unnecessary. Whoever controls this ship can write his own ticket, so I'll take it up alone and there'll be no danger of a doublecross, no doubt as to who will write the ticket."

Cullin reached out and turned the red knob to the right. "No pilot is needed," he said. "You've made the ship foolproof."

"How did you manage to keep Vickson from taking the ship up before you ever got to it?"

"He was selected, Knight, years ago. For all his passing of the tests for superior mental stability, Vickson is a man who places a very high value on his own life. Of all the men who had full access to the ship, Vickson was the best suited to our purpose. There are various ways of persuading various types of men and compelling them to co-operate. With Vickson it was very easy and simple—we used the y drug.

"Perhaps you've heard rumors of it. Our own scientists whipped it up for us several years ago, and it's very efficient. Thirty days after the administration of the drug the subject is stricken with intense pain. This pain increases by the hour and only the antidote, made from a batch of the original drug, can stop the increasing pain and eventual death. We have occasionally let Vickson wait a few hours extra just to keep him convinced of the desirability of wholehearted co-operation with us. Had he been foolish enough to take the ship he would have died in a great deal of agony within six hours, since everything was timed very carefully, including the last administration of the y drug."

"And what becomes of Vickson now?"

"I wouldn't know." Cullin shrugged his shoulders with disinterest. "He's served his purpose for me—I have no further use for him."

"And no antidote for him?"

"I rather doubt that the good citizens of what is left of Center will permit him to suffer very long."

No, thought Knight, they won't, but it was Cullin who had planned it, coldly, deliberately—

"I've planned this for a long time," Cullin said, as though he had been reading Knight's mind. "All my life I've played second-fiddle to someone else. Now, the world will dance to *my* tune."

Knight looked at him sharply and Cullin laughed with genuine mirth. "No, I'm not insane. This ship is my whip; I'll use the threat of it to whip the world into billions of gentle, obedient horses."

"Obedience seems to be a mania with you."

"It produces the desired results. That's why I liked your robot; no threats were necessary, no y drugs. It accepted orders without question and carried them out without question."

The bullets were no longer banging against the door, Knight noticed. That would mean that the Center forces had gathered in strength and had drawn in closer; that the paratroopers had no time to spare for watching the door. Cullin liked the unquestioning obedience of a robot and he, Knight, could not keep him from giving the order to the drive control that would lift the ship. The robotic brain that was the drive control would obey instantly and without question, but if Cullin should not word his command in the proper manner—

"Once more I'm leaving you. Listen while I give the order to your own ship."

Cullin smiled once more, triumphant and exultant, and gave the order: "Ship's drive control—accelerate!"

It was the command Knight had hoped he would give. It was a command the robotic brain would obey instantly and Cullin could never countermand.

It required slightly less than three seconds for the primary activation of the ship's drive, then the thrust of acceleration came and the ship hurled itself upward. Cullin was shoved deep into the cushioned seat by it, pinned and chained by it. He tried vainly to speak, the horror of sudden realization and fear in his eyes, then the blankness of unconsciousness clouded them. Knight turned away from the viewscreen. Cullin would be conscious when he returned to it later in the day. Cullin would not die for a long, long time—the doctor in the control room was very competent.

He went to the door and stepped outside. The ship was gone, already beyond sight, and the last of the paratroopers were throwing down their guns and surrendering to the Center forces that surrounded them. The planes were gone; back to carriers somewhere in the Pacific, he presumed, there to depend upon the threat of the disintegrator rays to shield them and the carriers from retaliation.

But there would be no war. Russo-Asia had put all her eggs in one basket and one wrong word had sent that basket away forever.

Someone was lying near Lab 4; motionless on the ground, his rimless glasses knocked askew by the bullet that had killed him and looking mild and apologetic, even in death. Knight felt a sense of relief. Vickson had paid the penalty and it had been gentle compared with the penalty Cullin would pay. It was as it should be.

"Blacky."

June was coming toward him, a cartridge belt sagging from her waist and a rifle in her hands.

"We've lost, haven't we?" she asked, stopping before him. "They took the ship and we couldn't stop them."

"The ship will never come back," he said. He looked down at her, her grimy hands clutching the rifle, her clothes torn and her face scratched and dirty and tear-streaked. He saw that most of the clips were gone from the cartridge belt.

"They got Tim," she said. "They must have killed him in the first bombing. I ought to go back and try to help—there are so many people in need of help and it's what Connie would want me to do. But first"—she looked up at him, tears suddenly threatening to wash a new channel through the dirt on her face—"can't we take her—home?"

He took the rifle she still held and let his hand rest on her shoulder.

"First, we'll take Connie home."

5

The doctor's pre-flight training had included the order to keep the pilot informed of each man's physical condition.

How long had it been since the doctor last changed the words on the pilot's communications panel? Was his time finally within short minutes of its end? It was no longer hours, but minutes. The words read: OBSERVER HAS A LIFE EXPECTANCY OF ONE HOUR AT PRESENT ACCELERATION. DEATH FOR OBSERVER WILL RESULT UNLESS ACCELERATION IS REDUCED WITHIN THAT PERIOD.

How many days and weeks had gone by since he had first given the fatal command to the drive control? It had been Vickson who had done the thing that would so soon culminate in his death. Vickson, the mild and apologetic. Vickson had feared that he would be deemed dispensable, and this had been his means of revenge. Vickson had told him how to word the command to the drive control: "Ship's drive control—accelerate!"

Vickson had known that the robotic drive control would continue to accelerate until full acceleration was reached. Vickson had known full acceleration would be maintained until he ordered it reduced. Vickson had known that the first surge of acceleration would render him speechless and unconscious. Vickson had known that the robot doctor in the control room would do the only thing possible to save his life while under full acceleration: by-pass his heart with a mechanical heart, and put it in conjunction with a mechanical lung that frothed and aerated his blood. Vickson had known he would live a long time that way, with the doctor watching over him and administering nutrients into his bloodstream. Nutrients—and the antihysteria drug that had been designed to keep the observer's mind clear and logical so that he could meet any emergency!

How long had it been since the viewscreen shifted into the red and then turned black as the ship exceeded the speed of light?

They had watched him until the ship's speed had become too great. Knight, and others he did not know. He had tried to appeal to them to do something; pleading mutely, with all the power of his terrified mind. They had done nothing—what could they do? The robot had been ordered to destroy the units that enabled the ground-control station to control the ship, and machines did not make mistakes when carrying out orders.

Knight had spoken to him once: "You wanted obedience, Cullin—now you have it. You climbed a long way up by forcing human beings to behave like machines. But you were wrong in one respect; no human can ever be forced to behave exactly like a machine, and no machine can ever be constructed that will behave exactly like a human. Machines are the servants of humans, not their equals. There will always be a gulf between Flesh and Steel. Read those five words on the panel before you and you will understand."

How many minutes did he have left? The doctor knew he wanted to live, and it knew it had only to reduce the acceleration to save his life. It was intelligent and it knew what he wanted, but it was obedient and it was waiting to be ordered to reduce the acceleration.

It was watching him, waiting for him to give the order, and it knew he could not speak without lungs!

Once he had wanted obedience, without question, without initiative of thought. Now, he had it. Now he understood what Knight had meant. The full, bitter lesson was in the five words on the panel before him, and he was trying to laugh without lungs when he died, his eyes fixed on it and his lips drawn back in a grim travesty of a smile.

It was a good ship, built to travel almost forever, and it hurled itself on through the galaxy at full acceleration; on and on until the galaxy was a great pinwheel of white fire behind it and there was nothing before it.

On and on, faster and faster, into the black void of Nothing; without reason or purpose while a dark-eyed robot stared at a skeleton that was grinning mirthlessly at a five-word sentence:

A MACHINE DOES NOT *CARE.*

Editor's note: And here we come to the end, the backdrop of reality that Godwin never forgot. There are times I think "The Cold Equations" may be the greatest science fiction story ever written. But it's not a story I read very often. And I'm glad that I started, at the age of thirteen, with The Survivors.

THE COLD EQUATIONS

He was not alone.

There was nothing to indicate the fact but the white hand of the tiny gauge on the board before him. The control room was empty but for himself; there was no sound other than the murmur of the drives—but the white hand had moved. It had been on zero when the little ship was launched from the *Stardust*; now, an hour later, it had crept up. There was something in the supplies closet across the room, it was saying, some kind of a body that radiated heat.

It could be but one kind of a body—a living, human body.

He leaned back in the pilot's chair and drew a deep, slow breath, considering what he would have to do. He was an EDS pilot, inured to the sight of death, long since accustomed to it and to viewing the dying of another man with an objective lack of emotion, and he had no choice in what he must do. There could be no alternative—but it required a few moments of conditioning for even an EDS pilot to prepare himself to walk across the room and coldly, deliberately, take the life of a man he had yet to meet.

He would, of course, do it. It was the law, stated very bluntly and definitely in grim Paragraph L, Section 8, of Interstellar Regulations: *Any stowaway discovered in an EDS shall be jettisoned immediately following discovery.*

It was the law, and there could be no appeal.

✧   ✧   ✧

It was a law not of men's choosing but made imperative by the circumstances of the space frontier. Galactic expansion had followed the development of the hyperspace drive and as men scattered wide across the frontier there had come the problem of contact with the isolated first-colonies and exploration parties. The huge hyperspace cruisers were the product of the combined genius and effort of Earth and were long and expensive in the building. They were not available in such numbers that small colonies could possess them. The cruisers carried the colonists to their new worlds and made periodic visits, running on tight schedules, but they could not stop and turn aside to visit colonies scheduled to be visited at another time; such a delay would destroy their schedule and produce a confusion and uncertainty that would wreck the complex interdependence between old Earth and the new worlds of the frontier.

Some method of delivering supplies or assistance when an emergency occurred on a world not scheduled for a visit had been needed and the Emergency Dispatch Ships had been the answer. Small and collapsible, they occupied little room in the hold of the cruiser; made of light metal and plastics, they were driven by a small rocket drive that consumed relatively little fuel. Each cruiser carried four EDS's and when a call for aid was received the nearest cruiser would drop into normal space long enough to launch an EDS with the needed supplies or personnel, then vanish again as it continued on its course.

The cruisers, powered by nuclear converters, did not use the liquid rocket fuel but nuclear converters were far too large and complex to permit their installation in the EDS. The cruisers were forced by necessity to carry a limited amount of the bulky rocket fuel and the fuel was rationed with care; the cruiser's computers determining the exact amount of fuel each EDS would require for its mission. The computers considered the course coordinates, the mass of the EDS, the mass of pilot and cargo; they were very precise and accurate and omitted nothing from their calculations. They could not, however, foresee, and allow for, the added mass of a stowaway.

The *Stardust* had received the request from one of the exploration parties stationed on Woden; the six men of the party already being stricken with the fever carried by the green *kala* midges and their own supply of serum destroyed by the tornado that had torn through their camp. The *Stardust* had gone through the usual procedure; dropping into normal space to launch the EDS with the fever serum, then vanishing again in hyperspace. Now, an hour later, the gauge was saying there was something more than the small carton of serum in the supplies closet.

He let his eyes rest on the narrow white door of the closet. There, just inside, another man lived and breathed and was beginning to feel assured that discovery of his presence would now be too late for the pilot to alter the situation. It *was* too late—for the man behind the door it was far later than he thought and in a way he would find terrible to believe.

There could be no alternative. Additional fuel would be used during the hours of deceleration to compensate for the added mass of the stowaway; infinitesimal increments of fuel that would not be missed until the ship had almost reached its destination. Then, at some distance above the ground that might be as near as a thousand feet or as far as tens of thousands of feet, depending upon the mass of ship and cargo and the preceding period of deceleration, the unmissed increments of fuel would make their absence known; the EDS would expend its last drops of fuel with a sputter and go into whistling free fall. Ship and pilot and stowaway would merge together upon impact as a wreckage of metal and plastic, flesh and blood, driven deep into the soil. The stowaway had signed his own death warrant when he concealed himself on the ship; he could not be permitted to take seven others with him.

He looked again at the telltale white hand, then rose to his feet. What he must do would be unpleasant for both of them; the sooner it was over, the better. He stepped across the control room, to stand by the white door.

"Come out!" His command was harsh and abrupt above the murmur of the drive.

It seemed he could hear the whisper of a furtive movement inside the closet, then nothing. He visualized the stowaway cowering closer into one corner, suddenly worried by the possible consequences of his act and his self-assurance evaporating.

"I said *out!*"

He heard the stowaway move to obey and he waited with his eyes alert on the door and his hand near the blaster at his side.

The door opened and the stowaway stepped through it, smiling. "All right—I give up. Now what?"

It was a girl.

He stared without speaking, his hand dropping away from the blaster and acceptance of what he saw coming like a heavy and unexpected physical blow. The stowaway was not a man— she was a girl in her teens, standing before him in little white gypsy sandals with the top of her brown, curly head hardly higher than his shoulder, with a faint, sweet scent of perfume coming from her and her smiling face tilted up so her eyes could look unknowing and unafraid into his as she waited for his answer.

Now what? Had it been asked in the deep, defiant voice of a man he would have answered it with action, quick and efficient. He would have taken the stowaway's identification disk and ordered him into the air lock. Had the stowaway refused to obey, he would have used the blaster. It would not have taken long; within a minute the body would have been ejected into space— had the stowaway been a man.

He returned to the pilot's chair and motioned her to seat herself on the boxlike bulk of the drive-control units that set against the wall beside him. She obeyed, his silence making the smile fade into the meek and guilty expression of a pup that has been caught in mischief and knows it must be punished.

"You still haven't told me," she said. "I'm guilty, so what happens to me now? Do I pay a fine, or what?"

"What are you doing here?" he asked. "Why did you stow away on this EDS?"

"I wanted to see my brother. He's with the government survey crew on Woden and I haven't seen him for ten years, not since he left Earth to go into government survey work."

"What was your destination on the *Stardust?*"

"Mimir. I have a position waiting for me there. My brother has been sending money home all the time to us—my father and mother and I—and he paid for a special course in linguistics I was taking. I graduated sooner than expected and I was offered this job on Mimir. I knew it would be almost a year before Gerry's job was done on Woden so he could come on to Mimir and that's why I hid in the closet, there. There was plenty of room for me and I was willing to pay the fine. There were only the two of us kids—Gerry and I—and I haven't seen him for so long, and I didn't want to wait another year when I could see him now, even though I knew I would be breaking some kind of a regulation when I did it."

I knew I would be breaking some kind of a regulation— In a way, she could not be blamed for her ignorance of the law; she was of Earth and had not realized that the laws of the space frontier must, of necessity, be as hard and relentless as the environment that gave them birth. Yet, to protect such as her from the results of their own ignorance of the frontier, there had been a sign over the door that led to the section of the *Stardust* that housed the EDS; a sign that was plain for all to see and heed:

UNAUTHORIZED PERSONNEL
KEEP OUT!

"Does your brother know that you took passage on the *Stardust* for Mimir?"

"Oh, yes. I sent him a spacegram telling him about my graduation and about going to Mimir on the *Stardust* a month before I left Earth. I already knew Mimir was where he would be stationed in a little over a year. He gets a promotion then, and he'll be based on Mimir and not have to stay out a year at a time on field trips, like he does now."

There were two different survey groups on Woden, and he asked, "What is his name?"

"Cross—Gerry Cross. He's in Group Two—that was the way his address read. Do you know him?"

Group One had requested the serum; Group Two was eight thousand miles away, across the Western Sea.

"No, I've never met him," he said, then turned to the control board and cut the deceleration to a fraction of a gravity; knowing as he did so that it could not avert the ultimate end, yet doing the only thing he could do to prolong that ultimate end. The sensation was like that of the ship suddenly dropping and the girl's involuntary movement of surprise half lifted her from the seat.

"We're going faster now, aren't we?" she asked. "Why are we doing that?"

He told her the truth. "To save fuel for a little while."

"You mean, we don't have very much?"

He delayed the answer he must give her so soon to ask: "How did you manage to stow away?"

"I just sort of walked in when no one was looking my way," she said. "I was practicing my Gelanese on the native girl who does the cleaning in the Ship's Supply office when someone came in with an order for supplies for the survey crew on Woden. I slipped into the closet there after the ship was ready to go and just before you came in. It was an impulse of the moment to stow away, so I could get to see Gerry—and from the way you keep looking at me so grim, I'm not sure it was a very wise impulse.

"But I'll be a model criminal—or do I mean prisoner?" She smiled at him again. "I intended to pay for my keep on top of paying the fine. I can cook and I can patch clothes for everyone and I know how to do all kinds of useful things, even a little bit about nursing."

There was one more question to ask:

"Did you know what the supplies were that the survey crew ordered?"

"Why, no. Equipment they needed in their work, I supposed."

Why couldn't she have been a man with some ulterior motive? A fugitive from justice, hoping to lose himself on a raw new world; an opportunist, seeking transportation to the new colonies where he might find golden fleece for the taking; a crackpot, with a mission—

Perhaps once in his lifetime an EDS pilot would find such a stowaway on his ship; warped men, mean and selfish men, brutal and dangerous men—but never, before, a smiling, blue-eyed girl who was willing to pay her fine and work for her keep that she might see her brother.

He turned to the board and turned the switch that would signal the *Stardust*. The call would be futile but he could not, until he had exhausted that one vain hope, seize her and thrust her into the air lock as he would an animal—or a man. The delay, in the meantime, would not be dangerous with the EDS decelerating at fractional gravity.

A voice spoke from the communicator. "*Stardust*. Identify yourself and proceed."

"Barton, EDS 34G11. Emergency. Give me Commander Delhart."

There was a faint confusion of noises as the request went through the proper channels. The girl was watching him, no longer smiling.

"Are you going to order them to come back after me?" she asked.

The communicator clicked and there was the sound of a distant voice saying, "Commander, the EDS requests—"

"Are they coming back after me?" she asked again. "Won't I get to see my brother, after all?"

"Barton?" The blunt, gruff voice of Commander Delhart came from the communicator. "What's this about an emergency?"

"A stowaway," he answered.

"A stowaway?" There was a slight surprise to the question. "That's rather unusual—but why the 'emergency' call? You discovered him in time so there should be no appreciable danger and I presume you've informed Ship's Records so his nearest relatives can be notified."

"That's why I had to call you, first. The stowaway is still aboard and the circumstances are so different—"

"Different?" the commander interrupted, impatience in his voice. "How can they be different? You know you have a limited supply of fuel; you also know the law, as well as I do: 'Any stowaway discovered in an EDS shall be jettisoned immediately following discovery.'"

There was the sound of a sharply indrawn breath from the girl. "*What does he mean?*"

"The stowaway is a girl."

"*What?*"

"She wanted to see her brother. She's only a kid and she didn't know what she was really doing."

"I see." All the curtness was gone from the commander's voice. "So you called me in the hope I could do something?" Without waiting for an answer he went on. "I'm sorry—I can do nothing. This cruiser must maintain its schedule; the life of not one person but the lives of many depend on it. I know how you feel but I'm powerless to help you. I'll have you connected with Ship's Records."

The communicator faded to a faint rustle of sound and he turned back to the girl. She was leaning forward on the bench, almost rigid, her eyes fixed wide and frightened.

"What did he mean, to go through with it? To jettison me . . . to go through with it—what did he mean? Not the way it sounded . . . he couldn't have. What did he mean . . . what did he really mean?"

Her time was too short for the comfort of a lie to be more than a cruelly fleeting delusion.

"He meant it the way it sounded."

"*No!*" She recoiled from him as though he had struck her, one hand half upraised as though to fend him off and stark unwillingness to believe in her eyes.

"It will have to be."

"No! You're joking—you're insane! You can't mean it!"

"I'm sorry." He spoke slowly to her, gently. "I should have told you before—I should have, but I had to do what I could first; I had to call the *Stardust*. You heard what the commander said."

"But you can't—if you make me leave the ship, I'll *die*."

"I know."

She searched his face and the unwillingness to believe left her eyes, giving way slowly to a look of dazed terror.

"You—know?" She spoke the words far apart, numb and wonderingly.

"I know. It has to be like that."

"You mean it—you really mean it." She sagged back against the wall, small and limp like a little rag doll and all the protesting and disbelief gone. "You're going to do it—you're going to make me die?"

"I'm sorry," he said again. "You'll never know how sorry I am. It has to be that way and no human in the universe can change it."

"You're going to make me die and I didn't do anything to die for—I didn't *do* anything—"

He sighed, deep and weary. "I know you didn't, child. I know you didn't—"

"EDS." The communicator rapped brisk and metallic. "This is Ship's Records. Give us all information on subject's identification disk."

He got out of his chair to stand over her. She clutched the edge of the seat, her upturned face white under the brown hair and the lipstick standing out like a blood-red cupid's bow.

"*Now?*"

"I want your identification disk," he said.

She released the edge of the seat and fumbled at the chain that suspended the plastic disk from her neck with fingers that were trembling and awkward. He reached down and unfastened the clasp for her, than returned with the disk to his chair.

"Here's your data, Records: Identification Number T837—"

"One moment," Records interrupted. "This is to be filed on the gray card, of course?"

"Yes."

"And the time of the execution?"

"I'll tell you later."

"Later? This is highly irregular; the time of the subject's death is required before—"

He kept the thickness out of his voice with an effort. "Then we'll do it in a highly irregular manner—you'll hear the disk read, first. The subject is a girl and she's listening to everything that's said. Are you capable of understanding that?"

There was a brief, almost shocked, silence, then Records said meekly: "Sorry. Go ahead."

He began to read the disk, reading it slowly to delay the inevitable for as long as possible, trying to help her by giving her what little time he could to recover from her first terror and let it resolve into the calm of acceptance and resignation.

"Number T8374 dash Y54. Name: Marilyn Lee Cross. Sex: Female. Born: July 7, 2160. *She was only eighteen.* Height: 5-3. Weight: 110. *Such a slight weight, yet enough to add fatally to the mass of the shell-thin bubble that was an EDS.* Hair: Brown. Eyes: Blue. Complexion: Light. Blood Type: O. *Irrelevant data.* Destination: Port City, Mimir. *Invalid data—*"

He finished and said, "I'll call you later," then turned once again to the girl. She was huddled back against the wall, watching him with a look of numb and wondering fascination.

✧   ✧   ✧

"They're waiting for you to kill me, aren't they? They want me dead, don't they? You and everybody on the cruiser wants me dead, don't you?" Then the numbness broke and her voice was that of a frightened and bewildered child. "Everybody wants me dead and I didn't *do* anything. I didn't hurt anyone—I only wanted to see my brother."

"It's not the way you think—it isn't that way, at all," he said. "Nobody wants it this way; nobody would ever let it be this way if it was humanly possible to change it."

"Then why is it! I don't understand. Why is it?"

"This ship is carrying *kala* fever serum to Group One on Woden. Their own supply was destroyed by a tornado. Group Two—the crew your brother is in—is eight thousand miles away across the Western Sea and their helicopters can't cross it to help Group One. The fever is invariably fatal unless the serum can be had in time, and the six men in Group One will die unless this ship reaches them on schedule. These little ships are always given barely enough fuel to reach their destination and if you stay aboard your added weight will cause it to use up all its fuel before it reaches the ground. It will crash, then, and you and I will die and so will the six men waiting for the fever serum."

It was a full minute before she spoke, and as she considered his words the expression of numbness left her eyes.

"Is that it?" she asked at last. "Just that the ship doesn't have enough fuel?"

"Yes."

"I can go alone or I can take seven others with me—is that the way it is?"

"That's the way it is."

"And nobody wants me to have to die?"

"Nobody."

"Then maybe—Are you sure nothing can be done about it? Wouldn't people help me if they could?"

"Everyone would like to help you but there is nothing anyone can do. I did the only thing I could do when I called the *Stardust.*"

"And it won't come back—but there might be other cruisers, mightn't there? Isn't there any hope at all that there might be someone, somewhere, who could do something to help me?"

She was leaning forward a little in her eagerness as she waited for his answer.

"No."

The word was like the drop of a cold stone and she again leaned back against the wall, the hope and eagerness leaving her face. "You're sure—you *know* you're sure?"

"I'm sure. There are no other cruisers within forty light-years; there is nothing and no one to change things."

She dropped her gaze to her lap and began twisting a pleat of her skirt between her fingers, saying no more as her mind began to adapt itself to the grim knowledge.

It was better so; with the going of all hope would go the fear; with the going of all hope would come resignation. She needed time and she could have so little of it. How much?

The EDS's were not equipped with hull-cooling units; their speed had to be reduced to a moderate level before entering the atmosphere. They were decelerating at .10 gravity; approaching their destination at a far higher speed than the computers had calculated on. The *Stardust* had been quite near Woden when she launched the EDS; their present velocity was putting them nearer by the second. There would be a critical point, soon to be reached, when he would have to resume deceleration. When he did so the girl's weight would be multiplied by the gravities of deceleration, would become, suddenly, a factor of paramount importance; the factor the computers had been ignorant of when they determined the amount of fuel the EDS should have. She would have to go when deceleration began; it could be no other way. When would that be—how long could he let her stay?

"How long can I stay?"

He winced involuntarily from the words that were so like an echo of his own thoughts. How long? He didn't know; he would have to ask the ship's computers. Each EDS was given a meager surplus of fuel to compensate for unfavorable conditions within the atmosphere and relatively little fuel was being consumed for the time being. The memory banks of the computers would still contain all data pertaining to the course set for the EDS; such data would not be erased until the EDS reached its destination. He had only to give the computers the new data; the girl's weight and the exact time at which he had reduced the deceleration to .10.

"Barton." Commander Delhart's voice came abruptly from the communicator, as he opened his mouth to call the *Stardust*. "A check with Records shows me you haven't completed your report. Did you reduce the deceleration?"

So the commander knew what he was trying to do.

"I'm decelerating at point ten," he answered. "I cut the deceleration at seventeen fifty and the weight is a hundred and ten. I would like to stay at point ten as long as the computers say I can. Will you give them the question?"

It was contrary to regulations for an EDS pilot to make any changes in the course or degree of deceleration the computers had set for him but the commander made no mention of the violation, neither did he ask the reason for it. It was not necessary for him to ask; he had not become commander of an interstellar cruiser without both intelligence and an understanding of human nature. He said only: "I'll have that given the computers."

The communicator fell silent and he and the girl waited, neither of them speaking. They would not have to wait long; the computers would give the answer within moments of the asking. The new factors would be fed into the steel maw of the first bank and the electrical impulses would go through the complex circuits. Here and there a relay might click, a tiny cog turn over, but it would be essentially the electrical impulses that found the answer; formless, mindless, invisible, determining with utter precision how long the pale girl beside him might live. Then a second steel maw would spit out the answer.

The chronometer on the instrument board read 18:10 when the commander spoke again.

"You will resume deceleration at nineteen ten."

She looked toward the chronometer, then quickly away from it. "Is that when . . . when I go?" she asked. He nodded and she dropped her eyes to her lap again.

"I'll have the course corrections given you," the commander said. "Ordinarily I would never permit anything like this but I understand your position. There is nothing I can do, other than what I've just done, and you will not deviate from these new instructions. You will complete your report at nineteen ten. Now—here are the course corrections."

The voice of some unknown technician read them to him and

he wrote them down on the pad clipped to the edge of the control board. There would, he saw, be periods of deceleration when he neared the atmosphere when the deceleration would be five gravities—and at five gravities, one hundred and ten pounds would become five hundred fifty pounds.

The technician finished and he terminated the contact with a brief acknowledgement. Then, hesitating a moment, he reached out and shut off the communicator. It was 18:13 and he would have nothing to report until 19:10. In the meantime, it somehow seemed indecent to permit others to hear what she might say in her last hour.

He began to check the instrument readings, going over them with unnecessary slowness. She would have to accept the circumstances and there was nothing he could do to help her into acceptance; words of sympathy would only delay it.

It was 18:20 when she stirred from her motionlessness and spoke.

"So that's the way it has to be with me?"

He swung around to face her. "You understand now, don't you? No one would ever let it be like this if it could be changed."

"I understand," she said. Some of the color had returned to her face and the lipstick no longer stood out so vividly red. "There isn't enough fuel for me to stay; when I hid on this ship I got into something I didn't know anything about and now I have to pay for it."

She had violated a man-made law that said KEEP OUT but the penalty was not of men's making or desire and it was a penalty men could not revoke. A physical law had decreed: *h amount of fuel will power an EDS with a mass of m safely to its destination;* and a second physical law had decreed: *h amount of fuel will not power an EDS with a mass of m plus x safely to its destination.*

EDS's obeyed only physical laws and no amount of human sympathy for her could alter the second law.

"But I'm afraid. I don't want to die—not now. I want to live and nobody is doing anything to help me; everybody is letting me go ahead and acting just like nothing was going to happen to me. I'm going to die and nobody *cares.*"

"We all do," he said. "I do and the commander does and the

clerk in Ship's Records; we all care and each of us did what little he could to help you. It wasn't enough—it was almost nothing— but it was all we could do."

"Not enough fuel—I can understand that," she said, as though she had not heard his own words. "But to have to die for it. *Me*, alone—"

How hard it must be for her to accept the fact. She had never known danger of death; had never known the environments where the lives of men could be as fragile and fleeting as sea foam tossed against a rocky shore. She belonged on gentle Earth, in that secure and peaceful society where she could be young and gay and laughing with the others of her kind; where life was precious and well-guarded and there was always the assurance that tomorrow would come. She belonged in that world of soft winds and warm suns, music and moonlight and gracious manners and not on the hard, bleak frontier.

"How did it happen to me, so terribly quickly? An hour ago I was on the *Stardust*, going to Mimir. Now the *Stardust* is going on without me and I'm going to die and I'll never see Gerry and Mama and Daddy again—I'll never see anything again."

He hesitated, wondering how he could explain it to her so she would really understand and not feel she had, somehow, been the victim of a reasonlessly cruel injustice. She did not know what the frontier was like; she thought in terms of safe-and-secure Earth. Pretty girls were not jettisoned on Earth; there was a law against it. On Earth her plight would have filled the newscasts and a fast black Patrol ship would have been racing to her rescue. Everyone, everywhere, would have known of Marilyn Lee Cross and no effort would have been spared to save her life. But this was not Earth and there were no Patrol ships; only the *Stardust*, leaving them behind at many times the speed of light. There was no one to help her, there would be no Marilyn Lee Cross smiling from the newscasts tomorrow. Marilyn Lee Cross would be but a poignant memory for an EDS pilot and a name on a gray card in Ship's Records.

"It's different here; it's not like back on Earth," he said. "It isn't that no one cares; it's that no one can do anything to help. The frontier is big and here along its rim the colonies and exploration parties are scattered so thin and far between. On Woden, for example, there are only sixteen men—sixteen men on an entire world. The exploration parties, the survey crews, the little first-colonies—they're all fighting alien environments, trying to make a way for those who will follow after. The environments fight back and those who go first usually make mistakes only once. There is no margin of safety along the rim of the frontier; there can't be until the way is made for the others who will come later, until the new worlds are tamed and settled. Until then men will have to pay the penalty for making mistakes with no one to help them because there is no one *to* help them."

"I was going to Mimir," she said. "I didn't know about the frontier; I was only going to Mimir and *it's* safe."

"Mimir is safe but you left the cruiser that was taking you there."

She was silent for a little while. "It was all so wonderful at first; there was plenty of room for me on this ship and I would be seeing Gerry so soon . . . I didn't know about the fuel, didn't know what would happen to me—"

Her words trailed away and he turned his attention to the viewscreen, not wanting to stare at her as she fought her way through the black horror of fear toward the calm gray of acceptance.

Woden was a ball, enshrouded in the blue haze of its atmosphere, swimming in space against the background of star-sprinkled dead blackness. The great mass of Manning's Continent sprawled like a gigantic hourglass in the Eastern Sea with the western half of the Eastern Continent still visible. There was a thin line of shadow along the right-hand edge of the globe and the Eastern Continent was disappearing into it as the planet turned on its axis. An hour before the entire continent had been in view, now a thousand miles of it had gone into the thin edge of shadow and around to the night that lay on the other side of the world. The dark blue spot that was Lotus Lake was approaching the shadow. It was somewhere near the southern edge of the lake that Group Two had their camp. It would be night there, soon, and quick behind the coming of night the rotation of Woden on its axis would put Group Two beyond the reach of the ship's radio.

He would have to tell her before it was too late for her to

talk to her brother. In a way, it would be better for both of them should they not do so but it was not for him to decide. To each of them the last words would be something to hold and cherish, something that would cut like the blade of a knife yet would be infinitely precious to remember, she for her own brief moments to live and he for the rest of his life.

He held down the button that would flash the grid lines on the viewscreen and used the known diameter of the planet to estimate the distance the southern tip of Lotus Lake had yet to go until it passed beyond radio range. It was approximately five hundred miles. Five hundred miles; thirty minutes—and the chronometer read 18:30. Allowing for error in estimating, it could not be later than 19:05 that the turning of Woden would cut off her brother's voice.

The first border of the Western Continent was already in sight along the left side of the world. Four thousand miles across it lay the shore of the Western Sea and the Camp of Group One. It had been in the Western Sea that the tornado had originated, to strike with such fury at the camp and destroy half their prefabricated buildings, including the one that housed the medical supplies. Two days before the tornado had not existed; it had been no more than great gentle masses of air out over the calm Western Sea. Group One had gone about their routine survey work, unaware of the meeting of the air masses out at sea, unaware of the force the union was spawning. It had struck their camp without warning; a thundering, roaring destruction that sought to annihilate all that lay before it. It had passed on, leaving the wreckage in its wake. It had destroyed the labor of months and had doomed six men to die and then, as though its task was accomplished, it once more began to resolve into gentle masses of air. But for all its deadliness, it had destroyed with neither malice nor intent. It had been a blind and mindless force, obeying the laws of nature, and it would have followed the same course with the same fury had men never existed.

Existence required Order and there was order; the laws of nature, irrevocable and immutable. Men could learn to use them but men could not change them. The circumference of a circle was always pi times the diameter and no science of Man would ever make it otherwise. The combination of chemical A with chemical B under condition C invariably produced reaction D.

The law of gravitation was a rigid equation and it made no distinction between the fall of a leaf and the ponderous circling of a binary star system. The nuclear conversion process powered the cruisers that carried men to the stars; the same process in the form of a nova would destroy a world with equal efficiency. The laws *were*, and the universe moved in obedience to them. Along the frontier were arrayed all the forces of nature and sometimes they destroyed those who were fighting their way outward from Earth. The men of the frontier had long ago learned the bitter futility of cursing the forces that would destroy them for the forces were blind and deaf; the futility of looking to the heavens for mercy, for the stars of the galaxy swung in their long, long sweep of two hundred million years, as inexorably controlled as they by the laws that knew neither hatred nor compassion.

The men of the frontier knew—but how was a girl from Earth to fully understand? *H amount of fuel will not power an EDS with a mass of m plus x safely to its destination.* To himself and her brother and parents she was a sweet-faced girl in her teens; to the laws of nature she was *x*, the unwanted factor in a cold equation.

She stirred again on the seat. "Could I write a letter? I want to write to Mama and Daddy and I'd like to talk to Gerry. Could you let me talk to him over your radio there?"

"I'll try to get him," he said.

He switched on the normal-space transmitter and pressed the signal button. Someone answered the buzzer almost immediately.

"Hello. How's it going with you fellows now—is the EDS on its way?"

"This isn't Group One; this is the EDS," he said. "Is Gerry Cross there?"

"Gerry? He and two others went out in the helicopter this morning and aren't back yet. It's almost sundown, though, and he ought to be back right away—in less than an hour at the most."

"Can you connect me through to the radio in his 'copter?"

"Huh-uh. It's been out of commission for two months—some printed circuits went haywire and we can't get any more until the next cruiser stops by. Is it something important—bad news for him, or something?"

"Yes—it's very important. When he comes in get him to the transmitter as soon as you possibly can."

"I'll do that; I'll have one of the boys waiting at the field with a truck. Is there anything else I can do?"

"No, I guess that's all. Get him there as soon as you can and signal me."

He turned the volume to an inaudible minimum, an act that would not affect the functioning of the signal buzzer, and unclipped the pad of paper from the control board. He tore off the sheet containing his flight instructions and handed the pad to her, together with pencil.

"I'd better write to Gerry, too," she said as she took them. "He might not get back to camp in time."

She began to write, her fingers still clumsy and uncertain in the way they handled the pencil and the top of it trembling a little as she poised it between words. He turned back to the viewscreen, to stare at it without seeing it.

She was a lonely little child, trying to say her last good-by, and she would lay out her heart to them. She would tell them how much she loved them and she would tell them to not feel badly about it, that it was only something that must happen eventually to everyone and she was not afraid. The last would be a lie and it would be there to read between the sprawling, uneven lines; a valiant little lie that would make the hurt all the greater for them.

Her brother was of the frontier and he would understand. He would not hate the EDS pilot for doing nothing to prevent her going; he would know there had been nothing the pilot could do. He would understand, though the understanding would not soften the shock and pain when he learned his sister was gone. But the others, her father and mother—they would not understand. They were of Earth and they would think in the manner of those who had never lived where the safety margin of life was a thin, thin line—and sometimes not at all. What would they think of the face-less, unknown pilot who had sent her to her death?

They would hate him with cold and terrible intensity but it really didn't matter. He would never see them, never know them. He would have only the memories to remind him; only the nights to fear, when a blue-eyed girl in gypsy sandals would come in his dreams to die again—

✧   ✧   ✧

He scowled at the viewscreen and tried to force his thoughts into less emotional channels. There was nothing he could do to help her. She had unknowingly subjected herself to the penalty of a law that recognized neither innocence nor youth nor beauty, that was incapable of sympathy or leniency. Regret was illogical—and yet, could knowing it to be illogical ever keep it away?

She stopped occasionally, as though trying to find the right words to tell them what she wanted them to know, then the pencil would resume its whispering to the paper. It was 18:37 when she folded the letter in a square and wrote a name on it. She began writing another, twice looking up at the chronometer as though she feared the black hand might reach its rendezvous before she had finished. It was 18:45 when she folded it as she had done the first letter and wrote a name and address on it.

She held the letters out to him. "Will you take care of these and see that they're enveloped and mailed?"

"Of course." He took them from her hand and placed them in a pocket of his gray uniform shirt.

"These can't be sent off until the next cruiser stops by and the *Stardust* will have long since told them about me, won't it?" she asked. He nodded and she went on, "That makes the letters not important in one way but in another way they're very important—to me, and to them."

"I know. I understand, and I'll take care of them."

She glanced at the chronometer, then back at him. "It seems to move faster all the time, doesn't it?"

He said nothing, unable to think of anything to say, and she asked, "Do you think Gerry will come back to camp in time?"

"I think so. They said he should be in right away."

She began to roll the pencil back and forth between her palms. "I hope he does. I feel sick and scared and I want to hear his voice again and maybe I won't feel so alone. I'm a coward and I can't help it."

"No," he said, "you're not a coward. You're afraid, but you're not a coward."

"Is there a difference?"

He nodded. "A lot of difference."

"I feel so alone. I never did feel like this before; like I was all by myself and there was nobody to care what happened to me. Always, before, there was Mama and Daddy there and my friends around me. I had lots of friends, and they had a going-away party for me the night before I left."

Friends and music and laughter for her to remember—and on the viewscreen Lotus Lake was going into the shadow.

"Is it the same with Gerry?" she asked. "I mean, if he should make a mistake, would he have to die for it, all alone and with no one to help him?"

"It's the same with all along the frontier; it will always be like that so long as there is a frontier."

"Gerry didn't tell us. He said the pay was good and he sent money home all the time because Daddy's little shop just brought in a bare living but he didn't tell us it was like this."

"He didn't tell you his work was dangerous?"

"Well—yes. He mentioned that, but we didn't understand. I always thought danger along the frontier was something that was a lot of fun; an exciting adventure, like in the three-D shows." A wan smile touched her face for a moment. "Only it's not, is it? It's not the same at all, because when it's real you can't go home after the show is over."

"No," he said. "No, you can't."

Her glance flicked from the chronometer to the door of the air lock then down to the pad and pencil she still held. She shifted her position slightly to lay them on the bench beside her, moving one foot out a little. For the first time he saw that she was not wearing Vegan gypsy sandals but only cheap imitations; the expensive Vegan leather was some kind of grained plastic, the silver buckle was gilded iron, the jewels were colored glass. *Daddy's little shop just brought in a bare living—* She must have left college in her second year, to take the course in linguistics that would enable her to make her own way and help her brother provide for her parents, earning what she could by part-time work after classes were over. Her personal possessions on the *Stardust* would be taken back to her parents—they would neither be of much value nor occupy much storage space on the return voyage.

"Isn't it—" She stopped, and he looked at her questioningly. "Isn't it cold in here?" she asked, almost apologetically. "Doesn't it seem cold to you?"

"Why, yes," he said. He saw by the main temperature gauge that the room was at precisely normal temperature. "Yes, it's colder than it should be."

"I wish Gerry would get back before it's too late. Do you really think he will, and you didn't just say so to make me feel better?"

"I think he will—they said he would be in pretty soon." On the viewscreen Lotus Lake had gone into the shadow but for the thin blue line of its western edge and it was apparent he had overestimated the time she would have in which to talk to her brother. Reluctantly, he said to her, "His camp will be out of radio range in a few minutes; he's on that part of Woden that's in the shadow"—he indicated the viewscreen—"and the turning of Woden will put him beyond contact. There may not be much time left when he comes in—not much time to talk to him before he fades out. I wish I could do something about it—I would call him right now if I could."

"Not even as much time as I will have to stay?"

"I'm afraid not."

"Then—" She straightened and looked toward the air lock with pale resolution. "Then I'll go when Gerry passes beyond range. I won't wait any longer after that—I won't have anything to wait for."

Again there was nothing he could say.

"Maybe I shouldn't wait at all. Maybe I'm selfish—maybe it would be better for Gerry if you just told him about it afterward."

There was an unconscious pleading for denial in the way she spoke and he said, "He wouldn't want you to do that, to not wait for him."

"It's already coming dark where he is, isn't it? There will be all the long night before him, and Mama and Daddy don't know yet that I won't ever be coming back like I promised them I would. I've caused everyone I love to be hurt, haven't I? I didn't want to—I didn't intend to."

"It wasn't your fault," he said. "It wasn't your fault. They'll know that. They'll understand."

"At first I was so afraid to die that I was a coward and thought only of myself. Now, I see how selfish I was. The terrible thing about dying like this is not that I'll be gone but that I'll never see them again; never be able to tell them that I didn't take them for granted; never be able to tell them I knew of the sacrifices they made to make my life happier, and I knew all the things they did for me and that I loved them so much more than I ever told them. I've never told them any of those things. You don't tell them such things when you're young and your life is all before you—you're afraid of sounding sentimental and silly.

"But it's so different when you have to die—you wish you had told them while you could and you wish you could tell them you're sorry for all the little mean things you ever did or said to them. You wish you could tell them that you didn't really mean to ever hurt their feelings and for them to only remember that you always loved them far more than you ever let them know."

"You don't have to tell them that," he said. "They will know— they've always known it."

"Are you sure?" she asked. "How can you be sure? My people are strangers to you."

"Wherever you go, human nature and human hearts are the same."

"And they will know what I want them to know—that I love them?"

"They've always known it, in a way far better than you could ever put in words for them."

"I keep remembering the things they did for me, and it's the little things they did that seem to be the most important to me, now. Like Gerry—he sent me a bracelet of fire-rubies on my sixteenth birthday. It was beautiful—it must have cost him a month's pay. Yet, I remember him more for what he did the night my kitten got run over in the street. I was only six years old and he held me in his arms and wiped away my tears and told me not to cry, that Flossy was gone for just a little while, for just long enough to get herself a new fur coat and she would be on the foot of my bed the very next morning. I believed him and quit crying and went to sleep dreaming about my kitten coming back. When I woke up the next morning, there was Flossy on the foot of my bed in a brand-new white fur coat, just like he had said she would be.

"It wasn't until a long time later that Mama told me Gerry had got the pet-shop owner out of bed at four in the morning and, when the man got mad about it, Gerry told him he was either going to go down and sell him the white kitten right then or he'd break his neck."

"It's always the little things you remember people by; all the little things they did because they wanted to do them for you. You've done the same for Gerry and your father and mother; all kinds of things that you've forgotten about but that they will never forget."

"I hope I have. I would like for them to remember me like that."

"They will."

"I wish—" She swallowed. "The way I'll die—I wish they wouldn't ever think of that. I've read how people look who die in space—their insides all ruptured and exploded and their lungs out between their teeth and then, a few seconds later, they're all dry and shapeless and horribly ugly. I don't want them to ever think of me as something dead and horrible, like that."

"You're their own, their child and their sister. They could never think of you other than the way you would want them to; the way you looked the last time they saw you."

"I'm still afraid," she said. "I can't help it, but I don't want Gerry to know it. If he gets back in time, I'm going to act like I'm not afraid at all and—"

The signal buzzer interrupted her, quick and imperative.

"Gerry!" She came to her feet. "It's Gerry, now!"

He spun the volume control knob and asked: "Gerry Cross?"

"Yes," her brother answered, an undertone of tenseness to his reply. "The bad news—what is it?"

She answered for him, standing close behind him and leaning down a little toward the communicator, her hand resting small and cold on his shoulder.

"Hello, Gerry." There was only a faint quaver to betray the careful casualness of her voice. "I wanted to see you—"

"Marilyn!" There was sudden and terrible apprehension in the way he spoke her name. "What are you doing on that EDS?"

"I wanted to see you," she said again. "I wanted to see you, so I hid on this ship—"

"You *hid* on it?"

"I'm a stowaway . . . I didn't know what it would mean—"

"*Marilyn!*" It was the cry of a man who calls hopeless and

desperate to someone already and forever gone from him. "What have you done?"

"I . . . it's not—" Then her own composure broke and the cold little hand gripped his shoulder convulsively. "Don't, Gerry—I only wanted to see you; I didn't intend to hurt you. Please, Gerry, don't feel like that—"

Something warm and wet splashed on his wrist and he slid out of the chair, to help her into it and swing the microphone down to her own level.

"Don't feel like that—Don't let me go knowing you feel like that—"

The sob she had tried to hold back choked in her throat and her brother spoke to her. "Don't cry, Marilyn." His voice was suddenly deep and infinitely gentle, with all the pain held out of it. "Don't cry, sis—you mustn't do that. It's all right, honey— everything is all right."

"I—" Her lower lip quivered and she bit into it. "I didn't want you to feel that way—I just wanted us to say good-by because I have to go in a minute."

"Sure—sure. That's the way it will be, sis. I didn't mean to sound the way I did." Then his voice changed to a tone of quick and urgent demand. "EDS—have you called the *Stardust*? Did you check with the computers?"

"I called the *Stardust* almost an hour ago. It can't turn back, there are no other cruisers within forty light-years, and there isn't enough fuel."

"Are you sure that the computers had the correct data—sure of everything?"

"Yes—do you think I could ever let it happen if I wasn't sure? I did everything I could do. If there was anything at all I could do now, I would do it."

"He tried to help me, Gerry." Her lower lip was no longer trembling and the short sleeves of her blouse were wet where she had dried her tears. "No one can help me and I'm not going to cry any more and everything will be all right with you and Daddy and Mama, won't it?"

"Sure—sure it will. We'll make out fine."

Her brother's words were beginning to come in more faintly and he turned the volume control to maximum. "He's going out of range," he said to her. "He'll be gone within another minute."

"You're fading out, Gerry," she said. "You're going out of range. I wanted to tell you—but I can't, now. We must say good-by so soon—but maybe I'll see you again. Maybe I'll come to you in your dreams with my hair in braids and crying because the kitten in my arms is dead; maybe I'll be the touch of a breeze that whispers to you as it goes by; maybe I'll be one of those gold-winged larks you told me about, singing my silly head off to you; maybe, at times, I'll be nothing you can see but you will know I'm there beside you. Think of me like that, Gerry; always like that and not—the other way."

Dimmed to a whisper by the turning of Woden, the answer came back:

"Always like that, Marilyn—always like that and never any other way."

"Our time is up, Gerry—I have to go, now. Good—" Her voice broke in mid-word and her mouth tried to twist into crying. She pressed her hand hard against it and when she spoke again the words came clear and true:

"Good-by, Gerry."

Faint and ineffably poignant and tender, the last words came from the cold metal of the communicator:

"Good-by, little sister—"

She sat motionless in the hush that followed, as though listening to the shadow-echoes of the words as they died away, then she turned away from the communicator, toward the air lock, and he pulled down the black lever beside him. The inner door of the air lock slid swiftly open, to reveal the bare little cell that was waiting for her, and she walked to it.

She walked with her head up and the brown curls brushing her shoulders, with the white sandals stepping as sure and steady as the fractional gravity would permit and the gilded buckles twinkling with little lights of blue and red and crystal. He let her walk alone and made no move to help her, knowing she would not want it that way. She stepped into the air lock and turned to face him, only the pulse in her throat to betray the wild beating of her heart.

"I'm ready," she said.

He pushed the lever up and the door slid its quick barrier between them, enclosing her in black and utter darkness for her last moments of life. It clicked as it locked in place and he jerked down the red lever. There was a slight waver to the ship as the air gushed from the lock, a vibration to the wall as though something had bumped the outer door in passing, then there was nothing and the ship was dropping true and steady again. He shoved the red lever back to close the door on the empty air lock and turned away, to walk to the pilot's chair with the slow steps of a man old and weary.

Back in the pilot's chair he pressed the signal button of the normal-space transmitter. There was no response; he had expected none. Her brother would have to wait through the night until the turning of Woden permitted contact through Group One.

It was not yet time to resume deceleration and he waited while the ship dropped endlessly downward with him and the drives purred softly. He saw that the white hand of the supplies closet temperature gauge was on zero. A cold equation had been balanced and he was alone on the ship. Something shapeless and ugly was hurrying ahead of him, going to Woden where its brother was waiting through the night, but the empty ship still lived for a little while with the presence of the girl who had not known about the forces that killed with neither hatred nor malice. It seemed, almost, that she still sat small and bewildered and frightened on the metal box beside him, her words echoing hauntingly clear in the void she had left behind her:

I didn't do anything to die for—I didn't do anything—

AFTERWORD:
Sometimes It All Just Works
by David Drake

My parents' thirteenth birthday present to me, a collection of SF paperbacks bought from a guy going into the Navy, included an anthology titled *Five Tales for Tomorrow*. I've since learned that the paperback was a selection from *Best SF of 1955*, but I was just getting into SF at the time; all the names and ideas were new to me, and I had a thirteen-year-old's appreciation of style (that is, effectively no appreciation at all).

Till I dug out the volume a couple days ago, I couldn't have told you what the other four stories in the anthology were (though one of them, Simak's *How-2*, is justly famous). I say "the other four" because the second of the five was "The Cold Equations."

A few years ago Ramsey Campbell asked me to put together my list of the ten greatest horror stories of all time; the first story I thought of was "The Cold Equations." For me at least, the question isn't even arguable.

I've read a lot of Godwin since 1958. None of it is similar to "The Cold Equations" in tone, nor is any of it even remotely comparable to "The Cold Equations" in impact. Though (as you know if you've read this volume) much of Godwin's work is very good, all the rest of it put together wouldn't have kept him from the obscurity that's covered truly excellent contemporary writers like Wyman Guin and Ralph Williams (the pen name of Ralph Slone).

But Godwin *did* write "The Cold Equations." Eric suggests it may be the best science fiction story ever written. That's true, but it's even more likely to be the best *known* science fiction story ever written.

What follows is my guess as to how Godwin came to write something so uncharacteristic (and by the way, he never tried to duplicate that one enormous success). The plot is lifted directly from "A Weighty Decision," a story in the May-June, 1952, issue of the EC comic *Weird Science*. I don't believe that coincidence could have created plots so similar in detail.

But before I'd read "A Weighty Decision," I'd heard the rumor that Godwin offered the story to *Astounding* with a happy ending: the pilot manages to strip enough out of the ship to allow himself to land safely with the girl aboard. John Campbell read the story and told Godwin to change the ending so that the girl can't be saved. Godwin obeyed, and we have the story as it stands.

I believe the rumor for a number of reasons. Campbell was notoriously fond of telling his writers to change some critical point of a story before he bought it. (He did that in 1940 to my friend Manly Wade Wellman, which is why Manly sold "Twice in Time" to *Startling Stories* instead of *Astounding*—after he'd told Campbell to go piss up a rope.) Further, the story with a happy ending would be exactly the sort of triumph over enormous adversity story which Godwin generally wrote.

Finally, the plot is such an obvious steal from the comic that I think Godwin would have concealed it better if he hadn't intended to use a completely different ending. I can also imagine that Godwin wouldn't have expressed his qualms at changing the ending to Campbell, who wouldn't have winked at direct plagiarism. (Not that EC had any legitimate gripe: Bill Gaines laughed in later years about the way he and his staff at EC stole plots from SF stories and ran them without credit.)

So a good but not great writer, through a series of chances, came to write an outstanding story; perhaps the most outstanding SF story ever written. I don't know about the rest of you, but personally I take comfort in the notion.

Dave Drake
david-drake.com

AFTERWORD
by Barry Malzberg

David Drake's remarkable short essay illumines the comment from A.J. Budrys' which I quoted in my preface, making what would otherwise seem an arcane reference completely understandable. ("'The Cold Equations' was the best short story that Godwin ever wrote and he didn't write it.")

It is clearly on the record that a 1952 story, "A Dangerous Situation," appearing in the comic book *Weird Science*, uses the central theme and circumstance of "The Cold Equations." Although, in the *Weird Science* version, the stowaway is the pilot's fiancée who hid on the ship so that she could give him a nice surprise—*her* "nice surprise" is that she is jettisoned just as thoroughly as Godwin's heroine.

There is myth—but no concrete evidence—that Godwin, in the belief that Campbell (to whom he had just begun selling stories; "The Cold Equations" was his fourth appearance in the magazine in a period of less than a year) would never publish an ending this despairing, changed the *Weird Science* story so that the girl was saved. But Campbell, having none of it, flogged Godwin through numerous revisions until Godwin was forced to accept the implications of his own material (the universe is vast and uncaring and has no room for pity, sympathy or even awareness of the human condition) and reinstalled the original ending.

We are not sure of this . . . The first collection of Campbell's letters, published in 1985, contains a letter to Isaac Asimov in which Campbell says, "I had Godwin really sweating over that story," but there are no specifics. It would be a pretty and resonant thing to believe that Campbell, all on his own, found the proper ending and made Godwin more of a copyist than he would have otherwise been, but we will probably never know.

What we do know is that Godwin's story, published in the August 1954 issue of *Astounding*, found an enormous response. As I said in my preface, and according to Campbell (a letter from that collection), it generated more mail than any story previously had—most of it apparently from anguished men who insisted that the girl could have been saved. (Harry Harrison in an introduction to the story in his *Astounding* anthology in 1972, said that the response to this story from *ASF*'s overwhelmingly male readership proved that males were clearly the more truly sentimental and teary gender.)

Campbell then showed Godwin his appreciation by the apparent rejection of his stories over a period of more than seven years until "—And Devious The Line of Duty" appeared in the December 1961 issue of *Analog*. One more story appeared in the magazine exactly a year later, and that was it—although Campbell edited the magazine for another nine years and Godwin himself lived another nineteen.

Did someone perhaps tip off Campbell to the *Weird Science* story after the fact? We can speculate entertainingly and uselessly over the imponderable Campbell but we shall never know. Campbell certainly had an authoritarian and vindictive mode (John Brunner and Fritz Leiber, regular contributors who suddenly became contributors no more, have testified to that). But Godwin did sell to him again; and Campbell, in a letter to Scott Meredith rejecting a 1966 Godwin story (Godwin came to the Scott Meredith Agency in that year) expressed unhappiness with the outcome and said, "I'm glad to see he's back to writing, I've been trying to get him to do that for years."

So, who knows? Science fiction is in many ways imponderable; our apocrypha have often overcome the apparent truth. The history of science fiction, compiled offstage and in its interstices, can never truly be known.

Godwin's story, certainly the most famous of the so-called *five most famous science fiction stories* (okay, for the record, the other four are: Bradbury's "Sound of Thunder," Asimov's "Nightfall," Daniel Keyes' "Flowers for Algernon" and Arthur Clarke's "The Star") was signed by an obscure writer; none of Godwin's other stories is well known or often reprinted. The fact that two of the five most famous stories are by writers otherwise unnoted within the field and regarded in all of its precincts as "one-story writers" is highly provocative and says a great deal about science fiction itself. But that would be another essay.

How did this happen?

My answer, years ago, was that Godwin was a writer who at the age of thirty-nine, with no definable history and no estimable future, had been—as a soprano said about a Puccini aria in *Girl of the Golden West*—"kissed by God"; that Puccini and Godwin had not been creating at that moment so much as they had been listening; and Godwin's failure to produce anything remotely as memorable (not true of Puccini) makes the mysterious answer the only explanation.

That seemed reasonable enough before I knew of *Weird Science*. Now I am not so sure. This story and its provenance become more elusive and mysterious the more carefully they are considered. As *The New York Review of Science Fiction* debate made clear, there is less of a settled body of opinion on this story than there was ten or thirty years ago. This of itself is not an explanation or definition of a masterpiece; but it is certainly a quality whose absence means no masterpiece.

Beyond "The Cold Equations" are twenty short stories and three novels written by Godwin. Some of the stories—I opt for "The Gulf Between" and "Mother of Invention"—are quite competent. And the two prison planet novels (*The Survivors* and its sequel, *The Space Barbarians*) are memorable enough to have been optioned for film by the respectable Howard Chaikin only a few years ago.

The third novel, *Beyond Another Sun*, was written before Godwin came to the Scott Meredith Agency, was marketed everywhere by the agency for five years, finally sold to a bottom-line publisher in 1971 for a thousand dollars and barely issued . . . I've never myself seen a published copy nor have I ever read or met anyone who had a good word to say of that novel. (Although, in fairness, I should mention that the editor of this volume, Eric Flint, thinks it would have made a good novelette—unfortunately, Godwin tried to expand a too-slender framework into a full-length novel.)

Godwin, without "The Cold Equations," is a mid-range writer of the kind formed and framed by the 1950s. Some of those writers are clearly better than he, others not so good, and almost all of them have been forgotten by all than old science fiction fans. In deference to those writers or their estates I won't call the roster, but I would note Godwin's astonishing similarity in one way to the otherwise forgotten Jerome L. Bixby, 1923–1998, who also wrote one extraordinary and memorable story—"It's a Good Life"—and is otherwise unknown. But . . . "It's a Good Life" has faded; "The Cold Equations" has not.

With "The Cold Equations"—and it is his story; he signed it, and there is no other fair ascription—Godwin comes as close to permanence as any writer to emerge from science fiction. If there are SF readers, if there is such a medium a millennium from now, Isaac Asimov and Arthur Clarke and "The Cold Equations" will still be read. The story has not only outlasted Godwin and almost all his contemporaries, it may outlast science fiction itself.

It is a mystery, this work, in the way that Puccini's great arias—my favorite is the Dove song which comes very early in the first act of *Rondine*—are mysteries. The marks on paper which cue the performer or reader are absolutely no indicator of the power, the tormenting, haunting, overwhelming power of the creation. For this we honor the creator, even if the creator was (as Mozart said of himself) only "taking dictation," was only the medium. What passed through Tom Godwin in one night or one week or one month in late 1953 was what Richard Strauss and Nietzche called "The World Riddle," the *muss ess sein* which Beethoven scrawled epigraphically on the opus 135 Quartet.

"Must it be?"

Yes, Beethoven and Godwin respond, yes it must be. It must be and here we all are: in its enclosure.

31 December 2001
New Jersey